A former journalist for National Public Radio in the US, and two-time winner of the Pushcart Prize, Anna Solomon's short fiction and essays have appeared in many publications, including the *New York Times Magazine*. She was born and raised in Gloucester, Massachusetts, and lives in Brooklyn, New York, with her husband and two children.

You can discover more about the author at www.annasolomon.com

LEAVING LUCY PEAR

One night in 1917, Beatrice Haven creeps out of her uncle's house on Cape Ann, Massachusetts, and leaves her newborn baby at the foot of a pear tree, then watches as another woman claims the child as her own. The unwed daughter of wealthy Jewish industrialists and a gifted pianist bound for Radcliffe, Bea plans to leave her shameful secret behind and make a fresh start . . . Ten years later, Bea's hopes for her future remain unfulfilled. When she returns to her uncle's house, seeking a refuge from her unhappiness, she discovers far more when the rum-running manager of the local quarry inadvertently unites her with Emma Murphy, the headstrong Irish Catholic woman who has been raising her abandoned child — now a bright, bold, cross-dressing girl named Lucy Pear, with secrets of her own.

ANNA SOLOMON

LEAVING LUCY PEAR

Complete and Unabridged

CHARNWOOD
Leicester

First published in Great Britain in 2016 by
Blackfriars
An imprint of Little, Brown Book Group
London

First Charnwood Edition
published 2017
by arrangement with
Little, Brown Book Group
London

A catalogue record for this book is available
from the British Library.

ISBN 978–1–4448–3360–7

Published by
F. A. Thorpe (Publishing)
Anstey, Leicestershire

Set by Words & Graphics Ltd.
Anstey, Leicestershire
Printed and bound in Great Britain by
T. J. International Ltd., Padstow, Cornwall

This book is printed on acid-free paper

To Mike

The Last Word of a Blue Bird

As I went out a Crow
In a low voice said, 'Oh,
I was looking for you.
How do you do?
I just came to tell you
To tell Lesley (will you?)
That her little Bluebird
Wanted me to bring word
That the north wind last night
That made the stars bright
And made ice on the trough
Almost made him cough
His tail feathers off.
He just had to fly!
But he sent her Good-by,
And said to be good,
And wear her red hood,
And look for skunk tracks
In the snow with an ax —
And do everything!
And perhaps in the spring
He would come back and sing.'

ROBERT FROST

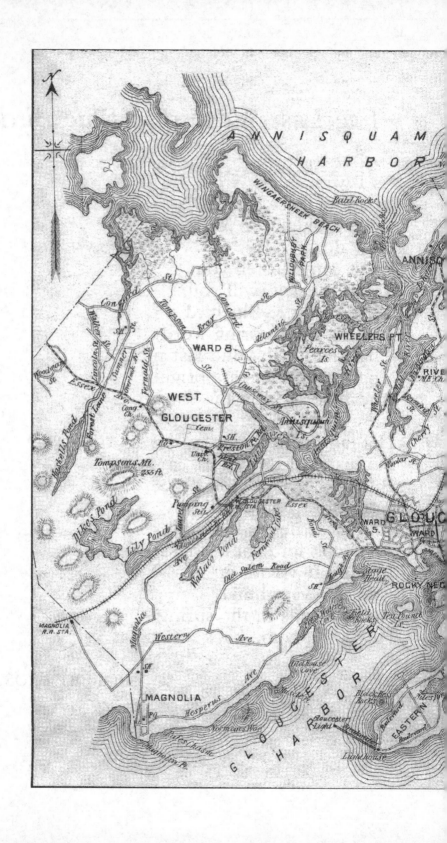

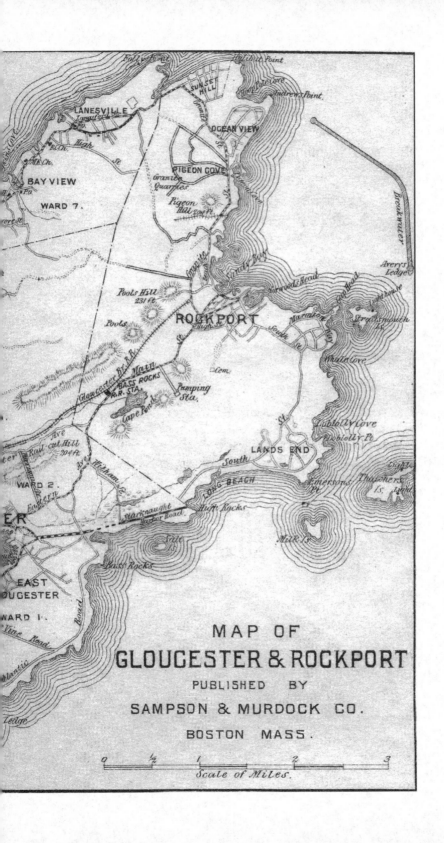

MAP OF
GLOUCESTER & ROCKPORT
PUBLISHED BY
SAMPSON & MURDOCK CO.
BOSTON MASS.

Scale of Miles.

Part One

Part One

1917

If they were coming, this was the night. The pears had stayed yellow and hard for so long that Bea had started to despair, but they were finally ready to pick. The moon was a quarter full. The afternoon's wind had gone limp. Midnight came and went. Bea counted to five hundred for extra measure — silently, so she wouldn't wake the nurse — then she took up the infant from its bassinet, wrapped it in her aunt Vera's angora shawl, and crept down the cellar stairs in her bare feet.

The stairs to the cellar were granite, and cold. The original wooden ones had burned with the original wooden house in 1873. Bea did not know about the fire but she could smell it, because the cellar was the one part of the house that hadn't needed rebuilding and its walls retained the flavor of ash. She moved toward the bulkhead door as fast as she could, feeling along the wall with her free hand, careful not to bump the handles of shovels and hoes, though the shovels and hoes had been through far worse. They had witnessed flood and fire. They had been variously cared for and abused by generations of gardeners, had been used to plant tulips and to dig graves. They had even, once upon a time, been in the presence of another unwed mother and her infant. Knowing this might have put Bea's own suffering in perspective. But she did not know and she had not been taught perspective. She was eighteen, the daughter of ascendant Boston Jews who had sent her away to Eastern Point in a black, curtained limousine the day she started to show.

The bulkhead door was heavier than she expected, its diagonal slope demanding that it be lifted as much as pushed. She had unlocked it from the outside before going to bed but she hadn't tested its weight and now the thing didn't budge. She pressed harder. The cellar was her only way out — she had tested the doors on the first floor and every one either shrieked or squeaked or groaned. She pushed again. If she put the baby down, it would cry. Bea started to pant with panic. The cellar roof seemed to be dropping, the walls squeezing. She climbed the bulkhead steps until she was bent nearly in two, the infant squeezed into the small space between her thighs and chest, and tried to open the door with her back. Her legs shook. Sweat sprang at her neck. She was still soft and weak from the birth two weeks before, her right eye bloodshot though she had no memory of pushing, no memory of any of it, nothing until a baby was being handed to her, clean and silent, like a doll her mother had bought. She was lucky, Bea understood — Aunt Vera had hired a doctor who had studied in Germany with the father of twilight sleep. There had been morphine, there had been scopolamine — these, according to Aunt Vera, would do more to liberate women than the vote. Bea understood that she was supposed to understand herself to be lucky. She

4

understood that she must have pushed, and that she should be glad not to remember. She pushed now, using her neck, her shoulders, every muscle in her body. At last the door gave an inch, then two, then lightened so quickly Bea was following it — she had to scramble to catch up before it slammed on the ground outside. She looked behind her, above. The hinge had given a sharp cry. She went stiff waiting for another sound, the nurse's heavy footsteps, her heavy call: *Beatrice?* She waited until her breath came and quieted her heart. Then she stepped out into the night.

★ ★ ★

Through the near trees she could see the far ones in the orchard down below. Slowly, her eyes adjusted, and she saw the pears themselves, their waxy orbs glowing greenly in the three-quarter dark. Her mouth watered and Bea, embarrassed by this bodily secretion, turned her thoughts to her Plan.

Walk to orchard.
Wake infant.
Nurse infant.
Change infant.
Check inside paper sack: extra diapers, two
    bottles, four cans of Borden's evaporated
    milk, five twenty-dollar bills.
Set infant under most plentiful tree.
Run.

Around her left wrist, on a leather cord, Bea

wore the very loud whistle Aunt Vera used to scare squirrels off the bird feeders. If they weren't gentle with the infant, she would blow it. Also, she would blow it if they turned out not to be who she thought they were. Bea had relied on Uncle Ira for her information, and Uncle Ira was prone to telling tales. Nevertheless, Bea had chosen to believe him. It happened every year, he said. When the moon was bright enough to see by but not to be easily seen, the air still enough not to carry sound or scent. The pears on the verge of starting to drop. He never heard or saw a thing, but the next morning he would look out his window and down the hill and there, where the day before the pears had packed the branches like sparrows, there would be only leaves and the gray, fleshy stubs from which the pears had grown. Uncle Ira smiled, describing this. They might be giraffes, he mused. Giants! Ira harbored a kind of love for the trespassers who stole his pears. They made him feel benevolent.

But really, he said, Catholics. A poor Irish family who had found a market for pears. And Bea believed him, maybe because she had to. She didn't know any Catholics. Catholics weren't Jews, but they were like Jews in that they weren't Protestants. So there was that. And back home Bea had seen the Irish children walking in packs through the common and envied them, even the poor ones, the company. There looked to be a certain freedom in being one of many: the right to go unnoticed, unattended. Neglect, Bea's mother would call it, she who had rarely let Bea out of her sight.

6

Until she had, quite suddenly.

And look at the consequences.

Bea steadied herself against one of the near trees, a tall, straight pine so bare of low branches it entered her consciousness as more human than plant. An idea came to her of sliding down its rough side, lying down on the cushion its needles made beneath her feet, and falling back to sleep with the baby in her arms.

The infant snorted. Bea wouldn't have guessed that babies snorted but this one snorted all the time, followed by a tremulous sigh. The sigh came. Bea shifted the infant to her shoulder. High above them, a branch creaked and shifted, making way for moonlight. Already its angle had changed. If Bea waited for the people to arrive, she would lose her resolve, or she would keep it and be seen and the people would tell Uncle Ira and he would tell her parents and her mother would make her give the baby to the awful woman who had come last month from the Orphanage for Jewish Children, reeking of camphor and assuring Aunt Vera and Uncle Ira that she did not believe in spoiling, kissing, or otherwise unnecessarily touching babies.

She began to walk. Her neck was wet with the baby's breath and to counter the sensation, and whatever emotion it might lead to, she did what she had trained herself to do over the months of carrying the baby, as rigorously as she had ever trained herself to play a Beethoven sonata or pen a thank-you card in the microscopic, finger-cramping script that satisfied her mother: she thought of other things. The pear trees, which she could see more clearly with every step. They were Braffets, she knew, not because she understood anything about fruit or trees but because Uncle Ira talked about his pears all the time, as though they were the children he wished he'd had, braver and brighter than his own. *Have you seen the Braffets, battling the frost? Look at those Braffets, blossoming like little gods. Who knew I would be so lucky to have such Braffets.* Thirty-one years ago, he had imported the trees from Sussex, England, paying their fare not in cargo but in third class, where each one, wrapped in burlap, its roots watered daily by a hired boy, occupied its own bunk. *The Braffets are in the orchard, fermenting the revolution.* Bea tightened her hold on the bundle of baby and shawl. She had reached the stone wall that marked the orchard's western boundary. She squinted into the dark, straining to hear the first sounds of feet and wheelbarrows, but heard nothing apart from the lazy slap of water on the rocky beach down below. The pears waited on their branches. Vera's exotic fish swam silently in their little pond. The infant made no sound but Bea covered its mouth with her hand anyway, half knowing its lips would move to suck her palm, half pretending to be surprised at the warm, wet mouth as it burrowed and groped. *Braffet*, she said in her mind. *Braffet pears were named after a duchess. Braffet pears appear on the branch a bold yellow and turn green when ripe. Braffet pears are often marred by rough brownish gray patches but these do not affect*

8

their taste or texture beneath the skin. All this Bea recited silently as she unbuttoned her dress to her waist, shrugged one shoulder from its sleeve, and lowered the waking infant so it could suck.

She gasped as the mouth clamped onto her nipple, but the pain was a distraction, too, welcome in its own way. If the choice had been up to the Orphanage for Jewish Children woman, the infant would have been taken away before Bea even woke up. Aunt Vera was the one who noticed Bea, during the woman's visit, turn bone white. Vera was weak but she had summoned the stick-straight posture she had been taught at Miss Winsor's School and argued for a two-week delay. They would hire a wet nurse, she promised. And maybe because Vera was so ill, or so rich, or both, the woman relented. But then Aunt Vera hired a regular nurse and shocked Bea by putting the baby to her breast and Bea had gone along, in part because it justified her holding the baby, which she was desperate if terrified to do, and in part because the whole business was so uncomfortable it called up in her a resentment and resenting the baby had been a relief.

As the sucking went on, the pain quieted. She leaned forward, trying to make out the gap in the honeysuckle that was the lower entrance to the orchard. Still she saw no one. She heard nothing new. The baby pulled at her breast until the pain abandoned her entirely, leaving behind a fluttering twinge that was recognizable to Bea, despite herself, as pleasure.

A crack sounded from beyond the gap. Bea held her breath. She heard no footsteps on the road, no wheels scraping the dirt ruts. She had assumed they would push wheelbarrows for the pears, but the scuffling she heard now came from the small woods across the road. Beyond the woods were the rocks that led down to the harbor. So they had come by boat. Bea stuck a finger in the infant's mouth, dislodged it from her breast, and started to walk toward the pear trees. The infant wailed. Bea stuck her finger back in its mouth and the baby sucked again, quiet, but the echo of its cry winged out over the trees. Bea's blood began to pound. She worked to breathe, even to swallow, but her throat was full of the pounding; each step she took through the tall grass exploded in her ears. She looked back at the house. Vera's hearing was weak and Uncle Ira slept like a stone, but the nurse was always half awake, it seemed, springing catlike when the infant so much as stirred.

Bea was looking back so intently she didn't see the root that threw her forward. She caught herself with one hand but the infant's head fell back roughly, as the nurse had instructed her it was never supposed to do. The baby howled. Bea filled its mouth again with her finger, bounced it, shushed in its ear.

In her fall she reached the pear tree she had chosen yesterday. She came down to the orchard in daylight, wanting to be sure that if for some reason the people picked from only one tree this year, they would find the baby waiting under it. She chose this one, and felt certain in her choice. But now she couldn't see well and the infant struggled in her arms and the scent of pears was so strong she thought she would gag. Maybe the next tree produced the finest pears. Maybe this tree was understood to be the runt and the people wouldn't even bother with it. Why had Bea thought herself capable of judging anything, let alone the worth of a tree?

Voices now, shout-whispers through the trees. *Get up*, said her mother. *Give the thing back to the nurse. Go to sleep. Wait for the lady from the orphanage. You're a good girl. You used to be. Don't let a small mistake ruin your life.* Aunt Vera said, *Keep the baby, if it upsets you so much. We'll raise it together.* But that was a lie because Aunt Vera was dying. *Do what you want,* Uncle Ira said. *You think your parents ever do a thing they don't want?* But Bea didn't know what she wanted. She wanted to go back, she supposed, to before the lieutenant, before he smiled at her, before he pushed her against the wall, before he forced himself on her. *Handsome,* her mother had murmured in her ear that night. *Handsome,* she murmured now. Bea wanted to go back to when her greatest struggle was picking her way through Liszt. But she couldn't go back and Aunt Vera would die soon and she didn't trust Uncle Ira to defend her, when the time came; for all his talk, he snapped like a stick in front of her father. So if Bea kept the baby it would be taken anyway, only it would be the hideous orphanage woman who got it.

The small woods trembled with the people's coming and Bea allowed herself a look down. Across the baby's cheeks, she could trace the rash that had bloomed its second day of life, ferociously red and raw. Bea had convinced herself that the rash was a direct result of her unsuitability as a mother, and that it wouldn't go away until she gave the thing up. She touched its cheek now, letting her fingers skid over the tiny bumps. They had receded, just as the nurse had said they would. The nurse couldn't have known how her words, meant to comfort, would rattle Bea. The rash was perfectly common, she had said, nothing to trouble over. It would clear up soon and the girl would have Bea's skin, 'coffee 'n' cream,' the nurse's *R* rolling like water. 'Baby girl,' she had cooed while Bea pretended not to listen. *Baby girl. Darlin'. Luv. Girl.*

Cradling it now as the people came closer, Bea experienced time slowing into a long, stuttering wave, her life at once paused and hurtling forward, her vision stretching to see the infant growing at an alarming rate, lengthening and fattening in her arms until it outgrew her grasp and unfurled to stand before her. It was so undeniably a girl, just like Bea — a girl in an orchard in the middle of the night — that Bea felt her own heart grow. She felt as if her ribs would crack.

Rubbish, said her mother. *Sentiment*. In three weeks Bea would recommence her musical instruction at the conservatory and enter the freshman class at Radcliffe, where she would continue her studies in the liberal arts and wear

12

a brace to hold in her stomach and go to dances with the Harvard boys and act like all the other girls, as if she'd never lost a thing.

A crunching from the road — feet on gravel, close now. Bea's breast went taut with goose bumps, reminding her of her exposure, and in the rapid, mindless act of buttoning her dress she was freed of decision. The baby's eyes were closed. Bea's arms shook as she set the bundle down in a clump of grass. The approaching footsteps were gentle, she told herself. The people were gentle thieves and they were Irish, like the nurse — they would know, she decided, how to care for babies. She had the whistle in case they didn't. She stood, her shaking violent now and in every bone of her body so that it seemed to her that she must be audible. She clamped her jaw tight against its rattling. Then she ran, a pounding, rattling heart-bone, and threw herself down behind the stone wall.

★ ★ ★

They emerged from the gap in a silent swarm, tall and short, in dark, shapeless clothing, their faces and hands pale. Bea could not determine, at first, a leader. They carried ladders, three figures to each, held tight at their sides as they headed for the trees. They were like fairies, Bea thought, until she heard a man's voice, quiet but clear: 'Get off your blasted arses and up those trees.' Bea positioned Aunt Vera's whistle in her hand. The ladders rose, their tops narrower than their bottoms, and Bea nearly shrieked, thinking

13

of the tiny body, thinking she should have wrapped it in something brighter than Aunt Vera's shawl, should have set it farther out from the trunk of the tree so it would catch the moonlight, or farther in so it wouldn't get trampled. She couldn't remember now at what distance she had set it. She rose on her knees, peering above the wall. She counted eight of them, maybe more. The ladders were planted but she hadn't heard the baby howl in pain and a new fear struck her — that they wouldn't find it at all. They would collect their pears and depart in their boats and the baby would still be lying there, sound asleep. Bea would have to collect it, and decide all over again what to do, and feel not only humiliation — that she was used to now — but failure.

She watched the pears fall off the trees. It was like that, as if they were simply falling, so quickly did they disappear down the ladders. The smallest figures — children — stood at the bottom, gathering the pears onto tarps, dragging these out of the way when they were full, then laying down new ones. The entire operation was carried out with an efficiency that Bea's father, Henry Haven, would have appreciated, the sort of efficiency he spent his days (and many nights) trying to achieve at the Haven Shoe Factory. *Astounding*, he might say, in the tepid voice he used to deliver praise so as not to please or, heaven forbid, flatter the recipient.

'Clear here.'

'On to the next one.'

'Quickly!'

14

'My foot!'

'Shut it.' This was said by the man who'd given the first order, in a calm, heavy voice.

'Ow!'

'Shut it.'

'Lay off 'im, Rolly. He'll shush if you lay off.'

'I'll lay off when I'm dead.'

But the man was quiet. It was a woman who had reprimanded him, in an accent like the nurse's, her voice uncommonly deep, and kind, it seemed to Bea. It was the sort of voice, Bea thought hopefully, that could only belong to the sort of woman for whom mothering comes naturally. So unlike Bea's mother's voice, which betrayed her unhappiness, or Aunt Vera's, fluty with distraction.

Bea didn't think to wonder what her own voice was like. She clung to the woman's kindness, longed to hear her speak again. She wished there were a way to get her attention without the others seeing. Still the baby had made no noise. This could be a sign, Bea thought, that it wanted her, and no one else. Or maybe she had nursed it too well and sent it into a stupor, knowing what she was doing without admitting it to herself.

'Mum!' A boy's voice.

'Shh.'

'Over here. Look!'

'What?'

'Come!'

'What.'

'Look!'

'Oh.'

15

'What is it?'

'A baby,' the child said.

'Christ.'

'Brand-new.'

'I don't care how new it is. We've got work to do.'

'Put it over there now.' The woman's voice. 'Over here.' Bea could see one figure pushing another, smaller one. The taller one, the woman, had a small child on her back. 'Set it down there. Let's finish.'

'What about the baby?'

'Shh.'

The boy left the bundle at the edge of the field, not twenty feet from where Bea hid. She fought a rising nausea. This she hadn't considered — that they might find the baby *and* leave it.

She traveled in her mind to Boston, the baby in her arms. She walked down Chestnut Street, up the stairs to her parents' narrow townhouse, and stared at the brass knocker. She stared for so long that all its facets came forward, intricacies she had not known she knew: three rosebuds arranged vertically, each slightly larger than the one below it; four paisley curls rising from the top, evoking a lion's mane. To her left was the mezuzah, a slim silver cylinder meant to go unnoticed. Bea in the orchard waited with Bea on the stairs, until her parents' maid, Estelle, opened the door.

Estelle stared. A visit from President Wilson wouldn't have surprised her more — that was plain on her face. Also plain was her pleasure.

16

She took the infant in her arms, held the pale face to her dark one, and slapped Bea gently on the cheek.

If Estelle was the whole story, Bea would survive it. She might even choose it. But Estelle was Lillian's before she was Bea's — after making Bea a strong cup of tea she would have to take her to her mother, who would be standing in her closet or sitting at her vanity in her girdle and brassiere, rageful with indecision. The sight of Bea and the baby would fell her — within seconds she would be flat on her back in bed, weeping. She had wept when Bea, at ten, came in second in the Young Ladies' Composition for Piano Competition, wept two years later when Bea's breasts grew to be 'larger than ladylike.' Bea had never grown immune to her mother's weeping. She had devised an expression, hard as a brick, that made her appear so, but inside she crumpled like a dropped puppet.

Her father wouldn't come home until late. By then Estelle would have propped Lillian on pillows and helped make up her face. Henry would see her puffiness. He would see Bea and the infant and feel an unscheduled joy unlock beneath his ribs, but he would suppress his smile. Lillian would ask Bea the question she had been waiting for Henry's arrival to ask. Did anyone see you walk down the street? Bea would say yes, everyone had seen, whether it was true or not, just to get the full devastation over with. Lillian would return to her weeping and Bea would go find Estelle and nurse the baby and begin living like a leper in her parents' house.

17

In the orchard, dew seeped through Bea's nightgown, wetting her knees. She looked up at the moon's tall, untroubled distance. If she knew how to pray, she thought, she would pray. Instead she held her breath and avoided looking toward the bundle in the grass.

'Clear here.'

'Here, too.'

'Ladders down!'

'Help him with that tarp.'

'This handle's broke.'

'Poor you.'

'I need a hand on this ladder.'

'Give 'im a hand — let's go!'

Small mountains of pears began to slide toward the gap. Bea started to cry.

A figure fell off from the group, and another — the woman with the child on her back, and the boy who had found the baby. They walked toward the bundle with high, quiet steps. The woman picked it up.

'Can we call it Pear?' the child asked.

'Hush.'

The woman dropped her face into the blanket, as if sniffing. Bea thought she was trying to decide, but the woman was already decided. She knew the story of Ruth, even if Bea didn't. A second later, she and the boy and the child and the baby were gone, following the others through the gap and disappearing into the woods. Soon Bea heard the sound of boats being dragged off the rocks. The high, whining creak of oars in their locks, moving offshore. Another whine, coming from Bea herself, a piercing, involuntary sound running from her stomach to her throat: all she could do not to wail. She clamped a hand to her mouth, then vomited into her cupped palm as quietly as she could.

1

1927

The Stanton Quarry was 230 feet deep and half a mile long, the largest granite operation on Cape Ann, and since the woods around it had been cleared to make room for derricks and cutting sheds and garymanders and the locomotive that hauled the rock down to the piers, a man could now stand in the corner office of the Stanton Granite Company headquarters and see the wide, whitecapped sweep of the Ipswich Bay. On the clearest days, he could see all the way to New Hampshire or, if he squeezed himself against the office's western wall and looked due north, as Josiah Story did now — his cheek taking on the shape of the wood paneling — the whaleish hump of Mount Agamenticus in Maine. Josiah waited for revelation. On his desk sat an optimistically thick stack of paper, all blank except for one sentence: *I did not come to Gloucester, I was born here, just like my dear wife Susannah was born here, and just how our children and grandchildren will be.*

Maybe it wasn't a very good sentence, as far as sentences went. Josiah didn't worry about that. Susannah would fix his grammar, smooth any awkwardness, tweeze out just enough but not too much of his townie roots, clean him up, as she always did. And he liked the idea behind the sentence. He thought it established not only his nativity but his inescapable devotion to the place, and he guessed that was important when a person was running for mayor. The trouble came when he tried to speak the sentence aloud and his tongue went limp on the word 'children,' which he and Susannah had been trying and failing to produce for the entire seven years and three months they had been married. He knew the numbers because Susannah kept track in a small leather journal and updated him on their progress, or rather lack thereof, each month. She might have kept track of the days and hours, too, though if so, she spared him that. Josiah did want children. The thought of their smooth heads running around provoked a drumming in his chest — he liked the idea of two, one boy, one girl, disturbing the order of his and Susannah's house. But he also liked order. He liked quiet, it turned out, a discovery since leaving his clamorous childhood home. He didn't mourn, as Susannah did, on a daily basis, the dreamed children's absence. But then he tried that first sentence and his mouth wouldn't do it — his tongue simply stopped, a flaccid rebellion. The children flung themselves at him with their sweet-smelling hair and noisemaking and he felt at once a crush of grief and the cold humiliation of having told a lie.

'Sir?' Through the door came the muffled plea of Josiah's assistant, who was already being bombarded by men waiting to see Josiah. It was Friday morning. By ten o'clock, the line might be twenty deep. He had arrived hours ago, when the sky was still pink, determined to finish the speech before anyone arrived.

'Just a minute,' Josiah called. He removed his face from the wall, straightened his jacket, and, to bolster himself, took a minute to regard the activity down in the pit. From this height, a ten-foot slab of granite rising through the air on dog hooks appeared light as a child's toy. The ladders looked like matchsticks, the men on the ledges like ants, their movements — swinging hammers, setting drills, maneuvering hooks — barely visible. *Here you are*, Josiah told himself. Running the quarry. Running for mayor. Last winter, his father-in-law, Caleb Stanton, had retired from the company's day-to-day business and put Josiah in charge and here he was, in Caleb's warm, leather-scented office, entrusted with Friday Favors, a tradition begun years ago by Caleb to enhance the company's reputation. Caleb, it seemed, had created or invented almost everything in Josiah's life, including his mayoral aspirations, for Caleb himself was too old now to run, and besides, too many powerful people envied him. Josiah, the rookie, the native-born son-in-law, was the perfect foil. So what if he had left school after eighth grade, like most of his friends? He had spent more time in front of the bathroom mirror than his mother and three brothers combined, regarding his strong chin and sky blue eyes, the both-feet-planted-shoulders-back bearing he had never been taught, and now a muckraker at the *Gloucester Daily Times* had dug up proof that Josiah's opponent in the mayoral race, Frankie

22

Fiumara, once attended a rally for the socialist Eugene Debs. That Fiumara was Italian didn't help him. Nicola Sacco and Bartolomeo Vanzetti were once again dominating the news: the findings of Governor Fuller's Lowell commission were soon due, the public waiting to see if the shoemaker and fishmonger would finally be executed. It had been seven years since their first trial for the murder of a payroll clerk and his guard in South Braintree, and six since their second, and still, though no evidence linked them clearly to the crime, the anarchists remained in prison. Around the world, people had risen up in protest. They had marched, gone on strike, bombed American embassies, named streets and cigarettes after the men. The cry was foul play: Sacco and Vanzetti had been tried for their politics and convicted for their foreignness. All this might have worked in Fiumara's favor — Gloucester was full of Italians. But there were more Irish, and plenty of blue-blood WASPs, and still more people who, though it didn't make them proud, simply didn't like the look of the two wops. And so Josiah Story, boy from Mason Street, was likely to be mayor, if he could just give a few decent speeches and rally the women's vote.

The women were still new to voting. The women were key. And Josiah had a plan to win them over, by eking an endorsement out of a leading dry named Beatrice Cohn. *See?* Josiah urged himself. *Here you are. With a plan. It's April. Almost spring. All these men are here to see you.*

23

The door opened, then shut again, letting in a brief roar from the waiting room. Josiah didn't turn at first. He waited to hear his assistant say, 'It's time, sir.' Then he turned.

Sam Turpa was a tall, skinny boy who would stoop like that until he filled out in the chest and shoulders. Josiah had chosen him for the job because he was loyal, because he was Finnish — the quarrymen liked seeing one of their own in a decent suit up in the office — and because Josiah did not trust himself to keep a woman at his side all day, as Caleb had. Josiah's eyes were the wandering kind. Back in the day, before Susannah, other parts of him had wandered, too. He was prone to a pretty smile, flattery. And so, no women. Susannah suffered enough.

'Who's here?'

'A Mr. Taylor, sir, and his brother. An Italian named Buzzi who says you said you had a job? Various innkeepers. A lobsterman . . . '

'The Italian is pronounced 'Boozy,' I think.'

The boy nodded, too harried to appreciate the joke. 'Who should I send in?'

'Shall,' Josiah said, correcting Sam as Caleb had once corrected him. 'Who *shall* you send in.' He gave the boy an apologetic smile, reached up to ruffle his straw-colored hair, seized with longing, then moved away, toward the porthole window. 'Let's see.'

He recognized Buzzi right away, a carver from Naples who'd come to Josiah's door a month ago, saying he could turn stone into lilies. There were the 'hotel' men looking for alcohol and whores, as if Josiah had been born with both in

24

his pockets. He could locate them, of course, but it would require telephone calls, perhaps a drive. If he were his blacksmith father, he would turn his sign around, go upstairs to his small apartment, and sleep. His father, though not a lazy man, had no stamina for negotiating, even on the price of his work. But Josiah wasn't his father. He had surpassed his father. A couple years ago, Josiah had offered him a job heating the iron rims for the garymander wheels and his father had declined, complaining that Josiah worked his men too hard. 'It's not me, it's old Stanton,' Josiah explained. His father simpered. 'Said like a future dictator,' he said, and went back to the hammer he'd been mending.

Josiah met with Buzzi first, then a ship captain who had sixty cases of full-strength, authentically labeled brandy waiting four miles offshore in need of runners, then a pair of young men who had done some running for Josiah in the past and were eager to do more. Deals were falling into place. He liked the game of it, the exercise of working out what the men would owe him in return, making them think, as his father-in-law advised, that they were getting a good deal. 'They have no idea,' he said, 'how much money you have access to. They can't fathom it. They hear 'rich' and they think a stand of timber, a heap of clams. They don't know that they are worth more to you than you will ever make yourself to them.' Caleb's choice of words wasn't lost on Josiah: how much money you have *access to*. But this was part of what he liked about Friday Favors: that he wasn't required to be himself, exactly, but a representative for someone else. He was like a playactor giving play money away.

He was about to have Sam send in the Taylors when a woman entered the waiting room, followed by one child, then another. By the time the door had shut behind them, there were seven, ranging from nearly grown to a toddler, all standing in a quiet line against the back wall. Their mother wore a plain dress and badly worn shoes. Her hair had been blown by the wind, and though she was making a great effort to gather it into a bun and tuck it behind her ears, Josiah found himself cheered by her minimal success. All that hair made her appear beautiful. Or maybe she was beautiful. And her children — they were so well behaved, so patient. Their sheer mass, that many small, warm bodies in a row, gave him a little chill. The waiting room had gone quiet at the arrival of the family.

'I'll see the woman,' Josiah said.

'The Irish lady, sir?'

'Is there any other?'

'But she's just arrived.'

'The others will wait.'

'And the children, sir?'

'Not the children.'

'They've come with the lady, sir.'

'They'll wait peacefully.'

'There's barely standing room, sir.'

'Send some of the others outside.' Josiah's need to see the woman up close was inexplicable but overwhelming. A clear, sharp stab. Hunger after years of being overfed.

'It's cold, sir.'

'Then see about ordering some hats! Certainly we should provide them with hats when they come to ask for money.'

Sam stared. 'Are you in earnest, sir?'

'No! Truthfully I don't care. If you want to give them hats, give them hats. Just bring in the woman.' And with a force he regretted, he pushed Sam out the door.

* * *

Once the woman was seated across from him, Josiah couldn't think what to say. Everything about her appealed to him — her high cheekbones, her small breasts, her teeth protruding, just slightly, in front of her bottom lip. She hadn't managed to fix her hair, and so she looked at him through a fringe of yellow, her gaze polite but unflinching.

'You wished to see me, Mr. Story?'

Josiah stared. 'Your eyes are the color of our stone,' he said before he could stop himself, and because he couldn't explain why he'd said it, he felt compelled to keep talking. 'Olive green. Very rare. Very valuable. When my father-in-law bought this spot, he had no idea. He thought it would last a year, maybe two, thought he would cut it for paving stones, ship it to New York, be done with it. But twenty feet down the rock came up green. Almost no seams or knots. So here we are, still cutting. People pay us to ship as far as Washington, D.C., and Chicago. They want the biggest slabs

27

so they can turn the stuff into monuments.'

Josiah stopped. The woman looked perplexed. He realized he hadn't stood when she entered, or asked her name, or shaken her hand. Now he stood, causing her to stand, the mechanics relieving them for a moment of each other's eyes until, upright, they appeared ready to part.

'Call me Josiah,' he said, extending his hand.

'Emma Murphy.'

Her skin was dry and rough but she didn't look away. He thought of the creams Susannah kept lined up like little dolls on her chest of drawers. He waited to feel repelled by Emma Murphy's hand, but the feeling didn't come. He saw that he hadn't been exaggerating: her eyes really were the color of Stanton stone. They were so strange, and yet so perfectly matched to the quarry, that looking at them gave him a haunted feeling, as though she had worn these eyes especially for this visit, and as he looked and she looked back he saw the closest derrick reflected in each of her eyes so that two tiny derricks looked back at him, their identical arms going through their identical slow motions, and before the shrunken derricks Josiah felt oddly free. His sentence floated into his mind — *I did not come to Gloucester, I was born here . . .* — and floated out just as easily.

He dropped her hand and motioned her to sit, all the while working to regain his sobriety.

'What can I do for you, Mrs. Murphy?'

'I've come with a proposition.'

He waited. A patch of pink crept up her neck. Clearly she hadn't done anything like this before.

28

She didn't know that confidence was key — you had to appear entirely certain that what you had Josiah would want. The derricks were gone from her eyes now — they'd been replaced by sky and a bright, blank distress. 'I'm listening,' he offered.

'Are you familiar with perry, sir? It's a fermented drink, made from pears.'

'Like cider?'

'But less common. People will pay more for it.'

'Is that right?' He sounded interested in the money, but that wasn't how he felt. He had noticed a small mole on Emma Murphy's right cheek.

'We've everything we need to run an operation, sir.'

He waited again.

'Except the press. And the bottles. And possibly a small shed, for cover.'

'Of course.'

'But we're not starting from nothing. I know someone who's been making the stuff for years. We'd offer you ten percent.'

'And who is *we*?'

'My family. The Murphys. Of Leverett Street, sir.'

'Josiah,' he said.

'Yes.'

'Will you say it?'

'Is that necessary? My family includes myself, my husband, and my children. I've nine.'

Josiah went to the window. The children stood against the wall in a tight line, their hair as pale and thin and blown as their mother's, except for one girl in the middle whose hair was nearly black. To an onlooker, her dark eyes appeared dense and unfocused, but in fact she was calculating the number of jugs of perry they would have to sell before she could siphon off enough money to buy a train ticket to Canada. And Josiah was thinking about how Emma Murphy, clearly, was not a stranger to infidelity.

'I count only seven,' he said.

'The others are grown, sir.'

'And does your husband know you're here?'

'He's fishing, out at the Grand Banks.'

'So he doesn't know?'

'He will.'

Josiah returned to his desk. He searched her face for coyness or deceit but found neither, only a frank nervousness he wanted to soothe.

'And his name would be?'

'Roland Murphy.'

'Roland Murphy the fisherman, out on a long trip. And you're an aspiring cider woman.'

'Perry. Sir. We intend to wet the cape in it. We can give you ten percent.'

Josiah nodded, trying to appear calm, though her words aroused him. He tried to focus on the 10 percent, hoping money would bring him back to his role. He laughed, as he was supposed to. 'Forty,' he countered.

'Fifteen?'

'Thirty,' he said, frowning. He snapped his mind back to Susannah, who would be preparing to eat her lunch now, fully dressed and alone; this afternoon, if it was the right time of month, she would pull back the coverlet on their bed and lay down a fresh towel as a rag — Turkish cotton, bought at Stearns — in preparation for his coming home. Susannah, who was a better businessman than him and who would tell him not to be sorry for Emma Murphy, not to go lower than 40 percent, not to frown but to smile when he negotiated. He focused on Emma Murphy's overbite and said, 'Last offer.'

She nodded. Then she surprised him by smiling. Her smile wasn't happy but matter-of-fact, obligatory, exposing a tall, pink gum line. 'Thirty,' she agreed, and it took all his strength to stop staring at her mouth.

'And your boys out there. Would they like jobs in the quarry this summer? Twenty hours, maybe thirty? That's the most I can get away with these days, for kids. We don't usually hire them at all anymore. But yours — are they as bright as they look?'

Emma Murphy narrowed her eyes. 'That's very generous. I'll consider,' she said, in the exact tone his mother had always used to pretend to consider turning down help.

'Okay, then,' he said, instead of *Very well, then,* which was what he'd learned to say from his father-in-law. 'I'll see that you get what you need, for the press.'

She stood. She was older than he'd realized, maybe eight or ten years his senior, and taller, too, and he was struck, looking up at her (her mistake in standing before he'd stood irritating and attracting him), at how completely unknown she was to him. He loved Susannah. She was as essential, as inextricable from his life as his own

31

hands or feet; it was the roll of her body toward him each morning, her long, horsey braid in his face, her Lady Esther Four-Purpose Face Cream-scented skin that righted him and sent him out into the day whole. He loved Susannah as much as he ever had — it wasn't the amount but rather the nature of his love that had changed. He felt for her now what he imagined one might feel for a sister. Most days, that passed in his mind as enough.

'I may come myself,' he said to Emma Murphy.

'You oughtn't.' Finally, she looked away.

'True,' he said, opening the door and showing her out with a sweep of his arm that would appear dismissive to an onlooker. 'But I may.'

2

Washington Street wound through Lanesville as close to the coves as a road could run, rearing up with the hills, skidding this way and that as the stone walls dictated. The earliest walls had been built before the road. You could still see where they had been taken apart to make way for the new lanes that climbed from Washington Street to the woods. These — among them Leverett Street — were not so new anymore, though many of the houses lining them still looked temporary: built hastily for quarrymen, their walls were thin, their doorsteps missing roofs to shield a person from the rain, their roofs cheap paper requiring frequent patching, lending the houses a disheveled appearance, even if they were well cared for.

The Murphy house was somewhere in the middle, better or worse cared for depending on the year, and Roland's mood, and how old the oldest boys living at home were at a given time. At this time it was suffering one of its more neglected moments because Emma Murphy and her children were spending all their energies on the perry shack and Roland was away. Seven paces from the house — a few more, if you were a child — in the small yard that separated their house from the next, shaded by an old, swaybacked oak tree and assorted beech and bramble that had grown up alongside it, an outline of a cellar had been knifed into the dirt. Here Liam and Jeffrey dug with their father's big shovels while Janie and Anne, using the oak's trunk as a vertical sort of sawhorse, measured pine planks for the shack's walls, and the youngest ones, Maggie and Joshua, dug with shells at the cellar's boundary. Their other sister, Lucy Pear, had taken them to Plum Cove Beach to find the shells. She was the one who had measured the cellar's outline and thought of using a knife — their hoe was too dull — and then cut the outline herself. She was the one who had bushwhacked through the trees dividing their yard from the next and asked Mr. Davies if he was planning to use the pile of knotty pine boards behind his house.

The boards were discards from a barn he was done building, and Mr. Davies was kind. Still, the girl's audacity astonished Emma. Lucy had always seemed older than her years, but she had not always seemed capable of brashness. As an infant she had been so calm that Emma worried she would get trampled — for a time, she even convinced herself that Lucy might be dumb, that she had been left because of a defect or injury and that no one but Emma would ever want her. This was when Roland was still telling Emma to find the baby another home: *Drop her at the orphanage at Salem, come on now.* As a mother of five, soon to be six, Emma knew he was right. She was sorry — she saw how hard he worked, saw his daily, degrading amazement: it was never enough. But Lucy's calm, the way she looked at Emma as she sucked, not tugging or bucking, only looking, her fawn-colored cheeks sighing in and out, her dark eyes locked on Emma's until, without warning, they rolled gratefully back, opened up a hole in Emma, a new, bloody tunnel through her heart.

Roland disapproved of the nursing, too. But Emma argued it was cheaper than evaporated milk, and this was true, so she got her way, and soon enough Roland fell for Lucy, too, stopping to watch her suck, tickling the bottoms of her feet. At first Emma's breasts, having weaned Jeffrey three months before, gave only a watery trickle, but then milk began to flow, and Lucy drank steadily, with that strange, almost unnerving calm. Even her fussing was gentle, more coo than cry.

Emma wondered if Lucy was dumb because then keeping Lucy could pass for a kind of selflessness. But Lucy turned out not to be at all dumb, only even-tempered and kind. She had the steady energy of a woman by the time she was eight, along with a boy's knack for physical work, for pieces and parts and how they fit together, how things worked. Now almost ten, she had become a leader among the children. She led them now, pointing with a hammer to show her sisters how to measure straight despite the board's knots. Emma sat on a stump trying to read a pamphlet she'd sent away for — blandly titled PEAR VARIETIES, though its real subject was perry — but Lucy's voice kept distracting her. 'Like that. No, a little to the right. Yes, there. Good. But now you have to check the angle . . . ' Emma looked to see Janie's

35

reaction — always she watched to see if her other girls would grow tired of Lucy's bossing. But she had her way about her. And Janie, while not a pushover, liked clear direction. She did as Lucy said, then tucked her pencil proudly behind her ear. Emma smiled. She was glad for the distraction. Perry was more complicated than she had thought. It was not simply cider made with pears. Pears had to stand longer than apples before you crushed them, and then the pulp had to stand before you crushed it. There were tannins to clear and possible 'hazes' that could ruin it and 'gravity' to check and other things Emma didn't understand. She had little memory or patience for such details, or any details at all, really — though the neighbors might have guessed otherwise, Emma had tunneled through the years of boiling potatoes in time for supper and captaining the transfer of clothing from larger to smaller children and overseeing the basic hygiene and nail clipping of nine children perpetually on the verge of chaos. There was little grace involved. And now the perry seemed to require particular perry pears, not eating pears, but they would have to use eating pears because that's all that was grown on Cape Ann, so perhaps the instructions would have to be adjusted — but how? She could not ask the perry maker she had boasted to Josiah Story about. She knew the man because she had been selling him their stolen pears over the years, but now she would be competing with him. He would not give her a recipe or help her solve yet another problem: their timing was off. The fermentation process was much longer than Emma had realized. The perry would not be ready this fall — not even close. What had she been thinking? Of money, of course. She had not understood.

'You look worried.'

Lucy came without warning, swinging her hammer silently against her palm.

Emma removed her teeth from her lower lip, attempted another smile. 'No,' she said, 'not worried.'

Lucy knelt down next to Emma's stump. 'Josiah Story's not coming, is he.'

'He'll come,' Emma said. She reached to ruffle Lucy's hair as if to comfort her, though it was Emma who took comfort in this gesture, the dark mass of Lucy's curls surrounding her hand like a nest. Josiah Story was the other problem. A week had passed but he had not delivered the money, as he had said he would. They had the boards, but everything else they needed his money to buy. And not only the press and the jugs and barrels and paper for a roof but something the pamphlet called a scratcher, to pulp the pears. Emma had not known to mention a scratcher in his office. She had known almost nothing. They had only ever taken pears from the Eastern Point orchard — some for eating, most to sell to the perry maker. Yet here they were, planning to hit four fields in West Parish, three in Essex, and one as far as Ipswich. Emma and Lucy had consulted maps. They even had a Schedule of Ripeness drawn up, based on the exposures of the fields. 'We intend to wet the cape in it,' she had said. It made her queasy now, the ignorance of her ambition.

Lucy set down her hammer. She took the pamphlet from Emma's lap and began to page through it. 'What're tannins?'

'I don't know,' Emma admitted. 'I haven't gotten that far. And they likely don't explain it.'

'What about bacteria?'

Emma shrugged. 'We'll figure it out.'

They were quiet as Lucy read. Joshua whined. Maggie laughed. The boys' shovels scraped in rhythm. Emma watched a male cardinal — the first of the season — flit into the fading tangle of a forsythia bush, poke around, and fly off again.

'If you look at this, it seems like they're saying it won't be ready until next year.'

'I know.'

'You know?'

'I know now. I didn't know before.'

Lucy freed her hair from Emma's hand and stood. 'What about Da? He'll be back before we get it in the barrels.'

'I'll handle that,' Emma said, though she had no way of predicting when Roland might return. The boat he had left on was heading for the Grand Banks, but only after it dropped Roland and a couple others in Eastport, Maine. There, they planned to night fish for sardines and herring. More lucratively, they would provide shore watch for the speedboats running whiskey in from the mother ships anchored at the twelve-mile line, just beyond the Coast Guard's jurisdiction. Roland might be gone as many as ten weeks, or as few as six. He would come back on a different boat — they wouldn't know he was coming until he walked in the door. 'We'll take the long view,' Emma said. She pulled Lucy into an awkward hug, the girl's hip against her ear. 'It'll be okay.'

'Maybe,' Lucy said, standing stiffly in Emma's embrace. Her hip had grown a little curve, which Emma felt against her ear. How, Emma thought, had she not noticed this? 'If Josiah Story ever comes.'

'He'll come,' Emma said again, though she wasn't sure at all.

But he did come, the next day, in a butter yellow car half the length of the Murphy house, with a wad of cash he slipped into Emma's hand. He talked business: Where would Emma buy the press and how many barrels were needed, and didn't the boys want the jobs he'd offered? But when it was time to go he reached into his pocket again and, taking Emma's hand as if to shake it, slipped into her palm a silver chain, one of a dozen or more — they all looked the same to him — that Susannah Story kept in a little box she almost never bothered to open. Emma didn't know where the necklace came from. She felt it shiver coolly against her palm, felt her palm break instantaneously into sweat. She was too surprised to refuse. Even if she hadn't been, the children were watching. All she could think to do as he drove off was wave, and call, 'Thank you!' and wave some more, a stilted wave, her hand fisted around the necklace as it wiggled. But the other one was full of money, so she didn't have a choice.

3

In 1915, tired of buying and selling railroads in the Middle West and West, Caleb Stanton stood upon a parcel of land overlooking the Essex River and told the brokers and lawyers and architects gathered around, 'To live here would be to live in a painting.' He smiled. His throat ached. He was dismayed not by the land — the land was perfect — but by himself. He still had ideas about hunting lions in Africa, or sailing to the Galapagos. He could do those things now — he hadn't remarried, his younger son was at Harvard, his older one quietly taking over his own railroad company, Susannah sixteen and willing to travel with him anywhere — yet here he was, looking at the painting that was to become his life. He understood then that he was like his father: his hands were small, he couldn't grow a full beard, he was too practical to be truly reckless, and he preferred staying over going. His father had stayed in Maine, and now Caleb would stay in Gloucester. His adventure would be to purchase a rock ledge — a most immovable thing — and blow it to pieces.

The place, for the most part, had brought him pleasure. The view was a gentle one: the far dunes rising to form the mouth of the Essex River, the double hump of Hog Island's furry ridge, the beached dories of the clam diggers out at the flats, the salt marsh unfurling like a rust-colored carpet. The estate itself was laid out in the English style, with a slight, but only slight, asymmetry. There was a rose garden, a carriage house, a gardener's shack, a crescent-shaped swimming pool, and a bathhouse. There was Caleb's house, and the house he built for Susannah. There were a dozen old pine trees he had not cut down, and lawns running down to the rocks. It was easy to look out at his gracious bay and manicured land and see the logic of it all. It was easy to feel at peace.

And at night, when the logic was swallowed, when the gravel paths grew spectral and the pines rose up like a mountain range, a different pleasure worked at him. The barks of harbor seals sounded like feral dogs roaming the plain. A cat in heat became a moaning puma. Coyotes howled themselves into wolves, raccoons clawed themselves into boars as they ransacked the gardener's compost heap. The noises sent delicious tremors into Caleb's limbs — the wildness he'd longed for was here! Over time, he started taking long naps during the day so that at night he could be transported.

This was how, one night in the spring of 1927, he came to hear the loping of large bodies and think: *LIONS!!!*

Then he spotted them — humans — scurrying toward the bathhouse, arm in arm.

He was furious that first time, not only that Josiah and Susannah had broken his spell but that they did so for flagrantly intimate purposes. He had thought they were over trying to have children. It had been such a bad time, when

41

Susannah's stomach did not grow and her sadness came in, fogging her eyes and dulling her skin. She had always been the strongest of his three children — though he never would have said so to the boys — but she seemed to him suddenly, hauntingly frail. She reminded him for the first time of her mother, his late wife, Berenice, who had been ill almost the whole time he had known her, and this reminded him of all he'd been unable to fix.

Caleb had put Susannah and Josiah's reproductive efforts out of his mind and hoped they had, too. Yet he heard the lions again a few nights later, and again a few nights after that. In his chair by the window he seized with disgust and pity.

But tonight, the fourth time, the light behind the slatted door flickered. It was a candle, Caleb realized. They had lit a candle. He melted as if Susannah were a child again, pulling on his pant leg, looking up at him with her hazel eyes. Yesterday afternoon, he had gone out to the garden and seen that the tulips had opened. He had seen a mourning dove furiously building her nest under the eave of the gardener's shack, one seemingly inadequate twig after another, her efforts miraculously adding up to shelter. And now the candle. It was enough to recall him to his kindest self, to cause him to bring his forearm to his nose and smell the oils the sun had brought up in his skin. He gasped. Whenever someone gasped in novels (which Caleb indulged in between biography and history, having developed a regimen — history, biography, history, biography, novel, history, biography, and so on — that satisfied his idea of rigor) it struck Caleb as theatrical and false, but he had gasped like a woman and now he stood, gawking at the candle. He recalled his body, which he had neglected. He thought, *This is a fine moment for new life to begin.* Then he released the sleeve of his pajamas and closed the drape.

4

Emma could not think of Roland until it was through, and then — wending around her howling guilt, bracing herself against the shock of having committed once again a sin her mother would have disowned her for, not to mention Mary, oh — it was to wonder: would he care? He would want to smash their heads in, he would threaten to tell the parish, ruin her, but would he *care*? Beyond his rage, would it be Emma that he wanted? He would want his Wife, yes, his Girl, an idea of her that went back to the South End saloon where he had found her working as a barmaid, allowing a pinch here or there in exchange for extra tips. He had been one of the pinchers until he fell in love with her and wheedled and begged, claiming he was now too respectable for pinching. Through the weeks of their engagement and the early months of their marriage, when Emma was learning Roland's many base habits, she kept waiting for him to use her beginnings against her. But he never had, a mercy that reminded her, when she needed reminding, of Roland's fundamental goodness. Sometimes, in tender moments between them, he even romanced her with memories of her bar days. *Not a shred of sentiment in you*, he'd growl proudly in her ear. *So practical*, his hand finding its way under the hem of her dress.

She believed he was right. Her sentiment had been bled out of her: incompletely by her tough, corn-haired mother; more starkly as she watched her father lose his work; and finally, wholly, when she left Banagher with her cousins and landed in Boston with nothing but her name. It was Eimhear then but became Emma within days.

And so she told herself, as she lay in Josiah Story's office-thin arms on a deep white sofa in a bathhouse larger than her entire house, covered in an unimaginably soft quilt he called an afghan, that if Roland were ever to find out — though he must never find out — she could explain it as a sort of business agreement. An abhorrent, blasphemous agreement, but a practical one. She slept with the man in exchange for the perry press, a shack to house it, jobs for the boys down at the quarry. She would not tell about the necklace. She would say nothing of the hand cream he had given her tonight — their fourth night, she had not been able to keep from knowing, in the same way she always knew to the penny how much money she had in the jar under her bed, and always knew the number and ages of her children, even when Roland forgot. A reflex, to count and track and measure, and so, *Night four*, she'd thought as she lay low in Story's backseat, bracing herself when they hit the bumps on Concord Street, and just as she started to berate herself, *How can this be? Shame!* Story's pale hand fell her way across the backseat, wagging the bottle of cream like a toy, and she grabbed it, the fancy cut glass imprinting flowers into her palm, the scent of flowers making her sneeze. He laughed. 'Massage it into your hands,' he said in his slow, strange, satisfied way. And she did.

This was the new trouble in her life. This was what she had known the first night she woke to the milky arc of Story's headlights sweeping the walls of her house: she was susceptible. For as long as Emma could remember, she had been the opposite, anchored and hard. Her earliest memories were of infants crying, of holding, changing, feeding them. She prided herself on her steadiness, her lack of surprise no matter what occurred. There was the filthy South End, there was Roland, there was Gloucester, there was the little drafty house in the woods whose chimney liked to catch on fire, there were Emma's hands always figuring out what to do. The children were never planned but neither were they unexpected; even Lucy Pear, of whom Emma had had no warning, had not come as a shock. She fed them all, clothed them, washed their messes, didn't blink at their cries, watched her oldest two go off and fall for a little bit of attention, an adventure. Juliet was married to a successful cabinetmaker now. Peter was up in Canada. And through it all Roland had been gone more than he'd been home and Emma had never, not once, felt lust when she looked at another man, or complained about Roland's comings and goings, or allowed the children to speak of missing him, or warned the older boys off becoming fishermen themselves. It was as if she'd believed, if she held the world at a constant distance, that it would hold her back, if not close then at least upright and unscathed.

She had ignored his flirtations in his office, resisted answering his eyes the afternoon he came to the house bearing the wad of cash and the necklace, but then she had woken to those lights. Lost motorist was her first thought, because automobiles so seldom drove that far up the road and because it went by twice before settling into an idle. Then she rose to her knees and recognized the whitewalls of the Duesenberg's six tires.

His being there was so bold — so stupid, Roland would say — that she found herself smiling. What made him so certain he'd wake her and not the children? What made him think she wouldn't shoot him, let alone that she'd be willing to get in his car? She was unaccustomed to such optimism. Yet it shone on her and made her feel supple, and as though she had no choice but to go out and meet it.

She crept out the back door. Her rope cut, just like that.

Massage it into your hands.

Roland would call Story's way of talking *fancy*, like the bottle, but Emma heard it wasn't simply that; she heard the effort it took him to push certain words around his mouth. *Off-gone*, he'd said, drawing the heavenly blanket over her, and she could feel him go hot at the exotic syllables. They lay under it now, their sweat cooling, the bathhouse flickering whitely around them. Four nights and still she knew almost nothing about the man, apart from what anyone could easily know. He ran the quarry but didn't own it. He had a wife and a house that looked large enough for four, maybe five bedrooms, but no children. She assumed a sorrow in him. But anyone could do that.

'Are you sleeping?' he asked.

'No.' She touched the back of the hand that rested on her stomach. It was hairless, and soft, everything that Roland's was not. She wasn't certain that she felt a great desire for these hands, but they fascinated her, and they touched her as though she fascinated them.

'Don't worry,' she said. 'I won't fall asleep.'

'I'm not worried.'

A scurrying beyond the door made them sit up. The sound stopped, then began again on the roof, louder, before resolving into the pattern of a chipmunk or squirrel. They lay back down, Emma's head on his chest, which was nearly as hairless as his hands. A sudden vertigo washed through her, guilt and revulsion entwined. She sat up.

'Your wife must sleep well, for you not to worry,' she said.

'Very well, yes. It was part of her education, when she was small. She and her brothers would roam all over with their father — this was for timber, and then the railroad — staying in hotels or strangers' houses, she and her brothers sharing beds, and she would find a way to sleep, no matter what. Sometimes, she says, they would be directly over a depot, where the men repaired the engines all night, clanking and banging. One time she slept through the whistle of a night train they were meant to board, and her brothers

48

carried her between them onto the train, set her down on her bunk, watched her sleep through the night all the way to Omaha, then carried her to the house of their father's friend, where she slept right through the rooster's crow in the morning.' He paused. 'She tells it better than me. Susannah's a very good storyteller.'

'You tell it fine,' Emma said. He loved his wife, she thought, but not in the way he should have — not in the way that would have made him ashamed to go on about her to Emma in such bland, friendly detail. Last time he had told her about Susannah's childhood pets, and the time before that about Susannah's love of the stars and her skills with a telescope, and the time before that — the first time — about Susannah's remarkable strength as a swimmer. Somehow the more sweet things Story told her about Susannah, the more unreal she became to Emma. She was a tale of a wife, a character.

Emma let herself touch his hair. It was as soft and thick as felt. She hooked one of his curls, then watched it spring back.

Story stopped her hand. 'Do you think my hair needs cutting?'

Emma waited, thinking the question must be a joke. But Story didn't laugh — against her ear, beneath the skin and bones of his chest, his heart sent up its steady effort. She considered him. His hair was different, certainly, from the rest of him. It flopped in his eyes, crept down his neck, ferned out across his ears so they showed through only occasionally, like buried treasure. Emma liked the overall effect. She thought the moppish wilds of his hair suited his broad brow and strong jaw, kept things in proportion. And maybe it was also true that all this hairiness made up in some way for his hairlessness elsewhere, and for this pristine, white cave of a room, for everything about the current situation that reminded her how far she was from home. Emma's father and uncles had all been hairy. She cut her children's hair so infrequently that the boys wound up looking like girls — they had to put the scissors into her hands, remind her. And when Roland returned from his trips looking and smelling like a woolly mammoth, when other women would have shaved and scrubbed and scolded, Emma wanted him more frankly at those times than at any other.

'Is it such a difficult question?'

No, Emma could say, *no, it's not so difficult and no, your hair doesn't need cutting, in my opinion*. But lurking behind his plaintive tone she grew aware of Susannah in the room, not the faultless myth of Susannah but the real one who must not have liked her husband looking frowsy. Susannah was with them as unmistakably as the candle and the ridiculously heavy white robes on their hooks, which Story had asked Emma not to use because he really didn't know her at all, didn't know that she would never even think to wear another person's robe. Emma shivered with disgust. She had no intention of entering into a debate with Susannah — however indirectly — about her husband's hairstyle.

'No,' she said. 'And yes, it does need cutting.'

He groaned and was on top of her, catching

the afghan in his teeth and backing down the couch, uncovering her as he went. The wool tickled, raised her hairs, made Emma gasp despite herself. How could it be? And yet it was. Later, composed, she wouldn't be able to explain it to herself. She would decide it was time to go to confession. (She had not been in nearly three weeks.) But now, here, she was on her back in a glowing bathhouse, a man she barely knew biting her hip bone, licking it, now her legs opened and she was barely required to give in because she already had.

★　★　★

'Will the children miss you?' he asked, once they were cooling again under the afghan.

'If they wake. Maybe. But they won't wake.' They were like Susannah, she thought, trained early to sleep through anything. And this was mostly true. But it was also what Emma had to tell herself, to stave off the part of her that wondered, as she lay here on a white sofa in West Parish, divided from them by the winding, dark river: *What if?* She was hateful, to have left them.

His chin nodded against her. 'Do the boys like their duties?'

'They tell me you've moved them straight to carrying drills. You didn't have to do that. I thought you'd make them water boys.'

'You want them in mortal danger?'

'Of course not.'

She was quiet for a moment. 'Let's not talk about the boys.'

'All right. Let's talk about you. You came to me with a proposition, now I have one for you. A position, to be exact, nursing a wealthy old man. Thirty dollars a week, funded by yours truly. You can't spend all day making a perry shack, can you?'

She lifted her head to look him in the eye. Thirty dollars was more than many men were paid, more than Emma made in a month cleaning rooms at the Blue Heron Hotel, and that job had lasted only one summer, two years ago. They wanted younger, unattached women who wouldn't frown, as Emma had, when guests leered at their too-short uniforms. Emma had knocked at other hotels. She had inquired at restaurants and tennis clubs. She had applied for situations she had no real skill at: assistant to a seamstress, arranger in a flower shop. She had looked until Roland had made her stop looking. He was embarrassed by his wife roaming about, embarrassed by their need, which had grown sharp that summer after he showed up late too many times to the boat he'd worked on for a dozen years, furred and sloshing in his boots, violent with remorse. Roland had always liked to drink, but without warning he'd become a drinker. The men came to Emma for help, but what could Emma do? Since then he had worked shoveling gurry on the docks, and sometimes pulling traps for the few lobstermen willing to take him. He worked at everything that was offered to him, but it still wasn't enough, even with fewer children in the house. Peter had sent money from Canada a couple times, which

Emma had used for food and clothing, hiding it from Roland until it ran out. She grew a kitchen garden but the rabbits and deer and coyotes always managed to outwit her fence and make off with half the crop. She tapped a few maple trees out back but Roland insisted they have store sugar on birthdays and there was always a birthday. Juliet offered to help with groceries but Emma refused her even as she wished that Juliet would simply stuff flour, sugar, and butter into Emma's pantry without her permission. Emma was not as proud as Roland. She had put her perry idea into action as soon as he left for the Grand Banks. But her anxieties about the perry were only growing. She worried they didn't have enough manpower for the rowing (to Ipswich!) and picking and pressing, worried people wouldn't pay as much as she was counting on, worried that even if they could squeeze a good drink out of the wrong pears, it was too late in the wet game to introduce a whole new libation to the market. By next year — when this year's crop would be ready — it would be even later. She worried about Roland, who might come home in the middle of their pressing, as Lucy said, and, ashamed they'd had to do it, put an end to the whole thing. Then he would feel regret, which would increase his shame, which would cause misery for them all.

She could share none of this with Josiah Story, of course. He was their patron. And they were not giving up: the shack was nearly finished, the picking schedule fine-tuned. They were forging gamely ahead. But the idea of a regular job, a well-paying job, had Emma's heart pounding.

'Thirty dollars?' Emma twisted her mouth, wanting Story to interpret the wobble in her voice as equivocation, wary of how many things she had already taken from him. She found one of the few hairs on his chest and tweezed at it with her fingers. 'I'm not a nurse, but I could probably manage. What's in it for you?'

'Ouch. It's politics.'

'It's politics. You think I don't understand politics?'

'I think politics are boring. But if you insist. The man's niece, Beatrice Cohn, she's a leading dry down in Boston, statewide really, very popular, very charismatic, made quite a stir among her own. She made friends with the Christian ladies. Now she's living up in Gloucester, taking care of her uncle. I saw her speak at the Ladies' Sewing Circle last month. She's had to care for her uncle instead of focusing on her work. The 'cause,' as they call it.' Mr. Story sighed. 'I figure I relieve her of the burden, maybe she gets me the woman's vote in November.'

'I thought you were a shoo-in.'

'That's what they say. They haven't heard me talk.'

'You talk fine.' *You talk fancy*, she almost said, but stopped herself. She didn't know — it had taken her years to know, with Roland — how much teasing this man could take.

He shook his head. 'Do you want the job or not?'

'It's odd, don't you think? You funding my

perry operation, me helping you pose as a dry?'

'There are worse sorts of corruption, don't you think? Nursing isn't such a sin.'

'What if I turn out to be terrible at it?'

He lifted himself onto his elbows. 'You have nine children, don't you?'

'It's not the same,' she said. But she was tiring of her protest. She was thinking of Joshua, who at three hadn't tasted currants or worn shoes that fit.

'So where is it?' she asked. 'Will I have to take the bus?'

'Out on Eastern Point. The Hirsch estate. Hirsch is the uncle. I'll drive you,' Mr. Story added, but Emma barely heard. She pushed off him, grabbing the afghan to cover her breasts. 'Hirsch' was like a curse word among the Murphys: spoken only inside the home and when strictly necessary. Hirsch was their secret. Or Emma had thought it a secret. Now, eyes shut, willing herself to shrink, she waited to hear Story describe her sins to her. The pears were nothing compared with what she was doing now, with him. Taking what the rich would not use anyway — she had barely flushed when she first confessed it and, because her penance had been a single Hail Mary, she never felt the need to confess it again. Even so, they did not talk of it: the dories they 'borrowed' from Flanders' Boat Yard once a year, the armfuls of fruit that didn't belong to them, the canvas tarps mended so many times the children affectionately referred to them as 'rags.' And most tender, most treacherous: Lucy Pear, before she was Lucy

55

Pear, alone in the Hirsch orchard in a preposterously sumptuous blanket. For nearly a decade Emma had kept that blanket in her box, under the bed, rarely thinking of it, but now it occurred to her that this had been a terrible mistake. The blanket had followed her here: it swam dreamily across her skin, a fluffy, luxurious trap.

But when Emma opened her eyes, the afghan was only the afghan. Story's eyes were innocent and bemused. He laughed. He touched her jaw, closed her mouth for her. 'Are you squeamish of Jews, Mrs. Murphy?'

Emma worked her tongue drily, moved her head back and forth.

'If it doesn't work — if the endorsement doesn't come through — I won't blame you. All right? I promise. Forget the politics. Just consider it me, wanting to do something for you.'

Emma managed a weak nod. As terrified as she was, a flame had been lit, the possibility of seeing Lucy's mother — if this woman was her — brought within her reach.

'Can't a man do something for the sake of doing it?' he asked.

Josiah sat up. He considered this a fair question, if not an entirely honest one within the context of this particular conversation. He would have liked it to be honest. He would have liked to be touched again by Emma's rough hands that the cream had not salved. He had allowed her to undress him tonight. He didn't think anyone but his mother had ever done that. He reached for her. But as he did so his nakedness

56

became fully apparent to her — it plucked Emma out of her shock. With Roland it was usually dark, the children asleep, or they were hasty about it, clothed. They hadn't seen each other naked in years. She wrapped the afghan around her and moved toward her dress, which lay rumpled on the floor. The hem, she saw, had begun to fray. One sleeve was torn at the elbow. She steadied herself with these defects, with thoughts of a needle and thread, all the while toeing into her dress, wriggling it up over her hips and shoulders, avoiding Story's eyes. She buttoned her last button, noting that it needed tightening. She was not a skilled seamstress, but she could sew a button, tuck a hem. She took comfort in an image of herself at the kitchen table with a needle and thread, the clear, honest effort, her daily life intact. 'Of course,' she said. 'You can do anything you want. Will you take me home?'

5

One week later, Josiah Story and Emma Murphy were fully clothed in his Duesenberg, blearing past Annisquam, Riverdale, Bayview, winding toward Eastern Point. In the backseat, Emma might have been a statue. Josiah, as he drove, noted the skyward point of her posture, the carved ridges of her neck muscles, the bone of her jaw, and told himself that if she appeared a little distant today, a little haughty, it was only proof that she was not too common or too old for him, that he was allowed to want her in the way he did. That morning, over coffee, he had told Susannah his plan to win Beatrice Cohn's endorsement with a nurse and she smiled. 'You look embarrassed,' she said. 'I think it's smart. It's a smart gesture, Joe.' He had left out his familiarity with the nurse, of course, so her words gutted him, made him take her hands and kiss them, hiding his face. Now the pain had thinned to a chafing in his throat, a disturbance in his groin that wasn't altogether unpleasant. Susannah's smile grated on him: the confidence a lifetime of money granted her even when she was being conned. He watched Emma in the rearview mirror and fantasized that her stiffness was part of a game they were playing, the game of emerging together into broad daylight, visible to passing drivers and loitering men, to the children playing along the road. Here was the munificent Josiah Story, delivering a nurse to someone in need. No one would see Emma's secret litheness, the way she gave under him, her soft stomach, her strong hands, the calluses on her feet that brushed against him like sandpaper. Josiah saw all this. The straighter Emma sat, the harder her gaze as she refused to meet his eye, the more naked she became for him. She was like an animal he'd caught. He caressed the wheel and squirmed.

★ ★ ★

Emma had never been to Eastern Point by land. Past downtown, the car turned sharply, hugging the shore, and for a mile or so she recognized nothing of the boatyards or artists' cottages that clung barnacle-like to the high-tide line above Smith's Cove. All this had been sheltered from the Murphy family as they rowed darkly past on the other side of Rocky Neck.

Beyond the cove, the road grew narrow and great privets sprang up, towering walls of green that briefly distracted Emma: could they be as soft as they appeared? One saw nothing through their denseness. Then a curve swung the car and the Dog Bar Breakwater came into view, a half-mile bed of flint against the horizon. This Emma knew well, for even at night it hung in front of their boats, the harbor's limit, their silent guide: other markings might change over the course of a year, but the breakwater stood still, telling them by its distance when they had reached the Hirsch rocks.

Emma's stomach fisted again, a hot knot. All night she had lain awake. Three times in the past week she had walked down to the coffee shop and asked Mrs. Sven if she could use the telephone. She had picked up the earpiece and heard the operator's voice. She would tell Josiah Story she had changed her mind. 'Hello?' The earpiece was heavy and cold. Emma stood against the wall in the back of the shop but the men at the counter watched her anyway, baldly curious. 'Can I help you?' She hung up. She would take the bus to the quarry, tell him in person. But even as she tripped out of Sven's she knew she could not do that, knew she could not walk into Josiah Story's office again with a straight face. His wife might be there — she was often there, he'd said. A good Company Wife.

Hedges on one side, a stone wall on the other, not plopped together like Lanesville's walls but tall and mortared, solid, the car moving too fast for Emma to track where they were — she could no longer see the breakwater. She heard Roland's voice: *Slow it down!* His admonishment when the oars rubbed too hastily in their locks. *Slower! You're making a hullabaloo!*

He was talking to her now. He could see her in the backseat of Josiah Story's car, flying past hedges. She had been a bad wife. Vile. And now — what kind of mother was she? What was she doing? When Lucy was a baby, a woman had hovered at the fringes of Emma's thoughts, without face or name, a receptacle for whatever Emma might feel for her at any given moment. Pity. Incomprehension. Disgust. Pity again. She

60

even felt guilty toward her, as if Emma had stolen Lucy against the woman's wishes. Her guilt, perhaps, helped explain why the Murphys had not found another orchard for their pears. Maybe, though her heart did not stop clanging the entire time they picked, Emma felt she had to give the woman the chance to take Lucy back. Maybe, too, each time the woman didn't come, Lucy became more irrevocably, rightfully, hers.

She made her a servant of the house, rather than a daughter. Always Emma returned to pity, settled there — it was easiest on her heart. Then, for years, the shadow woman had retreated, replaced by the reality of Lucy, her ever-growing body, the habits of her tenderness, her deer-quiet footsteps in the house. Lucy belonged there as firmly as any threshold or drawer. They were so far from the beginning now. Why risk going back? What was wrong with Emma that she could not say, *Turn the car around, I've changed my mind?* But the car was slowing and turning up a long, sycamore-lined drive, and Emma saw, up ahead, the old gravel path the Murphys tiptoed across each year. The Duesenberg sailed it without pause, knowing nothing of the sharp pebbles and ruts. Through the sycamores, Emma saw the pear trees, in full flower. She wiped her hands on her skirt. Despite her stillness and the mild day, she was sticking to the seat; creeks of sweat ran from her underarms. The house came into view, the first time she had seen it in daylight: mortar flaking, hedges mushrooming, shutters missing slats, an ailing monument of stone. A woman's figure appeared at an upstairs window and Emma's fear cracked open.

'Tah-dah!'

A poem came to Emma, one her mother had sung to her and her siblings to scare them off straying:

Come away, O human child
To the waters and the wild.
With a faery, hand in hand,
For the world's more full of weeping than
    you can understand.

'Emma?'

She had not sung it to her own children. It was too sad.

'Here we are!'

The figure was gone from the window. Story's eyes in the rearview mirror twitched with nerves. He had trimmed his hair, Emma realized. Or more likely Susannah had trimmed it. His nape was visible: a dark, clean point.

'Did you tell her' — Emma's voice a husk until she cleared it, began again — 'Did you tell her we were coming?'

'I told her I was coming. With a little gift.'

'A gift?'

'I don't know what I said. A token of my appreciation for all her hard, important work. And so on.'

Emma's annoyance was swamped by dread as the front door to the house opened and the figure from upstairs stepped out into the sunlight. Sweat pooled in Emma's elbow cracks and between her thighs. Even from a distance, the resemblance was unmistakable. There was Lucy's formidable brow, her dark, springy hair, her stance: feet flat, toes out, arms loose at her sides. Lucy had been the only person Emma knew to stand comfortably like that. Not an hour ago, Lucy had stood like that in the yard, her hammer cocked in one hand, her head cocked to one side, watching as Emma ducked into the Duesenberg. Emma had not told the children where she would be working, only that the new job was on the other side of town.

'Emma? She's waiting.'

'You might have loaned me some boats,' she said. 'Instead of all this. We could use a couple boats.' She swiped at her forehead with her forearm, wiped her forearm with her other hand, tried to wring her hand out, with little success. Story was too nervous to notice, she thought, but the woman would, the real woman with a face and a name who was staring down at the car now, waiting. Beatrice Cohn. Emma wished her back into facelessness even as she felt herself rising from the car. She felt her legs lift, one after the other, up the stone path, felt her fear slammed aside by a greater force. Now that she was here, her need to see Lucy's mother, to know, was like a rope pulling her by the neck — she was nearly foaming with it. She must look preposterous, she thought, her gait halting, undecided. She did not know that from where Beatrice Cohn stood, she appeared perfectly natural, and of a piece. She looked like a poor, lovely, heavily perspiring Irishwoman treading cautiously in a place she had never been before.

'Good morning, Mrs. Cohn,' called Story, his voice over-bright. 'I'm ten minutes early. I like to be on time, always — out of respect. For your time, I mean. I hope we're not troubling you.'

Beatrice Cohn smiled flatly, not even glancing at Emma. Lucy's grace was drowned in the woman's skinniness. She was all angles. 'You couldn't trouble me, Mr . . . Forgive me. It's *Stanton*, isn't it?' she asked, and as Story coughed up a good-natured chuckle, Emma nearly bit her tongue. She realized with shock that she had met Mrs. Cohn before: two summers ago, on a meltingly hot day, when a group of women in plain, dark, throat-strangling dresses knocked at the Murphy door and urged Emma to deny her husband 'intimate pleasures' if he would not deny himself 'the pleasure of drink.' Emma had moved to shut the door but one woman, this woman, caught it with her foot and pushed a small package, wrapped in butcher paper, into Emma's hand. *At least deny him more children*, she had said, in the same nasal, Brahman accent with which she had just mocked Story. Sweat had fallen from her nose, slid into her tight collar. How could Emma not have recognized her? *You think he wants more children?* she'd asked, before she kicked the woman's foot out of the way, slammed the door, and pulled the curtains. She was instantly horrified by what she had confessed, and to a stranger. Worse, it was not Roland she had spoken for but herself. When the women knocked again, she ignored them. She was Emma Murphy, of Leverett Street, of Church of

64

the Sacred Heart. She did not even know what the package contained. But she kept it, and opened it, and discovered inside a thing she had not known existed: one Mensinga brand rubber diaphragm and shocking, illustrated instructions for how to deploy it. She had used it, every time, ever since.

'Mrs. Cohn,' Story was saying. 'Let me introduce you to Mrs. Emma Murphy. With your uncle ill, I thought you could use the help. Nursing him, I mean. So that your energies don't have to be divided from your work. Divided? Diverted. You understand. Yes?' He clapped Emma on the back with comradely force.

Again, the flat smile dribbled back. 'My uncle is a very private man,' said Mrs. Cohn. She appraised Emma quickly, top to bottom. Flyaway hair pinned plainly, Emma thought. Sweaty. Scrappy. Dull brown shoes. Mrs. Cohn gave no sign of recognizing her. Through the open doorway loomed a hallway crowded with impractical chairs and chests. A towering grandfather clock. A chandelier whose lower regions Emma could just make out, glittering seas of treasure she might be asked to dust. She was squeezed by a sudden hatred — she saw the design of Beatrice Cohn's life with startling clarity. Mrs. Cohn had a hundred bedrooms and her snide accent and enough wealth to hire an entire city of nannies and she had dumped her child on Emma, shed her like an extra pair of shoes to charity, and then — then! — she had made a career out of 'saving' poor women and

65

children, a pitiful stab at redemption, even as Emma fed and bathed and dressed and disciplined and loved her daughter, until the day she had the gall to come along and chastise *Emma* for having too many kids. She had suffered that deadening dress but it was all a choice, a lark — Leverett Street must have seemed to her a ripe kind of underworld, and she its guardian. Emma tasted bile looking at the dress the woman wore today — lavishly flowered, silk so nice it must have been imported (even Emma could tell this), green and pink and black at ten o'clock in the morning. Her stance — feet flat, toes out, arms loose — struck Emma as a cold thing now. When Lucy stood like that, it was an offering, the kind of stillness that said, *Come in.* But on Mrs. Cohn, the effect was the opposite. *You couldn't trouble me, Mr. Stanton.*

Emma had given so much for this woman. She had let her be the servant, envisioned her need being greater than Emma's own. But Beatrice Cohn was a rich Jew. Beatrice Cohn needed nothing. She glanced at Emma — her little *gift* — as if Emma were barely there. She had forgotten that she had once been desperate, that someone had saved her. Someone! Emma was struck by an urge to hit her, followed by an understanding that Story's money wasn't all she wanted by being here. She wanted to trouble Beatrice Cohn's smooth exterior, poke holes in the myth of her goodness. She wanted to remind her.

'I'm a good caretaker,' she heard herself say, in her most motherly, mollifying voice, 'and very discreet. And of course,' her knees weakly curtsying, 'you can always change your mind.'

Tears rose in Mrs. Cohn's eyes, as shocking as if she'd begun to sob. Emma looked to Story, but he wore the same diligent grin he'd worn the whole time, oblivious. Emma had caused the tears, she knew. *You can always change your mind.* She had provoked a memory, needled, hurt the woman before she had even really tried. The effortlessness of it startled her. But Beatrice Cohn's tears disappeared as abruptly as they had come on, simply dropped back behind her skin, water behind a wall. She smiled at Emma, her mouth closed but still a smile, disorienting Emma to such a degree that for a second she thought, *She knows who I am.*

'I don't see why we can't give it a try,' Mrs. Cohn said in her clipped, humorless way, unaware of her blatant rhyme, and now, as she and Story began to make arrangements, Emma saw her smile more clearly. There was no complicity in it, only charity. It was the smile she had worn on Emma's stoop, the one she must have worn on all the stoops she visited where women with plain hair and brown shoes answered their flimsy doors. So Emma's pity for Lucy's mother had been fantasy, but hers for Emma was real. As she nodded at Story, her smile stuck, a studied, stale thing, and Emma saw the thought that must keep Beatrice Cohn's heart going, despite its early shame. She was thinking, correctly: *The poor woman, married to a drunk.* She was surrendering to Story for Emma's sake.

6

On Saturday mornings, Lillian Haven played bridge at the Draper House on Commonwealth Avenue with the College Club. She went to be among the Protestant women, to maintain her place among them, however tenuous it might be, to let their scents (understated), their voices (soft), their movements (slight), their entire atmosphere, seep in and inflect her. She went for the chamber music, too, especially the violin, and for the sandwiches: tiny triangles of cucumber or cream cheese or shrimp pressed between bread so impossibly white and airy she felt transformed (almost) just holding one. Pinkie out, mouth closed, she bit her tongue so as not to salivate.

She could have done without the bridge, or any other game. Games worked against Lillian because she always wanted too badly to win and was never able to hide this, and so the other women trusted her, the sole Jew, even less than they would have.

They all liked to win, of course. Their very presence in the Draper House was a testament to their having won the right to be there on Saturday mornings, for three hours, before the men arrived. They hired their own musicians — all male — and drank coffee, not tea. But this was a collective triumph. It was a point they'd made, like winning the right to vote, though Draper House had come later and seemed to many of them just as significant. Whereas the way Lillian sat forward in her leather club chair, cards pressed to her collarbone, lips drastically pursed, clearly had nothing to do with anyone but Lillian.

'I've had the thought' — Evelyn Sharp's hand paused en route to laying down her next card — 'we should bring our granddaughters one weekend. Show them what women can do, when we put our minds to it.'

Penelope Lockhart clucked. 'What a lovely idea. I don't know why I didn't think of it myself.'

The others murmured in agreement. Lillian murmured, too, though she was looking at Evelyn's hand, at the slender, tan fingers, the freckles she'd contracted sailing in her youth. She focused on Evelyn's freckles to avoid the envy that slithered through her heart. Lillian had no granddaughter, nor any grandsons either. She cleared her throat, an almost but not quite involuntary nudge to Evelyn, who at last laid down her card with an infuriatingly opaque expression. Lillian flared her nostrils but Evelyn didn't see; she and Penelope had begun to plot the granddaughters' visit.

Lillian's husband told her she was like a boot, laced too tightly — a foot didn't have a chance, in or out. He told her if her parents had had the money to send her to Miss Winsor's, or the English to get her a scholarship, then she wouldn't have such a great need for friendship anyway. But Lillian hadn't gone to Miss Winsor's, or anywhere else. She'd pinned hems

69

for her mother, kneeling at the feet of men and women who weren't much better off than her parents, all of them shtetl folk in one way or another, all trying to pretend that Boston didn't terrify them. Even then, Lillian was disdainful of the cheap, prickly fabrics. She had been eleven when her family came from Bialystok, had survived an eight-year desert of pinning and pubescence, until Henry found her standing outside Elizabeth Pimm's School for Secretaries, her knuckles white from gripping the gate. He said he had seen her beauty right away — she would never succeed in seeing it herself — and she had seen a sturdy, sunny, whistling, blue-eyed Jew in a finely tailored suit, intent on saving her.

The violinist was rotten this morning, sad when the score called for plaintive — there was a difference, Lillian knew — whiny as a fiddle on the high notes. They were playing Beethoven's Piano Trio in C-minor, opus 1, number 3, a piece Lillian's daughter, Beatrice, had played impeccably at age fourteen, and not just in the technical sense. Beatrice had a *feel* for music — not quite virtuosic, they never called her that (which Lillian had thought for the best, believing that those sorts of girls scared off the good men), but gifted, certainly, that's what the teachers at the conservatory said. Beatrice had heard music, understood it, made it bloom under her fingertips as naturally as if it were her real language, before English, before the scraps of Yiddish she had picked up from Lillian's parents despite Lillian's best efforts to make them speak

English in the girl's company, and, when that failed, to keep their visits short. Music was simpler, without accent or markings, nothing to be mispronounced or misunderstood because you were one sort of person and not another. That was its beauty, Lillian thought: the way a player, playing it, was both heard and obscured. This was freedom, it seemed to Lillian. This is what she heard when she listened to Beatrice play: her daughter was free.

Lillian had never told Beatrice any of this. She never told her that during Beatrice's lessons at the conservatory, Lillian didn't in fact go to Filene's Department Store, as she claimed, but to the conservatory's library, where she sat in one of the soundproof booths and listened to Mendelssohn, Liszt, Schumann, MacDowell. She studied the music; she taught herself how it worked. This is how she knew that the violinist was off, that the whole ensemble was decent but not worth half what the club paid for them.

Not that she would ever say so.

They had reached the finale now. The violin whined toward its crescendo, causing Lillian to chew her inner cheek, a habit she had developed as a teenager to avoid talking too much, or too loudly, or in too strong an accent, or to avoid unsavory expressions such as wincing, which is what she wanted to do now. A violin *is* a fiddle, she thought — it's just a whiny old street fiddle in disguise. It was like Lillian herself. This morning she had tried on eight different dresses before choosing the Lanvin she wore now, but even so she felt all wrong, misaligned and frumpy. She tasted shrimp in her throat, still strange to her after all these years, like some coppery, forbidden salt. The women were staring at her. She held her breath with shame — at her second-class status, at Bea's barrenness. 'Bea is expecting!' she heard herself say. 'Finally.' She waited, stunned at her lie. Then Penelope Lockhart began to clap, and the others followed, joyous in a way Lillian had never seen them. Pleased, yes, but this was joy! This was true feeling for Lillian. She experienced a sudden bloom of faith, a warm flower unfolding in her throat. It wasn't too late. It might even be true, she thought. Perhaps the boldness of her declaration, her very optimism, would make it true.

Then, as the women's cheers died and they began to ask their questions — *And when will the shower be? And how is she feeling?* — Lillian realized they had been staring at her because it was her turn. She missed her mother suddenly, with a force that surprised her. Her mother would have been in synagogue this morning, looking down on her father from the women's balcony, wearing a dowdy dress she had sewed herself, not a hint of embarrassment on her face.

7

One Saturday afternoon a month, after her card game, Bea's mother took the train up to Gloucester, calling it her 'little country holiday.' Lillian called everything related to Gloucester 'little,' including the milewide harbor, the hulking, barnacled fishing boats, the wharves that stretched the length of three city blocks. The car she hired at the depot to drive her out to the house, always the largest available, was 'my little car.' She was trying to say she found the place charming and quaint, Bea knew. Lillian was barely aware that in fact she found it common, inconsequential, striving, and sad. She was even less aware — at least Bea preferred to think so — that she had begun to associate these sentiments with Bea.

In preparation for her mother's visit, Bea closed her bedroom drapes, threw half the dresses from her closet onto the floor, and pulled a flannel dressing robe over a shapeless, blue-and-white-striped, mannish shift. Bea brought tea up to her uncle Ira, who sat in his wheelchair by the window. He'd left the window open so he wouldn't fall asleep but his eyes were closed, his nose whistling gently. At Bea's 'Tea!' his eyes fluttered, closed again, then opened fully before traveling, at a milky, meticulous, tender pace, Bea's length.

Bea knew how she appeared, the loose costume bagging around her, her hair uncut

73

since Lillian's hairdresser had given her a disastrously conceived row of bangs a few months ago. Bea's hair bushed around her head as she never allowed it in public or even, most days, out of self-respect, in private.

'Why do you always want to look a wreck for your mother?' Ira asked.

Bea set down the tea and shut the window. 'Because it drives her mad?'

'Maybe. Open the window, please. Or maybe because it makes you look mad.'

Bea opened the window. Ira was probably right. Ira often said aloud what Bea preferred not to say, or even to think when she could help it. Nine years ago, when she had stopped eating, gone mute, been pulled out of Radcliffe and sent to Fainwright Hospital, where she was diagnosed as 'undiagnosticated,' Lillian had become inexplicably kind to her. She'd sat with Bea for hours whether Bea spoke or not, sometimes in silence, a state that normally made Lillian squirm, sometimes reading to her from the papers about the local news and the war, assiduously skipping the gossip — though Lillian loved gossip — or any mention of music or Radcliffe. Bea had watched Lillian's eyes ferociously skimming on her behalf, perceived a new weight at her mother's jawline, a layer of softness and worry. It was as if Lillian had only thought she wanted Bea to 'go places' — by which she'd meant play piano at Isabella Stewart Gardner's salons, marry someone even richer than Henry, and bear children Lillian could dress and spoil — but discovered that she liked Bea better as a doll,

74

droopy on Luminal. And Bea discovered how good it felt to please her mother, which she had often almost succeeded at before Fainwright, but never quite. There had been Bea's face, for instance, which Lillian said would be stunning if only Bea would agree to get her nose reset; Bea's piano playing, which Lillian paid for and boasted about but never directly praised; Bea's expression when she played — lips mashed, brow squeezing the bridge of her nose — which Lillian swatted at, warning of wrinkles. Then there had been Lieutenant Seagrave, aide to the navy admiral her father was working to woo into a boot contract with Haven Shoes. It was the lieutenant, according to Lillian, who made the admiral's decisions. She worried the family's Jewishness would offend him — she pushed Bea on him as a kind of balm. *He's not so much older than you!* she'd said to Bea. (Though he was, by at least ten years.) *And see how handsome!* (He had the sort of straight, tall, very white teeth that reminded one of the skull underneath.) *And that name! Seagrave! A direct descendant of the Mayflower, I've been told.* Bea had pictured the lieutenant descending from the famous ship, literally floating down from its gunwales onto a rocky shore, his jacket's stiff hem whiffling in the breeze. Bea had flirted with him, as her mother clearly wanted, but then he'd forced himself on her, as her mother presumably did not want, and then she'd gotten pregnant, as her mother certainly did not want. It had been a disaster, a humiliation, a gross joke on them all. It had been worse than anything Bea had ever feared, worse — she'd had the thought — than if he'd murdered her. But thirteen months later, in the hospital bed at Fainwright, too washed out to ask questions or assign blame, her head hollow and gleaming, Bea was finally perfect. 'You'll come home,' her mother said. 'You'll join me at the clubs, make use of yourself. We'll find a patient man to marry you.'

Bea stood by the open window, watching Ira's face. It was too various, too much a collision of parts to be called objectively handsome, but Bea found her uncle's long, tunneled cheeks, the broad bulb of his nose, the pink skin at his temples where hair had once grown, his full, sorrowful mouth staggeringly lovely. He had sipped his tea — ginseng, to soothe his perpetual certainty that he was dying, procured by Bea from Chinatown on her last trip into Boston — and dozed off again, the hair in his nostrils trembling with each breath like live, warm forests. Out the window, the old hydrangeas bowed leggily toward the ground, their buds narrowly containing their blossoms. It had gotten to be June somehow. The breeze was gentle. Somehow the days had gone along, stacked up, and led here. What had Bea done in those days? In the towers made of days, where had she been? Inside, of course, exerting herself at this or that, but for what? In a few weeks, her cousins would come up from Boston and New York to drink themselves silly for the week leading up to Independence Day. Uncle Ira would stay upstairs, pretending he couldn't walk, and Bea would not out him. She hadn't decided yet what to do with Emma Murphy during that time, whether to pay her on top of Story's wages for the extra work or give her a week's holiday and spare her the circus.

Bea liked the woman, so far. She was good with Uncle Ira. She didn't speak to him in a baby voice. And she was competent — almost — at the housekeeping Bea had assigned her to occupy the hours when he slept. She made mistakes here and there — she'd used a good pillowcase as a rag and broken a vase and seemed to have little knack for organizing, or maybe it was categorizing, so that Bea had trouble locating items Emma had put away, and sometimes, it seemed, items Emma would have had no reason to put away: a single shoe of Bea's, shoved into a box with another pair, a pen placed on a shelf in the pantry. But Bea said nothing, in part because something in Emma's face warned her off, a willfulness that seemed to defy her broad, deferent cheekbones. Also, Bea didn't want Emma to correct herself. Her faults were a comfort to Bea. Bea could not be replaced.

She left Ira's gentle snores. She felt a little guilty, in the great room, as she grabbed up the pillows Emma had fluffed and arranged the day before and flung them into a heap next to the fireplace. Lillian would be here soon. Bea's skin twitched, like an animal sensing weather.

★   ★   ★

'What's the point of this?' Lillian asked almost as soon as she walked in. She pointed to the pillows, as Bea knew she would. 'Are you trying to live like an artist?'

She was thinking of Aunt Vera, of course, who had spent whole days painting a flower or a ship or nothing anyone recognized while the house went on without her, loud and unkempt, or who disappeared entirely. Once when Bea was nine she and her parents came up to visit on a summer afternoon to find that Vera had gone off on a fishing trip. She'd left nothing for a meal — Bea's cousins' mouths were black from eating blackberries all day. Uncle Ira laughed proudly as he described 'the locals' Vera had met down at Raymond's Beach, how she'd waded out to their skiff in her dress. He drove everyone to a clam shack in Essex by way of apology, but Henry hated clams — he hated eating anything that resembled the live version of itself. Lillian was so irritated she bought a glass of beer, thinking no one saw — Lillian said women who drank beer might as well have beards — and swilled it in one gulp down by the marsh behind the shack. Bea had seen.

'Here.' Bea marched over to the pillows, gathered them in her arms, and arranged them on the sofa, much as Emma had had them. Her mother's anger at Vera, she thought, had actually been jealousy. Lillian had wanted a Yankee name and the freedoms that came with it, the ability to sail and ski, fearlessness, immodesty, joy. It wasn't as if she kept house with any more vigilance than Vera had. She just paid Estelle to do it and hoped having it done would make her better. Her choice of a black maid, like nearly all her choices, was meant to affirm her own whiteness, despite being a Jew. 'Please, sit. Can I make you some tea?'

'I've been drinking coffee all morning.'

'Does that mean you do or don't want tea?'

Her mother smiled her thin half smile, which she must have thought polite but which settled over Bea like ice.

'No, thank you.'

Bea sat down on the carpet across from Lillian. So Lillian would refuse tea, so as not to let Bea do a single thing for her, and Bea wouldn't have any either, to match Lillian's refusal, and they would both sit there wishing they were drinking tea.

'How was whist this morning?'

'Bridge. It was fine.'

'Fine?' Bea repeated. Lillian put on a casual tone when she talked about Draper House, but Bea knew it would take a bomb dropping on her head for her to miss one of the games.

'There's something about being amidst a gathering of women and not fighting for anything anymore. We just sit there, and play cards, and chat. It's very . . . refreshing.'

'Do you mean boring?'

'No! I mean refreshing. I'm certain. These women are progressives, to be sure, but it's not on their sleeves.' Lillian pouted. 'Hmph,' she said, though on another day it might have been 'Uch' or 'Ugh' or 'Ack.' For as long as Bea could remember, Lillian had been trying on different social groups — and their mannerisms — like gowns. There had been the Polish Jews: not the

'Jewy' ones, like Lillian's own parents had been, but the 'happier' ones, as she called them, who outfitted their synagogues with organs and rarely went. There had been the suffragists, who'd seemed just about ready to take their sleeves off: Bea had watched them from the stairs, their corsetless middles spread out in her mother's chairs, their men's boots flattening the oriental carpet. Then Lillian got fed up with 'all that ugliness' and more fully embraced Henry's set, the German Jews, who might have liked the idea of suffrage if they thought it wouldn't lead directly to Prohibition. Many of their husbands were involved in selling liquor and besides, beyond that, beyond profit — these were women who liked to tell each other that profit wasn't everything — what did Jews need with temperance? They were temperate by nature. Their rituals taught — indeed, required — moderate consumption of alcohol. Jews didn't need anyone telling them. But the German Jews made Lillian especially anxious — she was like them in many respects and yet so obviously, irretrievably different — and so she drifted for a time over to the gentile Germans, who didn't question profit as a driving motive. Their husbands were brewers, their fathers had been brewers, their sons would be brewers: they wouldn't have set foot in a voting machine if a gun was put to their heads. Lillian was attracted to their singular sense of priority, to their wealth, their music, their salons. Then America entered the war and suddenly the same women were Huns and spies and Lillian tiptoed away and installed herself among the quietly rich Protestant women who knew by then that they would win suffrage. Bea didn't know how Lillian passed among these women, or how she was tolerated by them if that was more the case. She continued keeping up with the German Jews, too, out of an obligation to Henry and because they threw the best parties. Lillian could fit anywhere, it seemed to Bea. It was a knack she had, for performing, or maybe for believing. She adjusted her speech, sometimes incorrectly; she was formal in odd moments, informal in others, used too many words or too few, put her emphasis on the wrong syllable. But always, without fail, she persuaded people to let her in. She bought the right clothes and carried the right handbags. Today she nuzzled a Cartier on her lap as her eyes flitted around the musty, regal room. Vera's impassioned, derivative watercolors (her best work, a series of tiny nude women sculpted in clothes-hanger wire, sat in a forgotten box in the ash-scented cellar) hung among portraits of her sallow, oily ancestors, who stared into a middle distance of hutches, tables, cabinets, and drawers, on top of which stood groupings of objects that had lived together for so long they appeared like little families. On one side table was a piece of scrimshaw from the time of *Moby-Dick*, a tobacco humidor in the guise of a slave woman's head, a silver spoon from the Chicago World's Fair, and a rough clay bowl made and placed there by the most sensitive of the Hirsch children, Julian, decades ago, to test what went noticed in his house. Once upon a time Julian had been Bea's sweetheart, her fiancé, though that wasn't something one thought about if one could help it. His test was flawed in the end, and revealed little. Either his bowl had been noticed — Vera might have kept such a thing, to make a point — or it hadn't.

Lillian took the room in hungrily, as she did every time, frayed carpets, altitudinous cobwebs, confirming, Bea imagined, the relative order of her own life. She took a deep, ponderous breath before her gaze landed again on Bea.

'Is it really truly absolutely necessary that you sit on the floor, Bea-Bea?'

Bea moved without so much as a sigh to an armchair. She had known that sooner or later her mother would scold her, and that she would acquiesce. She had sat on the floor expressly in order for these things to happen. It satisfied her. It was like provoking a fly that was already trapped, just to see it dance and buzz. It must have satisfied Lillian, too, just like the ugly striped shift, both confirmation that Bea, if not ill, was still disturbed in some implacable way that Lillian — lucky Lillian with her stable, sour mood — would never comprehend.

'Your father told me you've taken a nurse.' Lillian might as well have said 'lover' for the titillation in her voice. Bea's frugality — associated, in Lillian's mind, with what she called Bea's 'prudiness' — was one of her favorite things to mock. It belonged with temperance itself, and the androgynous shift, and every other safe, loveless thing Bea embraced.

'She was brought to me, by an aspiring

politician. He wants the woman's vote.'

Lillian sniffed. 'Such a little town. Yet you like it here. Or is it just a seeming?'

Bea shrugged. 'Ira's getting sicker.'

'You say you summer here, but your summers have gotten long. Last year you came to visit us for a week in mid-August, then returned here until October. You've been to the city twice since March. Your father wants to know if you'll even come back to the city this fall.'

'He should come and ask me.'

'Bea.'

'I don't know yet what I'll do.'

Lillian hadn't heard. She was craning her neck, her eyes lit with fright. 'What is that noise?'

She was referring to the sound of a whistle buoy that had been installed a week ago in the water off the point. The buoy had been quiet all morning, but the wind must have picked up, rocking the thing, making it shriek.

'Isn't it awful? This is nothing. You should hear it when it's really blowing out there. Makes me want to tear my hair.'

Lillian eyed her cautiously. 'If it helps to say so, your father misses you. It makes him moronic.'

Bea laughed. 'Morose.'

Lillian's embarrassment was embarrassing to behold. Her nostrils flared, the gully between her eyes deepened — she looked, in the instant before she recovered herself, like a pawing bull. 'Albert must miss you, too,' she said.

'He was here last weekend.' Bea said this breezily, and Lillian chirped, 'Oh! Good!' in response, but her left, ungovernable eyebrow rose, betraying her doubt. Bea's husband, Albert, was her closest friend — he was one of her only friends — but he hadn't come to Gloucester in three weeks and Bea neither faulted him nor allowed herself to miss him. Gloucester was her choice, her place. It was nowhere Albert would ever have visited on his own, preferring the city to anything other than the city, disliking 'natural nature,' as he called it, darkness, and the smell of low tide. This wasn't all. When it came to his weekends — during the week he worked as a loyal, ascendant banker at First National of Boston — Albert preferred to spend them in the company of men.

Though Bea had known this before she married him, it had taken Lillian years to fully grasp the situation, took her catching Albert kissing a man in the toilet at Congregation Adath Israel's Benefit for Orphans to understand why Albert and Bea didn't fight in the way of most married people, and why Bea's stomach remained flat.

Lillian claimed she'd walked into the men's by mistake, but who could believe that?

She understood now. Still, she did not see how Albert's being 'like that' should preclude the couple from having children. And she was incapable of spending more than thirty minutes in Bea's presence without asking her about these children. She was about to ask now, Bea could tell, because just before asking Lillian licked the corners of her lips, where her Tre-Jur Divine Scarlet lipstick had pilled. Her tongue was audibly dry, like a cat's.

'Just because he . . . Just because you . . . Just because you had one too soon doesn't mean you can't allow yourself another.'

'Do we have to talk about this?'

They never used the word 'baby.' Bea's parents assumed it had gone to the orphanage and Uncle Ira had never told them otherwise, never told how he had called the place, pretending to be Henry, and explained that there had been a change. Lillian had not even told the doctors at Fainwright about the baby. The baby had been erased from the official record.

'What would you like to talk about? Do you have anything to tell me? Anything new? News? Other people's children have children, they go places, they buy something outrageous. Why are you squinting, Bea? Their husbands get promoted. Which I know Albert does but only because *his* mother tells me.'

'That's good of her.'

'Beatrice. Look at you. You look . . . ' A screech from the whistle buoy interrupted her. She tightened her grip on her bag. 'Why don't you ever wear any of the dresses I bring?'

Bea looked around for a gentler place to rest her eyes. She chose the humidor, about the size of a rugby ball, painted brown for skin, black for the slave woman's chunky hair, white for her bulging eyes, red for her massive lips. Bea and her cousins used to play with her, taking the top of her head off and putting it back on, off and on, making the porcelain rub and grind, until Vera would say, *Leave the poor woman alone.*

85

'Don't judge,' she told her mother.

'I'm not judging.'

'You are.' Bea was judging, too. Her shift was ugly, and made of a potato-sack fabric that was starting to itch. It was an absurd costume, she thought. She wished she were wearing the black silk kimono Lillian had brought on her last visit.

Lillian sniffed. 'How is it she never bought a single comfortable chair?' She shifted on her haunches. 'So I'm judging, so what? So I judge. So do all the mothers. What I'm saying is you don't have to punish yourself.'

'I'm taking care of Ira.' Bea considered this the truth and it was. Also, she was escaping (mostly successfully) from her work for the Woman's Christian Temperance Union, though she barely admitted this to herself and would never say so to her mother.

'You're taking care of Ira,' Lillian repeated. 'Did it ever strike you, Beatrice, that you would be happier if you weren't so set on being *good*? Come back to the city. Make a new kindle with Albert, see what comes of it. Ira doesn't need you anymore, now that you have this nurse, this . . . '

'Emma. She's not actually a nurse.'

'What is she, then?'

'A mother, of nine.'

Lillian's jaw fell, then recovered. 'Nevertheless. She takes good care of him, yes?'

'She's not family. You can't have forgotten, Mother, how well Uncle Ira has always cared for me.'

Lillian appeared to consider Bea's forehead.

86

She closed her eyes, acknowledging the insult, then sprang them open, as if willing a new scene. 'But all those children, Bea. They must fulfill her, don't you think? Don't you think it would, going home to that, after a long day's work?'

'I wouldn't know,' Bea said. 'Based on my experience, which as you know amounts to nothing, I have no idea if she's fulfilled.' She nearly said, *I think she's having an affair*, to make a point about children not ensuring salvation in a life, but that was none of Lillian's business. Twice more Josiah Story had delivered Emma to Bea himself instead of sending her with the usual driver, and though he busied himself wooing Bea toward an endorsement in his clunky, surprisingly charming way while Emma stood silently, hands clasped, Bea sensed an almost visible charge between them. Her suspicion made Bea feel tender toward Emma. Not that she was in favor of adultery, only that she knew it happened. Women came to her all the time, thinking they would keep their talk to drink, invariably stumbling on into matters that used to shock Bea until they didn't anymore. She had come to think of marriage as an island all its own, tidy and firm when viewed from a distance, unknowable except to the ones who lived there.

'Beatrice. Bea-Bea. It's been so long since your last . . . episode. Years, if I'm not misled.'

'Mistaken.' Bea apologized with her eyes. 'And no, you're not. It's been three years.'

'You appear almost entirely well, Bea-Bea.'

'Is that meant to be a compliment?'

'I only mean, apart from certain, *keskasay*,

differences. The cause, which I'll never understand. You know I never meant for that to happen, I brought you to the clubs so you might have a little fun. These clothes you insist on wearing. But apart from all that. It's not too late. You think you're old but believe me you'll realize when you get old you weren't old. You still have your skin. You might be happy. You know there are doctors now, psychiatrists, I've heard about it from women, various women you'd never expect — suspect? — a variety of women, and you just go there for an hour or so and they ask you questions and you talk. Dynamic something or other but my point is it's quite easy, and normal, that's what I'm trying to say, all kinds of women you'd never suspect and you just lie there and answer their questions and apparently your childhood is much more interesting than you ever knew . . . ' Lillian trailed off.

'Have you been?' Bea asked.

Lillian reddened. 'Your father would laugh.'

This was not the answer Bea had expected. Her mother's eyes looked black and small; they sparkled with desperation. Bea pictured her splayed on some bearded man's couch. Was that what she wanted? Bea did not know how to talk to Lillian about Lillian. Sunlight crept up her mother's skirt. Bea knew this moment well, knew that behind her the room's western windows were filling with light. She had lain on the sofa where her mother now sat more times than she could count, watching the sun conduct this same fall from noon. The familiarity softened Bea. She knew the light would strike

88

Lillian's face soon, blinding her.

'You never know,' Bea said.

'I know.'

Lillian's hands flushed now with sunlight; her death grip on the Cartier became apparent. Bea smiled hopefully, but Lillian was looking elsewhere. She said, 'I used to think my mother didn't like me. She would slap my hands when I sewed. I was terrible at sewing. Or I was terrible at it because she slapped my hands. I don't know. The only stories she told me were about wretched people living awful lives. She said these were her parents but I didn't believe her — I thought she was making the stories up, to scare me. Or ashame me. She would say I should have been born to a queen. I took this as an insult. But later — I am talking about much later, when she was dead — I realized she wasn't just talking about me. *She* wanted to be the queen! She would never have said so. However. I think it's true. My mother wanted to be a queen. When she slapped me, I would say, 'Then why make me do it?' and she would just point at whatever I was working on. She didn't know the answer. I — ' Lillian closed her eyes — the sun had reached them, fire in her lashes. 'Do you remember how your *bubbe* pointed, Bea?' Lillian laughed. 'At everything. It gave her away to the very end.' Lillian shaded her eyes and peered shyly across at Bea. 'Do you remember?'

Bea nodded.

'It isn't easy, to raise a child. But Bea, won't you be disappointed?'

It took Bea a minute to understand. Her first

thought was *Mother, I am already so disappointed.* She lived with her uncle instead of her husband. She didn't play piano. She hadn't lasted a semester at college. She had abandoned her baby! She had failed to recover. Her work — whose central purpose, it had begun to seem to her, if you stripped away the beaten women and penniless children and stumbling Negroes, everything worthy of a poster, was to keep dark foreigners from defiling the country (the same people Bea and Lillian's people had been not so long ago) — had outlived Bea's need for it, certainly her interest in it; it had swept her along in its tide and pinned her against a podium, an accidental, celebrated naysayer. Yes! She was disappointed. Yes! She had only to think it and the disappointments flung themselves at her throat almost as fast as Bea could hammer them back down. Her mother looked at her tenderly and Bea felt swollen and strangled. She nearly began to speak. *I am already so disappointed.* She was stopped by fear: fear that if she started talking about herself, she would never stop; fear that her pain would fall out of her, grotesque, hairless, gasping, and she would not be able to stuff it back in. It was this fear, in part, that had gotten her to Fainwright. Which was disgraceful, Bea knew, but nevertheless true: it was far less frightening to collapse and be carried off and cared for than it was to talk. It would be less frightening right now to slip onto the floor like an empty sack than to look into her mother's black eyes and begin to talk. The fact that she talked all the time, that she was paid to talk,

90

wasn't lost on her. She was a master at talking about other women's lives — she plied their heartbreaks, massaged their anecdotes, crafted satisfying, persuasive conclusions. If only she could talk about her own life with so little fuss. Lillian had done it, after all, just now. Lillian, of all people, had tried to share something of herself with Bea. But the whistle buoy pierced the silence and Bea tensed, grew skeptical. She looked at the humidor with its impossibly large, red lips and decided that Lillian had not been sharing, she had been imparting a lesson, all of it coming back around to wanting Bea to have another baby. Which Bea neither wanted nor deserved. She had told herself this so regularly — *don't want, don't deserve* — she had been so focused on putting off her mother, that Bea couldn't recognize a change inside herself, a minute yet radical sifting, a rearrangement at her very core, where a tiny fist of longing for a child grew.

So Bea, her throat in agony, kept hammering. 'I'm fine,' she said.

'Are you hot, Bea-Bea? I'm almost certain I could find a glass of water in this house.'

Bea shook her head.

'Bea-Bea. You're like a boot, laced too tight.'

This was something Henry had said to Lillian, clearly. Bea wished she didn't know this, but she did, and knowing it caused the remaining closeness she'd felt with her mother to evaporate.

'I'm fine,' she said. 'Truly.'

'If you say so.' Lillian smiled her half smile.

'How is Uncle Ira?'

'The same. Oakes and Rose and Julian are coming next week.'

'How are they?'

'I don't know.'

'Dumb,' Lillian said. 'Oakes and Rose anyway. You could use those two in one of your campaigns. They're a fine example of what drink will do.'

'Rose is a doctor,' Bea said, grateful to Lillian for leaving Julian out of it. 'And Oakes was dumb as a child. Ask Uncle Ira.'

'I wouldn't want to bother him,' Lillian said. Her eyes roamed toward the ceiling, then back down. She had only once gone upstairs to see Vera when she was sick. Lillian had shrunk even from her own parents when they got old, Bea remembered, touching them only with her fingertips, visibly working to narrow her nose against their odors. 'He's the same, yes, sleeping, most likely? I ought to go soon, anyway, if I want to make the next train. I'll come back next week, maybe your father will come with me, or not, you know the store is doing quite well, those silly boots he made for the war, Bert Lacey wore them in his latest picture and now the young men love them, they wear them to all the functions and then they show up in the *Herald* and the *Globe* and then the poorer boys want them, too, so the store is busy.'

Lillian stood. She looked beautiful, thought Bea, though she knew, when her mother got home, that she would change her dress five more times and watch her nose in the mirror for an hour before agreeing to go down for supper.

'Do you need a car?' Bea asked, standing.

'No. I told the driver to wait.'

In the drive sat a taxicab. *Of course*, Bea thought. She wondered why she bothered throwing her dresses on the floor whenever Lillian came only to have to pick them all up an hour later. Her mother never asked to see Bea's room. She didn't even know there was one devoted to her in this house — not one of her cousins' rooms, her own.

Lillian started for the door. 'That bookend,' she said, pointing at a glass lion on a high shelf. 'Where is its other one? Where is its friend?' She shrugged and said offhandedly, 'You look fine, Bea-Bea.'

'Thank you.'

Lillian paused. She closed her eyes. A ripple of some emotion passed across her forehead. Then her eyes snapped open and she said, 'Your cousins, you know, they weren't so stupid. You were just very smart.'

★ ★ ★

Ira was not asleep. He watched Lillian's hired car disappear down the drive. It would head off the point, past Niles Beach — here he imagined his sister-in-law thinking, *How picaresque!* in a way she considered generous, not realizing either of her mistakes — and back to the train station, where she would sit in her car until, at the last possible minute, with the southbound whistle bearing down, she would yell at the driver to

93

open her door, thinking to herself, *These people.*

Tomorrow, perhaps, in the *Gloucester Daily Times*, there would be an entry in the social register: *Mrs. Beatrice Cohn entertained Mrs. Lillian Haven, of Boston, at the home of Ira Hirsch on Eastern Point.* Which would be the truth, if the truth were made of facts. Ira knew the difference, having been a newspaperman himself. More accurately, the lackey writing the social register might write, *Mrs. Lillian Haven, née Kunkel, socialite Jewess from Boston posing as a WASP, took the 12 o'clock train up to Gloucester yesterday to psychologically abuse her daughter, Mrs. Beatrice Cohn, née Haven, at the home of dying widower Ira Hirsch, née Heschel.*

Ira smiled. He had thought newspapers were going to shit when he retired, but now — except for the *Freiheit* and a few others — they read like veritable graveyards. There was the inane and endless coverage of the Snyder-Gray murder, the driveling deification of Lindbergh, the four-inch headlines devoted to the opening of the Roxy while the Mississippi flood, half a million homeless, was already dead in the back pages. This Kehoe fellow out in Michigan blew up a school, killed forty-two people, almost all children, and a couple days later the *New York Times* forgot about it. And what about Sacco and Vanzetti, still awaiting execution? Felix Frankfurter's piece in the *Atlantic* in March had destroyed the case against them, then last month a bomb had been sent to Governor Fuller's house. But the papers, after a day or two of condemnation and platitude, had returned to detailing Lindbergh's youthful smile. If that wasn't complete bull . . .

It was also possible, Ira considered, that he just wasn't interested anymore in what most people considered 'news.' Or perhaps he had transcended it, via age or grief or immobility. He thought Vera would have something to say about the difference — or maybe similarity — between not being interested in something and having transcended it. She would remind him to laugh at himself. But it was hard to laugh at himself, by himself. So Ira smiled, and continued. To clarify, the entry might go on: *Ira's brother, the shoe man Henry Haven, née Heschel, also called himself Hirsch once upon a time, until he met Lillian Kunkel, who insisted on Haven. And that was the beginning of the split between the Heschel brothers. Henry Haven made himself a fortune, and Ira Hirsch married into one, which allowed him to continue thinking of himself as a Marxist and a few even though he lived in a very large house, sent away to England for his pear trees because the name 'Braffet' gave him a thrill, and entertained men and women whose blood ran mostly blue. True, they were often artists, like his wife, Vera, née Victoria Bent Oakes, but artists in the safest sense of the word, for they could take great risks while risking very little.* But this was roaming from the point. The point was Ira's younger brother, Henry, whom Ira had not seen in years. Was that possible? It was. *Ira Hirsch's brother, Henry Haven, the shoe man, did not accompany his wife to Gloucester*

95

yesterday, not because he cannot find time to make the trip, but because he cannot forgive his brother his kindness to Beatrice Cohn, who comes to the Hirsch home during bouts of 'instability' because this is where she wants to come. Henry Haven is too ashamed to forgive Ira Hirsch, and Ira Hirsch is too angry to forgive Henry Haven.

That would be a fair place to end. It would be honest, at least — it was where things stood and would probably go on standing until he and Henry were both dead. Ira could hear Bea downstairs, rearranging things, no doubt choosing a nice dress, putting herself back in order. He would have liked to fall asleep again — his chest hurt — but his chest hurt, so he couldn't fall asleep. He could call for Bea, and she would rub his feet, and he would drift off again maybe, but if he drifted off with Bea rubbing his feet in the stew he was in now, he was likely to dream the dream in which Vera's angora shawl floated by on the outgoing tide, the dead baby wrapped within. This was what Ira had never told Henry and Lillian, for Bea's sake, for his own, for theirs, too: the child was gone the day after the pear people came, along with Vera's shawl, which Ira had bought for her in a little Paris shop. Bea had used the pear thieves, Ira figured, as distraction; she'd gone down the hill in the other direction and drowned the thing off the rocks. Ira had seen something, that afternoon, drifting out toward Thacher Island. That had not been a dream, the listless something forty feet or so offshore, too distant for Ira to see clearly. It might have been a dead gull, or a man's shirt buoyed by driftwood. Still, the fact remained: the baby was gone.

He questioned his niece, but she appeared paralyzed; she wouldn't even open her mouth. Ira had slapped her — the only time. Then he'd seen that the front of her dress was wet. Her milk was leaking. *I'm sorry*, he'd said, wishing Vera weren't too sick that day to help the girl, wishing, as Bea began to weep, that he had the courage to hold her. Instead he'd called for the nurse and left the room.

A month after that, Vera died. And her dying became associated in his mind with the baby's, so that in his dream he would sometimes see, wrapped in Vera's shawl, where the swollen lump of the baby's face should be, Vera's face, her lemon-colored hair wound around her neck, her expression peaceful, almost saintly, as it had been when he'd found her.

Ira touched the pain in his chest. Vera wasn't part of the story anymore, he knew. He had told her she could leave, her last night, to make it easier for her. He had never regretted that. Yet he missed her. He doubted he would live long enough to stop missing her. Whereas Henry, he predicted, would live forever and barely be cognizant of what he had, or lost, along the way. Ira watched a fishing boat trudge into the harbor, its gunwales low, laden. He heard the call of the new buoy. It didn't bother him as it did Bea. He found it comforting, actually: that the buoy was out there, calling with the water and the wind, keeping Ira apprised of what was going on in the world. He let his eyes close.

Today Beatrice Cohn lives with her uncle, Ira Hirsch, on Eastern Point and he is uncertain that she will ever leave. He doesn't want her to leave, for his own sake, but he wants her to want to, for hers. He would never say this to her. Also he would never tell her that even after all these years, he cannot tell if she is actually unstable, or just very sad.

8

And Albert Cohn, he wasn't with another man. He was alone, in his underwear, at Bea's writing table. He was a large man, and the table was very small, with fussy legs that knobbed into his calves and a sliding leaf — stuck for years in its fully extended position — that was slowly but steadily purpling his elbow. Albert could have chosen somewhere else to write his letter; the house on Acorn Street was full of horizontal surfaces. But the table helped solidify his resolve. It was like a perpetual pinch, urging him on.

He was writing to Bea, to tell her that he wanted to live alone. This was his first problem: his basic purpose was undermined by the fact that he already *was* living alone. He'd been living alone for months and could continue living alone, doing whatever in hell he wanted, until Uncle Ira died, or — if Bea decided to stay on in Gloucester, which she might, for all sorts of reasons, some known to her, some not — maybe forever.

So what was it he wanted to tell her? He didn't even know what he meant: living alone. Everyone was always living alone, if you wanted to get depressing about it. If he didn't live here alone, he would live somewhere else alone. If he lived with another man, as he allowed himself to imagine in the narrow crawl spaces that intersected rational thought, he would: (a) still

99

be alone, because everyone was; (b) perhaps cease to exist, because he didn't know any men who lived in this way; and (c) be miserable, because the man he wanted to live with had just last week told Albert he didn't want to see him ever again.

Dear Bea, I'm so sorry

Dear Bea, I'm not sure exactly what I'm writing to say

Dear Bea, I'm not even sure that this will upset you, what I have to say, which makes it all the more confusing — to know how to say it, or even to know why I should bother saying it

Albert was hungry. This was another problem; he hadn't left the house all week and was very, very hungry. He rubbed his calf. He traced the ridges the table leg had left in his skin. He was asking for a divorce, he supposed. But the word was so dramatic, and final; it seemed to belong to another marriage than theirs. He could imagine Bea reading it and bursting into laughter.

He released his calf, winced, took up another piece of stationery, made for Bea's confirmation ceremony fourteen years ago. Lillian had chosen the shade of pink, and the embossed initials: *BTH*. Beatrice Theodosia Haven, Theodosia for Feigel, who had been Lillian's or Henry's grandmother, Albert couldn't remember which. He also couldn't remember how they'd gotten Theodosia out of Feigel (they had drawn the *T* from the Hebrew equivalent of Feigel, Tsipporah) but the distance between the words represented for him part of the problem. Bea was so attached, on the one hand, and so utterly unattached, on the other.

Even when they met, at Congregation Adath Israel's Purim Ball, where Albert played one of Vashti's handmaidens with such gusto and so much chest hair that he found himself attacked afterward by a herd of young women, Bea was not among them. It wasn't until the party was winding down and Albert, having extracted himself, was walking toward the men's room, that he felt a hand on his elbow and found himself being steered toward an out-of-the-way window by Beatrice Haven, who wasn't known to bat her eyelashes at a man, let alone touch him. She started to introduce herself, but Albert smiled and said, 'I know who you are. No Booze Beatrice. I'm Albert Cohn, who likes to drink.'

Bea did not blink. 'But do you like women, Mr. Cohn?'

He unhooked himself from her arm. 'Excuse me?'

'Do you prefer us?'

'That depends on the context.'

'In the context of marriage, Mr. Cohn.'

'I don't prefer to be married.'

'And what if the woman, hypothetically, didn't want to be married either?'

Albert, looking around the room, lowered his voice. 'And why wouldn't this hypothetical woman want to be married?'

'Let's say she was strange. Or lonely.'

'If she were lonely, wouldn't she want to marry?'

'That would depend on the nature of her loneliness.'

'I see.' Albert nodded, trying to look sober, but he'd drunk a lot of whiskey and the conversation was so far from anything he'd ever participated in. A kind of giddiness swept through him.

'Forget loneliness,' Bea said. 'Let's say she'd simply had enough of men.'

'She's a man hater.'

'If we must call her that.'

'She hates men. Except for a man like me.'

Bea didn't answer.

'But her mother wants her to marry,' he said. 'Her mother has wanted her to marry since she could walk.'

'Her mother must be like his mother,' she said.

Albert took off his wig. He'd forgotten he had it on. 'Is this a proposal?'

'I've never known a woman to propose.'

'And I've never heard of a woman who wanted to marry a fairy. Not knowingly, anyway.'

'Well, then.' Bea flushed. 'Consider me down on one knee.'

He scratched behind one ear, then the other. The wig had made him itchy, and the scratching was straightforward and satisfying. He kept at it, needing more as he went. 'I barely know you.'

'You know of me.'

'I know you spend a great deal of time trying to rid the world of my second-favorite vice.'

'That's only politics.'

'If that's only politics, you're quite an actress.'

He watched her watching him, her eyes taking in his tutu and his woman's shoes.

Nothing more had been said that night. Albert took her hand as if he'd done it a hundred times before, and turned them to face the room.

Dear Bea,

Out the window, just visible through the budding tree that flanked the opposite townhouse, was Lillian and Henry's house one block over on Chestnut Street, their windows turning purple as they caught the sun. Albert guessed Henry would hate him, and Lillian would act as if she hated him, too, while secretly she would soften toward him, relieved. Albert didn't think he should care what his in-laws thought, and yet he did, which was yet another problem, not what they thought but his caring, or it was emblematic of his largest problem, which was, he supposed, if he was going to be honest — he took out a fresh piece of paper — what he really wanted to tell Bea.

There was a secret court

Albert's senior year at Harvard, there had been a secret court. It was convened after the suicide of a student named Cyril Wilcox, who had been involved — according to his brother — in homosexual activities. (Cyril's brother informed Harvard's acting dean of this only after he'd gone and beat up Cyril's lover.) Thus the court, consisting of the dean, a professor of hygiene, and several others, began interviewing reputedly homosexual students about their practices of masturbation, habits of cross-dressing, uses of slang, parties attended and with whom, etc. After thirty such interviews, the court reported its findings to President Abbott Lawrence Lowell and, based on the evidence, expelled eight students, one of whom, Eugene

103

Cummings, killed himself in Stillman Infirmary a few days later.

I was not called in

It could be said — it would be said — that no one knew what had gone on. But the court knew. President Lowell (the same man Governor Fuller had just appointed to sit on the Sacco and Vanzetti commission) knew. And the boys knew: the ones who were refused positive references by Harvard and therefore rejected by other colleges; the ones who had perjured themselves before the court and denied all kissing, mutual masturbation, fondling, and dancing; and the ones like Albert, who had stayed so far away, kept his head so low, and pretended so earnestly to himself that he was nothing like Wilcox or Cummings that he never got called in.

I watched

A wretchedness had flattened Albert when he heard about Cummings, a spine-wracking fever had forced him to bed for a day. But then he'd stood up, moved on, watched his back, gotten his job at the bank, accepted and framed and hung his indecipherable diploma, married Bea a year later, and so on and so forth. Then last year he'd run into one of the boys who'd been expelled, Tederick Whitlock III, onetime champion sailor and heir, tending bar at the Green Lamp (an underground coupling of the establishments formerly known as the Lighted Lamp and Green Shutters). Albert didn't recognize Teddy at first, changed as he was, fluid and toothy where he'd been stiff and grim, his shirt open to his bony, aristocratic chest. Older. But Teddy recognized

Albert. He took Albert's money, rose on his toes to lean across the bar, and said, *You fuck.*

They'd taken up together. Teddy beat on Albert, screwed him, bit him, called him names, and Albert, so much bigger than Teddy, took it as his punishment. For months this went on and Albert thought it would continue going on, a mutual convenience. But then Teddy had questions. He wanted to talk. He wanted Albert to say why he'd lied and when Albert said he hadn't lied, Teddy said of course he had, and when Albert said he'd had to, Teddy refused to hit him — he said calmly, *We all had to.* Albert said Teddy's breeding afforded him leniency in the world, that he didn't know what it was to be a Jew, and Teddy reminded him that he'd been disowned. He hadn't seen his siblings in years. Albert said, *At least you're free,* and Teddy laughed a quiet, mean laugh and Albert realized he'd fallen in love with Teddy, which had never happened to him before in such an appalling, unfixable way. But Teddy was done. Teddy said he'd met a boy, *and I really mean a boy,* and then he said it wasn't the boy at all, actually, it was Albert he didn't want any more to do with because Albert was despicable and Albert shouldn't go to the Green Lamp anymore either, because that was Teddy's livelihood. Albert worked at First National and Teddy worked at the Green Lamp, *because I'm so fucking free,* and Albert should at least respect that.

So. Albert hadn't bathed. He'd barely eaten. The whiskey was long gone. And now he'd been sitting at Bea's awful writing desk for hours without managing to finish a single sentence because Teddy was right, Albert was despicable, and stupid, too, not only in the sense that he'd never learned Latin but in the sense that he couldn't sustain a thought long enough to figure out what it was that he wanted to say to Bea. The city was coming to life outside, Saturday picnics and paddleboats, children's balls pounding the paving bricks. People had to know about Albert, of course, but they wouldn't *know* unless he did something. What would he do, stick his head out the window, holler? Telling Bea about the court would accomplish nothing, he admitted. She, too, was very good at keeping secrets — she would allow it to slide in between them, another piece of furniture in the sham house of their marriage. And even if people *knew*, say the boys at the bank, what good would it do now? Teddy was gone and the Green Lamp, too, buried along with Cyril and Cummings beneath the paving bricks and the cobblestone walks and the granite curbs of the city, the fusty air and old trees, all of it pressing down on Albert, all of it propping him up.

His stomach whimpered. He was aware of it as an organ, gaunt walled and angry, requiring his attention. He wondered if this was what drew Bea to eat so little, if she stayed hungry because hunger helped one stop thinking of other things, its hard lump like a ballast, steadying you. He thought he could almost cry from hunger. He thought, *I don't want Bea to stay in Gloucester forever. I would like her to come back.* 'What are you waiting for?!' shouted one of the boys down in the street. 'Throw the fucking ball!' *Hunger*, thought Albert. *My stomach is crying*. On Monday he would go into work, say he had recovered from his illness, make it so. He fisted the sheets of paper into a ball, retrieved himself from the table, dressed, and walked toward Charles Street, to find something to eat.

9

'I'll tell Mum,' Liam threatened for the twentieth time that week.

'You won't,' Lucy said.

'Give me a penny.'

'Oh, fine.' She gave one to Liam and one to Jeffrey, too.

They were on their way home from the quarry, cutting through the beech and pine woods above Washington Street. The shade cooled them and they quickly fell into not talking, their feet navigating the rocks and roots on the forest floor. There was a path somewhere near here, but they never took the path.

Lucy Pear was nine and wished she could stay nine forever. She easily hid, beneath a pair of suspenders and one of her brothers' vests, her newly, barely swollen breasts, which she hoped against all likelihood were done growing. Her hair she would gladly have cut, except that their mother would ask questions. The rest of it wasn't so difficult, to walk like a boy, and work like a boy, and keep her mouth shut. She was Johnny Murphy. She counted her first week's pay by touch, in the pocket of her brother's trousers: five dollars and twenty-five cents. An astounding sum, given that they worked only in the afternoons. A ticket to Canada was twenty-eight dollars and thirty-one cents, Lucy had learned from her sister Juliet, who lived in Rockport now, with three children of her own. Juliet was the oldest of the children, and very resourceful, and because she would never have thought to leave Cape Ann herself, she was the perfect target for Lucy's questions.

How much is a ticket to Canada?

That depends. Handing Lucy a cookie. Chuckling. *Where are you pretending to go? Will you need a berth?*

Where did Peter go?

Their brother Peter had gone to Canada the year before. He was ten years Lucy's senior, an outwardly tough boy, almost a man now. Lucy trusted him. She imagined living with him, in Canada, imagined that he would be like a brother-father to her. In Canada, apparently, they had turned the schools into breweries, the grass into moonshine; they had laid tracks straight from the distilleries to the border. Everyone was getting rich.

Quebec. Juliet said it *Kebeck,* as if she were French.

To make the trip, Lucy calculated that she needed thirty for the ticket, ten for food, and ten extra to get by until she found Peter. The perry, their mother had explained matter-of-factly and too late, oblivious to the panic rising in Lucy's throat, wouldn't be ready until next year. So when the quarry jobs came along, Lucy thought, *Why not?* If she kept up the work at the quarry, she might be gone before the pears even hit the press. Maybe, if a storm came up or the fish were scarce, before Roland even returned from his trip.

109

In the yard, their three sisters — with help from the youngest boy, Joshua — were working on the shack that would hold the press. Three walls were up, the fourth in progress, a pine door resting on its side against the cedar tree. Beneath where the floor would be, she and Liam and Jeffrey had been digging a secret cellar. The way down to the cellar would be through a 'turnip bin,' which would be just like the potato bin beside it except that its bottom would drop out. Voilà! Lucy's latest idea was to put the scratcher in the shack above and the press in the cellar below and devise a detachable chute that would carry the pulp straight down into the press. They would press the juice, let it ferment into perry in wooden barrels, then funnel off the perry into jugs. The jugs and barrels had already been ordered — like everything else — with funds from Josiah Story.

'Hello, boys!' Janie sang in greeting, and Lucy was seized by an urge to jump into her sister's arms. Instead she took off her cap, let her hair swing down, and said, 'Hulloh,' in a deep voice, which made them laugh, Janie and Anne and Maggie and Joshua, too, though he didn't understand what was funny. She missed them all already. Her continued devotion to the perry — despite her understanding that she wouldn't profit from it — was her way of apologizing to them, in advance. She hoped that next year, when the jugs were ready to sell, they would see that all her bossing — the lists she made for them each morning, her inspections at the end of the day — had been for them.

Lucy knew — Lucy was not blind — that she was not a Murphy by blood. There was the fact that she was barely older than Janie. (She'd been told that her middle name came from her having been born right around that year's pears, but Janie's birthday was barely nine months after that.) There was Lucy Pear herself. She was dark where they were light, round where they were straight. At her nape there was a fur, very soft but very dark, which spread out on either side of her spine like the wings of a skate. In school, children used to taunt her, ask where her parents had bought her, or what monkey her mother had fucked. *Fucking Catholics*, they would say, even some of the ones who were Catholic. *Fucking Catholic rabbits*. Then Peter had come to school one day. He was seventeen, already working the Jones Creek clam flats, but he walked into the school yard, grabbed the worst of the bullies by the collar, knocked his nose to the right, and blew his wind out in one punch. *What's it to you?* he said tenderly, showing that he had the stamina to inflict far worse. And no one had bothered Lucy since.

Among the family, it had never needed to be spoken. The older ones must have known the story, and the younger ones must have wondered, once they were old enough to notice what other people noticed. Lucy had allowed herself to wonder only in the briefest, most hidden of ways — her eyes flashing open in the dark, a line between lines in her primer, a

111

particular tree branching into two in a particular way. Then it was gone — the beginning, the question of the beginning, the beginning of the question. She stuffed it away like her brothers would a dirty photograph.

It seemed unnecessary. It seemed a betrayal. Then she turned nine and Roland bumped into her one night, in passing. The force knocked her to the opposite wall. He walked on. She thought it was a mistake; Roland touched none of his children, not even on the head or hands, as if to preclude some idea — his own? the neighbors'? — that he must beat them. But the next evening, passing her in the same doorway, he touched her arm, the upper part where she was soft: with one finger he drew a straight line down, quick but hard enough to leave a mark. Since then, every so often, he poked or pushed her in this way: without warning, and on an almost-but-not-quite-private part of her, and so silently and inscrutably, Lucy wondered if she had dreamed it. She felt pain, but only briefly. The next day, Roland would smile at her. He had a sudden, toothy smile not a single one of them could resist, the kind of smile that if seen only once a month made amends for the other twenty-nine days, his eyes shining as impishly as a child's. Maybe she had it wrong. She said nothing. Complaints were not tolerated, and besides, who would believe that Roland had behaved so strangely? He was tempestuous and prone to shouting, but this was not like that. This was like another man, like Roland's dark, quiet cousin emerging, but only for Lucy. This was, undoubtedly, Roland's punishment for her having wondered. Worse, each time he did it, she wondered more. Which would only lead, she feared, to more punishment. And so, it seemed, she was trapped. Which was why she planned to go to Canada, to Peter.

Lucy let Anne and Maggie comb her hair. The yard smelled of pinesap, and more faintly of fish — down at the cove, a field of cod had been laid out on racks to dry. If Quebec was inland, she thought, maybe it wouldn't stink of fish. From the top of the hill, the crazy old widow Mrs. Greely called for her crazy cats. *Beast! Lover! Old man!* Lucy counted the money again, gave one penny to each of her siblings, for their labors on the shack, which she was supposedly in charge of. Then she went inside to wash her face and change into her dress before their mother came home.

10

After the fire of 1873, the Bent heirs had been heartbroken and brash and, in the rebuilding, had overlooked or dismissed a number of elements, some trivial, like a weather vane that would have been stolen anyway when young men from neighboring towns started stealing such things decades later, and some more important, like gutters. The original house wore 240 feet of copper gutter, a glorious, greening skirt you could see from across the harbor. But now there were none at all, and when it rained hard, as it did today, the whole house appeared to be crying.

Inside, the furniture and rugs perspired: the resulting odor was mosslike and sweet. Bea had been watching the rain since she woke, a straight, windless, dumping rain that drove holes into the grass and formed lakes in the driveway. She'd watched, mesmerized, until Emma ran in saying, 'Sorry! Dammit. Oh! Sorry! I'm soaking the floor, I hate the rain,' looser in mood than Bea had seen her, and Bea smiled. 'I know!' she agreed, though she didn't hate rain. It was a relief now and then, particularly in summer when the sun and birds and sparkle off the harbor started to feel a little pushy, even depressing, if one didn't feel just the same. Also, the rain drowned out the terrible sound of the whistle buoy. Bea could see the buoy, if she walked out to the road's end and lifted Ira's binoculars to her eyes: a finger of steel rising out of the water. Seeing its mournful sound come from its rocking and its rocking come from the sea, the plain, material order of the thing, temporarily eased her loathing of it. But at night, waking in the dark, she felt as if a great bird had been sent to harass her, a braying, whining creature with talons bigger than her own feet. At the thought of her own feet, Bea would become aware of a cramping there — she would try and fail to move her toes. And because this was a problem she had experienced before, at Fainwright and on several occasions since, always resolving by morning, she told herself it must be benign. *All in your head!* she heard Nurse Lugton say. But then another voice would enter, like an actor onto a stage, a character more vigilant and afraid, convincing Bea that this time she was in for it — this time she would be paralyzed. Her feet would grow hard as rocks and she would sit up, to make sure she could still do that, then she would swing her legs off the bed and lower herself onto her feet, to see if she could do that, and her feet, somehow, would hold her, they felt balled and worthless but they went on functioning as feet, and she would say, out loud, 'Damn whistle,' as if adding a real voice to the room might jar her out of the debate in her head. She would lie down again and try to fall back to sleep. Sometimes she could but often she couldn't and she would lie and sit and lie awake like this, harassed by the buoy, for hours.

But the rain washed out the sound of the buoy

and Bea hoped it would continue all day and through the night. She had loaned Emma a dry dress and now Emma stood in front of her, wearing it, a drapey, pinkish brown silk thing, *very modern*, Lillian had said, presenting it to Bea, *what all the young women are wearing*, 'young' hit hard as a challenge to Bea, and Bea was thinking how much better it looked on Emma, even though Emma had to be at least ten years older than Bea, because Emma was taller and her skin pale enough to set off the pinkish brown whereas on Bea the color seemed to merge with her skin and the fabric caught on her hips and it looked, generally, like a dress wearing a woman rather than the other way around.

'I'll have to give you that dress,' she said.

'No,' said Emma. 'You shouldn't even let me wear it. It's not a dress for working in.'

'Don't work today.'

'Of course I'll work. Ira . . . '

'He's taking a tub. When he's out, yes. For now, sit?'

Emma frowned. Bea wasn't sure what had caused such a need in her this morning for company — it had flown in with Emma, a damp hollow in her throat.

'Please. Sit with me.'

Emma continued to stand, arms crossed at her breasts, the small, perky kind Lillian had wanted for Bea. 'I'm a good deal older than you, Mrs. Cohn.'

'Meaning what?'

'I'm not certain. I apologize for saying it.'

'Meaning you should be the one telling me

116

what to do? Or that you don't want to sit with me?'

'I didn't say that.'

'No.' Bea was sorry. Emma was clearly uncomfortable in the dress, and with the idea of making small talk with her boss. All the energy she'd arrived with was gone. Bea would have excused her, in another circumstance. But in this one, she didn't want to be alone.

'How about a compromise,' she said. 'You make tea — that counts as work. Then you drink it with me.'

Emma didn't move.

'Are you worried I'll tell on you?' Bea laughed. 'I don't owe Josiah Stanton that much.'

'Story.'

'What?'

'His name is Josiah Story.'

'Right.' Bea was now certain they were having an affair. 'Doesn't he bring you here to woo me? Wouldn't he want you to do what I want, even if it's sitting with me, pretending to be my friend?'

★ ★ ★

They sat at the card table in the parlor, by the window. They were quiet for a while, listening to the rain hammer the earth, watching it jump back up and fall again. Bea reached into the piano bench nearby, withdrew a small bottle of Lydia E. Pinkham's Vegetable Compound, poured more than the recommended dose into her tea, then positioned it over Emma's cup. 'Yes?'

'Thank you.' Emma bit her lip. 'I've heard this stuff is twenty proof.'

'If that's the case, I'm sure I never heard it. I didn't hear you say it, either.'

Emma took a sip and smiled politely.

'Well?' Bea asked.

'It's bitter, if you don't mind my saying so.'

'It's also perfectly legal.' Bea held up the bottle. 'See? 'Health of Woman Is the Hope of the Race.' My aunt Vera introduced me to Mrs. Pinkham's when I was sixteen.' She slurped loudly, then exhaled in an exaggerated fashion. 'And you? Is it true what they say about the Irish?'

'What's that they say?'

There wasn't even a hint of mischief in Emma's face. 'I'm sorry, that was a joke,' Bea said, but Emma went on looking as unmoved as a plate and Bea, feeling desperate, said, 'Why don't you tell me about yourself? Where are you from?' in a bright, stupid voice. It was the same voice — it was the same two questions — she and the other Ladies used to start a conversation with the women who came to them for advice, about husbands or contraception or children or other feminine quandaries of which Bea had little actual experience. She advised them nonetheless. But Emma hadn't come to her for advice. She muttered, 'Ireland.'

'Oh!' Bea flushed. 'Yes, I meant . . . ' She poured more Pinkham's into Emma's cup, then into her own. 'Why don't you ask me the questions.'

Emma sipped her tea slowly. 'I think it's best if

118

I don't. Why don't we talk about Mr. Hirsch? I think we might bring his bed downstairs soon. It's getting harder for him to make the trip, even once a day. He shouldn't be . . . so removed.'

'My uncle can walk perfectly fine when he wants to,' Bea said. 'Am I that boring?'

'I don't find you at all boring, Mrs. Cohn.'

'Well, then. Ask away.'

Emma sipped again, set down her cup, and looked up toward the ceiling. 'There's a leak,' she said.

Bea followed Emma's gaze. She waited, doubtful. Slowly, almost imperceptibly, a drop of water began to form. It grew to the size of a pea, then a marble, seeming at once to cling to the ceiling and to hold it up, an exquisitely controlled little thing, until it dropped and spatted apart on Aunt Vera's oriental carpet.

'It's an old roof,' she said. 'I'll tell the man who fixes these things.'

'I'll go get a bucket.'

'Don't trouble yourself.' Bea slipped her saucer out from under her cup and handed it to Emma. 'Here.'

Emma looked at the saucer, then at Bea. She walked to the corner and placed it under the leak, taking some time to figure out how best to lower herself in the silk dress — bending at the waist first, then attempting a squat, and at last going down gently onto her knees. By the time she returned to the table, Bea had drunk the rest of her tea and poured them both some more Pinkham's. She was starting to feel a little drifty. 'Now. What do you want to know?'

119

Emma looked at her lap. She crossed her legs one way, then the other. Then she snatched up her teacup, swallowed what was left in two gulps, and met Bea's eyes. 'What is it you would like to tell me, Mrs. Cohn?'

'I . . . ' Bea was unprepared. 'I'm from Boston?'

'And why don't you live there, with your husband?'

'Uncle Ira . . . '

'But don't you miss him?'

'I do. Of course. But. Maybe you know. Your husband's often gone, isn't he?'

She poured, and Emma drank. 'I miss him awfully,' Emma said without emotion. 'I barely know how to live without him.' She made a briefly pitiful expression of forlornness before continuing: 'And what about children, Mrs. Cohn? Did you never think to have any?'

'Albert didn't want them. He thought it would interfere.'

Emma looked away, toward the pinging of the leak into the saucer. Bea knew she had turned into a woman about whom others say, *She doesn't like children* and *It's hard to imagine her ever having been one.* She used this to her professional advantage, setting herself apart from the maternal melodrama that had defined the cause for years, the mothers on their knees, singing and weeping. She wore to her talks a man's tuxedo jacket and spectacles — though she didn't need them — and ironed her hair back so severely people speculated she might have Indian blood in her. Bea had

120

envisaged her costume, she'd sussed out her niche, at the very first meeting Lillian brought her to, after 'the trouble' (with the baby) and 'the episode' (with her nerves). Lillian had had to drag her there, saying it wasn't too late for Bea to make something of herself and that it would do her good to think about someone else for a change. She'd had no idea how far Bea would take this.

Bea was a success. A public, well-armored success. Never mind that in the early spring, when she'd last been working in the office of the Boston chapter, she found herself unable to focus on what the women who came to her were saying. She was looking at their children. She was distracted by their beauty. Even children who wouldn't grow into beautiful adults were somehow beautiful.

'In a way, I have children,' she heard herself say to Emma. 'All the children whose fathers beat their mothers, or don't come home at night, or can't stay sober long enough to earn a decent wage. My work. I do it for them.'

Emma regarded her blankly for a moment, then she stood, carried her teacup over to the saucer on the floor, dumped the rainwater from the saucer into her cup, and put the saucer back. 'I should check on your uncle,' she said curtly, her back still to Bea, her long, motherly back, and Bea felt so acutely aware of her own insignificance that she curled her fingers around her thumbs just to feel herself. Then, as often happened, she went toward the bad feeling instead of away from it. She said to Emma's back, 'I don't even know if I'd have been a good mother.'

Emma opened the window near the card table and emptied her cup out into the yard. The room was loud with rain, then she shut the window and it was quiet again, except for the drip in the corner, which dripped faster now.

'Why do you say that?'

'Nerves. It's nothing.'

Emma poured more Pinkham's, drank hers, and looked skeptically at Bea. 'I really should go check — '

'When I was very young, maybe seven or eight, I woke up in the middle of the night to go to the toilet. And just as I was about to open the door, or just as it did open, in that moment when it went from being closed to being open, that point you can't pinpoint where something solid becomes air — do you know what I mean? — in that moment, I saw all these green lights, flickering. And I was sure, suddenly, that there was this whole other life going on behind the door, a world, really, a tiny, very old forest, not a Massachusetts wood but a dripping, savage forest full of lizards and monkeys and lions and half-dressed people who were calling to me to join them.'

Bea paused. Emma watched her blankly, hands neatly folded in her lap. The only sign of her tipsiness was one pinkie, on her left hand, which kept jumping up, then lying back down. 'And?'

'And.' Where had Bea been going? She had been talking to talk, to keep Emma from leaving.

She hadn't told this story to anyone. It wasn't a story, really, just a fantasy she'd had as a kid. It had nothing to do with her nerves, or her balled-up feet. Yet talking about it she felt at ease, much as she had felt answering the doctors' questions at Fainwright, telling them what she knew they wanted to hear. It was like talking about a subject that was at once her and not her at all — as if, the more she talked, the further the subject grew from her, making it easier to talk. 'I was scared. But also tempted. I started waking up every night just to stand at the bathroom door and be scared. I waited for something to happen. I didn't know if I was supposed to make it happen, by opening the door, or if the people were supposed to come for me — if the door might just disappear and I would be in the forest. I had this idea that my grandparents might be there, too, my mother's parents, who were dead. I waited like that every night for a week, maybe longer, and then I wouldn't be able to sleep afterward because I was too excited and still hadn't relieved myself.'

'And then you went in?'

'No. I never went in.'

Emma was quiet for a while. 'Most children imagine things,' she said finally.

Bea looked out at the rain. She felt accused, but of what? Emma was already up again, making the trip to the saucer, but this time, when she returned, instead of dumping her cup out the window, she set it on the table, picked up the Pinkham's, and drank from the bottle's spout so delicately that when she set it down, Bea

123

wondered if what she'd seen had really happened. Emma looked at Bea. 'So your nerves,' she said gently. 'They're the reason you don't have a child?'

Bea cringed at the tenderness in Emma's voice. A moment ago, she had wanted Emma to believe her. She had even wanted to tell her something more, maybe something truer, but now Bea sensed a kind of greed in her, this fecund mother of nine, a ravenousness for any and all information. Bea had already said too much. She had exposed herself as Lillian had warned her never to do to the help. If Emma chose, she could make sure the whole North Shore knew by sunset that Beatrice Haven Cohn had a nervous disorder and regretted being childless.

Bea finished her Pinkham's and set down her cup. She sat very straight. Just above the ground the rain was frenzied — it was impossible to tell which drops were going up and which down. She waited until she felt the vertebrae in her neck pop, then she said, in a calm, syrupy voice, 'Thankfully, I've had the opportunity to give back in other ways. I've helped women and children less fortunate than myself and for that I'm grateful.' She smiled a smile she despised — her mother's don't-pretend-you-don't-understand-me smile. 'We all make *compromises*, as I'm sure you know.'

Emma didn't smile back.

'I meant to ask,' Bea went on, 'what you've done with the pillowcases. What kind of method you've devised. I find one of each pair, but not

124

the match. It's as if they're off doing who knows what with the other missing ones. I can't understand it.'

Emma's pinkie jumped. 'I'll see what I can do, Mrs. Cohn.'

'Also, my spectacles. I don't need them, which means I can see perfectly well that they're not where I left them.' How she hated herself! 'And there's a bookend you must have dusted, a lion. Wherever you've taken it, I hope you'll put it back with its mate.'

They were silent for a minute. Bea felt very lonely.

'That leak is getting worse, Mrs. Cohn.'

'I can hear.'

'Do you think . . . ' Emma looked stricken.

'What?'

'Isn't your uncle's bathroom in that corner, upstairs?'

It took Bea a moment to understand. Then they ran together toward the stairs, their legs, weak with Pinkham's, struggling to catch up.

11

Emma sat low in the Duesenberg's backseat as one of Story's two drivers — the short one, a round-faced Italian called Buzzi whose woolly caterpillar eyebrows danced and kissed in the rearview mirror — told her about the latest craze to hit Rum Row: a purplish, syrupy concoction that originated in Jamaica, was shipped to the Bahamas for 'modification,' then showed up on America's shores in pearl-colored bottles marked SWEET RELEASE RUM.

It seemed a bad sign, that he thought her the kind of woman one could say such things to. Wasn't she still Emma Murphy, of Leverett Street, of Church of the Sacred Heart? Maybe he knew about the perry press, but perry wasn't brandy or whiskey and she and Story had made a straight deal for it. Buzzi wasn't supposed to know about their other dealings. He had dropped her off this morning talking about baseball. Maybe for him nothing had changed since then — maybe the name of the drink didn't even register as vulgar. But after Mrs. Cohn's awful smile and her trilled, nasty *compromises*, everything Emma encountered seemed slightly skewed and salacious, as if she wore a pair of dark, twisted glasses. Buzzi winked at Emma and she had to hug herself she felt so exposed. She was still wearing Mrs. Cohn's dress, a ridiculous getup for a nurse and now wet, too, at the

shoulders from the rain as she'd run to the car
— Mrs. Cohn had not offered her an umbrella
— and at the sleeves from Mr. Hirsch's
bathwater.

He was fine. He had fallen asleep as the bath
filled around him, but he was too large a man to
drown like that. On his face was an expression of
such pure, sleepy contentment that for a
moment, she and Mrs. Cohn looked at each
other, half drunk, and smiled. A simple moment
passed. Then Emma got to work turning off the
water and waking the man, who began talking at
once, as if he'd only blinked, about how flood
was better than fire, and did they know about the
time Vera's great-grandfather, Brink Bent III, too
busy in love with a milkmaid, abandoned a
candle on his windowsill? This was in 1870-
something. He burned the house down but kept
the help, and a couple years later the same girl
bore him a bastard child whom Brink visited,
every Sunday, in the old barn. The kid became
one of Brink's gardeners. Mr. Hirsch laughed. 'I
never heard that story,' Mrs. Cohn said with a far
look in her eye, and Emma, who was doing her
best to position herself between Mrs. Cohn and
the sight of her uncle's willy floating like
pickleweed, who was thinking, *Is there no end to
these people's woes?* had to say, 'A towel please.'
Then she had to prod Mrs. Cohn to find her
uncle's clothes while Emma mopped the floor.
The water had risen a full inch before clearing
the threshold and running into the hallway, but
when Emma showed Mrs. Cohn a cracked tile,
Mrs. Cohn waved her off. She said she would

call the man who took care of 'that.'

'You know a woman called Ameralda Norris?' Buzzi asked. He had moved on from the subject of the rum and was working through his docket of local news.

'No,' Emma said.

'This woman has been hiding bottles in her chimney soot and selling them outta her wood box. Very clever. Very brave. I think so. I really do. But I am only a lonely roly-poly stone carver driving a woman around. This is why I ask *you*. Do you agree? That this Ameralda Norris is clever and brave?'

Emma said nothing. The windshield wipers thumped.

'She got the ax last night. Four pigs. Took her to the station with another woman what's been making wine in her cellar.' Buzzi chuckled. His dirty teeth filled the mirror, followed by his gleaming eyes. 'I woulda like to know these women,' he said, and Emma shivered. She sank lower in the seat. 'It's not as if they're dead,' she said.

Buzzi laughed again. 'You are true, Mrs. Emma, you are true,' he said, beaming at her, and Emma's cheeks burned at how wrong he was. She couldn't help feeling that Mrs. Cohn had set her up for just this moment. *The pillowcases, off doing who knows what . . . The lion, back with its mate . . .* So Mrs. Cohn knew about Emma and Story or she had guessed or it was simply so obvious — Emma was so obviously a compromising woman — that Mrs. Cohn had never thought otherwise. It was as if all the years of Emma's virtue since her bar days had been erased.

At the Washington Street railroad crossing, the car had to wait. A man peeked out from under his umbrella, called hello to Buzzi, then caught Emma's eye in the backseat and ran on. *Oh!* Emma started to shake. Everyone knew this was Josiah Story's car. They knew nurses did not wear silk dresses. (At the door Emma had asked for her dress and Mrs. Cohn said, as if she were giving Emma a car, 'Oh no, you keep it, I'll have your old one cleaned and get it back to you next week. My cousins will be in town, did I mention that? In the meantime feel free to wear this one as often as you like!') People would suspect Emma wasn't only being ferried back and forth from her place of employment. Roland would find out. How could she have been so stupid? Not only stupid. Impulsive. Profane. The rain on the roof grew louder. It was Story's fault, Story with his broad forehead and his straight nose and his mouth never giving him away until the moment he kissed her. She had gone to him for money and offered him a commission in return and that was that, that was all she had intended, she was almost entirely certain that that had been all, yet now every few nights he picked her up in his Duesenberg, wrapped her legs around his waist, and turned from a plain man into an agonized, ecstatic one. It was thrilling, to see a public face rupture in front of you, for you. She would have to stop the whole business. Thank you very much but I'm not a tart so you can take back your jobs and your money, too. Thank you

129

very much but we've managed, my husband and me, the money may come and go but the children have never been hungry. Thank you very much, Mr. Story. Please don't come near my house again.

The train bellowed and was past. Emma had the urge to open the door and run but she was miles from home in a deafening rain wearing a nude-colored silk dress and if anything said *poor tart* more clearly than a woman running in a silk dress in the rain, well.

So Emma stayed where she was, and Buzzi drove, his voice muffled by the rain that flooded the windshield despite the steady beating of the wipers. They drove across the Goose Cove Bridge, past the glimpse of the Annisquam Yacht Club, the sleek sailboats rocking in the rain, their masts suddenly, unmistakably phallic, and Emma felt her determination grow. The next time Story came for her, she would tell him. She couldn't simply be bought. It couldn't be that simple.

Part Two

12

The house changed when the Hirsch children arrived. First was Oakes — née Irving — the larger and louder of the boys, with his shy wife, their two children, a nanny, and a cook. Then Rose, alone as always, dragging a carpetbag so hideous it could be taken only as judgment on Oakes's leather trunks. And last Julian, with his French and very pregnant wife, Brigitte, whose long sequined skirt (unlike anything heretofore seen on Eastern Point), when she first climbed from the car, caught the sun and flung rainbows that Oakes's children tried to catch, their screams strikingly close in pitch to that of the whistle buoy.

The whistle buoy howled often and more shrilly. A wind had come up from the south.

Within a day, shoes and tennis rackets and hats and books and watches and wine bottles and also one gold locket were flung around the house. From the harbor, sailors noticed the windows wide open, towels spilling out the sills, music drifting on the breeze. Oakes had brought his phonograph. Julian's wife played piano, badly. The children screamed with delight and despair. The cook tore the kitchen apart and put it back together. The nanny scowled at the dust and began to clean.

All this activity made the house's fading stand out as it did not when Bea and Ira were alone.

Wallpaper curled, paint crumbled, floors sagged at the corners. Bea and Ira themselves, the quiet routines they had built between them, the satisfactions of their bond and the safety of their fundamental distance, appeared dusty and frayed. Her cousins' arrival made Bea feel at once invaded and like the invader, abruptly aware that this was in fact not her house. Ira was not her father. Once upon a time she and Julian might have married but that hadn't happened and so she was — and would always be — Cousin Bea, the almost, the only child, the one they knew well and not at all, the one who had seemed to be going one place yet wound up in quite another, and because there had never been any discussion of the baby (even when she had been huge with it and living in their parents' house) she was separated from them by yet another valley.

She stayed upstairs with Ira and Emma, except when Julian came up to sit with his father. Then Bea slipped past him, able to meet his eyes only for a fraction of a second, a bright, hot instant that stretched into her girlhood and down to her toes, and walked down to the point and out the granite bed of the breakwater where the noise of the house was far away and the water beat hard enough between the stones to drown out the whistle buoy, seeing his long, angular face. She fixated on the place where his tall nose met his brow, the place he would furrow once upon a time when they played their duets, where his purpose, and his feeling, seemed most strongly to reside. Two wrinkles had grooved the skin there now.

Bea played backgammon with Rose a few times, listening as her cousin gossiped, envying the way Rose sat in her chair with one leg flung over the arm and her skirt stuffed brazenly between her legs. Bea asked polite questions of Oakes's wife, Adeline, who had been a scholarship girl at Miss Winsor's and appeared perpetually appalled by the entire family: their flagrant, neglected wealth, the wet rings they left on tables without looking back. Bea listened to Oakes brag about his recent conquests as the communications director for Haven Shoes, which seemed to involve trailing along to lunches, handing out cigars, spinning tales about the wonders of the patented rubber Haven heel, ensuring the company its weekly ad spot in the upper right-hand corner of page three of the *Globe*, and more generally doing Henry's bidding. Oakes saw Bea's father more than she did, and in this he held some interest for her, but when she suggested he encourage Henry to come out for the Fourth, Oakes said, 'Sure, I'll ask,' gave a vague snort, and changed the subject to Sacco and Vanzetti and — his favorite subject — the 'foreign element.'

A couple times, she put on a bathing suit and set out with her cousins for the yacht club. She had not swum in years and was genuinely excited to dive into the pool. She indulged a hope that everything there, which she trusted remained the same — the old teak lounge chairs with their scratchy, striped cushions, the people standing around with yellow, sour cocktails while the children splashed and dove — would return them to their childhoods, if not to the time then to the sensation of it, that transcendent floating platform on which you didn't look forward or back but existed only as you were. Cold water, hot sun, salt stinging your eyes.

But Brigitte had to walk very slowly, which meant Julian walked slowly with her, which left Bea, walking ahead with the others, with the feeling that he was watching her from behind, which led to all sorts of other feelings. They were eleven or twelve when Julian's shoulder, rubbing against hers as they sat on the piano bench, flooded her legs with a heat so startling she had to close her eyes. They played for years like that, their shoulders touching, legs touching, feet touching at the pedals, a vibration humming between them, making the music really very good — everyone agreed that it was good. Sometimes, when others left the room, they kissed, kisses that began as pecks and devolved quickly into huge, wet messes. Then, one evening, he said, *Let's get married*. She laughed, but only for an instant. Of course. It was done often enough: first cousins. It might be done quietly, but it was done. He would finish Harvard, she would finish Radcliffe, then they would marry. It was so obvious. Who else? Bea kissed him hard, nodding yes, then Lillian called for her to leave and she pushed off him and ran, close to vomiting with excitement.

She was seventeen. Two weeks later the lieutenant came with his boot-loving admiral and the next time she saw Julian — she at the Hirsch

136

house for her 'rest,' he home from Harvard for a weekend — her stomach had started to bulge. He wouldn't look at her. He felt betrayed, she knew, but she wished he felt something else. She wished he felt complicit in some way, wished he would wonder if their secret engagement caused their trouble. An immaculate conception! It was an absurd but irresistible fantasy: Julian smiling at her knowingly; their marrying sooner than planned; their raising the child together. She watched him desperately for a sign of recognition but he hadn't once, not even when he brought her glasses of water as Vera instructed him to do, looked her in the eye. Now he'd said little more to her all week than 'Looking good, Bea. What a pleasure,' as though she were his great-aunt, and he plodded behind her with his beautiful, bursting wife, likely noting that Bea owned no sandals, only covered shoes, or that the robe she wore over her bathing suit was one of Ira's old ones, for she didn't have a swimming robe either. And so forth. No doubt he would pity her her frizzy hair, compared with his own smooth locks, which of all the gifts Vera had passed on to her children were the most instrumental in allowing them to fit in at the club, whereas Bea would stand out. She had always stood out. Despite the name Haven, despite all her parents' efforts to tame and gloss themselves and their daughter, still her cousins won, because their mother was not a Jew.

She turned back, citing some need of Ira's, or an order of business for the cause — the word gross in her mouth, her cheeks raging with

137

humiliation. But they didn't notice. Or she was so good at hiding — how many years she had spent hiding! — that they couldn't see. 'B'bye, Bea-Bea,' they called cheerfully. 'B'bye, see you later!'

She returned, and took off her dry suit, and sat in her room. Ira was asleep. Emma was helping Helen, the nanny, set up a game or make beds — of course she liked the help better than she liked Bea. Everyone was doing what they ought to be doing except Bea, who dreamed of the pool and of Julian kissing her and of Oakes's deep, fat voice filling the house as she sat on her bed listening to the whistle buoy wail.

13

Where did Emma go?

Into the window slid the big moon, bathing Lucy's face in blue. Next to her Janie rolled away. Lucy kneed her gently in the bottom. She willed her awake but Janie sighed and slept on. Lucy woke every night, at some point — this had been true for as long as she could remember. Usually she fell back to sleep without trouble. But every time the long, yellow car came for Emma, a jolt ran through her: her heart started to thump and her back to sweat; she woke as fully as if it were noon. The headlights filled the trees outside her window, so bright they seemed to be laughing at the moon. She heard the house's misfitted back door close. Another thud, a car door. The crunch of tires as Mr. Story's car pulled away down the road.

Lucy had thought — she had hoped — all that was over. For a while, the car had stopped coming. Now its rumbling would not leave her chest.

Why would Emma run away like that?

Lucy couldn't help but feel that Emma's sneaking off had something to do with her, just as she felt an unaccountable anger at Emma for Roland's nastiness toward her, his bizarre pokings and proddings. She was too young to try to account for such things; instead she experienced them as an old nick, a sharp silence in her bones. She had been pulled from sleep, then abandoned. Janie and the others did not stir. Up the hill, Mrs. Greely hollered: 'Lover!'

Outside, the air had cooled. Lucy kept to the far edge of the road, where any child knew to walk when her feet were bare — here the granite chips had been worn to a fine, velvety dust. She passed the Davies' dark house, then the Solttis', then Mrs. Greely's. Here the lights were on. Lucy heard the sound of a piano being struck, apparently at random, the notes darting into the night like a riddle.

Five minutes into the woods, the noise had faded. Lucy's eyes adjusted. She found her boulder and climbed to the top. She did not bother feeling her mossy seat for rainwater — except for a couple stormy days there had been little rain since May. The Mississippi River, she knew, had flooded. But she did not understand where that was, or what it meant. She sat, and thought about Emma. Lucy understood only about half of what adults said. She did not know, for instance, what it meant that Mr. Greely had died of a 'venereal disease.' But she thought she understood what Emma meant when Lucy overheard her say: *He wandered around on her.* Mr. Greely had gone off somewhere in secret, just like Emma was going off somewhere in secret. That much was clear. Less clear to Lucy was whom Emma was wandering around on. Roland, probably, but he wasn't home, so did it count? And if not, wasn't she wandering around on the children? What did she do as she wandered? And why was she doing it with Mr.

Story? Lucy recognized the car from the quarry. She had heard two men in the carving sheds arguing about Josiah Story: one said, *You can't expect a guy gets handed a silver spoon and turns it down,* the other, *Don't think he's your friend, he's a sellout. I wouldn't vote him in for mayor if he paid me, which he probably would, he's such a whore.* Lucy had not observed Josiah Story closely — she tried to keep her eyes down at the quarry. He was funding their perry operation, of course. There was that. But Emma never took him inside the shack. She climbed into his car and rode away.

Lucy would have liked to ask Peter. If she focused her eyes the right way in the moonlight, the forest floor looked made of fish skin, each leaf a glinting scale. Peter would see this, too, she thought. Yet when she called him up, when she sat him next to her on the rock with his perpetual smirk and his shrewd green eyes, his heavy fist curling out to knock her in the shoulder, she knew she wouldn't dare ask him about Emma. And it was this, more than what she'd actually seen — she hadn't seen anything, after all, but the car, and Emma fleeing — it was her understanding that she could not ask Peter that told Lucy something bad was going on. And though she didn't know what the something was, knowing *that* it was seemed to make her somehow bad, too.

The air darkened as the moon went behind a cloud. The trees appeared to thicken, the ferns that grew from the boulder's lower crack to grow a full foot, black creatures stretching toward her through the night. People liked to call Cape Ann the Rock, and sometimes, like now, Lucy could feel it: how hard the place was, hanging off the world with its back up. She wished she was like Janie and the others, sleeping through to morning, not realizing anything was amiss. Lucy's knowing about Emma was another thing that separated her from them. It was lonely, being the only one awake, the one protecting their mother's secret. She felt guilty for keeping it, guilty at her gladness that Roland was away, guilty that the family was not as it seemed to be, guilty for being one of them and also outside, looking in, seeing the seams but not how to stitch them up.

Mrs. Greely's house was dark when Lucy left the woods. She crawled in beside Janie and fell quickly back to sleep. She was only nine, after all — she never did manage to stay up until Emma came home. Instead, she would wake with the others, eat Emma's oatmeal, return Emma's sleepless smile. Always, Emma needed Lucy to smile back — this was a need as clear to Lucy as her own need for food, a need that preceded her first memories or words. In smiling, Lucy would forgive her, because Emma needed that, too, and because Lucy, after all, had her own secrets. The quarry. Canada. She was getting closer each day.

14

The Annisquam River was tidal from both mouths, water flowing toward itself and away, the harbor at one end, Ipswich Bay at the other, both saltwater, an infinite exchange. The river cut the Rock from the mainland. It was what made the cape an island. Emma knew this. She was from away and so she knew, because to get here you had to cross the river. But Josiah had lived most of his life not leaving the island, not knowing where the river went. Eight years ago, when Susannah walked past him outside his father's shop and decided against all reason and familial threat that he was the man she wanted to marry, he didn't even know the river had a northern mouth. He was scared of the water and so had not traveled the Annisquam by boat, and he had never been shown Cape Ann on a map. But soon he found himself in Caleb Stanton's house, wandering the map-lined halls, half lost and half evading the mystery of cocktails-on-the-terrace. Some maps showed places Caleb had conquered in his rail and timber days, others the European cities to which he'd traveled with his children, others — these under glass — exotic places like Africa and the Amazon. When Josiah first came to the map of Cape Ann it might as well have been Cape Horn — he did not recognize it as the place he lived. Other capes and islands looked like moons or squirrels or whales or hearts, but this place — though Josiah could divine a finger here, a mouth there — lacked any coherent shape. It was lumpish, and ragged. And slicing its disorder in two was the tortuous river, represented by the blackest of inks, its many dead-end tributaries obscuring its outlets. A dark, defiant vein. Josiah got stuck there, mesmerized, until Susannah found him, and laughed. She had a beautiful laugh, chimelike and knowing, and she took his arm with a certainty that soothed him even as he knew that she was the one who had caused him to feel uncertain. She was revealing the world to him like sunlight to a dark room and he felt toward her alternately grateful and petulant. He let her lead him out to the terrace, where he drank his first gin and tonic and listened to his future father-in-law talk of profits and paving stones while Josiah thought about the map's lumps and the river and the vast woods he had glimpsed at the center of the island, and when he could get back to them unnoticed.

'Are you going through?'

Emma looked past him, in the direction of the cut, where the river let out into the harbor, or the harbor squeezed into the river, depending on the tide.

'I don't know.' Josiah spoke weakly, the unmoving oars heavy in his hands, his feet still spasming from gripping the floor of his father's boat. The boat was his gift to Emma, to apologize for disappearing — he hadn't been to Leverett Street for nearly two weeks — and also, most urgently, to distract himself from Susannah, who was pregnant, and hopeful, and, Josiah felt sure, bound to miscarry again. The boat was meant to affirm his power, showcase his munificence — it was something he knew he could succeed at. Or he'd thought he could. He had forgotten about his fear of the water, forgotten what it was to float above the dark surface, unable to see underneath, the jellies and fins and claws and kelp, forgotten how his own soul seemed to crouch down there, ready to jump. *Raaaow!* And how queasy it made him, as if cut from his roots, how there was no middle, no almost: two feet from shore and you were adrift. There was a reason Josiah had followed his father into the shop while his brothers took up fishing, but he hadn't been on a boat in years and had managed to forget. So here he was, on the Annisquam in the middle of the night, attempting to row out against an incoming tide, trying and utterly failing to impress Emma, who exuded a kind of rage as she sat. He had been giddy imagining himself and Emma in the boat — the boat she had asked for, a boat for catching pears, a pearing boat! — gliding soundlessly across the black water, an Indian warrior and his princess, or something like that. He had presented the boat with a patrician sweep of his arm, offering to row her all the way out to the harbor, but as soon as he started rowing, he'd slammed into a moored dory, tangled an oar in a lobster line, and been cowardly enough to blame both on his father's poor upkeep of the boat. Emma hadn't even stuck out an arm to fend off the dory, and now she stewed silently, her eyes bled of their strange green color in the dark, and between their boat and the cut was a black stretch of water pushing them back, or in Josiah's case forward, and this he'd also forgotten: the general awkwardness of rowing, how everything ahead of you is at your back and everything behind you at your front, then and now, here and then, a baffling arrangement. The cramp in his toes left an ache. A firework whistled somewhere, practice for the holiday. It was the first of July. At the Hirsch house, at the other end of the harbor, there was talk of where they would buy lobsters, and what had happened to the old crackers, and whether there were enough hammers in the cellar to open the beasts that way. But here, in the silence that followed the firework, Josiah heard a very distant cry of warning.

It was the whistle buoy, Emma knew but did not say. She was still angry at Josiah, and furious at herself. Her mind had been made up never to go with him again. He made it easy at first by staying away, until he made it harder, the mystery of his prolonged absence its own seduction. But even tonight, when she heard the car, she promised herself she would be good, exert her will, be like her mother, whom she had managed to emulate most of her life, a practical, disciplined woman with little patience for ambiguity. It should be easy not to rise for him, Emma thought — she was tired from all the extra work at the Hirsch house, the cousins, the children. It should be easy to gird herself to her bed. And yet. What if he punished her, took away her job? For the first time in her life Emma had enough money. Not a lot, but enough. This was like having needles removed from her skin — it was a shocking, wondrous absence, not to perform the constant arithmetic of debt. Still, Emma balled the corner of her pillow into her fist, stayed flat. She was not a whore. She shut her eyes. Into her mind slid an image of Mrs. Cohn looking at her cousin Julian with such obvious desire that Emma, thinking of them, was filled with despair. Bea-Bea, her cousins called her. Bea-Bea! It was a sort of warning, to think of Mrs. Cohn's unhappiness, not Emma's mother's sort of warning, but another, powerful one. Emma had opened her eyes and there were the trees spiraling with light, and the Duesenberg's headlights boring into the wall of her bedroom, one illuminating the rusty path of an old leak, the other a small hole the boys had made years ago, fighting over something. She flooded with want.

'Maybe this is far enough,' Josiah said. 'You get the feel of it. The other one' — he was loaning her one of his brother's boats, too — 'is the same. Your average skiffs. But you said you needed boats. And they should hold a lot of pears.'

He wanted her to thank him, Emma knew. Just as he wanted her to tell him to turn around, release him from his obvious suffering. But how could she do that when he caused her so much torment?

Again the whistle buoy sounded. Emma liked the buoy's noise, though she wouldn't have said

147

so to Mrs. Cohn. It put her in mind of the malt-house horn in Banagher, and of her own old innocence, as a girl. Eimhear.

'I'd like to see the harbor,' she said.

Josiah's arms began again to lift and pull. The oars banged in the rusted locks, his knees knocked into Emma's, the boat clanged miserably on. But why, he thought, should he be so unhappy? He didn't used to be unhappy, and now, by all accounts, he should be happier than he'd been then. He knew the map of Cape Ann by heart. He had two of his own, one on the wall outside his and Susannah's bedroom, and another — showing the names of roads and streets — that he kept in the glove compartment of his Duesenberg. He knew where Bayview became Lanesville and where Lanesville became Folly Cove, knew which kinds of people lived on which streets, knew about the hermits and witches supposedly living up in Dogtown, knew Magnolia from West Parish, knew where the prostitutes were and how to make a phone call, knew the view from the bell tower atop City Hall. Soon, if all went as planned, he would have his own office in the room beneath the tower. His men at the quarry (except for Sam Turpa, he hoped) would probably vote for Fiumara, even the ones who weren't Italian — to them it was a vote for Sacco and Vanzetti, a vote for themselves — but his men did not matter in the big picture. Josiah would still win. Susannah was pregnant. He might be a father. A father and a mayor, writing a check to dredge the cut, which was officially known as Blynman Canal. Josiah knew

148

this, too, because Caleb had made the annual and entirely uncontroversial dredging of the Blynman a centerpiece of Josiah's platform.

Caleb had written Josiah's speech in the end, after Josiah admitted the night before he was supposed to make it that he had written nothing at all. (He would never show anyone that first sentence.) The speech was good, Josiah thought, but giving it had made him feel ridiculous, like a character in costume, the upright one that speechified about canals and temperance while his other one, the down-low one who wheeled and dealt in his office, went on undermining everything this one had to say.

This, he supposed, was maybe part of why he was unhappy. But nobody seemed to notice. Even his father believed in Josiah For Mayor. Josiah had gone to him back when Caleb first proposed the idea, had worn to his father's shop the suit Susannah had bought him on her last trip to Boston, and his camel and white two-tone brogues, still stiff from the box. Some part of him must have meant to offend his father, ply his insecurities, incite his judgment and gall, so that Josiah would not have to feel any of this himself. He expected his father to rant about the vileness of elected officials. But Giles Story was not himself that day, or else he had changed. He was smitten by the notion of seeing the name 'Story' on campaign signs all over town. He especially liked the idea of seeing it added to the company billboard out on Washington Street, which he was sure would happen if Josiah won his campaign. STANTON & STORY GRANITE

COMPANY. Giles went straight to the shop telephone — he was usually stingy with the telephone — and rang a friend who made signs.

And so. Josiah ran for mayor. He tried for fatherhood. He rowed.

'How are the children?' he asked, to ask something. Emma didn't answer. He considered asking why her husband had been off 'fishing' for nearly two months now, when the longest ice could last in a hold was two or three weeks. Or maybe he would tell her how her daughter, the different, dark one, was working at the quarry dressed up as a boy, and how Josiah had seen through her disguise right away but hadn't said a thing, and wouldn't — he was that magnanimous! Maybe then Emma would forgive him.

Or not. She was looking at him now, harshly. She asked, 'Have I been of use to you, Mr. Story?'

'I wish you would stop calling me that.'

'I know. Have I?'

'I don't know what you mean.'

'Has Beatrice Cohn agreed to endorse you?'

'She's working on a speech. I thought I'd told you.'

'No.'

'I'm sorry.'

She chewed her lip with her big front teeth. He loved to lick those teeth, just as he'd known he would the first time they met. Josiah stopped rowing. He heard the roil of the cut now. He had forgotten that, too, the river's agitation as it squeezed between the stone walls, how it churned with square waves, how a boat could

150

jump and slide in the narrow passage. He rested the oars on the gunwales, hung his head on his neck. The tide began to push them back.

'You're afraid,' Emma said. Her tone was gentler now — not accusatory but matter of fact.

'The Feds are out some nights, patrolling,' he said. He wondered why hadn't he thought of this excuse before. 'And the Coast Guard's got seaplanes stationed on Ten Pound Island. Smack in the middle of the harbor.'

'Not afraid like that.' Emma lifted his chin with her finger and made him look at her. The dark pools of her eyes glistened — they seemed not to watch Josiah so much as take him in. She was the one who saw his unhappiness, he realized, saw that he was split in pieces.

'Susannah's pregnant,' he said. 'That's why I didn't come. I'm sorry.'

Emma's finger dropped. 'That's good,' she said. 'That's very good.'

'It's only three months in. Further than before, but still. She's too excited. She's talking about names.' Josiah stopped, conscious of Emma's having retreated. He had not meant to talk about Susannah. The whole point was not to think of her, to trade her flat, taut stomach for Emma's soft one, to assert himself, to take charge! How pathetic it seemed now.

The sound of jeers and whistles made him turn. He saw dark shapes on the drawbridge above the cut. Early revelers, perhaps the firework setters. He and Emma wouldn't be seen from this distance, but they couldn't risk going closer, either. They could not row through, thank

God. Something landed on his neck and Josiah reached back to feel the nubby slime of a rotting tomato. He was always being saved like this, in ways he had not thought to want, from dangers he had not foreseen. Before he could react — he fingered the tomato, stunned — Emma had grabbed the oars, shoved him off the bench into the bow, and turned the boat around. She was far better at rowing than he. She started to pull and like that the stuff between them fizzed again, Josiah's punishment complete, her hand's imprint on his chest a hot desertion, his prick rising. Another tomato hit the stern but Emma rowed fast and well with the tide, her back rocking toward him and away. Stuffed onto the tiny bow bench, Josiah felt he had been stolen. He felt helpless and safe. They reached the sagging dock in a quarter of the time it had taken him to row them out, an instant, a blink, so that when he had cleated the line it seemed they had never left. His agony was erased. He let her wrestle him onto the dock, roll him off into the marsh, and pin him against the stabby grass, leaving bright red nicks in his back, which Susannah, he knew with glad and grievous certainty, would not notice.

15

July third. The Hirsch children's visit slid into its ninth day. They would be in Gloucester four more before returning to their cities. Ira sat with Lillian at his bedroom window, watching his grandsons play ball on the lawn below as their mother watched from the terrace. Adeline had the nanny but rarely left her with the children, whether out of fear or discomfort or a genuine desire to be close to them herself, he couldn't tell. She was the opposite of Vera, who didn't hire anyone to take care of the children or take much care of them herself. So the nanny sat in the shade for appearances while Adeline watched her own children. Julian had gone for a swim at the club while Brigitte napped. Oakes was somewhere. He couldn't be heard for once. The whistle buoy was quiet, too. It was a hot, still day, the children the only ones moving. A sailboat tried to tack. It heeled, it sat — one of the boys from the club would have to go tow it in.

'There she is.' Lillian pointed to the far end of the lawn, where Bea had appeared from between the trees that lined the drive. Unless she was with the others, Bea always walked the drive, not through the orchard. Around her neck she wore Ira's binoculars, which she had begun carrying all the time now, claiming she was looking at the whistle buoy, and sometimes birds. She had left early this morning, when she heard that Lillian was coming, and Ira was surprised to see her back. He guessed she might have run into Julian, and fled.

'There she is,' he agreed.

'I don't know why Albert couldn't grace her with a visit.'

'He's coming tomorrow.'

'Why not today? It's Sunday, for God's sake. Mph.'

'It's very hard for Julian,' Ira said. 'Bea. How she's changed. He still won't admit that she doesn't play. He comes home expecting her to be sixteen.'

Lillian turned to face him.

'And Bea. She still has a crush on him, you know.'

Lillian's red mouth fell open sarcastically, a mockery of a mouth falling open. 'You busybody man. Of course she doesn't.'

Ira nearly shouted, *She does!* He wanted to wring her neck. But his insistence would do Bea no good. What did he need Lillian to know for anyway? Company, he supposed. Another elder. He was torn between his son's happiness — that beautiful wife, their first baby due soon, the boy settled in a good if uninspired job at the *Post* — and his niece's, which was as elusive as Julian's was evident. He wanted Bea to have something she wanted. He found himself wondering in odd moments: whom did he love more? He knew his loyalty should be with his son. The fact that it wasn't that simple Ira blamed on his brother, who was not even here for the Fourth of July, who said he had to go sailing with clients in Boston Harbor to 'seal a deal.' Even his language was rote, as if he'd stopped actually thinking. Forget feeling. At this point Henry had all but abandoned Bea here.

'She's happy,' Lillian said, and Ira almost felt bad for her. She might have gone sailing, too, one presumed.

Bea walked across the lawn with her hand above her eyes, the sun glinting off the top of her head. Her hair was not slicked back as usual. Since her cousins' arrival she had let it puff into its natural state, which at first Ira interpreted as a sign of comfort, even confidence, but now, as the days wore on, saw as a kind of giving up. She wandered, lost. She flinched every time the whistle buoy called.

'You know, it might be good for you to try to walk, just a little.' Lillian's hand clapped Ira's knee and bounced off. He could see her surprise at his boniness, though she tried to hide it in a brave smile. 'You could lean on me,' she said cheerfully. 'I can help you.'

She was being honest. Ira could see this. He could also see that she was bored up here, that she wanted him to walk with her so she could go down and join the action, have a good kvell over Brigitte's baby, aggravate Bea. It was impossible, looking straight into Lillian's dark, angling eyes, for Ira not to think of Vera. People said time eased grief, and it was true that Ira's came less frequently now, but when it came, it was still a blow to his gut, a wave spitting his heart onto the shore.

They heard a loud grunt, then 'Oh!' from the older boy and 'Oh no!' from Adeline. Bea had collapsed on top of the older one, Jack, who had smashed into her as he ran for the ball. 'Oh my goodness!' Adeline cried, running toward the heap of limbs. Lillian ran, too. In an instant, she was gone. Ira tensed as if to stand but stayed where he was, his pulse too quick even to try.

* * *

Down below, in the grass, it wasn't such a disaster. When her knees buckled at the boy's force, Bea felt a queer joy unspool in her. The grass was soft, the boy underneath her slick with sweat. He gawked at her in fright and she laughed — her laughter pealed up from her ribs, opened her face, made her teeth ache with fresh air. Tentatively, Jack smiled back. Then everyone was running and shouting, Emma and Helen now, too, everyone converging, and the boy wiggled himself out from under her and fled, but not before Bea grabbed one of his calves and gave it a playful squeeze. At least she meant it to be playful — she could have lain there forever, holding that beautiful, strong muscle. But he wiggled and scrambled and she let him go, running toward his ball, as the women crowded above her, chirping madly, blocking out the sun.

* * *

On the screened porch, where she was sent against her will to recuperate, Rose handed Bea

156

a copy of *The President's Daughter*, easily the trashiest book Bea had ever read. She skimmed at first, but Nan Britton told the story of her affair with President Harding in such lurid detail, even Bea could not resist it — she took a glass of lemonade from Rose and forgot about her altogether until Rose, sitting behind Bea's copy of *To the Lighthouse*, interrupted a passage Bea was reading about what went on in a very small closet in the White House by saying, 'I'm not happy, Bea-Bea.'

Bea looked up. From her perch on a large wicker chair, in nothing but her bathing suit and an unbuttoned man's shirt, Rose looked very small. It was hard to imagine her working as a physician, but that was what she did most days: put on her starched white coat, high-heeled boots, and lipstick and went to work among her male colleagues. Bea assumed it was a bold, fulfilled life, a natural extension of the young Rose who'd worn trousers belted provocatively at her waist and joined the Socialist Club at Smith. Once she had taught Bea a Negro spiritual, another time a ballad about Seneca Falls.

'What do you mean?'

'My sexual encounters are so infrequent, and cold.'

Bea put down the Britton book.

'Here,' Rose said. She poured more lemonade and Bea drank it. Rose lit a cigarette and went on, 'I used to think sexual freedom meant doing whatever you wanted, with whomever you wanted, whenever you wanted to, but now I wonder if I'd be better off married.'

'Uh-huh.' The lemonade was spiked, Bea realized. Between the rum and the crash and the heat of the day she was woozy. She would have liked to curl up in her own chair, read smut until her eyes closed, sleep all afternoon. The only person who had ever used the word 'sexual' in front of her was one doctor at Fainwright. *And your sexual intimacy, it was forced, yes?*

'I think I thought my sexual self was a man. Not homosexual, I don't mean that, I mean voracious, craving variety, impossible to pin down. I think I was wrong.'

Bea nodded. Yes. *Yes,* she nodded at Fainwright.

'I've been reading Freud,' Rose said. 'You're not so sucked into the temperance vortex that you haven't heard of Freud, right?'

This was why Bea couldn't complain about the lemonade, which was rapidly loosening her mind. 'Yes, I've heard of Freud. I've read him, actually.' In fact Freud had been read to her, by a fellow patient whose name Bea couldn't remember now, a poet who said that Freud was the future, that the Europeans knew it but Fainwright was stuck in the last century with its Swedish exercise machines and pummeling shower cages and ice wraps. Bea remembered little of the Freud passage now. She remembered mostly that the poet was a tall, handsome woman with dark, billowing eyebrows whom Bea found surprisingly beautiful, even alluring. And she remembered — the memory cut like a scythe through the dense field of all she had forgotten — one doctor saying to another, 'Don't you see

158

how centrally Ms. Haven's poor appetite functions in this case? Wouldn't it make sense that a girl who wishes to repress her memory of her first sexual encounter, an encounter against her will, would attempt to rid herself of womanly flesh?' She remembered his pride, his sweaty face, how he had swaggered out of the conference room without looking at her. She was humiliated now, remembering this.

Rose swished lemonade in her mouth, puffed out her cheeks, swallowed loudly, exhaled. 'I just think I actually want one man, one man who knows how to please me. I'm tired of pleasing myself. It's so . . . boring. After a while.'

Bea could no longer look at Rose. She knew but did not know what Rose was talking about. She took up her book again, whiffled through the pages. She found herself imagining, where Rose's feet were tucked up underneath her, men's hands there, men's mouths. She found herself thinking of the lieutenant fingering her dress off her shoulder, pulling up her skirt, pushing her against the wall.

'Bea-Bea.' Rose giggled. 'You look terrified.'

'My mother,' Bea whispered.

'Your mother is outside talking with Brigitte, pretending that she is French and that Brigitte's baby is yours. Your mother can't hear us. And neither can mine. But Albert, for instance. I mean, doesn't he . . . make you happy? Tell me he makes you happy. When you actually see each other, of course.' She scrunched her nose. 'So maybe that isn't the best example.'

Bea was stuck on Rose's nonchalant mention

159

of Vera. What was wrong with Bea that she should miss Rose's mother more than Rose did? Bea used to think everyone must have a mother they loved better than their own, but now she wasn't sure — who else took refuge in her aunt's house ten years after the aunt had died? She said, 'I'm probably a bad example in every way.'

'Still, he's there. If you wanted him.'

'Yes.'

'He's very handsome.'

'He's very handsome.'

'If I were you . . . ' Rose trailed off. 'Of course, I have no idea. It couldn't have been easy for you.' She was quiet. They heard the boys shouting as Helen and Emma ferried them toward the club. Brigitte laughed at something Lillian said. 'I just think, and what I'm trying to say, what I didn't say but what I want to say, is I'm going to do better with what I've got. No more looking back, no more regrets. Mark my word, and hold me to it, Bea-Bea, by next year I'm going to be married. I'm going to find a man and marry him and stop being so mean and lonely.' She pressed her lips together, then resettled herself on the chair, her thighs where they had pressed into the wicker hatched with stripes. 'I have to admit,' she said, shaking *To the Lighthouse*, 'I don't understand this book at all. Do you?'

Bea had finished the book last week and had not stopped thinking about it but she did not think that understanding — the way Rose meant it — was its point. She understood that Mrs. Ramsay was her mother and that she, Bea, was 'the sudden silent trout' pinned against the glass (if she read again she would see they were not pinned but 'hanging,' but that was the difference between this kind of understanding and Rose's), and Bea understood that the book as a whole was about her own life and that other people probably understood it to be about theirs. But her understanding in this way was vague — the book had stayed with her through the week like a glowing, invisible pet she could not risk touching. 'I think it's about memory,' she said. 'And about how the present is always becoming the past, both in our consciousness of it and in reality. And about the confusion, or maybe the elision, between the two, and also between reality and a person's vision of reality. Very little happens but a lot is happening. A character can stand with a foot on a threshold and her whole world shifts.' Bea had not known how good it would feel to talk about the book. The only educated women she spoke with on a regular basis — club women she courted at benefits or after her speeches — talked about Virginia Woolf like Lillian and her friends fawned over Parisian silk. 'Also, it's about women and men,' Bea concluded, starting to worry that she was making little sense. 'And whether or not the children will get to the lighthouse.'

Rose smiled. 'You're so sweet, Bea-Bea. I hope we'll be better friends, don't you?' She raised her glass and Bea raised hers, though she felt less exultant and more simply awake, and glowing, as if the glow had now entered her. She clinked before Rose even began her toast: 'To Albert's visit. To marriage. To Independence Day!'

161

16

In her father's attic, sweat soaking her dress, Susannah Story knelt beside a ceramic light-house her father had bought for her in Maine. The lighthouse was white, with a wide black stripe around the middle and a black turret on top. At night when she was a child and they weren't traveling, her father would light a candle and place it through the lighthouse's door and the thin walls would glow in a way that reminded her of skin, as if a person or animal had been emptied out and lit from within. The candle was meant to help her fall asleep, but Susannah didn't need help with that — it was her brothers in the next room who were afraid, her older brothers who remembered their mother well and called out sometimes in the night like babies. Susannah had been four when she died and remembered little of her. The lighthouse scared her more than the dark did. She would carry it into her brothers' room and in the morning they would put it back in hers. In this way Caleb didn't have to know and everyone slept.

Susannah squinted into the corners of the attic. She was looking for the box of tiny American flags, to plant around the lawn for her father's party tomorrow. Her plan was to take them out of the box and carry them down in little bunches. She was not supposed to carry anything at all, not supposed to swim or walk too fast or ride in a car. She probably wasn't supposed to climb the drop-down ladder to the attic, either, or scavenge in a sweltering attic. Even the dust motes looked lethargic, tumbling through the steamy air.

Turn a corner, bump into another rule, another shaking head, another set of hands, cold metal — this was the path to motherhood, as far as Susannah could tell. It was Susannah's path at least. But she couldn't bear to listen to the doctors anymore, to stay in bed, have tea brought to her, read a novel, nap. It made her feel like an old woman, made her feel sick. Susannah could not believe her barrenness was a sickness, or even that she was barren — she was pregnant, after all! She had several friends who had borne children — 'friends' perhaps a stretch, though she liked these women and they seemed to like her, the wives of Josiah's business cohorts, who were not exactly his friends either; his friends were back on Mason Street, where he rarely had time to go. The point was none of those women had spent their days in bed. They were educated, like Susannah, if not at college then by tutors. Their ambitions ranged, however rangily, beyond their children, a hazy, appetizing swirl of benefit dances and easels and bagging trousers. They were too busy to lie in bed. Susannah wanted to be busy, too. She was happiest busy: swimming, shopping, visiting the quarry, advising Josiah. She missed the men standing from their benches to greet her, missed the smell of dynamite and dust. Her legs bounced when she sat, twitched when she lay

163

down. Besides, she had stayed in bed last time, and what difference had it made?

She found the box of flags on top of a steamer trunk. Her sweat was monumental now, stinging her eyes, dripping from her fingers and nose, slicking the floor. She breathed deeply. It felt good. It would have felt even better if she could dive into the ocean afterward. The tide was high. Maybe she would. Maybe she would dive off the dock — or, a fair concession, jump — and be instantly cleansed, one salt replaced with another, her mood remade. Ten minutes would be enough, even five. Then she would go home, take a bath, get in bed, and wait for Josiah to come home. She would pretend to have lain in bed all day like a good patient and ask Josiah questions about the quarry without betraying her longing for it. If he asked about tomorrow's party she would tell him the long table linens were pressed and that her father had fetched the flags, the minor lie a precaution in case she miscarried again, for no matter how gentle Josiah was about her losses, she knew he — like her doctors — must blame her in some way. Then they would share a nice supper and go to sleep holding each other's hand (his left, her right) and though at some point in the night he might leave the bed for a few hours, in the morning he would be there, his rumpled face against her hair.

She knew about Josiah's affair. Of course she did. Not the details but the basic fact of it. She was not stupid. She had noticed when he took her necklace. And she did not always sleep as

164

well as she had when she was a child. Josiah assumed it of her but he was simply nostalgic for something he'd never even known, pining for the myth of her.

She loved this about Josiah: his capacity for belief, his willingness to be swept up in a good tale.

Susannah opened the box and grabbed a bunch of flags, then she dropped the flags back down and picked up the whole box. It was not that heavy. On her way to the ladder she picked up the lighthouse, too. Josiah would like it, she thought, and he would like the story that went along with it. And maybe, just maybe, there would be a child, and the child would like the lighthouse, and sleep with it, as Susannah's brothers had.

With both her hands occupied, the ladder proved a bit tricky, but the rungs were flat and Susannah welcomed the challenge, shifting her weight into her toes, winging her elbows for balance. Her skin rose into goose bumps as she reached the bottom.

'Susannah?'

Her father. He was galloping up the stairs from the first floor, his short legs like springs. He spent his days in his office, with the door closed. Susannah had not considered his emergence a possibility. He was looking at her, and past her, at the ladder, with unmistakable anger.

'I was only going to get the flags,' she said. 'I'm fine.' And she was. She was better than fine. In her mind she was swimming already. But her father would not see this. He would see only the heat in her cheeks, the sweat rolling down her skin.

'Susannah,' he growled. He took the box from her, then the lighthouse. 'You know you're not — '

'Please don't tell.'

'Tell who?'

This was meant to be a joke but sent a jolt of injury through her, that he should regard Josiah with such insouciance. Yet she allowed her father to take her hand and lead her: down the stairs, out the door. She walked toward her house, feeling his eyes on her the whole way. 'Go to bed!' he shouted as she opened her door. She flashed him an obedient smile and waved good-bye.

Inside, the air was cool, and slightly dank. It was an odd house, large in the new way but built like one of the older Colonials on Bray or Lufkin, the windows small, the clapboards thin, the floorboards wide and already creaky, built to relieve her father's embarrassment at having built such an opulent, modern house himself. There was no back door, no way to get down to the bay without her father seeing. Susannah moved slowly up the narrow stairs, the steps disingenuously sized for smaller, centuries-old feet. She paused, thinking of her father's anger, and of what he would do if he learned about Josiah's nocturnal flights. He could not possibly understand Susannah's inaction. She would not understand it if another woman told her: how such a thing could occur and you could just go on, inside and out, as if nothing had changed. It wasn't that she liked it, or that she hadn't been glad when for a week or so he seemed to have stopped. And it wasn't that she felt tepid toward Josiah. He was still the most beautiful man she had met. This morning, half asleep, he had rubbed her shoulders in bed, grunting softly about the water boys wanting raises like their counterparts had gotten at Babson's, about Sam Turpa's brother who'd lost his two fingers fishing and needed work, about the Sacco and Vanzetti mess, and she had wanted him awfully, deep in her legs, as badly as she wanted to swim. But that was the biggest no-no, the no-no even Susannah fully believed in, because really how could you have it both ways? She had given him her advice — give them the raises, find the brother a job, but stand (gently) firm against Anarchy disguised as Labor, don't let your men be seduced, offer a few little perks, a midmorning break, a once-a-month dinner, fire a ringleader or two in warning. She watched him dress. He went down to breakfast and she stayed on her stomach, wishing it were big enough already that she could not lie on it, waiting for desire to drain away.

Susannah was a rational woman. She knew, based on her observations of the world, that a man's running around was never ended by a wife's interfering, unless she outright killed him. This was part of what stopped her from accusing and berating Josiah. Also, she had her father's loyalty, which was intense and pure and had been this way for so long, sitting on her shoulders like a fur, warm but heavy, very heavy,

167

that she did not require loyalty in and of itself — she knew it was not an end. But most powerful was the fact that she blamed Josiah's behavior on herself. Back when she first spotted him outside the blacksmith shop she experienced her attraction to him simply: the man had the poise of the rugby player with none of the arrogance. Yet something more mercenary had driven her, too, however unaware of it she imagined herself at the time: in Josiah's innocence, in his willingness to be shaped and molded, she saw the potential for a kind of power, for herself. She had courted him as a man courts, promising wealth, fine clothing, a beautiful house. She had created him, in a sense, set him up to be the sort of man he now was, and he had gone along, bossing at the quarry, running for mayor, and — now — running around on her. Meanwhile she had failed to give him a family. So. How could she blame him? Susannah saw his affair as his right — she saw her ignoring it as a kind of apology.

Slowly up the narrow stairs she went, meeting each foot with the other before attempting another step, like a caricature of a heavily pregnant woman, though she looked the same as she always had. She bent at the knee more than was necessary, so as to feel and use the strength of her thighs. How she wanted to swim! But maybe this was her trouble. Maybe her mother had given up all her strength to Susannah so that Susannah had two times as much as a normal woman, which meant she could swim long distances and endure her husband's infidelity and bear her own barrenness with equanimity for so many years but not, never, any children. Maybe it was all tangled up like that, one strength another weakness, and if only she could happily lie in bed all day and weep to her husband all night and make him promise never to stray again, her pregnancy would continue, she would not bleed, and the next thing to come out of her would be a child.

She did not believe this. But there was a kind of promise in pretending to believe it, because then, maybe, something could be fixed. From her bedroom window she could see the river opening out to the bay, the tapering white lips of the beaches on either side, Crane and Coffin's, the dunes. The view was broken by the tops of pine trees, for her father ordered trees cut based on the view from his house, which stood higher on the hill. The trees thrashed in the hot breeze, interrupting the white sand, any idea of true expanse. This was sight in New England, Susannah thought, always broken, hemmed in. Her father had taken them to places where you could see endless sky or mountains wherever you went, but then he had brought her back here.

She climbed into bed and waited for her husband to come home.

17

Yes, the wind was up again. In Riverdale, as children readied their costumes and farmers chose the animals they would drag through the Horribles Parade, the inlets frothed with whitecaps. At Lanes Cove, where fish gathered by the thousands to wait out the breakers, the Murphy children caught so many so quickly for their Independence Day dinner they started handing them off to passersby. In the small living space within the Eastern Point lighthouse, the lighthouse keeper, who had been raised two hundred miles inland in Virginia, cursed the whistle buoy for making his son cry. Outside, his tomatoes were still green — tomatoes didn't ripen until August in Massachusetts. He held his son and sang loudly, to compete with the whistle buoy and every Yankee roaming Cape Ann tonight: 'Oh I wish I was in Dixie. Hooray! Hooray!' And the gulls heard him and sang along, carrying the song across the breakwater.

★　★　★

Over at the Hirsch house they grew restless as the sun went down. They were tired of backgammon, agitated by the wind and the whistle buoy, itchy for the real show to begin, but the big fireworks show was still one night off, so they gathered in the great room with the air of the condemned, desperate for any kind of entertainment. Oakes paced the perimeter of the room with a Chesterfield behind each ear, shouting about taxes and what a fine president Coolidge was but when would he abolish the income tax for *everyone?* Julian was at the piano, repeating the first measures of Chopin's Prelude Number 17, distracted by Brigitte, who sat in the largest wing chair caressing her inside-out navel almost continually through her clinging dress. On the pink love seat across from her sat Rose and Bea, trying not to stare. Helen and Emma came and went with drinks — Bea had given in to Oakes and Rose and asked Emma to stay for the evening. Ira lay supine and snoring on a nearby couch, while Adeline tried to occupy Jack, who had come downstairs complaining he could not sleep, with a game of cards.

'And the estate tax!' Oakes shouted, his eyes darting like a rabbit's. 'What a load of bull crap. None of you commies think it matters, but watch — the Feds are going to filch this house!'

'That's not how it works, Irving.' Rose rolled her eyes. But when they landed again they were trained on Brigitte's stomach, betraying an earnest, mortified longing.

'I feel like a . . . *baleine?*' Brigitte said sweetly, staring back at Rose. She rubbed her navel in circles, like a genie rubbing a snail, until she smiled and cried out, 'A whale! I feel like a whale!'

'You look lovely,' Bea said firmly. She understood almost nothing about Brigitte. All the categories by which one typically categorized

171

a person — money, education, religion — Bea had no idea how they manifested in the French. Even Brigitte's clothes were mysterious. Bea couldn't tell if the sequins were elegant or cheap, or if the uneven coloring in the fabrics was intentional. Apparently, Brigitte was a painter. She spoke some English but used it mostly to make perfectly apparent observations: *You cut your front hairs!* she'd squealed when she greeted Bea, referring to the disastrous bangs, which Bea kept forgetting — why? — to pin back or iron. To Julian, Brigitte spoke in rapid rivers of French that Bea didn't think he could possibly understand, not the subtleties, not the sort of things you would need to understand. During the war, he had worked as an assistant to Frederick Palmer in Paris, 'managing' news from the front, which entailed putting legs back on soldiers, erasing reports of missing coats and food, and miraculously losing horrific photographs. But they had translators. Maybe he loved Brigitte because she was a painter, like Vera, or because of her accent and the plush, pushy way she moved her mouth. Maybe her minimal English was itself an appeal. Maybe Julian had no need for more words when he came home from the *Post*. Ira called the *Post* job a 'velvet coffin' — he said when Palmer stepped down and Julian returned to New York, he was disillusioned from having sold out his convictions, too fatigued to become the real journalist he had intended. Bea had believed this because it was convenient — it allowed her to think of Julian as unfulfilled. But of course Ira's own journalistic ambitions had not been fully realized, so there may have been some confusion in the verdicts he reached about his son. What Bea saw was not unhappiness. Julian looked at Brigitte, grinned, and began the prelude once again.

'Lovely,' Rose agreed, but her voice was drowned out by Oakes, who called to Julian, 'Will you stop playing whatever you're playing over and over again? What about something more appropriate, more cheerful? 'Yankee Doodle, Keep It Up'?'

Julian kept his head low and did not stop. Onward he piddled for a phrase, then circled back, teasing — Bea could not help but feel teased. The sound of Julian's old lightness on the keys slid between her ribs and quivered there. Number 17 had been one of her favorites.

Oakes started walking again. 'On my way to work I pass this yard, every day, where this Eye-talian man and his wife have a garden. A little kitchen garden right out on the street, covered in soot.' He glanced at Ira, whose eyes were still closed. 'So last month I see this guy's got a project under way, he's digging up something big and I stop and watch, wanting to see, you know, and he digs and digs and finally he pulls out this bundle, about the size of a child, and I'm thinking, this guy's a murderer, an absolute madman, he's unwrapping a corpse in his yard in broad daylight! But then he gets the cloth off and it's a tree! A fucking tree.'

'Sweetheart, please,' Adeline said.

'So?' Rose said. 'What's your point?'

'My point? It's a waste of time! You should have seen how long it took him to plant this thing again, then water it. In and out of the house with a tiny bucket!'

'It's probably a lemon tree,' Rose said. 'Something that can't survive the winters here.'

'I don't care what it is! Why doesn't the guy get a job? If he loves this tree so much, why not take it back to Italy? These anarchist wops kill a man . . . '

'Two men. Read the paper, Irving. And there's little evidence that they killed him.'

'Two men! Even better. They kill them and then here we are, however many fucking years later, and people — *Americans!* — are going crazy to save them. How in hell can they be innocent?'

'It's not about innocence. It's about the fact that they've been convicted on account of their politics. It's about the powerful trying to rout out people who don't buy in to their power. It's about process . . . '

'Process!'

'Yes, Irving! Process! A fair and just trial. For the new as well as the old, the poor as well as the rich. I'm sure to you that sounds very un-American.'

Oakes groaned. He pulled a Chesterfield from his ear, lit it, exhaled. 'I don't even know half the time what the fuck you're saying, Rose. My point is why does this guy with his crappy little house spend his time taking care of a tree that's not even supposed to grow here in the first place?'

Emma and Helen, on the threshold of the

room, did not enter. Julian played more slowly, so that Number 17, meant to be allegretto, began to sound like a dirge.

'I think it's sweet,' Adeline said. 'It's like his baby.'

Bea felt sorry for her. Why had she married Oakes? Bea imagined that when they met, Oakes told Adeline first about his mother dying and second about his taking her middle name for himself and that Adeline took these facts to mean that Oakes was a particular kind of man, sensitive and loyal, perhaps like her own father but wealthy. She appeared bewildered by him now. Still, Adeline had to be terribly naive to have fallen so quickly for Oakes — that or far smarter than she appeared, out for Oakes's money, in which case she didn't need Bea's pity. There was an undeniable comfort in watching Adeline's unease — she was more an outsider than Bea.

'On to a new topic!' cried Rose. 'I'm afraid we'll have to change our plans for a bake at Brace's Cove tomorrow. I hear there's a red tide on the clam flats.'

'It's not a red tide,' Oakes said. 'Just red tide — there's red tide in the Annisquam. Or wherever. You sound like a tourist.'

'I am a tourist. So are you.'

'We're summer people.'

'And that's better.'

'Of course it's better!' Oakes pounded the mantel. 'Summer people descended of year-round people, old people, real people! Bents! Of course it's better. Have you heard what that

175

interior designer from Boston is doing over at that mansion down on the harbor? Whole rooms wallpapered in circus print. New wings just to show off the wallpaper. His friends are all artists. A bunch of faggots. And I bet they get better booze than us, too. This' — he held up a bottle — 'I have my doubts. I suspect Cousin Bea's been watering it down while we sleep, gradually tricking us into abstinence!'

Breathing wildly, Oakes stared with triumph at Bea. Julian played so slowly now that each note fell dully before the next began, absorbing and irritating her: she could not help straining, in her mind, to pull the notes into line.

'Oh, shut it, Irving,' Rose said. 'Though perhaps you could keep Emma on tomorrow, Bea-Bea. We could use the extra help.' Rose threw up her arms as Vera had, with more vigor and drama than a situation called for. She could not stop herself from saying what she said next. In her regular life she dressed herself, shopped for herself, cooked for herself, amused herself, soothed herself; then there were her patients, needing her, and the other doctors, needling her. And most of the time this was all right by Rose. She kept waking and dressing and going and coming. But when she boarded the train to Gloucester, whatever it was that kept her upright through her days seemed to snap. She wanted desperately to be taken care of. She spoke loudly: 'I don't mean to sound like a brat, but this *is* my vacation. Couldn't her children look after each other for a couple more days? We looked after each other. They'll survive.'

Bea looked to Emma. But Emma and Helen were gathering empty glasses, moving in their discreet, superior way around the room. Emma would not pardon Bea for her cousin's rudeness. 'I've given Emma the holiday with her children,' Bea said with as much equanimity as she could manage. She was struggling not to jump each time Julian began again. Brigitte's bejeweled hand circled her stomach. Bea would leave, she decided. She would leave before she cried.

But before she could leave, Jack stuffed something into his nose and began to weep. The object was quickly determined by Adeline to be one of Vera's collectibles: specifically, a finger-sized silver dolphin whose splayed tail had gone up the unfortunate boy's nostril while it's bottlenose hung down like a tusk.

It was none of Bea's business, really. So she had had a moment with Jack earlier that day. He probably didn't remember it — or if he did, the memory terrified him. She terrified him. Bea watched Adeline tug reasonably at the dolphin, wiggling it this way and that, Adeline who had grown up on a farm: among this family her knowledge of basic repair made her the equivalent of an engineer. Surely she was capable of removing a trinket from her son's nose without any assistance. Yet Bea, an auntish confidence surging through her, went and crouched down next to the mother and son. 'Is it stuck?' she asked in what she understood to be a chummy, cheery voice, but as with the squeeze of the calf, her judgment was off. Her voice was shrill. And the question itself turned out to be exactly the wrong thing to ask because upon hearing it Jack fell to the floor, where he began to thrash and yowl: 'I'm stuck! I'm stuck!'

There were moments that seemed to conspire to undo you, as if time and space knew your precise dimensions, knew how to surround, squeeze, mock, and scold you in the most effective, soul-crushing way. Bea leaped into a frenzy of action. She ran for mineral oil, and when that didn't work, tweezers, and when this didn't work, she found a magnet in a kitchen drawer. Back into the great room she ran, waving the magnet absurdly, conscious of her unfashion-ably long skirt, her hair loosening and wild, her childlessness. She dropped to the floor. The boy rolled. The magnet landed in his ear. A trail of mineral oil ran snotlike across his cheek. He shouted, 'Get away from me!'

Bea fought the urge to slap him. It had come on suddenly, bearing down like a train, scattering her intentions. She took the boy by the shoulders, tried to make him still. 'I'm trying to help you,' she said. 'You can't just go sticking things inside you!'

His eyes were his mother's: blue and plain, their odd opacity suggesting self-sufficiency. He had stopped writhing and looked at Bea not with gratitude, as she must have fantasized, or terror, as she feared, but worse, with what appeared to be forgiveness: he seemed to know, in a child's crude way of knowing, that Bea had no idea what she was doing, and that she was ashamed.

Bea was pulled back by Adeline, who growled softly in her ear, 'Let him be.' She tried not to

178

look anywhere but the rug: its mute, whorling repetition. She felt the neat dents Adeline's fingers had left in her arm, like little egg cups. Jack had quieted as soon as his mother took Bea's place. The piano was quiet, too.

Slowly, willing herself insect small, Bea made her way back to the love seat. She could recover, she told herself. Her cousins would pretend they had seen nothing of what happened, just as they had always pretended. She hated the idea of any of them pitying her. And she couldn't leave the party now, in defeat. She didn't want to leave. All that waited for her up in her room was the listless, half-finished speech she'd been writing for Josiah Story and the latest issue of the *Radcliffe Quarterly*, which Lillian had brought on her last visit. Why did the *Quarterly* still come to her parents' house? Bea threw it out every time Lillian gave it to her, but then, always, she wound up creeping up on the trash bin, fishing it out, and reading it all in one sitting, a forbidden, painful sweet, all those cheerful mothers and acceptably brave career women with their polite little boasts, their references to jokes Bea had not been in on.

She smoothed her skirt and briefly closed her eyes, thinking this might be the moment for her to give Brigitte the locket she had found upstairs on the hallway floor a few days ago. The locket was engraved *BH* and held a tiny photograph of Julian in one side, while the other, empty, presumably waited for a picture of the baby. Bea could return it to Brigitte now, a public demonstration of just how fine she was:

179

untroubled by the thing with the boy, not even jealous of Brigitte. Here she was, returning her locket! Bea opened her eyes, feeling almost calm, only to see Brigitte's hand in its slow caress, her huge, hard stomach resting in her lap. Bea had not touched her stomach when she was pregnant. It had not seemed like hers to touch. It was like a moon that had attached itself to her, unreachable even in its closeness. She tried to ignore it, but even then it changed everything, reduced her world to black and white, then and now, now and after, later, when? Toward the end, when it was as big as Brigitte's, she could see, even through her dress — she never looked at it bare — the baby's parts jumping and jabbing. Despite her determination not to, she felt the baby wriggling. Once she felt what must have been hiccups. Bea hadn't told even Vera what that felt like, those gentle astonishing taps: Hello. Hello! She went for a walk so as not to notice, but all she could do was notice; she was shrunk to sensation, as if her eyes, her ears, her breath itself, had been replaced by a baby's hiccups. Now she watched Brigitte's stomach for signs of movement. The glow that had followed Bea, then entered her, had grown painfully bright. She felt herself drifting toward its other face: not what was still possible but all she had lost.

Jack was crying again. He had his mother by the hands, blocking her efforts to free the dolphin. Adeline sang to him calmly but her dress was dark at the armpits, her face purple with strain. Oakes said something about baseball. Julian started to play again, 'Frère

180

Jacques' now, for the child. 'Ow!' shouted Jack. Adeline, straddling him, had managed to pin his hands down with her knees and was doubled over, her face next to his. Her plan was unclear. Would she yank the dolphin out with her teeth?

Her mouth opened. But instead of grabbing the dolphin she closed the boy's jaw, planted her mouth over his open nostril, and blew. Out came the dolphin in her other hand.

Brigitte gasped, and clapped. *'Le bébé!'* The boy began to sob. Adeline held him, and Oakes finally shut up. Julian returned to the prelude, broke through the beginning, moved on to where the melody opened up, the high G-sharps piercing and delicate at once, his eyes locked on Brigitte, who stood and moved toward him. Bea could not help but watch: Brigitte's stomach rising, her weighty swagger as she made her way across the room. Trapped on the love seat next to Rose, Bea waited for their good-night kiss. Instead, Brigitte fell into Julian's lap, pressed her back into his chest, lifted her face, closed her eyes, and cried (a girlish, private cry they all heard): *'Un bébé!'* And Julian, instead of looking embarrassed or tumbling off the bench at the bulk of her, did the most shocking thing. He reached around Brigitte, stroked her snail, and said back to her, with great tenderness, *'Un bébé.'*

Rose leaned close to Bea's ear. 'She does look like a whale, don't you think?'

Bea looked to Ira, a pit rising in her throat. She knew he must be awake now — the shouting, Bea's need, would have roused him.

But he lay still, eyes closed. He wouldn't rescue her from the despair that swelled inside her at the sight of that stomach, those hands, the odd pietà Adeline and Jack made on the floor, Rose's whispered insult echoing Bea's own smothered rage. She remembered huddling with Julian in the attic when they were still children, and inseparable, always hiding together — 'little phantoms,' the adults called them — and how she wished then that he was her brother, so she could have him near her all the time, how his smell, and his warm skin, seemed more familiar even than her own. Now his slender hands cupped Brigitte's vast stomach and Bea considered her options (attempting detachment, considering herself consider), to scream or to leave, and settled on a groan, hoping it would come out more quietly than it did.

Everyone stared. Bea didn't look up but she could feel them staring — she heard their thoughts traveling the room like arrows. *Poor cousin Bea. What's wrong now?*

The abrupt silence was punctured by the whistle buoy's wail.

'Play a song, Bea?' Julian's voice was kind — clearly he meant to help her — and Brigitte started playing a staccato 'Yankee Doodle,' as if to help her further. But they had made everything worse. Bea could not play.

'Come,' Brigitte said. 'A song of the freedom!'

'Independence,' Rose corrected. 'Oft confused, but not the same.'

'The freedom of the dolphin!' Oakes cried. 'It's brilliant!'

182

'Go on, Bea.' Ira spoke gently. Even Ira was in on it now, though he knew the piano for Bea was like alcohol for others, her desire for it verging on lust, disease. She had kept herself from it for so long that she couldn't imagine touching a key now without losing control.

She couldn't play. And she couldn't sit here with her fear flayed, her heart shrinking, as everyone shouted at her. So she stood. And with a jovial, almost peppy wave — hammering this, hammering that, mashing back tears, seeing double — she walked out. 'Good night, everyone, I've work to do, well done, Adeline, hurrah! Goodnightgoodnightgoodnight!'

★ ★ ★

Brigitte's bony rump cut off circulation to Julian's leg. Her playing was awful, and very loud. She had no shame! He was crazy for her. He loved that she sat there with her stomach knocking against the piano, banging out patriotic songs she barely understood. He worried a bit, too, at how little she had changed. Even her body, apart from her stomach, was exactly the same, long and lean, like a deer's. You could look at a girl like Adeline and see that she made a natural, good mother. But Brigitte might be more like Vera, always pulled to do something else, an unstoppable wind. Julian feared she might have the baby and forget about it, go off to paint or brew tea or knead clay or dance by herself in front of the mirror the way she liked to do, and just forget.

183

Then again, he could nuzzle into Brigitte — he nuzzled — and smell her perfume and sweat and want desperately to kiss the string of muscles that stood between her neck and shoulder. So. They could afford a nurse. So they would work it out.

But her playing really was so bad. She knew it was bad, Julian was almost certain, but it was impossible not to wonder. And it was impossible, wondering this, not to think of Cousin Bea's playing. She had been as gorgeous a pianist as Brigitte was a woman. Julian had tried to let her exit tonight roll off him, tried to focus on Brigitte, but Bea had a way of haunting him when they were in the same house, and Brigitte's neck was reminding him of Bea's arms, the way they'd been before the baby, that era so starkly ripped from this one that Julian could almost smell it, summer, boxwoods, saltwater-soaked towels. Before the baby, there had been a length of flesh at Bea's upper arms, just at the edge of her underarms, secret but not quite, and as she played Julian would watch this flesh, taut and shivering with her movement, and he would imagine, if she were to stop playing and lift her arms a bit more, the scent. This was his first fantasy of a sexual sort, which embarrassed him, because he assumed that other men did not desire women's armpits. Then he had asked her to marry him and left for school and come back to find her stuffed into the costume of a girl-woman expecting a child, all of her puffed, her skin marked with tiny pocks, those arms bloated, undone, and she seemed either to have no awareness of this or not to care, or Vera had been dressing her, because she wore a sleeveless dress with wide straps that only accentuated the tragic heft of her new arms. And now, ten years later, though she was skinny as a stick, her arms still bore the imprint of that time — they hung, the skin slack, so opposite Brigitte's tight belly when she undressed at night, the smooth, hard earth she offered up to his hands so that he could feel, if the timing was right, the jostling of their baby. Brigitte said she knew which were kicks and which punches but to Julian they were all the same — they were the baby, saying hello, hello. He was elated and terrified, watching Brigitte's stomach jump.

In Paris, before he'd met Brigitte, the pregnant Bea filled his mind. The most upsetting thing, somehow, was that within all her foreign, wobbling flesh, her face had looked younger than it had in years. She looked about twelve, he thought, the age she had been when he first noticed that she was a girl. Maybe seeing her next to Vera, who had aged so rapidly that summer, accentuated this effect — still, Bea seemed to have lost something, not only in years but in strength. She walked into his dreams as a six-year-old crying for some small treat she'd been denied, crying about how it wasn't fair, pleading with Julian to make her case to the grown-ups, but Julian, unable to discern whether the treat had been kept from her because she'd done something bad or because his aunt Lillian was in one of her moods, unable to tell how he might be punished if he helped her, did nothing.

Vera had told Julian that Bea had been forced, but Julian couldn't bear to listen to his mother talk about Bea in such intimate terms and besides, he couldn't quite believe her. Bea had always been so stubborn he couldn't imagine anyone making her do anything — and more than that, he could easily imagine Bea wanting to do what she had done. He had felt her turn his sloppy kisses into a worldly sharing of tongues, felt her teeth find his lower lip. Her wanting had been building for years.

Oakes said it was all bullshit, that if a girl couldn't keep her legs closed she was asking for it, but Julian didn't think he believed this either.

All he knew was that he missed her and blamed her.

In Paris, Ira wrote to him. *I hope you're fine, I figure you should want to know . . .* The words 'should want' brought tears to Julian's eyes — he felt his father in front of him looking straight into his heart, his missing, his general feelings of lack, the number of times he used the phrase on himself, *should want a different girl, should want to drink more heavily, should want what you have.* He should want to know, wrote Ira, that his cousin had had a 'break' of some kind. *I am told of no official diagnosis, you know Henry and his secrets though really it's Lillian who drives the hush-hush train, claims she wants to create less drama when of course she wants more, but I gather it was of the nervous or hysterical variety.* Ira didn't know or wouldn't share many details. He wrote that Bea was *resting now at a very upright kind of place, I do*

186

believe they call it a 'hospital' these days, there are pianos in every parlor, I went to visit, passed on your regards, hope you'll forgive me, but Bea-Bea refuses to play.

What was it Ira wanted Julian to forgive? That he spoke to Bea on Julian's behalf? That Bea wasn't playing piano? Or that Ira told him about this not playing? It was a bewildering thing to learn — harder to imagine, in some ways, than an asylum.

In his mind, in Paris, Bea continued to play. She had lost the weight. She looked her age again, tired but lovely in her uncommon, dark way, her face tilted over the keys as she worked out some problem. Julian felt as if he were the one who had discovered Bea's loveliness — he hoped and also worried that no one else would ever see it. He wondered if in her eyes now there was some sign of her breakdown. He looked out across a French café and one or two of the women looked back and he asked himself: if they were crazy, would he know?

Even more troubling was another question, grown out of silence, what Ira did not say: that Bea's baby had been born. Julian left in June, when Bea's walk turned heavy — she had to have been nearly as far along as Brigitte was now — but he heard nothing from home until September, when Ira wrote to tell him that Vera had died. Don't even think of coming back, you won't make the service and besides she wouldn't have wanted you to abandon your work. There was nothing about Bea, though she had to have had the baby by then. Julian forgave the

187

omission. He assumed his father wasn't thinking clearly. He himself was bushwhacking through the news of his mother's death: one day he didn't believe it; the next he forgot; the next he left his colleagues at their midday coffees and wandered the streets, indulging his isolation among the foreign faces until, finally, he cried. But then he got the second letter, about the asylum, and the silence about the baby became more pronounced, a black scrim he parted only to find more blackness. He dwelled there, trying to grow an explanation. He knew the silence was meant to mean that everything went as planned, birth, orphanage, etc., but he couldn't help feeling it meant just the opposite, for those items alone, he thought, would not have thrown Bea so profoundly off course. She was too stubborn, her ambition huge. (And outsized, if Julian was honest, for she was excellent but not a prodigy, not Amy Beach.) 'I'll get to Symphony Hall or die trying,' she liked to say with a studied drollness that was easy to see through.

But he had been in the business of checking facts (along with dismantling them, when necessary); he knew that a feeling was not a fact. In his letter to Ira, he wrote, *Everything went smoothly with Bea's condition, I assume?* knowing as he sent it off how vague and cowardly his words were. Months passed before Ira wrote again and he made no mention of Julian's question — Bea, he said, was at home again, better, apparently, though Lillian had not yet allowed him to visit.

Julian rooted at Brigitte's nape. She was

188

playing 'Grand Old Flag' now, leading the group in her scratchy soprano, 'The emblem of / The land I love!' She was so proud of having learned these words. Julian reminded himself that when he was back in New York, living his life, working at his uninspiring but entirely respectable work, scaling each day's minor pinnacles and faults, he rarely thought of Bea. In a couple days he and Brigitte would go back and set up the nursery and all this, Oakes and Rose, even Ira — though part of Julian wanted to take his father with him, his thinning calves where the hair had fallen out or rubbed away, his fingernails, their half-moons the pale pink of a baby girl's bonnet — would fade. Brigitte jiggled on his lap, mashed his femur, demanded he pay attention. Still, he could not shake the panic in Bea's eyes when he'd asked her to play. Tomorrow, he decided, he would take her aside in a quiet moment and tell her he was sorry, say it simply, *I'm sorry about the piano*, just that, not making her explain. *I'm sorry*, and walk away. Let her be. Stay away from the silent gap.

Julian breathed in Brigitte's flowery mushroom scent. He rubbed the painting callus on her thumb. He got so lost in her that when he heard a cry, it seemed at first to be coming from inside his wife. He raised his head, then his hand. 'Shh.'

Brigitte slowed but didn't stop her fingers.

Again, a cry, distant but distinct, clearly coming from upstairs. Bea.

'*Arrête!*' he barked.

Brigitte stopped. '*Merde*, Julian. What?'

189

'Didn't anyone else hear that?'

Oakes and Adeline and Rose, standing at the piano now, shook their heads. On the sofa, Ira looked to be asleep. '*Quoi? Where?*' asked Brigitte, and, when Julian didn't respond — having realized, not wanting to say — she lifted her hands, preparing to recommence. '*Allons-y!*' she cried. '*Voilà! L'independence!*'

★ ★ ★

Coming upon Mrs. Cohn rocking on her bed, Emma turned away out of shock and shame, only to look back with sudden recognition. Of course.

Mrs. Cohn sat cross-legged, a noise swelling from her as she rocked, her hands frantically working at something in her lap. The noise was part whine, part moan, part growl, part air hissing through her teeth. Her ears were stuffed with cotton. Next to her some kind of pamphlet appeared to have been beaten. Emma stood in the doorway for a moment, thinking she might leave unnoticed and return downstairs to Mr. Julian, who — obviously troubled — had sent her up with vague instructions: *See if Mrs. Cohn needs anything?* But Emma could not do that, not even to Mrs. Cohn. And she had been spotted. 'Emma!' cried Mrs. Cohn, pulling the cotton from her ears. She appeared like a tantrumming child, her eyes pink and streaming behind her knotted hair, her upper lip shining with snot. She threw the object in her lap in Emma's direction, then balled her hands into fists and beat her knees.

'Mrs. Cohn.' Emma's voice quavered. She swallowed, and began again. 'Calm down. Take a breath. It can't be so bad.'

Mrs. Cohn began a new round of moaning.

'You're panicking,' Emma said, and lowered herself to look in Mrs. Cohn's eyes. Nerves, she'd said. But nerves were not what Emma saw, nor madness. In Mrs. Cohn's tears she saw only misery. This was a relief. It even brought Emma a queer sense of satisfaction. She wasn't without pity. That was not the case. But her pity gave her a new sense of power. She held Mrs. Cohn's gaze, waiting until she saw something give, panic settling into despair. Then she bent to pick up what Mrs. Cohn had thrown: a tiny locket on a gold chain. *BH*. Beatrice Haven. Mrs. Cohn's maiden name. Emma unfastened the locket. Inside was a photograph of Mr. Julian. But it wasn't a youthful version of him, as she expected. It was Mr. Julian now. *BH* was for Brigitte Hirsch, she understood. She closed it.

'You're making a fool of yourself,' she said. 'You've got to forget him.'

Mrs. Cohn leaped. She was faster than Emma would have thought, catlike in her acceleration, powerful as she yanked the necklace from Emma's hands. She snapped the locket in two, and fell again onto the bed. 'You don't know anything,' she said, starting to rock again. 'You have no idea.'

Emma laughed before she could stop herself.

'Don't laugh!' Mrs. Cohn dropped her head and held it, her palms pressed against her ears,

191

her knees folded around her hands. She was like a cartoon, Emma thought, of a spoiled woman who had been a spoiled child.

'I know a lot,' Emma said. She was done, she decided. She was exhausted. She missed her children. In the last few days she had played with another family's children more than she had ever played with her own. She would leave now, tell the older Mr. Hirsch, let him figure out what to do. And Mr. Cohn, who was supposed to come up tomorrow for the holiday — if he was still here when Emma came back on the fifth. But no one else. They were singing downstairs now — Emma could hear them as she left the room, their dissonant, off-key chorus soaring into the upstairs hallway. Who sang that loudly when they clearly could not sing? Disgust rolled through her. 'That buoy's not going to bite you,' she said gruffly. 'Try to sleep.' She shut the door.

Emma could not know how much she sounded like Nurse Lugton, how the impatient rigor of her voice, and the unmistakable tenderness that rode its flank, would pitch Bea into another round of weeping. Other patients complained about Fainwright but to Bea it had been a great reprieve, for a time, not to strive. She liked her class in basket weaving, her hands in thoughtless motion. She liked watching the cows stand around at the hospital's little farm, their doomful eyes, liked the sweet smell in the greenhouse. The plants seemed to her exotic (though they were not), for she had never lived with plants. She wept now for the plants, and for Nurse Lugton. She wept as the whistle buoy careened through her earholes, as its screeching, predatory arrows burrowed in her brain. *Stop the whistle buoy*, she would cry, if Nurse Lugton were here. *Stop the whistle buoy*, though the whistle buoy was not a quarter of her suffering. It was Julian she cried for. It was Bea herself, Bea as she had been. But she could not speak of that, so she would cry whistle buoy, just as she had sobbed at Fainwright about the lieutenant — his rough hands, his pushing her against the wall, his forcing her — when really it was the baby she grieved.

'Every heart beats true, to the red, white, and blue!'

She lay down. She sat up. *Tut-tut!* Nurse Lugton commanded, her gruff alto a rope. She tried to hang on. She wadded the cotton balls again and stuffed them into her ears. She wiggled her toes, checking — they had not seized — and forced herself to walk to her desk, to pick up her pen. But the speech was so dull, and the *Quarterly* on the bed so bright, its crimson cover and raised seal beckoning. Until recently, the *Quarterly* had been printed in a flat, dull gray. At least there had been that.

Katherine Graver is getting on famously at Physicians and Surgeons. And speaking of doctors, Dina Papineau begins her internship in a Midwestern hospital shortly. What a lot they must know!

Hannah Bugbee reports that she has never been so busy or so happy in her life! College not excepted? She is to be the Song

Director at Aloha Camps next summer.

Our class is now the proud possessor of thirty-one infants and children, according to the secretary's records.

Dorothy Sprague is at the Hampton Institute again. I will quote from her own words: 'I am thoroughly absorbed in my work here of teaching to eager, interesting, appreciative human Negro boys and girls. I feel glad to be making a concrete difference rather than the quite lofty speeches I used to deliver on campus. I am not engaged. I am particularly happy that Radcliffe has proved open on the race question!'

Roberta Salter I have seen at the New York Radcliffe lunch very gay and enthusiastic. Her activities include choral singing and a course at the Metropolitan Museum. She enjoys entertaining and welcomes visitors — let Ro-Ro know if you are in New York!

What could Bea possibly add? She did not recognize a single name. Her blood rattled in her ears. She pulled out the cotton. The noise of the whistle buoy exploded in her chest: *What about youuuuu?* She had not graduated from Radcliffe. She had barely lasted ten weeks, and half her time there she spent fiddling with the wicked brace Lillian had had made for her. *Shrinks the stomach, strengthens the back, reforms a girlish posture!* the advertisements promised. The brace's top edge dug into her ribs, its bottom into her hip bones or, if she was sitting, into the

194

tops of her thighs. During her lessons at the conservatory, she shifted and sagged, her fingers cold, her stomach empty. A tiredness overtook her. She floated outside herself, the floating part watching the playing part falling asleep as it played. The music reeked of competence. Master B. smiled painfully. His disappointment was clear. She wasn't to be his star pupil after all; she would not make him famous. His certainty was like a blade through Bea's ribs. She had not been taught to bear up against people's judgments. She had been taught to take them seriously because until the trouble with the baby, she had only been judged well. She turned Master B.'s hostility on herself. Her supposed talent at the piano was a lie, her true mediocrity another secret she would have to keep. (She refused to perform.) The brace made her body a lie. Not a single person, not even Uncle Ira, knew the full truth. When she considered confessing to her roommate, an Eliza Dropstone from Needham, a kind, horsey, not-very-serious student who told Bea her secrets in a loud, conspiratorial whisper (she liked a boy, she couldn't understand a word Professor M. said, she had kissed her dog before she'd left home, but really kissed it, like a boy), Bea's throat began to close.

In her isolation, Bea felt absurd. She could say nothing without feeling she was lying. Her very being, the air she moved through, seemed to drip with falseness. Except when asked a direct question, she stopped talking. She did not join the clubs that met in the Yard. She did not join them because she did not talk and because the

195

brace made it impossible to sit on the ground and because she was too hungry to listen anyway. Hungry yet fat. She had assigned herself a diet of fruit and cottage cheese but each night, when she removed the brace before bed — a finicky and covert operation undertaken beneath her robe, facing the wall, so that her roommate wouldn't see — her stomach hung down her front like a third, misshapen breast.

A Harvard boy took an interest in her. Benjamin Levine. He learned Bea's schedule and began showing up outside the Garden Street gate after her last class on Wednesday afternoons. 'How do you do, Miss Haven.' Lifting his hat with a three-fingered squeeze, walking jauntily toward the square as if she'd agreed to follow. Bea found Benjamin Levine attractive. He had dark curls, olive skin, a mole on his right cheekbone. But she could see so little reason for him to like her — she barely spoke, she couldn't play piano, if he were to touch her waist he would find a knuckle-hard casement there, pushing him back — that she started to suspect he must be unlikable himself. She looked for points of ugliness and found them, in his somewhat comical high-step walk, his hairy knuckles, his narrow shoulders, his too-long trousers. Faults followed. He didn't like athletics. He'd never heard of Haven Shoes.

She stopped answering Benjamin Levine's questions. Then she stopped walking with him. She avoided the Garden Street gate and walked another way to her dormitory, until Benjamin found her one day on Appian Way and took her by the wrists. 'Is it that I'm poor?' he spat. 'Or do you not like your own kind of people?' By this he meant Jews, she knew, and she giggled out of embarrassment. Benjamin's face was warped with anger, and something more primal — was that desire? Students crossed the street to avoid them, whispering. Bea tried to pull away but Benjamin's grip was firm and she had to get into it then, bending her knees, pulling harder, finally flapping her elbows and twisting herself free with a grunt that surprised her. She breathed heavily. Benjamin stood back, hands raised, a gloss of fear in his eyes. Bea felt a stab of sorrow. But she was distracted by the sweat that had sprung under her arms. She was heated through as if she'd been running, which she hadn't done in so long, and this produced in her such a rush of rightness, a feeling that she had at last reentered her eighteen-year-old body, that her act of defiance (small as it was), her fighting off Benjamin (unthreatening as he was), overtook her regrets and was transformed into a point of triumph in her sea of failures, a declaration that solidified in the days that followed: Beatrice Haven was not susceptible to men.

That was a relief. A kind of stiffness settled over her. All the times Lillian had told Bea to 'make something' of herself, as if she were unformed clay, and now it seemed one part of her at least was formed, decided, drying.

Her loneliness was great. In the dining hall, she ate even less. Her hips and breasts shrank, the skin shrivelly. She told Lillian nothing and Lillian had not visited. All her smushing and crowding seemed transparent now, a show. She had merely been waiting for Bea to go do and learn all that she herself had been denied, but she didn't want to see it — she couldn't bear it. They spoke once a week, Bea in the phone closet on her dormitory's second-floor landing, answering Lillian's questions *(And do you like Master B.? Is he as good as they say? And is the food too rich? Are you managing to lose the weight?)* in polite, short sentences.

In the evenings, which came earlier, the college following the city into dusk, a silent sobbing overtook her. She would sleep then, in the hours after supper, and often well into the night. But when she woke, it was into a profound disorientation. The bed was turned the wrong way, the pillow too soft, its smell changed — and where was the bassinet? Trees through the window, branches bare, shock in her gut, summer turned. She must have left it somewhere! She must have forgotten. She could hear it struggling, tensing as if to cry, but when she reached for the light the light had been moved.

Finally, Bea would stop flailing. She would sit up, and listen. The sounds were only Eliza, snoring. Always Eliza. Bea told herself to breathe. But just as she had been unable to stop listening to the baby make its strange, incessant noises in the middle of the night, now she couldn't stop listening to Eliza's snores and thinking of the baby, and in her desperation not to think of the baby, Bea would think of Vera. It was Vera's fault that Bea had nursed the baby, roomed with the baby, absorbed the baby's sounds into her memory. If not for Vera, Bea would have been sent to the House for Unwed Mothers up in New Hampshire, where they would have whisked the thing away as soon as it was born. Oh, but she missed Vera! Her delayed grief for Vera was so overwhelming (Vera was the one Bea needed now, the one Bea could tell anything to and know she would still be loved) and her fear of grieving the baby so sharp (she hadn't *wanted* the baby, so why should she feel so bereft?) that she found herself locked in a kind of war, her need to cry and her fear of crying so powerfully opposed that she gagged. She covered her ears, trying to block out Eliza's breathing, until, gripped by a need to hear what she didn't want to hear in order to know that she wasn't hearing it, she would uncover her ears and Eliza's tender wheezes would once again erupt, pulling Bea back to the baby and Vera. On it went like this, Bea covering and uncovering, sucking great breaths through her nose to block out the sound, then holding her breath to hear it, holding her breath until she heard the thudding of her own blood, echoing the lieutenant's finish, *unh unh unh*.

One night she went to sleep in her brace, hoping it might hold her together, fend off the shell as it did through her days. Instead her lungs restricted, the panic arrived more quickly, evolved newly, climbed into her throat. If Eliza hadn't shaken her, Bea might not have recognized her own voice crying out — she might have gone on shrieking. But Eliza shook her, then switched on the light above Bea's bed.

Her face was pillow creased, childish. 'It's just a dream,' she said softly. 'You've had a bad dream.'

It was never a dream. But she couldn't tell that to Eliza, just as she couldn't tell it to Nurse Lugton, who came quickly with the Luminal. The crying at Radcliffe had not lasted long: the third time, Eliza brought her to the infirmary and that was the beginning of the end of Bea's time at college.

The whistle buoy cut into her remorse, its talons ringing through her body. Again she took up the cotton balls but could not stuff them in, for the party, too, rose into her room, beckoning and taunting: ' . . . the land I love . . . the home of the free and the brave!'

Bea wanted desperately at that moment to be someone who could sing badly. But she had become a temperance lady. The songs could be sung only on key. She longed for Nurse Lugton's hands on her shoulders — or her roommate's hands, Eliza's strong, horsey hands — these hands or those hands, shaking her from what they assumed were dreams. How Bea wanted to be held now. She rocked with this wanting, crying for Eliza Dropstone, who had sent to Fainwright a kind, apologetic letter to which Bea did not reply, and for Nurse Lugton with her *tut-tut* and her Luminal, and for Emma, who had left her, and for Julian, who had moved on, and for all the women in the *Quarterly*, for their hypothetical friendship, yes, but more so for their lives, for all the lives that might have been hers.

18

On the same coast, 1,033 miles to the south, in a leather chair in a corner office overlooking the Charleston Naval Shipyard, Admiral William Seagrave stared into a middle distance. His secretary's typing soothed him. A mug of lukewarm coffee stood on his large, flat palm. Through his window was the nearly lifeless yard, a few ships in dry dock. But Seagrave kept his attention on the dust motes that swam through a near patch of sunlight. He focused on the moisture that had gathered between the concave underside of the mug and his hand. It was a balancing act — not a difficult one, but nonetheless, a small challenge to occupy the middle-to-late part of his morning.

Admiral Seagrave wasn't without things to do. At any moment he could set down his coffee, review the morning's wires, find an underling in need of direction. He could ring Admiral M. and meet for an early luncheon at the club. But he had no desire to see Admiral M. — the talk would either be depressing, of the yard's possible closure, or pointless, of the men's respective wives and children. M. was married to a fat, homely woman he adored and Seagrave to a tall redhead everyone else adored. His children were six and four, two boys conceived on an impeccably respectful, optimistic schedule after the war. Seagrave loved his children, but looking at their photographs on his desk did not lighten his mood.

A telephone rang, the typewriter stopped abruptly, his coffee sloshed in its mug. He heard his secretary murmuring on the other side of the open door, then she knocked and poked her head through.

'I said you were busy, sir, but she insists. A Mrs. Henry Haven, sir? She says it's urgent. Annapolis put her through, so perhaps she's someone?'

Seagrave worked to place the name. He thought of his mother's friends, her inner circle first, then the next one out, and so on and so forth. Then his sister's set, up in Delaware. His mind raked the surface of his life. *I am nobody. Who are you?* It came to him. Boots. Haven Boots. 1916. A townhouse on Chestnut Street, Brahman to the bone, except they were Jews. Henry and Someone, he couldn't remember the wife's first name, and a daughter, who wasn't beautiful at first but became so as you looked at her, like a plain sunset unfurling. He saw her hips now: broad and beckoning. Her full mouth, her dark eyes. Bea-Bea, for Beatrice. But he couldn't picture the mother at all.

'Put her through,' he said. Then, 'Hello?'

'Hellooow?'

'Hello?'

'Lieutenant Seagrave! Excuse me. Admiral. I hear you made quite a hero of yourself in the war. This is Lillian Haven. I trust you'll remember.'

Lillian. He did remember her now, an

exuberant and severe woman with a strange, shifting accent that hadn't changed. She was beautiful, too, but in a more common way than her daughter: pale skin, black hair, lips as red as a stepmother in a fairy tale.

'I remember,' he said.

'Good for you to have made yourself a success.'

'Thank you.'

'It doesn't happen for everyone. As I'm sure you're aware.'

Admiral Seagrave wasn't a dull or deaf man. He was sensitive, perhaps to a fault. He waited, thinking of Charlie Sayles, down in the storage compartment, as the USS *Crain* listed drastically to port. Under Seagrave's command, the *Crain* had sunk more U-boats than any ship in the Atlantic, clearing the way for American supplies to reach France. He had done it nearly error free, the 'nearly' by now forgotten. He had been made admiral at thirty-six.

'I didn't call to flatter you, of course.'

'I wouldn't expect it. How can I help you, Mrs. Haven?'

'I'm so glad you asked. My daughter, Lieutenant — Admiral — I presume you remember her, too? Bea-Bea? Well, now she's called Beatrice, Beatrice Cohn. Married, you see. Happily married. Yet she suffers from a nervous condition, I'm afraid, and it's been made worse by one of those buoys, what do they call them, the ones that scream like banshees?'

'Whistle buoys?'

'That's right. A whistle buoy. This one is fairly

new, off Gloucester, Massachusetts. Eastern Point, to be precise. I heard it myself. I promise you, it's dreadful.'

'I see. I'm very sorry to hear about your troubles. But I'm afraid I don't see how I can be of assistance, Mrs. Haven.'

'Lillian.'

'Inshore navigational devices aren't my command. The Coast Guard . . .'

'But surely the Coast Guard and the navy have some kind of relationship? Surely a man in such a position as your own has some kind of . . . pull?'

All it took was that bit of coyness to remind him: she is the one who throws herself at him, almost as soon as he and the admiral arrive. She has heard, no doubt, about wunderkind Seagrave, the one who pulls the strings behind the admiral's back. Everywhere he and the admiral go, the wives of men who want things flutter their eyelashes at him. Mrs. Haven can't know that he's already settled on Haven Boots for the contract, that there is nothing comparable in quality and price for hundreds of miles up or down the eastern seaboard. Her husband was smart to call himself Haven — if he were Havenstein it wouldn't fly. But Haven it is, the decision is made, he and the admiral have come only to seal the deal. Even so, Lillian gets him by the bar and talks nonstop about *value*, also *valor* and *vim* and *virtue* — clearly she has stood in front of a mirror and watched herself utter the letter *V*. At one point, he is almost certain, she uses the word 'virile' to describe the patented brass eyelets Haven uses in all its boots. She keeps her Negro maid refilling his glass, then, when she must gauge him sufficiently soused, she steers him toward the girl, who stands by a window in an odd, arresting manner: legs apart, hips even, arms at her sides — almost like a soldier. She stares unflinchingly at him, seeming to know either everything or nothing at all. When he suggests they go for a walk, she smiles, a sudden, wet opening that takes his breath away.

Thinking of it now, Seagrave felt an ache in his groin. He sat straighter, took a long sip of coffee, and sloshed it around in his mouth, trying to wake up. 'Mine is not a pull I'm eager to abuse, Mrs. Haven.'

'Lillian. Please. But you see it wouldn't be abuse, Admiral. It would be a very average act of self-protection.'

He swallowed the sweet, cool coffee. 'I see.'

'Do you?'

He thought of the girl's new breasts, her purple nipples standing — all he'd had to do was blow in her ear.

'Let's make certain, shall we? The evening you visited us, admiral, back when you were merely a lieutenant, as I presume you'll recall, you and Bea-Bea went for a stroll, as you'll also recall? A breath of fresh air?'

'That was ten years ago, Mrs. Haven.' Was she trying to blackmail him? He'd done nothing extraordinary. He hadn't been married. It wouldn't work.

'Nine and a quarter, Admiral Seagrave. I know with such exactness because, you see, the advantage you took with my daughter, you see, there was . . . a consequence. Or shall I say, in your speak, a casualty of sorts. Do you understand me now? Do I need to translate?'

All this time, he'd been holding his coffee in one hand, his receiver in the other. Now he put the mug down. He looked at his empty hand. *What hands!* his mother had said, from the time he was twelve. *I've never seen such hands.* Her voice filled with awe and fear. His father, whose own average-sized hands sat in his lap, looking away with feigned disinterest. The word 'casualty' wormed through Seagrave's chest. No one but he had made the choice, once the U-boat blew a hole in the *Crain*'s hull, to section off the damaged part of the ship and with it Chief Engineer Sayles and Chief Jones. The sailors only reported the situation: the torpedo had hit the stern; the port storage compartments, where Sayles and Jones had gone to inspect a leaking pipe, were filling with water. Did the captain want them to attempt a rescue or shut the hatch? But it wasn't a choice. Not really. There wasn't time to go for Charlie. When the *Crain* limped into Cork Harbor, Seagrave was lauded for battening down just in time. The fact that Charlie was his closest friend was further proof of Seagrave's bravery — he had put the good of the ship over a life he held dear. It had been the most celebrated, worst mistake of his life.

Or so he'd thought. But a child? An older sibling to his sons, a child he'd never seen? His family would come unraveled. His wife . . . It was the sort of thing people lied about, of

206

course. And Mrs. Henry Haven was just the type. She was lying. She had to be.

'Admiral Seagrave. You haven't hung up on me?'

'No.'

'You'll understand me when I say that this whistle buoy is not a matter to be taken lightly. You'll have it removed.'

His gaze lifted involuntarily to the docks, where two men were coiling a rope. All else was still, the bone-dry ships waiting for repairs that might never come, the eastern coast beyond the harbor peacefully eroding.

'Think of your family, Admiral Seagrave.'

The line clicked, then there was silence, hot in his ear. His secretary poked her nose hopefully into his office. 'Sir? Admiral M. telephoned. He says the men are waiting for you down at the club.'

She was hungry, restless for her break. But Seagrave could not shake Mrs. Haven's voice. Even if she was lying — and he felt certain she was — that didn't mean she wasn't dangerous.

'Sir?'

'Yes. Fine. Tell them I'll be right down.'

And he went, just as Lillian sat down to her own lunch, shaking with triumph. She could have been a lawyer. She could have run a business, made history! *Good*, she thought, *good*. She pressed her napkin across her lap as if sitting down to high tea. She shook salt onto her herring, released by her proud moment from her usual shame. Only once a month, the day before she bled, did Lillian allow herself herring, *seledka*, her mother's old food. She needed it then, needed it as a person with a broken bone needed a splint. Her cycles were changing — sometimes now they didn't come at all — but Estelle could tell, Estelle tracked Lillian as if Lillian were a gathering storm. When her bleeding was through for good, Lillian thought, Estelle would continue with the herring without making Lillian ask for it. She would make a schedule and once a month she would set out Lillian's secret lunch — her herring, her crackers, her finger of whiskey — and leave her to it. Lillian liked being alone with her herring. She did not want Estelle to see just how much salt she poured on it, or how one had to lap with one's tongue to capture the herring and cracker in one bite.

But today, Estelle erred. She poked her head into the kitchen (Lillian did not eat in the dining room when she ate her herring) and asked, 'You need anything else, Mrs. Lillian? You all right?' She had heard Lillian's telephone call. She had seen her shaking. Estelle recalled the lieutenant as nothing but a gentleman, but gentlemen could fool you, she had to give Mrs. Lillian that, and besides, Estelle loved Bea as if she were kin. She worked for Mrs. Lillian in Mrs. Lillian's house but half the time she was thinking of the girl. So she rooted for her, and therefore for Mrs. Lillian, that the man would turn the thing off.

'Fine,' Lillian said. 'Go take your walk.' But her shaking grew worse. Estelle's interruption, her question, *You all right?* flipped her upside down, grayed the fish on her plate, made the stink unbearable. Lillian pushed it away. It was not triumph she felt now but desperation. He had not made any promise, after all — she had hung up before he could do that. She had felt like Buster Keaton rescuing Annabelle from the Union guards in *The General*. But she was not Buster Keaton, she was Mrs. Henry Haven, wife, mother. It was the mother in her who despaired now: for Bea, who would not talk to her about her episode, and for herself, who had so often done wrong by her daughter. Bea didn't know that Lillian knew this, but she did. She had known it for a long time, known it since the night she pushed the lieutenant on her. She knew it when she lied to the women at the Draper House about Bea being pregnant. (She was avoiding the place for a while, allowing them to think Bea had suffered a loss without having to say it herself.) Now her daughter at twenty-seven fell apart as if she were still eighteen and Lillian knew it more certainly, and more painfully — the pain was blinding. And because she was not a lawyer, or a businessman, because she was only a mother, her failure was total. *Some use you make of yourself*, her mother used to say. Dead so many years now. And still Lillian had not made herself of use.

She prayed, under her breath, for the whistle buoy's removal. Then she left the herring and went to bed.

19

The dismantling of Ira's bed was dismayingly easy — two pulls and it split into parts. Bea didn't understand exactly how Emma had been charged with the decision to move the bed downstairs, but she also didn't consider herself deserving of an explanation. She was embarrassed by her willful defiance of the facts, which now appeared plain: Ira had not been pretending lameness. He couldn't walk.

Emma and Albert had already carried down the headboard with its sizable posts, inflicting scratches and dents upon the walls as they went. Now Bea, trying to prevent more damage, was directing the journey of the footboard.

'There. No, there! This way, Emma! Albert, not there . . . '

'Bea! This is completely unhelpful.' Albert set his end on a stair and dragged his forearm across his brow. 'Did I never teach you left and right?'

Emma laughed. 'Don't tease her.'

Albert grinned up at Bea. 'Why don't you pour us some ice water? It's hot as hell.'

There wasn't space to get down around them, so Bea went back up, through the halls, down the back stairs, and into the cool of the kitchen. Like all the rooms in the house that had been built for servants, the kitchen faced north to little sunlight, and Bea found herself retreating here often on hot days. She pressed her forehead against the cabinet glass, letting Albert and Emma's banter trickle through her. She was in love with the sensation of being their hinge, despite knowing that their light, sweet talk was meant to soothe and keep her calm. She resented their eggshell treatment. So the night of July third had been a disaster. So she'd had another fit. Nearly two weeks had passed — why should it still stand shadowlike behind her, making everyone itch? Yet Bea understood. Bea couldn't shake it either. Even when she succeeded in forgetting, the absence of the whistle buoy reminded her: on a breezy day like this one, she tensed for a cry that never came.

All Lillian would say about that was 'Your nerves suffered, I pulled some threads.'

The icebox opened with a squeal, closed with a thud. (Vera had bought a refrigerator the year she died, but it had no freezer compartment, so Ira still had his ice delivered, and stored it in a seaweed-insulated chest.) Bea set the glasses on a tray, tied on an apron, and walked out upright and bright-eyed, calling, 'Come and get it!'

Albert and Emma stared. She couldn't remember now what she'd intended with the apron — to show that she could tease herself, too? To prove that she was *fine?*

She rattled the tray down onto the nearest table. 'I've got to get to work,' she said with a sigh, though she felt no actual regret. Her work steadied her. The speech for Josiah Story was still not finished, but that would sort itself out. The point was to drag herself back to her room, sit in the chair, and try. When she had woken on July

Fourth in the sludgy wake of her wailing the night before, and Emma's aseptic green eyes, and her exit, the door's heavy thud, even the door knowing its place better than Bea, all she could think to do was dress as Beatrice Haven Cohn, walk to her desk, phone the chapter as if they might convince her of her credibility — it was closed for the holiday, the operator reminded her — and get to work.

Before that, though, she had burned the *Radcliffe Quarterly* that had given her such trouble the night before and now mocked her from the trash bin, its pages spread obscenely. In retrospect, burning the *Quarterly* had been a mistake. The ashes in the waste bin made her look truly crazy. But that morning, it had seemed reasonable: if she couldn't make herself throw it away, she would destroy it.

'You can't work now,' Albert said. 'We need you on the frame.'

This was a relief. Bea didn't actually want to work. Albert carried one end, Bea and Emma the other. It was a heavy bed, made of oak for Vera and Ira's wedding. Bea had suggested having a new one delivered to the parlor, where Ira would be set up, but Ira had said he wouldn't sleep in another bed and Emma had told him not to worry, they would make it work. Incredibly, when Emma said that, Ira stopped worrying.

'Let's take a break,' Albert said. He looked at Bea, whose corner was sagging.

'I'm fine,' she said.

'You're fine, I'm fine, let's take a break.'

They rested halfway down the stairs.

'Ira!' Albert called. 'Could you bring us some water?'

'You'll excuse me, Mr. Cohn,' said Emma, 'but that's not a funny joke.'

'I disagree!'

They began again. Bea, who got little regular physical exercise apart from walking, was astonished by her weakness. That she could lift the bed at all seemed due merely to structural facts: her arm bones hung from her shoulder bones; her finger bones locked under the frame. When they finally set it down, she sat on top of it, watching her legs shake under her skirt. Her eyes swam with sweat. Emma brought more water and Bea drank — still, it took some time before she felt she could stand again. She propped up the headboard, then the footboard, as Albert and Emma put everything back together. Assembled, the bed made the parlor feel small, the seven-foot posts carved with pineapples and vines a sudden woods. They stood, regarding it.

'Why didn't you tell me he was so diminished?' asked Albert.

It took Bea a moment to realize that he was speaking to her. In her mouth, her sweat tasted bitter. 'I didn't know,' she said.

'Excuse me,' Emma said, starting to leave the room. 'I'll go get Mr. Hirsch.'

'I'll get him,' Bea said.

'I don't mind.'

'But I do.'

Bea went, leaving their wary looks. Upstairs, Ira was in his chair. Bea sat next to him, on the chest that held quilts, which would also be moved. She followed his gaze out the window, trying to guess what he was looking at. The harbor in the distance? The gray sycamores? The pear trees down in the orchard, heavy now with fruit, their leaves whiffling and steaming in the hot breeze? The pears would be ready for picking soon, still hard but green, ready to soften off the stem. She would have to leave before that, go to Boston for her usual week, return only after they were sure to be gone.

'Your bed's ready,' she said.

'I won't have the view.'

'I know.'

'Do you remember, when you were small, I took you to see a rock, around the other side of the lighthouse? If you get in just the right position, she comes into view, a Puritan woman, reclining?'

'Of course I remember. Mother Rock.'

Bea nearly went on. Mother Rock was where she'd been going on her frequent breaks from writing the speech. She took Ira's binoculars as she had earlier in the summer but now, instead of the whistle buoy to stare at, there was the woman's sharp nose, her tall forehead, her square, grimly set chin. There was nothing particularly motherly about her, but neither had there been, apparently, about the king of Denmark's mother, Ann, for whom the rock — and the whole cape — had been named. Bea liked the challenge of finding her. She liked climbing down from the thicket of beach rose, settling herself on a rock, adjusting her eyes until

214

the woman rose out of the rock. Sometimes she was plainly there, waiting. Other days Bea had to will and pry her into focus. The binoculars weren't necessary — the problem of Mother wasn't one of distance but perspective — but Bea wore them anyway, out of habit, and sometimes, once she'd been staring successfully at the profile for a while, she would lift them to her eyes and watch as the woman, magnified, was again obscured.

'I would like to see that rock again,' said Ira.

Bea touched his forearm, the hard tendons she'd allowed to pass for strength. 'You can't see it from the house,' she said. 'Even if we let you live up on the roof, you wouldn't be able to see it.'

'I mean I want to go down there. In my chair. Albert could do the final lift.'

Bea looked at him. 'You said you never wanted to go anywhere in your chair. You said, 'All I'll ever do in this undignified piece of crap is *stay right here*.''

Ira kept looking out the window. 'Emma changed my mind,' he said.

Albert was halfway down the drive, headed for a swim, when he heard Emma call, 'Mr. Cohn!'

He stood limply, soaked with sweat, unable to manage a step back in her direction. After reassembling the bed, he had moved the chest of blankets, then the wheelchair. Finally, he had left Bea and Ira sitting quietly in the great room like an old married couple, their backs to the newly appointed parlor with its fresh, morbid bed-sheets.

'Pardon me, Mr. Cohn, but you asked Mrs. Cohn why she didn't tell you about Ira, and she said she didn't know. And I thought you should know I think that's true. I believe it. I think she can't bear it.'

This was more than he'd heard Emma say. 'She's very attached to him,' he agreed.

Emma stood, as if expecting him to go on, then started to back-step toward the house. 'Have a nice swim. I've got to get home, to the children.'

'Thank you for coming on a Saturday. Will the same driver pick you up?'

'He will. That's fine. Will you stay the rest of the weekend?'

'I haven't decided,' Albert said, because he was used to suspending those sorts of decisions. But he knew that he would stay. He had come up each weekend since Bea's fit, to keep her company and to save her from Lillian doing the same. (*I'm fine*, Bea said, *but if I have to see my mother I might not be.*) It was a relief: focusing on someone else's trouble, carrying things.

'I think it's good for her,' Emma said. 'To have you here. Though perhaps it's not my place to say so.'

'How does she seem during the week?'

'Honestly, all right. Not chipper. But.'

Albert smiled. 'But she isn't a chipper person.'

'Does she — pardon me — but Mrs. Cohn said — does she ever — does she still talk about wanting a child?'

Albert, not knowing what else to do, looked at Emma's hands. They were large for a woman,

216

and visibly strong, and bore a disturbing number of scratches — nothing moving Ira's bed could have caused. 'She spoke with you about a child?' he asked.

Emma shrugged apologetically and started again to back away.

'Never,' Albert said. 'She's never said a thing about it.' Which was at once true, factually speaking, and also so bound up with lies — omissions, evasions — as to feel almost sinister. He pulled at the towel he'd hung around his neck, as if to hide the clawing of his heart, while Emma, visibly embarrassed, shook her head in a particularly vehement, sorry way, the way another Irish nurse had shaken her head at him long ago, overwhelming Albert with confusion. *Mr. Cohn, forgive me,* the nurse kept saying. She had shown up at his office at ten in the morning, a few weeks before he and Bea were to be married. She wouldn't talk until he shut the door. She saw the announcement in the papers, she said, recognized Bea's name, knew her picture unmistakably. She had seen her name through the years, a speech here or there. She had felt no obligation to anyone until now, she said, now she couldn't live with it — she tapped her firm bosom — if she didn't tell the girl's husband-to-be. *Forgive me, forgive me.* She told him about the baby, told him it was supposed to go to an orphanage but that one morning, before dawn, she went to fetch the infant for its usual diaper change and found it gone. *I woke the uncle. We looked everywhere, then found the mother down in the pear field, asleep in her*

217

nightgown. Filthy. Forgive me. But the baby . . . her head shaking that quick, almost angry shake, like a bird flushing. *The aunt dismissed me.*

Albert asked the woman her name, and when she wouldn't give it to him, he told her to leave. He decided she was probably lying, for one reason or another. Maybe she imagined Albert might pay her for the information, or maybe Bea's mother, unhappy with the match for a reason she had not expressed, had sent the woman to dissuade him. But after she left, he sat there for a long time, thinking about what he did and didn't know of Bea. He knew she was strange, stubborn, smart, rich, but that was about it. Since the Purim Ball months earlier, she had told him about Fainwright, but only in the haziest, most generic terms. So he wasn't entirely shocked that Bea might have another secret. A baby, though. He tried, sitting in his office, to locate inside himself the kind of horror, or at least judgment, that he knew such a situation called for. But he wasn't horrified. If anything, he found it a little comforting that her sin — if the story was true — was worse than his.

After the wedding, Bea took him up to Gloucester for the first time and Albert, seeing the pear trees, knew the nurse told the truth. Those trees were one of the reasons he didn't like coming to Gloucester. The past was past — that was how Albert preferred to live. But the instant Emma shook her head like that, like a flushing bird, his heart began to struggle, and now, as she turned toward the house, saying, 'Forgive me, I've got to get home,' Albert felt as if he were in a children's book in which one woman had come back disguised as another. He turned away and walked quickly in the direction of the road, his towel swinging, trying not to see, in his peripheral vision, through the line of trees that divided the drive from the orchard, the clinging, greening pears. That was Bea's story, not his. He still hoped to leave Bea, once she was feeling better. He concentrated on the water he was walking toward, how painful it would be at first, like jumping into nails, the cold taking his breath away, staking him where he was. Then he was in it, and it was in him, so cold, a narrow, stunning release. He swam to the first rocks, then, feeling strong, he swam to the second rocks. The water focused him, and he kept swimming, out of view of the Hirsch house, beyond Bea's reach, and past the lip of the cove and around and on until, lifting his face to catch his breath, he saw the house Teddy had once told him about, a 'sprawling, medieval, very homosexual place' with Chinese wallpaper and French moldings. Teddy had been to a party there once. You couldn't see the house from the road — Albert had tried — but from the water, well, there it was. And here was Albert, numb as a brick and filled with an escapist's courage, kicking the last few feet to the house's swimming raft, hauling himself up the ladder, and sitting on the warm wood, panting, letting the sun warm him, in full view.

20

Emma and the children were lost. A fog had dropped down, sudden and dense, blocking the moon. At first they had stayed to the edge of the river, but they must have swung into one of the creeks that looped and split and looped again and now they were spun around, nowhere. At least the tide was high, which allowed Emma and Liam to row the skiffs onto the marsh, where they rested in the tall grass, waiting, trying not to talk, the boats unnervingly echoey without any pears covering the floor. Emma knew she should have gotten them onto the marsh sooner, but she had been too frustrated to think clearly. When the fog fell, they had been within a quarter mile of tonight's orchard on Thurston Point, their only destination on the Annisquam and — theoretically — their easiest row. They were only a few nights into their two-week harvest schedule, the moon just fatter than half, the air still, their best night for a smooth pick. Missing tonight would require a rearrangement, maybe a reduction in overall pears and profits. (Emma had already decided they would have to skip the Hirsch orchard this year, though she had not come up with a way to explain this to the children.) Worse, it would bring them closer to the day Roland walked up the road, saw the heaps of pears waiting to be pulped on the floor of the shack, and quite possibly called it all off.

The fog was cool, the children silent and good, but Emma's insides jiggled and cried, *Damn fog, damn fog!* Not knowing when Roland would be home was like having a rope set around her neck that might or might not be yanked at any minute, dragging her back into her real life, even as that life started to feel like a dream and this one, the one she'd built in Roland's absence, like the real one. A couple evenings ago Emma stood in the back of the Gilbert Club, wearing a broad hat to hide her face, and listened while Mrs. Cohn regaled the crowd with reasons to be afraid — indolence, criminals, all that was new in America, etc. — though how Josiah Story would protect them from all this wasn't made entirely clear. Story followed Mrs. Cohn's speech with a few words of thanks and a couple of inarguable remarks, his hair slicked back, signs of Susannah all over him. With his handsome jaw, Emma thought, he could have stood there silently and the crowd would have cheered. Then he smiled a smile Emma knew wasn't real, stepped down from the stage, and kissed Susannah, seated in the front row. Emma left before Susannah could turn around, before Emma could see whether she had started to show. She was glad for them, but jealous, too, a feeling that lowered her to a new depth of self-repugnance.

What surprised her, though, as she started the walk downtown to catch the bus that would take her home, was the realization that she hadn't gone to see Susannah or Story as much as to see Mrs. Cohn. Emma hadn't been able to imagine Mrs. Cohn giving a speech but there she was, her hair flattened even more extravagantly than Story's, her face in unfamiliar relief, her eyes flashing behind spectacles. 'Your vote is your opportunity not to inspire but to influence, not to be trampled on by popular trends but to trample upon them!' Her voice was powerful where it often warbled, her message singular where she hedged and circled. Not too long ago, Emma would have tossed this off as hypocrisy; she would have felt a cruel pride at having proved Mrs. Cohn's falseness, for having seen her rocking on the bed, tearing at the locket, moaning uncontrollably. Instead, she found herself worrying for Mrs. Cohn, and for herself: her own slippery costumes, her lies. She'd taken the big hat off as soon as she was out of sight of the club, and spent more time than usual that night singing the children to sleep.

Lucy Pear watched her from the stern bench, where she sat beside Janie. She was oddly moody in recent days, almost furtive when Emma tried to look her in the eye, a change Emma connected to the girl's heavier hips — all that was coming earlier for her than it had for Emma's other girls. But the other children were growing up, too, at a disorienting pace — even Joshua strutted around the yard now, handing his sisters nails as they put the finishing touches on the perry shack. Meanwhile Emma went off to the Hirsch house to care for another family.

She set down the oars and rubbed at her hands, as if she might smooth the nicks and bruises that hundreds of pear branches had pounded into them. 'Shh,' whispered Janie, at

222

the sound Emma's hands made. 'Shh-shh,' Joshua said from the bow, and giggled. 'Hush!' hissed Lucy Pear, her eyes darting wildly, though there was nothing to look at but fog, multiplied. Even Liam and Jeffrey, three feet away in Story's father's boat, were barely visible: vague brushstrokes through the white-black shroud of the night.

'All of you, calm,' Emma whispered. 'Sing 'Molly Malone' to yourselves.'

Almost imperceptibly, the boats began to rock. Water slapped against the hulls, the marsh grass shifted and sighed. Emma knew they had gotten to the chorus — *Alive alive oh-ho, alive alive oh-ho, crying cockles and mussels, alive alive oh-ho . . .* — when the rhythm picked up slightly. She smiled. This, she knew, Roland would approve of. It had been his invention: Silent Singing. Sometimes he was sweet like that, in a way that could still make her swoon. He surprised her regularly, with little gifts: a rose 'borrowed' from Mrs. Parson's garden, or two sticks he'd whittled — when he was supposed to be gutting fish — for putting up her hair. This was the Roland she could not resist, the slyly rebellious man who long ago had come from a job painting boat bottoms at Niles Beach and told her how, on his lunch break, he had discovered a hidden field of pear trees.

'Mum?'

A third boat had materialized. It had simply slipped in beside them, holding two men. They might have been unicorns at first, the vision was so surreal, until Emma fully registered the guns raised at their ears. She swatted the children's heads down, felt her body depart itself, try to float.

'Federal agents, ma'am. Prohibition Bureau.'

'Mummy!' cried Joshua behind her, his voice muffled in her dress.

'Please. It's just me and my children. Will you put down the guns?'

The larger man, his jowls softening, returned his gun to its holster, but his companion, bouncing a skinny leg, only dropped his hand slightly.

'What's this?' he said, standing to peer into their boats.

'It's nothing,' Emma said.

The larger man, in front, grabbed the gunwale of Emma's boat and pulled her and the children in, as if reeling in fish. He leaned over to look, his shaggy head nearly brushing Lucy Pear, whose face twisted as if waiting to be hit — a fear Emma had not seen in her before. The man didn't notice. 'It really is,' he said as he peered into the boat. He looked quizzically at Emma. 'What are you doing out here?'

She shrugged. 'A tradition. The moon. We live just up the creek. We didn't expect a fog.'

'A tradition,' sneered the thin man. 'That's what they all say. What about the moon? It's not full, it's not new. It's nothing.'

'There's nothing in the boats, Finny,' said the large man. 'What's your name, ma'am?'

'O'Hara. Maryann O'Hara,' Emma said. When even Joshua didn't protest, she was relieved and disheartened. He was either so scared of the

224

men, or so cognizant of the family's guilt, or both, that he knew before he should have to keep his mouth shut.

'You want a ride?' asked the thin man, his gun bouncing on his thigh. 'Back *home?* We got power.' He jerked his head at an outboard motor strapped to the stern, which appeared to Emma like a large, ornate eggbeater.

'That's kind of you to offer,' Emma said. 'That's very kind.' She spoke slowly, trying to delay, so she could think — think! Why didn't she have a gun? What had Story been thinking, giving her these boats and not a gun? Roland had a gun but he'd taken it with him and besides, if she had a gun, what would she do with it? Even Liam, the oldest boy, could not reliably shoot a squirrel. So there was no gun and no one to shoot a gun and she had wasted time thinking of it. 'Thank you, but we're not far,' she said, wondering, as she said it, if maybe, if the men knew where they were and Emma told them how to go from here, she and the children could be dropped at the Thurston property, easy as that. But the Thurstons had no dock, and though their house was a distance from the creek, they might wake at the sound of a motor, and anyhow, wherever the men dropped them, they would surely wait to see — or hear, given the fog — Emma and the children enter a house. It would never work. She considered a sacrifice: she could ask the men to tow her and the kids back to the boatyard they had launched from, admit to 'borrowing' the boats — no need to get into the business of their being (sort of) legitimately borrowed — declare that as her wrongdoing and get on with it. But there was an itchiness about the skinny one. He was angry, maybe, at not yet having busted anything up tonight, or stewing about some other thing, needing someone to nab. Who knew what such a man would do? If not to her or the children, then to Buzzi, who would be waiting for them, asleep in the black Chrysler that Story's drivers used for such dealings, kind, bawdy Buzzi, who not tonight but regularly delivered other people to do other, more clearly illegal things. 'Thank you,' she repeated. 'We'll wait for the fog to clear.'

'Maybe I'm not being clear,' said the skinny man. 'It's our *pleasure* to escort you. Make sure a lady gets home safe.'

'I'm grateful for your concern, Officer, but it's our pleasure to stay.'

'I'm a federal agent!' He leaned forward, both hands on his gun, squinting at her. 'What. You the ones taking all them pears? The *serial harvesters?*' He laughed nastily.

'I haven't heard about that.'

'Local cops told us. Weren't supposed to. They kept it out the papers, *some* reason.' He scrunched his nose as if he'd smelled something bad, and Emma understood that Josiah Story must have been the reason. Her stomach rolled. 'You're doing something out here, lady.'

'We're waiting out the fog, sir.'

He spit over the side of the boat. It must have been a large, well-made wad because it sounded like a rock, hitting the water. 'Well, then. We'll just wait with you.'

Emma did not look at her children. Her breath was sour with panic. The fog was beginning to loosen into tendrils; slivers of black could be seen; the men's faces sharpened into view. The large one grinned. She calculated uselessly: if she admitted to the pear situation, their run would be over, the shack emptied, and Roland would come home to failure and scandal; if she tried for a lesser offense, having taken the skiffs, Buzzi might get caught up, and the local cops notified, who in turn would notify the boat owners, Story's brother and Story's father, who would question Story about Emma, which would likely lead to other revelations, about Emma's pears, both actual and metaphorical, which would make for another, worse sort of scandal.

A groan split the air, distant yet clear: a vast, creaking, cracking chorus, as if a forest were coming down all at once. The marsh shuddered.

'What the fuck was that?'

The men's eyes lit up. They might have licked their lips, their hunger was so clear. The big one yanked the motor to life, and they were gone.

Emma prayed, *O Lord. O Lord in heaven, thank you.* But as she watched the Feds disappear down the creek, as she heard the thrum of their motor die off, she knew that whoever or whatever had made that crashing sound — her first, implausible thought was a string of derricks collapsing — was in far more danger than she and the children had been and that this, their reprieve, had nothing to do with Jesus or Mary and everything to do with luck. Every one of her children had at some point

227

come close to disaster. They had almost poked their eyes out, almost chopped their fingers off, almost expired from fever. There was polio, there was the woodstove, there were Roland's axes, there was abandonment. Yet here they were, staring at her with astonishment. Adrenaline snaked up her legs. She gripped the oars hard to stop the shaking of her hands. The fog lifted, making way.

21

Under a blanket in the parlor, Ira read:

LOCAL CRAFT BELIEVED TOTAL LOSS

Sch. *Esmerelda J. Mendosa* Bound Home, Wrecks off Eastern Point

July 21 — Late last night, the *Esmerelda J. Mendosa*, returning from the Grand Banks, smashed upon Webber Rock.

Capt. Mendosa and five members of the crew abandoned ship and rowed in the ship's dories for shore. Two men are badly injured. Their names are given as Luis Pereira and Roland Murphy.

Residents of Eastern Point and beyond were awakened by the crash of the *Mendosa*, who lies now with her bow buried in rock, one mast fallen, a gaping hole in her side, and her engine room full of water.

According to members of the crew, the accident was due to dense fog. They could not see the signals from the lighthouses at Thacher Island or Eastern Point, and a whistle buoy they waited to hear had recently been removed from the water, leading them to believe the ship was farther offshore.

The *Esmerelda J. Mendosa* has on board

an estimated 4,500 pounds of fish. As of late this morning, men were making frantic efforts to save all they possibly could from the doomed vessel before the waves and water claimed her for their own.

The *Mendosa* was 90 feet long, 72 tons net, and insured for $30,000.

Ira's mind moved so quickly, so determined to leap and prove itself, to be nothing like his body, that he didn't at first notice the basic information contained in the article. He thought of the men, less than a mile from home, weighing whether to anchor or keep on. They would have been caught in fog before. They would have thought, *But this is only that again.*

It took Ira three tries to get through the article. He kept drifting, half dreaming.

Albert was wheeling him up the drive from a visit to Mother Rock (Mother was Vera). Through the line of sycamores Ira saw the pear trees, the fruit nearly ready to pick. He asked Albert to take him into the orchard, and Albert tried, but the field was bumpy so Ira had to sit and watch all that beauty — the late-July light playing with the leaves, the pears basking, the funny dignity they had about them — and not be able to get there himself. Albert picked a pear so Ira could feel the cool weight in his palm, but what Ira felt was guilt: this pear would not ripen well.

He shook himself to attention, straightened, read again. *The lighthouses* ... He forced himself: the sentence. It was convoluted, they were always writing convoluted sentences these days, ignoring the beauty of parallel structures, losing track of their subjects. *They . . . and a whistle buoy they . . . leading them to believe . . .*

It struck him with sublingual clarity, his stomach fisting, his heart knowing, before he thought, *Bea. Her fit. The whistle buoy.* He read the names of the injured crew again, and thought, *Emma. Roland Murphy. Bea, Emma.* A choice had to be made. Here he shone, his mind clearing, a fine, taut wire. In one case — Bea — there might be something to be done; in the other — Emma — if her husband was going to die, he would die. And of course, there was Bea-Bea. Ira's loyalty to his niece was a weight he couldn't remember not wearing. It dragged at him but held him steady, too, a sort of medal, reminding him of one thing he had always, mostly, gotten right.

He cleared his throat, took up the telephone, and asked the operator to put him through to his brother.

22

The first days went by in a green, quivering haze. The fog had left in its wake a cloudless sky and a gusting wind that threw the leaves into perpetual frenzy. Emma tripped through the clean air, winding from house to hospital and back, fighting an almost constant urge to cover her eyes, retreat back into fog, see nothing clearly. She succeeded mostly, a walking, winding body, tending, going, feeding, nodding, until nine days and nights had passed and Roland was brought home. She woke up then. She saw Roland sitting in the old nursing chair without most of his left leg, and the doctor kneeling before him, showing Emma how to clean and wrap the stump. She saw herself in the kitchen doorway, Joshua in her arms, her face worked into the easiest expression she could manage, though she was close to vomiting with what was in front of her: black stitching holding together a nearly unrecognizable, swollen, shining, ham-pink remainder of a leg.

'Like this,' said the doctor. 'Then this.' He was done with the alcohol — he was drawing small circles on the flesh with a wad of linen. 'Sometimes this helps with the pain. Mrs. Murphy?'

She nodded. 'I see,' she said, but she was looking at the side of Joshua's face, the curled scruff of his sideburn, the intricate, perfect tunneling of his ear. He was pointing behind her, into the kitchen, his hips rocking against her, *There, go.* 'You want a cookie?' she asked him quietly.

'A nurse can help,' said the doctor.

'We won't need a nurse,' Emma said quickly, before Roland could say it. But looking at him, she saw he was far from taking offense. It had been the same in the hospital: while Emma flinched at the facts, the clacking floors, the words themselves — *crushed, amputate, stump, stump, stump, stump* — Roland appeared to float in a distant, empty state. She thought it must be disbelief, but even here, in his own house, he seemed a punched-out version of his previous self, a balloon everyone had always feared would pop but that instead had quietly diminished. Maybe he was still in shock, and would return. Emma had often longed for Roland to be less irascible, but the reality of it, his peaceful bagginess, filled her with grief.

'If there's any redness . . . '

It's all red! Emma wanted to shout. *How do I distinguish between one red and another? How am I supposed to know what I'm doing?* She had managed well enough with Mr. Hirsch — she had bathed and inspected him, she had treated the spots gone sore from too much sitting, she had acted, despite her lack of experience, as his nurse. But she hadn't known him when he'd been another way.

'We'll keep a careful eye on it,' she told the doctor. 'Thank you.'

Roland reached his arms out for Joshua.

233

'Bring him here,' he said quietly.

'He wants a cookie,' Emma said.

'So bring him a cookie,' Roland said, his arms still out. Emma placed the boy in his lap and went. It was Roland's rule that the Murphy children did not eat outside the kitchen. When they did, he shouted and swore as if they'd set the house on fire. Emma made the children follow the rule when Roland was home and when he wasn't, to keep herself in the habit of enforcing it and to keep all of them in the habit of Roland. This summer, she had been especially strict about it, to compensate, she supposed, for her other, more significant rebellions. Walking out of the kitchen now with the cookie in her hand — its butter and sugar bought, like so much else, with funds from Josiah Story — she felt a mix of bewilderment and fear, as if Roland might turn on her at any moment and say, *Got you!*

'You know,' the doctor was saying, 'in a few months, you might be able to fit a prosthetic. Once the stump is healed. It takes strength, but you've got that.'

'I'm not going to pretend I've got a leg,' Roland said quietly.

The doctor looked to Emma. 'There's time,' she said, handing the cookie to Joshua and a five-dollar bill to the doctor.

He waved the money away. 'It's the least I can do, Mrs. Murphy.'

'Please.'

'Thank you, but no. Here.' He drew a vial out of his pocket and handed it to Emma. 'For night. For the pain.'

Emma bowed her head. Her neck knew the stretch now and went easily — it was all she could think to do when people insisted she take things, which they did almost constantly since Roland's accident or, as the papers had taken to calling it, his 'tragic mishap.' Strangers delivered cakes and flowers, friends came with toys for the children, neighbors brought more food than Emma could fit in the new refrigerator, a General Electric Monitor Top that the women from Sacred Heart had brought. Another parish brought Roland a crystal radio set, another a gramophone, and another a corner table on which to set them. They were competing to outgift Roland, who, along with the other maimed crewmate, Luis Pereira — whose face had been burned when the engine blew — had been turned into unwitting heroes after the cause of the *Mendosa*'s wreck became known. The *Boston Herald* had been the first to break the news: 'The tragically absent whistle buoy had been removed on account of temperance leader Beatrice Haven Cohn, who suffers, it has become apparent, from a nervous disorder.' Mrs. Cohn's mother, according to the paper, had previously boasted to a friend about her sway with the U.S. Navy, and this friend, seeing news of the wreck, had gone to the *Herald*. The next day, the story filled the front page of the *Gloucester Daily Times*, catapulting Roland into sainthood and — because the local press, more outraged about a wealthy outsider's ability to influence the navy than about whether the navy gave a damn about fishermen's lives, spared

235

Admiral Seagrave — instantly transforming Beatrice Cohn into the pariah the natives had been hungering for for years. She was a perfect symbol of wealth and recklessness, proof that those who summered on Cape Ann would also ruin the place. One cartoonist reimagined the Lady of Good Voyage, who stood atop the Portuguese church cradling her fishing boat, as a hawk-nosed woman cradling a bag of money. It was assumed that Emma felt the same as everyone else — more vehemently, if anything — but Roland's leg wasn't the only loss she had suffered. A few days after the wreck, a driver had arrived bearing a basket of bread baked by Susannah Story along with a cordial letter, on official campaign letterhead, from Mr. Josiah Story for Mayor, welcoming Mr. Murphy home and wishing him a quick and full recovery. Emma guessed that Story had written it himself, for the squat, scratchy hand, and the stupidity of his word choice — what was a 'full recovery' when you'd lost a leg? She missed him. She dreamed perverted dreams about him. In an entirely different way, she missed Mr. Hirsch, too. She could not go back to work for him — locals were picketing outside the mansion, apparently, demanding the whistle buoy's immediate return; his niece had caused (however indirectly) Roland's maiming — but neither could she have predicted how much she would miss the rhythm of her days there, the old man's curmudgeonly kindness, the seemingly simple act of going out into the world, working in it, returning from it, Emma, alone. And Mrs. Cohn, who to Emma's surprise had not absconded to Boston. Emma had been angry at Mrs. Cohn for so long that she wasn't particularly moved by her role in the wreck. Instead, now that Mrs. Cohn's undoing was complete to a degree Emma had not imagined, Emma found herself hoping she was all right. She was Lucy's mother, after all. And she was frail. But then Emma would think the same thought upside down: *She* was Lucy's mother, after all! Mrs. Cohn had left Lucy for Emma to raise. Mrs. Cohn flipped in Emma's mind like a playing card: heartless queen, sniveling girl. She had sent a check for one thousand dollars and Emma wanted to tear it up, eat it, and take it to the bank all at once. For now, she had put it in the box under her bed.

'Excuse me,' said the doctor, as he ducked out the door, 'but the boy should be sure to sit on the right side.' He nodded apologetically at Roland's lap. 'For now.'

Roland looked after him blankly. A warm breeze swept through the room, throwing the wiggling, waving light against the walls. The door closed. It was dark in the house. Joshua asked, his mouth full of cookie, 'When is Daddy's leg coming back?'

'Hush,' Emma said. She went to lift the boy, but Roland held tight. Emma could not remember ever seeing him with any of his children on his lap.

'It's not coming back,' he told Joshua. To Emma, he added, 'I'm not getting a fake one.'

'You don't have to decide now,' she said.

'I'm decided.'

'We'll see. You'll have to work again.'

'We could live a full year off people's pity.'

'Rolly!'

'And this Story character seems to be on our side.'

Emma had told him almost everything: the perry press, the jobs for the boys at the quarry. She knew he would find out from the children if not from her. She had told him, too, about her job at the Hirsch mansion, because she could not see how that would not come out in the papers (though it never did, for Mr. Hirsch and Mrs. Cohn were as discreet as they had claimed to be). She answered his questions — *What in hell? Did they make you clean? Do they really have horns? Did they suspect, about the pears?* — but offered no more, just as she did with the children when they asked about dying or intimacy. Like the children, Roland came back for more when he was ready. Yesterday, in the hospital, he'd emerged from a silence to ask, 'Did this Story character take a cut out of your nursing job?' and Emma had said, 'No,' without clarifying that Story himself had paid her wages or that he'd done it to gain Mrs. Cohn's favor or that now that Mrs. Cohn was despised, a political liability, he had no reason to continue doing such a thing, though he might pay Emma anyway if she asked him nicely. 'He's been very generous,' she said, fighting off thoughts of Story's pale, freckled shoulders.

'You've got something saved up?' he asked.

'Some. What about you?'

'I did all right. Those runners would rather

pay you in booze than cash, though. I had to put my foot down — '

'Somehow I'd bet you didn't put it down hard.'

'Hey!' Roland made a doleful face. 'I swear I did. But most of my stash went down with the fish. At least the whiskey's safe.' He shook his head, chuckling. He had explained to Emma that he had come back on the *Mendosa* because of its side business, and that the reason one of the ship's dories hadn't made it in until noon the day after the wreck was because as soon as the fog had cleared two men had rowed out to Thacher Island to stash a hundred cases of rye. 'You should see the place we picked it all up,' he said, and though he'd already told Emma twice what she knew he was about to tell again, she let him go on. 'This little island off Newfie, you see the warehouses before the rock, rising up like a city of booze. You'd think the place would sink with it.'

'Daddy?' Joshua asked, slapping at the chair where Roland's knee would have been, 'Where did it really go?'

'I'll take him outside,' Emma said, though she was wondering the same thing about the money Roland had made and whether he would in fact see any of the liquor profits. Men rarely liked Roland and she didn't know if his missing a leg would change that.

This time Roland let her take the boy. She saw him wince with relief. Joshua was too old for lifting but she held him anyway, wanting him close, and maybe tempting Roland to chastise her, to act like himself. It was a confusion, her desire for Roland to be as he'd been, a surface to push against, and her awareness for the first time that the surface could give way. She had brought her older boys up to be like their father, but now she worried her preparation had been inadequate. 'It's beautiful out,' she said, shifting Joshua to her other hip.

Roland twisted to look out the window. 'It's a beautiful day,' he said. 'Take him outside.'

'What about a wheelchair, Rolly?'

'It's not hard to get around in this house. The road's a load of gravel. Where would I go?'

'We could get a car.'

'A car. How would we get a car?'

Emma started to carry Joshua toward the door. She would treat the question as it was meant, a statement of impossibility. Even if she did deposit Mrs. Cohn's check, she didn't need to tell Roland about it: she had opened her own bank account in his absence.

Roland stuck out his right foot, blocking her way. 'Emma-bee,' he said, a thing he hadn't called her in years. 'We won't be going to the old place this year, I'm thinking.'

He meant the Hirsch estate, for pears. 'We haven't gone anywhere since you've been home,' she said.

'That'll have to change,' he said. 'You'll have to get on with things. But not there. All right?'

'Of course. I already decided that. But I think we're done, Rolly. They were so afraid that night. I was . . .'

Roland grabbed her free arm and pulled her

down hard, so that her ear was at his mouth. 'Emma-bee,' he said. 'The little one . . . Is she . . . This Cohn . . . She's . . . her mother?'

Even after there were more little ones, he had always called Lucy Pear the little one.

'Yes,' Emma said.

'She doesn't know.'

'No.'

'And Cohn doesn't know.'

'No.'

He nodded. 'Good.'

'Rolly, please, I'm going to fall over.' He let her go and she carried Joshua out into the crazy light.

★ ★ ★

Emma woke, her first thought a baby, before she realized. Roland whimpered in his sleep. It was after midnight, the time the Duesenberg would have been coming up the road. Maneuvering so that her legs stayed at a distance, Emma put her arm around her husband. He was sweating, his heart beating too fast like it did when he drank. But he hadn't had a drink. The doctor had set the whiskey bottles on a high shelf and told Emma to keep them there. *For now*, he added kindly, though Roland barely seemed to hear. He hadn't asked for a drink. But he had taken one of the pills. Gingerly, Emma turned him onto his back, undid the buttons of his shirt, and started working his arms out of the sleeves. He cried out and she stopped, looking at him, his bushy beard, his muscled shoulders, his chest twice the

241

bulk of Story's, testing to see what she felt. Still he didn't wake, so she went on, touching her face to his arms as she wriggled the sleeves toward his hands, reorienting herself, running a finger along his veins. Despite his sweat, he was clean from his hospital stay — she had to sniff at his armpits to find his scent. She expected him to wake then, but he slept, his face pinched as if fending off pain. 'Emma-bee' was the name Roland had used when he was sorry for something, and wanted nothing from her but forgiveness. Emma-bee was a girl, exempt from his desires.

She rolled him back onto his side. His skin cooled. His breathing slowed. She drew up the sheet and wrapped her arm over him again and this time, Roland took her hand and drew it into his chest. Still, she kept her lower half away. After the war, plenty of men were without legs or arms, but somehow Emma hadn't thought beyond them, to their wives.

23

Josiah woke for the third day to the smell of Susannah's blood-soaked cloths wafting up from the sheets and knew immediately that he could not stand to be there when she woke. The skin around her eyes was raw, her cheeks chalky with dried tears, that smell — like pennies in mud — unmistakable. Yet she had said nothing of a miscarriage, had gone on yesterday and the day before as if nothing at all out of the ordinary were happening. And maybe it felt that way to her, because it had happened so often before — maybe it seemed nothing needed saying. Or maybe she was afraid to say it, knowing by now how a thing like that didn't have to be exactly real until you said it. Josiah understood this, though Susannah didn't know he did, though the point was never, had never been, Josiah: he had experienced how speaking a thing made it irretrievable, shameful, how shared disappointment — the instant their eyes met — was a million times worse than bearing it on your own. He should feel sympathy for her, he knew. Always, always, he had been sympathetic! He had listened and kissed her and agreed to continue wanting what she wanted, he had agreed with everything she'd ever said. But now he was filled with rage: rage that she was keeping it from him, rage that she kept trying and trying, that she had never been taught as a child that you don't always get what you want (he forgot, in his rage, that she had wanted a mother), rage that she couldn't just *make* a goddamn baby. He pushed the Duesenberg faster than he had before — sixty miles per hour, sixty-five, seventy — jerked her roughly around the curves. He was dizzy with his anger, dizzy with the road, astonished as he wound toward Lanesville at how many other roads split off from the one he was on. He felt as he had when he'd first learned to drive, after he and Susannah were married: overwhelmed at every fork, stupid, hesitant. Only now he didn't hesitate, he mowed through his fear, drove like a battering ram, angry at Caleb, too, for what Josiah knew must be the man's judgments, that it was all Josiah's fault, Josiah's inferior bloodline, though the Stantons were so loyal to the Stantons they were practically inbred. Across the Cut Bridge Josiah gunned the engine, angry about the canal that ran underneath and the problem of dredging it and the speech Caleb had written for him, angry about all the words Caleb had taught him and that Josiah had repeated. He drove toward Lanesville, past the quarry, where he would soon be expected. His men were antsy, talking low about Sacco and Vanzetti. The Lowell commission had released its report: there would be no more appeals. At the sight of his slogan up on the wall —

JOSIAH STORY FOR MAYOR
PROSPERITY FOR ALL

244

— his rage grew, enveloping the inane nothingness of those words. They had nothing to do with him. And despite them, despite his posturing and compromises and confusion, it was looking like he might lose the race in the end anyway. Beatrice Cohn's whistle buoy fiasco was one problem. Then there were the socialist sympathies Sacco and Vanzetti were stirring up for Fiumara, whose supposed attendance at a Eugene Debs speech was starting to work in his favor. Josiah felt them stirring up in him, too. ('Stirring up' itself a phrase he must have learned to say and think from Caleb. Josiah would never have chosen it himself.) He wasn't even sure, if he were to act as himself, whom he would vote for.

On he drove, about to smash into everything, churches and stone walls, fences and flowerbeds, until at last he chose his fork, mounted Leverett, roared up through the overgrown trees. In the middle of the night, everything outside the tunnel of his headlights had appeared as emptiness but in fact the road teemed with branches and thorns, all grabbing for the car, pressing and scratching, until he arrived, his tires throwing pebbles, in the Murphys' yard.

Two girls and a boy walked out of the perry shack and stared. It struck Josiah then that he might be going mad, that he should reverse the Duesenberg, drive to the quarry, ask Sam to pour him a whiskey, and get to work. But one of the girls shouted, 'Mama!' and the boy ran toward the car, reaching a hand toward the freshly waxed hood so that Josiah was obliged to jump out, crying, 'Careful, son, it's hot!' the words tumbling him into a further valley of dissemblance. Then Emma was there, her body centered in the doorway, blocking any view, her green eyes lit with warning. He had not seen her in nearly three weeks.

'Mr. Story. Can I help you?'

'Good morning.'

'It's not even seven o'clock.'

'I realize,' Josiah said, though he hadn't. He heard himself say, 'I'm sorry for the . . . surprise. But I may have a new position for you. Beginning today.' He walked toward the door, drawn helplessly to her pink gums and small breasts even as her progeny scampered around him, the boy yanking on Josiah's trouser leg.

'I'm afraid I'm not available, Mr. Story. My husband needs my care.'

'Of course,' Josiah said, barely listening, only wanting to be closer to her.

'I'm afraid — '

'Emma? Who's there?'

'No one!' Emma called back into the house. 'Just Mr. Story.'

'Just? Bring him in!'

Emma flared her nostrils at Josiah. Then he was inside the Murphy house, his head close to the ceiling, his whole clumsy, stupid self very high above Mr. Murphy, who appeared, in the panicky, half-blind way Josiah took him in, like an old bear. Josiah didn't look at the man below his massive beard. 'My apologies, Mr. Murphy . . .'

'Nonsense. After all you've done for Emma.'

246

Josiah waited. Would there be a punch line? But Mr. Murphy looked sincere. Josiah laid a hand, palm up, between them, a cautious offering. 'I've found another position that might be perfect for her.'

'I'm grateful, Mr. Story, but as I said, Mr. Murphy . . . '

'Emma,' Roland said. 'You can't turn it down.'

'Rolly . . . '

'You'll take it, Emma.'

Emma's eyes had gone gray with anger. Josiah looked away and found the boy at his side, staring up at him. 'Mister, my daddy losed his leg we don't know where it is or if'n it'll come back I wished for Santa Claus to bring it but now is only summer but maybe you know where it is or do you know Santa to tell him to come early?' He inhaled as if he'd been at the bottom of a pond. Josiah smiled. *Yes!* he wanted to say. *I know Santa. I am Santa!* But the boy was being pulled outside by his sisters. 'Take him swimming at the cove,' Emma called after them. 'I'll be right out,' she said, looking at Josiah's feet.

He realized she meant for him to leave. 'We're much obliged,' Mr. Murphy said, and Josiah, with a tip of his hat, left. In the yard he watched the children grab up towels and thump the walls of the perry shack, calling, 'Lucy! Lucy! Come to the cove!' At the one, glassless window, the dark girl came into view. 'Johnny' hadn't been to work since the *Mendosa*; she couldn't go, Josiah realized, unless Emma went somewhere, too. The girl looked at Josiah now as if daring him to call

247

her out, her brown eyes a collision of toughness and fear. Her ambivalence about his seeing her — the caution that had kept her in the shack when he arrived, and whatever urge now brought her to the window to stare at him — was so visible to Josiah, and so familiar, that he nodded. She nodded back, ever so slightly, then ran down the hill with the others.

★ ★ ★

'There is no job,' Emma said as Josiah maneuvered slowly down the hill, unable to take his eyes off her face in the rearview mirror.

'That may be true, but I can get you one.'

'He's home. I can't . . . '

'Can't what? What are *you* talking about? I'm talking about a job.' He paused. He had no real desire to tease her, only to have her. 'Susannah's been home the whole time.'

'That's for you to sort out.'

Josiah chose a narrow, nameless dirt road. Almost all the nameless roads led up into the woods until they narrowed to the point of disappearance, and this one did the same. He cut the engine, allowing Emma's remark to sift through him, a lit coal finally landing in his dark, angry stomach. 'I need you to do something for me,' he said.

Emma scoffed. 'Really.'

He reached into his pocket and pulled out a scissors he'd grabbed on his way out of the house. He hadn't been sure he would have the courage but here he was, waving them at her

248

across the backseat.

'Careful! What are you doing?'

'Cut my hair.'

'No.'

'It's a mess,' he said, pushing the scissors toward her. In fact his hair had finally grown to how he liked it, but it wasn't Josiah Story for Mayor hair, and Susannah had told him yesterday that she would cut it today. But he was so angry at her he couldn't bear the idea, so angry he was taunting her by having Emma cut it. Of course in all likelihood Susannah wouldn't even notice, just as she hadn't noticed he'd been driving around in his one-of-a-kind Duesenberg with his lover, bringing her to their bathhouse instead of to a hotel, running naked — he'd run naked, more than once! — back to his own bed, his prick not even dry. Susannah's privilege finally their great equalizer, for it made her blind, and Josiah free.

'You barely have to touch me,' he said. 'I'll sit here, and you cut my hair. Anyway, what's with you, all of a sudden pure? Tell me this is your first time carrying on with a man. I've seen your dark girl. I'm not blind.'

Emma didn't move. 'What will Susannah say?'

Josiah turned on his knees, overcome by a sudden aggression. He forced the shears into Emma's hand, worked her fingers into position, squeezed her wrist, hard. Emma watched him. The fact that she didn't look alarmed made him sorry. 'I'm not any good at this, you'll see,' she said. But she swatted his hand away, told him to face forward, and,

249

from the backseat, started to cut.

'When she interrogates you,' she said, 'you won't be mentioning my name.'

'I don't even know your name.'

A little breeze touched the back of his neck — Emma's helpless half laughter, he knew, all nose, no sound.

'I'm sorry,' he said.

'Your campaign said so, in the condolence letter. I don't want to talk about it with you.'

The scissors thwacked at his ear. Hair fell into his lap.

'Have you gone to Mrs. Cohn yet, to ask her to withdraw her endorsement?'

'I went last week. She wouldn't come to the door.'

'You can't blame her for that.'

He lifted his head, to check her expression in the mirror, but she grabbed him by both ears and made him look straight ahead. 'So what will you do?'

'What will I do?'

'About Mrs. Cohn.'

'I don't know. I don't know what one does.'

'Do you have to know what one does?'

Josiah fingered the fallen hair. It was all different lengths. With Susannah, the entire business took less than five minutes, but Emma was jumping around, seemingly without a system or plan. She was snipping roughly at his sideburns. Susannah used a razor for these. Josiah's heart pummeled itself in its cage.

'You don't think,' Emma said. 'If you think, you'll know what to do.'

'I think!' Josiah said, touching his bangs, which felt poufy, like a duckling's.

'I haven't gotten to those yet. But I will. I'll be as thorough as Delilah.'

Josiah nodded. He had forgotten about Delilah, and Samson, too.

'Stop moving,' she said.

He stared at the woods in front of them. He was struck by the constant motion of the leaves and the utter stillness of the tree trunks. It was hard to believe they were attached to each other. His heart felt like the leaves today: trying to fly, flailing. 'I didn't bring you here to scold me,' he said.

'No, you brought me here to offer me a new position.'

'There is a position!' Josiah saw the scissors come for him, open, glinting. 'There will be. How cometh the pears?' he asked in a swaggery voice that only made his guilt more transparent.

'They don't,' she said. 'We've been busy.'

'I'm sorry. That was stupid.'

'Couldn't you renounce her or something? Mrs. Cohn, I mean.'

'What, withdraw for her?'

'No, withdraw your acceptance of her endorsement.'

'Disown her.'

'I guess. It sounds awful.'

'It does.'

They were quiet for a minute as Emma cut his bangs.

'You don't even want to be mayor, do you?'

A wheeze came from Josiah, nothing like the

laugh he intended. 'I didn't say that.'

'You probably don't know it.'

'All I said . . . My only point . . . She gave a very nice speech, on my behalf.'

'I read about it, yes. But speeches are what she does. If you wanted to win, it wouldn't be a question. You'd find a way out.'

At the Gilbert Club, he had watched Susannah watching him from the front row, her face so full of pride it seemed a mockery. After the speech, as he watched her exchange a beaming handshake with Beatrice Cohn, both women had looked at him and waved and he was sure they could see that his suit was in fact too big for him, see through the restrained, closed-mouth smile he'd been practicing in front of Susannah's full-length mirror to the boy on Mason Street, regarding himself in the tiny, unvented bathroom, making his brothers wait outside, dreaming of nothing but girls, beautiful girls, cute girls, short girls, tall girls, girls with small waists and large breasts or small breasts and large bottoms, all sorts of girls, but never one who lived beyond the neighborhood. The more costumes he wore, the more exposed he felt.

'I don't know,' he said. Susannah and Beatrice Cohn were mixed up in his mind, their way of waving with their fingers, their sheeny talk. 'I don't know what I'll do. I expect *you* hate her.'

'I'm expected to.' Emma tossed the scissors into the front seat and pushed his hair around with her hand. 'Done.'

He stretched to see himself, but at the first

glimpse of his new bangs — trimmed so close he could see his scalp — he sighed back down onto the leather seat.

'Good choice,' said Emma. 'Now. Where's my job?'

Her voice was firm, but her hand lingered on his head, traced a path down to his neck, drew a cool circle there with her fingertips. He knew each of her calluses now, followed their journey as a record might the gramophone's needle. He didn't know the roil inside Emma, how she needed the job for the money, yes, but also to get her out of the house, away from Roland. Barely a week home and already he was inching back into himself, drinking again — he had yelled at Jeffrey until the boy stood on a chair and fetched the liquor from the shelf. The doctor had stopped in and said Roland's pain should be easing, but Roland said it wasn't and insisted on taking the nighttime pills. Emma heard him weep in bed. Once she had rolled to hold him and he had rolled to her, his chest to hers, his eyes discomfitingly close and shining in the dark. 'I lost my leg,' he said. 'I lost my leg, I lost my leg, I lost my leg, Emma-bee,' until, his crying done, he took Emma's hand and led it to his prick. Now, when she heard him, Emma pretended to be asleep.

Once, before his trip, Roland asked why she wasn't yet carrying another child. Emma shrugged him off with possible explanations — Joshua was barely three, she was getting older — and hid the diaphragm more securely. But the question, she knew, would not be raised again.

During the day, Roland was quiet for long stretches, reading westerns Juliet brought him from the Rockport Library. Then he flashed into rages over a child tracking mud through the house or an empty bottle, rages made scarier somehow by the fact that he had to rage from his chair, which required that they come to him, as witnesses. They could not run away — his missing leg, his piteousness, was their trap. He pulled the children onto his lap and though Emma saw, in his face, a melting sorrow, a desire to be good, he handled them roughly, tickling and tossing them with gritted teeth. All except Lucy, whom he simply held, maybe because he feared losing her. The children would start school soon enough. They would not need Emma's protection. But what would Emma do?

Emma's fingers dipped inside Josiah's collar, scratched.

'When I was a kid,' he said, 'I dreamed of a girl like you.'

'An Irishwoman with nine children?'

'Yes. Exactly.' He turned to find her smiling just wide enough that he could see through to her gums. Then he climbed into the back.

That was how they started up again, sometimes in the afternoon, in the woods, sometimes at night, back at the Stanton estate, in the bathhouse. Roland never woke fully. He couldn't wake, for he continued to take the pills the doctor gave him for night. He said he was still in pain and Emma couldn't see how to disprove it — twice she had taken the vial to Perkins's to be refilled.

When they were done, Josiah lay picking tiny hairs off her stomach, fantasizing about making babies with her. There was hair in his mouth, and all over the car.

'You look ten years younger,' Emma said. 'She might kill you.'

Josiah nodded. He touched his head. He understood that he looked as vulnerable as a sheep after shearing. His heart bled and thumped.

'Did she lose the baby?' Emma asked.

Josiah nodded. His head rubbed against Emma's chin, which felt good, and she couldn't see his tears from here, so he kept nodding. They held each other for a while.

'They need help at Sven's,' he said finally. 'Pouring coffee. Think you could do that?'

Emma sat up. She looked at him with pity. 'You have a funny way of saying thank you. But sure. I can do anything.'

24

Lucy loved the quarry. She loved the thunderous blasts from deep in the pit, the derricks bent like fishing rods, the collective exhale — then applause! — as a mighty block arrived safely on shore. She loved the clinking of the old shims and pen hammers and points and pneumatic drill bits in her carry bag, and she loved making money. She loved the place even more for the fact that she and her brothers were the only children there that summer. At some of the smaller pits, a kid could still drill holes for half a penny, or scoop the drill dust out with a spoon before the men went in with their shims and wedges, or clear brush, but the Finns were done even with that. Their children would write and read. And the big companies were growing wary: they saw the labor laws moving in Washington, beat back yet breathing. So the Murphy kids, because Josiah Story was still in love with their mother, felt special. At times they felt like elves, dashing through the dirt and noise, from the quarries to the sheds, between the blacksmiths and the carvers, as the men coughed up dust and complained, though never about their coughs. The quarry was not the parochial place the local history books would later paint it to be. (Even the derricks were not local but made of Douglas fir shipped in from Washington and Oregon.) The men complained about the Association of

Granite Manufacturers, those shit-for-souls men who were on the lobby pot again trying to lower the minimum daily wage, and about concrete and steel, which were taking over the world and would soon kill stone, and, as the summer wore on, about Sacco and Vanzetti, who (as Josiah Story knew) stood in their minds for themselves, not because the quarrymen were anarchists (though some of them were) or Italian (though some of them were that, too), but because they knew if they were accused of a crime, they would be treated like dogs, too.

All this talk was part of the excitement for Lucy. At first she paid it only as much attention as she paid to the suspenders digging into her shoulders, or her ever-present fear that her hairpins would come undone, or the hard, heavy way she tried to walk. Which is to say she attended it as a way of neglecting the growing desperation she felt when she was not at the quarry. Roland was drinking again, his old self and his new one joining forces. He pulled the children in but roughly now, tickling them too hard, squeezing them to the bone. As Lucy sat on his lap he poked and pinched her, pinches that left welts: in the crease where her leg met her body, in the tender flesh near her armpit, on the undersides of her thighs, where there was more to pinch than there had been a year ago. No one noticed — if anything, he appeared to be more gentle with her than the others, not wrestling but just holding her, his fingers doing their quiet work — and she did not cry out. If she cried out, she feared he would do something worse. If she cried out, no one in the house would know what to do, not even Emma. Or maybe especially not Emma, who left the house early now for Sven's and came back late, who for the first time in Lucy's memory hummed to herself as she cooked and cleaned and bathed the little ones. She hummed to cheer them, Lucy supposed, but her hum was not cheerful and it had the opposite effect, on Lucy at least: the need for cheer proved how cheerless things had gotten. The more loudly Emma hummed the further Lucy felt from her, and from the other children, who often hummed along. They barely seemed to notice. It was that natural for them, a funnel pouring straight from their mother's throat to their own. Lucy wondered, sometimes, if Roland pinched them in almost-private places, too, if maybe they, like Lucy, endured him silently, if all of them together were like the idiot men in the story about the emperor's new clothes. She almost wished it sometimes, shamefully: that she was not the only one. But she did not believe it, because Joshua and Maggie would not have been able to hold back their tears and because the others, all of them, even as they wrestled their way out from him, even as Lucy perceived beats of fear in their eyes, laughed as they fled.

Lucy began to sense things she could not name. That Roland did not want to hurt her but to make some kind of mark. That if he outright hit her, he would give up some of his power. That his pinches were not unrelated to his being a man without a leg and her being a girl with two growing ones. A new heaviness had begun to gather in her legs, along with a fear that soon she would not be able to climb as nimbly, or run as fast.

It was a comfort to wear her brothers' clothes. She changed in the perry shack — Janie and Anne inspected, adjusted, nodded — then darted out and down through the woods, and she was as fast as ever, her feet finding the right rocks, her toes digging into roots, launching herself like a bird-boy toward the quarry.

It was her haven. The beating hammers, the filth, the men barely noticing her as they thanked her for a drill or laid a broken bit in her palm. On breaks she sat with Liam and Jeffrey on a pallet and watched the men hammering in the pit. She admired their strength but more so the steady, thoughtful way they worked — in her mind the care they took stood for a variety of kindness. Each man had his own system for hammering, depending on his size. A left-handed man and a right-handed man would stand together to bang in an especially large set. On the shallowest shelves they moved around each other as gently as deer.

★ ★ ★

The only risks the men took that summer they took in the sheds. Once the foreman had passed — and sometimes when he hadn't — they rested their tools and talked about Sacco and Vanzetti. They brought the papers and folded them ingeniously so they could pinch them between

259

their thighs and spread a given article open in their lap, peering down between jobs as if to stretch their necks. A juror's house had been bombed. The IWW was calling for strikes. Lucy began listening to their talk as she went in and out. She walked slowly to hear more. They talked about the *Mendosa*, too, which was connected, it seemed, to Sacco and Vanzetti, in that there were rich people to blame on both counts. They called Beatrice Cohn a mad bitch, and they called her a kike. One called her a cunt. One said he hoped she would marry Governor Fuller, and that the next bomb sent to Fuller's house would be a great success. One said if he was one of the men who got hurt (not noticing one of Roland Murphy's boys, listening, or not knowing he belonged to Roland Murphy) he would hitch a ride to her house and shoot her.

As Sacco and Vanzetti's day neared, as more facts came out about Beatrice Cohn and her factory-owning father, not to mention her conniving mother, the men's breaks grew longer, their courage greater. Lucy walked more slowly. The papers were not allowed in the Murphy house since the wreck. Who were these anarchists? Who was this woman Emma had worked for, and why had she dared work for the family they stole the pears from? One afternoon Gap Palazola, rushing for the outhouse, left his paper on the floor next to his bench. It was folded open to advertisements for garage doors and piano lessons and an adding machine and Lydia E. Pinkham's Vegetable Compound and there, in the far-right column, the second part of

260

an article about Beatrice Cohn. Above the article was a small photograph of the woman. It was so small Lucy had to squat, then squint, then bring the paper to her face, to make sure she was seeing it clearly. She was. She ripped it out and stuffed it into her pocket. 'Whatchyou doin'?' chuckled one of the blacksmiths. But Lucy was already walking toward the next shed, her carry bag clanking, so he muttered, 'Crazy kid,' repaired Gap's paper the best he could, and got back to work.

25

Bea drank Templeton Rye, two bottles of which Oakes had left in the pantry. She had begun by rationing it into a jigger and sipping slowly, then had moved on to Vera's crystal lowballs, which provided room for an ice cube, which allowed Bea to imagine herself drinking less even as she drank more, because by the end of a glass the stuff tasted mostly of water.

She wasn't at the end of a glass. It was nearly midnight and she had just poured herself another, plopped in an ice cube, plopped herself down on the edge of Ira's bed, and taken a large, stinging swallow. Before he fell asleep, they had argued again, Ira saying the people were right to hate her, which wasn't the same, he pointed out, as her deserving their hatred, and Bea saying if there was a difference then it had no effect on the hated, and why, anyway, couldn't he put aside his politics and see that she was suffering? 'I can't even begin to parse that question,' Ira had said, laughing in a way that might have seemed gentle to Bea if she weren't in such a grave mood, but she was and so she took it as admonishment.

He had drifted off. Again she had forgotten to change his sheets while he was out of the bed.

Drinking rye fast was a little like drinking fire.

She and Ira had been over every inch of the situation too many times to count. There was nothing left to talk about. Still, it was easier to talk than to sit by herself with her infinite circling, *If only this, if that, if that then this, if this then not that, if only* . . . the tired, torturous track she'd been circling since she was seventeen. The specifics were new — introducing the shiniest, latest-model engine, the shipwreck! — but the rails were the same, and they led, circling, back and back, a seamless heritage of regret, the genealogy of her mistakes, a lurid line in her mind from the shipwreck to the whistle buoy to her fit to her jealousy and disappointment to her first temperance meetings to dropping out of Radcliffe to more fits to leaving the baby like a parcel, all the way back to the lieutenant pressing her up against the wall.

Looking at it like this, Bea could see that Lillian was a monster, for it was Lillian who had thrown the lieutenant at her and Lillian who had taken Bea's complaints about the whistle buoy as a request to have it removed. It was Lillian, too, who had accepted Bea's dropping out, doted on her at Fainwright, watched as she quit the piano and fell into the movement. She had let Bea make decisions Bea was not prepared to make. She had manipulated, cajoled, done nothing, done too much.

Sitting on the bed, sucking Templeton through her teeth, Bea fantasized about killing her mother. This was not new, either — it was a familiar little detour off the circle, a daggerlike path leading to a cliff, off which she pushed Lillian, or on top of which she strangled Lillian before she pushed her off. This was satisfying, somewhat.

Ira whistle-snored. He slept on his back since being moved to the parlor, the blankets wearing into peaks at his feet, knees, belly. He was always cold. On his face was an expression of frank bemusement, the expression she'd associated him with and loved him for when she was a child. Watching him age was like watching herself, early in her adolescence: not wanting to see the disfiguring changes taking place yet unable to turn away.

She should remember to change the sheets when he was next out of the bed, or learn to change them with him in it, like a real nurse. Emma had done that, too, rolled him, understood how it was done. Now she would do it for her husband, Bea supposed.

She walked to the dark window, drawing close enough she could feel her breath coming back at her. Her nose, from this perspective, was bulbous, her eyes deep-set and dark. She felt watched. The house wasn't visible from the road, but yesterday another group of locals had marched up the drive, shouting and holding signs, demanding that Bea issue an apology. In the week since the *Mendosa*, she had removed herself almost entirely from public life. She had stepped down from her post in the Boston chapter, issuing a vague statement about Mabel Willebrandt in Washington having everything under control. Bea had withdrawn her endorsement of Josiah Story. She had sent cards and flowers and checks — for one thousand dollars each — to the families of the injured men. *To Roland and Emma Murphy . . .* Bea was so sorry. Still the picketers came. MURDERER. THINK FISHERMEN DON'T MATTER? GO HOME, KIKE. She and Ira had watched, the drapes drawn, and eventually, the people had left. This morning, Bea had drafted a letter to the *Gloucester Daily Times*. It had not been difficult, for she felt what she wrote she felt, a profound remorse. Yet she knew, as she handed it off to the mailman, who refused to look at her, how inadequate her words were, just as she had known, when she sent the flowers and cards and checks, that none of it would make any difference. Emma's husband and another man were still maimed. Bea could try to blame Lillian for that, but Lillian wasn't the one who'd had the fit. Lillian hadn't known, when she appealed to the navy, that there was sometimes a drama to Bea's episodes that seemed to stretch beyond her, a liminal moment in which she chose — albeit not quite willingly — to fall apart. Bea had never told anyone how sometimes falling apart before she fell apart seemed the only way for her not to *actually* fall apart, how screaming could be a refuge from having to talk, or think. That night, as she went upstairs, as the banister fell away from her palm and the rug in the hall wanted to trip her and the image of Julian rubbing Brigitte's belly lingered and the whistle buoy wailed and the music chased her — *. . . stuck a feather in his cap and called it macaroni!!!* — she had known, even as she tried the cotton balls, tried picking up her pen, that

265

she would let herself go, that she would unfasten herself as once upon a time she had unfastened her brace at Radcliffe and that her release would flood her with relief and shame.

She stepped back from the glass, took in her length, touched her hard boy's stomach through her nightgown, regarded her diminished breasts. She felt the usual stab of pride these facts brought her. But her face was not as she imagined it. There were dark cups under her eyes, there were lines etched into the skin around her mouth. She looked hollow and old, and above her hollow, old face was the frizzy grove of her lengthening but still grievous bangs pointing in all directions, the bangs she had let Lillian's hairdresser talk her into while Lillian sat with her own head wrapped in an inky turban so that her hair would remain forever black.

Bea drank slowly, watching herself warp through the thick-bottomed glass. Her tongue was tired and thick, her mind slowed to a sweet, fractal mud so that although for a moment she thought of the pears down below, heavy and green and . . . *In a few nights it will have been ten years, I shouldn't be here, wasn't supposed to stay this long, promised myself* . . . the thoughts swam out of her and in came Albert, saying, *That's fine, Bea. It'll all be fine.* He'd been calling her every day, to check in; tomorrow he would be back, for the weekend. She had told him about Josiah Story coming up the drive, to ask her to withdraw her endorsement, no doubt — which she would do, she said, before he could ask, of course she would do it. (To hear him ask

266

for it, that she couldn't do. The speech at the Gilbert Club had taken too much out of her, the women with their unpainted, upturned faces, trusting her. That felt like years ago now, though it had been just before the *Mendosa* went down.) She had told Albert about the rye, and how she'd fallen asleep on the floor the night before, and when he said, 'Fine, that's fine, Bea,' she knew she must be lost in a way she hadn't been lost before.

In the window, her reflection looked close to crying. But she didn't cry. She thought of Emma, surrounded by her children on the other side of the cape, and felt a pang of envy for what she imagined must be the clarity of Emma's grief, the simple square of her house. No matter the situation with Mr. Story — Bea didn't allow that to factor in. Emma was certain in her suffering and had come by it honestly and Bea envied her this. Which made her even more despicable, she knew, but there it was. There was her irreparable haircut, her old face, her bare feet so pale they appeared blue.

She turned off the light so she wouldn't have to look at herself anymore.

★ ★ ★

Somewhere between Folly Point and Hodgkins Cove, in a part of the woods called No Man's Land, in a cave blown into one wall of an old two-man pit that was mostly filled in now with scrap, a great quantity of whiskey was stored. The quality varied, depending on what was running — *Blues or herring?* the men liked to wink — but quantity could be counted on. 'Bottles'll be there' is how Lucy heard it said in one of the paving sheds. 'Eastern Point schmancies tonight. Story's got his pinkies in this one. 'Leven o'clock.'

She hid behind a boulder, leaning out to watch the men work. The wind had fallen, the night was hot. A bullfrog groaned. A pine needle came to rest on one of her hands. *I could hear a butterfly fart* is what Roland would say — it was that kind of night. When the last box was loaded, the men gathered on the other side of the trucks, their cigarettes twinkling, their voices soft, Lucy slipped into the middle truck, balled up on the floor between the front seat and the back — on the left side, where the seat above her was loaded with boxes — and waited.

The trucks kicked to life and rattled out of the woods, knocking Lucy's nose against the floorboards. She had been on the bus, but not in a car. It was very loud. When her face stopped bouncing, she knew they had turned onto Washington.

Frankie Silva found her with his foot. He was sitting on the other half of the seat, one arm stretched mightily across the wall of whiskey, a cigarette in his other hand, the most relaxed he'd felt in ages, when his left foot hit a thing that was not made of steel. He reached down and felt her cap. He slid his toe under her forehead, lifted it like a ball, then pulled her up by the nape, calling into the front, 'Got a boarder!' Lucy's hands flew to her head. She wore Liam's dark coat. Sweat filled her ears. 'Johnny Murphy,' she whispered. 'Please . . . '

'And I'm Frankie Silva.' The man snorted. 'That don't make no difference.'

But the caravan had already rounded the last bend before the Goose Cove Bridge, where Dirk Parsons collected his toll. What could they do? The road was narrow — there was no room to turn around. Even if there were, Dirk and his brothers had seen their headlamps and would know if they changed direction. And that was no guarantee anyway: there was one dirt road they could try through Dogtown, there was the long way up and around the cape, but men ran rogue tolls along those routes, too. There was too much booze in Lanesville not to collect on it, booze in other caves, booze underwater, booze in chimneys and woodpiles and trees. Ten thousand bottles of whiskey were buried in Salvatore Santorini's kitchen garden alone. The Feds came with steel rods, poking, poking, but they couldn't find every cache. (In 1983, Salvatore's great-grandson, digging for treasure, would pry up an unlabeled bottle of brown liquid and pour it into his boots.)

Dirk Parsons and his brothers had good rifles. Josiah Story had money invested in this trip. What could Frankie Silva do? He stuffed the kid back down, the drivers paid up, the caravan rolled on.

★ ★ ★

Through the yacht club gate Frankie rode with his foot on Lucy's back. 'Stay put,' he grumbled.

'Stay, we'll get you home. Won't tell nobody. Not worth our time. Stupid kid.'

She was gone before they got back for their second load. She did not run. She slipped like a shadow over the club's wall, clambered down through beach rose until the breakwater slid into view, judged by its distance how far she had to go, then stayed to the side of the road, to the hedges and walls, until she reached the gap in the honeysuckle.

It wasn't until she was through, to where the air was thick with sugar and the pears hung in her face, that she felt afraid. She had been too worried about getting there to fear being there. But the smell choked her, and the pears were so close, and she was alone, very alone, her aloneness as abruptly apparent as if until a moment ago Janie had walked beside her, as if the whole Murphy clan had been wading together into the field, the children grabbing at once for the low fruit, hissing, *Look how much I've grown! Last year I was only this high. Look!*

And Roland would laugh and say, *Who needs a doctor to measure you when we can go begging for pears? Now get to work!* And a glow would run among them as they started to pick, a shared, almost sacred kind of joy, like what happened when they went to church on Christmas Eve but even more so, even better, because the orchard, and the joy they felt there, was never spoken of.

Lucy listened. Could she flag down the trucks on their way off the point, beg Frankie Silva to take her back? In a few days she would turn ten.

Janie would bake her a cake. They would all sing to her. It could be as if she had never come here.

The night hung so still she heard her own breath. She heard her dress shift against Liam's coat. She heard the photograph she'd torn from the newspaper rustle deep in the coat's right pocket. She heard sweat roll off her nose and land in the grass.

She shed the coat. She pulled at a pear and it dropped into her palm like a stone. The stem was intact, the flesh firm under her thumb. Perfect. *Look!* she wanted to shout. *Look how easy that was, how tall I am. Look how brave I am. Look! Come get me. Come and take me home.*

She turned once, in a circle, as if Janie and Anne might be hiding behind the trees, tricking her, as if everything had been a trick and they would all come out now, Roland on his two legs and Emma all devotion and Lucy, too, before she had grown, before Roland started pinching her, before she had been split so definitively, irrevocably, from the others.

A noise. A crunching in the grass. She stopped. The crunching stopped. Of course. Her cheeks burned, her fear sang. She folded the pear into the coat, folded the coat in a neat pile on the ground, set her cap on top, pushed her hair into some kind of order, and walked on.

★　★　★

Lucy Pear walked past the place where she had been laid by her mother, and past the other place, where she had been laid by Emma. She fell into a hole — Vera's old fish pond — and climbed out. She climbed the stone wall, passed the great, comforting pine tree beneath which Bea had nearly lost her resolve, and found herself standing, exposed, on a long, rolling lawn, facing the sort of house she had glimpsed only in fairy tales. She did not see its neglect — the night was too dark and she was too young to have believed it anyway. She saw the terrace, built of granite so white it seemed to glow, and the tall windows lined with heavy drapes. Each window appeared taller than her own house! She saw the many chimneys, and the vases the size of children set out across the terrace, and the long car parked in the drive.

She crept across the lawn's lower edge, then up along its side. Her cheeks burned now with hope, her heart jigged, her mouth felt full of birds. This place! She might have come from it. She might belong to it. She might return.

Only as she reached the top of the lawn did the lower floor rise into view. The terrace had hidden it, but Lucy saw now: two lit windows. A woman on a bed, holding a glass.

Lucy knew right away. Even as she pulled herself over the railing, her cheeks began to cool. A chill swept through her. Weeds grew so densely in the terrace cracks they appeared to hold the stone together. She crouched behind a vase and watched the woman walk to the window and saw clearly that the woman's bare ankles were her ankles. The woman's skin was her skin. The woman was close to crying. It was the strangest thing, to watch a woman she had no memory of and know she was trying not to cry because that pinch in her brow, that flare of her nostrils, that was what Lucy's face did when she tried not to cry.

She heard the trucks leaving the point. She wanted to cry. Her mouth was salty with tears. As surely as she knew that Beatrice Cohn was her mother, she knew she could not knock at this window. How could that woman possibly help her? What had Lucy imagined? She had barely thought it through. She had gotten as far as asking for a train ticket. Tonight, just now, she had wanted to move in! But Beatrice Cohn looked as wrecked as the *Mendosa*. There were men who wanted to kill her. There was Roland's leg and Luis Pereira's face and Emma, who no longer worked here.

How could she have worked here in the first place?

And behind the woman in the bed lay a long lump, an old man, judging from the white scraps of hair fringing his bald head. The uncle, clearly, Hirsch. He had been the one Emma nursed. His name had been in the papers, too. Did Lucy's mother sleep in a bed with her own uncle? Was she as pitiful as that? Her stare, certainly, was pitiful, her eyes lit with misery. She swayed, as Roland used to do, when he stood drunk rather than sat drunk. She was staring, Lucy realized, at a dark window, lit from within. The only thing you could see standing at a window that way was yourself.

Lucy crawled closer. Against one of the house's dark windows she stood, and regarded

273

the woman's figure from the side, through the cloth of her nightgown. She was not like Emma, who joked she was built like a ruler. Beatrice Cohn was very thin but not at all straight, nor flat: her bottom lifted the gown behind her; her breasts were twice the size of Emma's; her thinness pulled at her curves, made them seem even more pronounced. Her nipples stood in a disconcerting, arrowlike way.

Lucy would have rather her mother had no breasts at all. Then at least Lucy might get her wish, to stay like a boy forever — at least some promise would have been eked from this encounter. She inched closer, trying to see the color of Mrs. Cohn's eyes, noting as she neared that she was still a head shorter than the woman. This was such a simple observation, the sort of thing people said all the time, *still a head shorter*, yet its very simplicity, its commonness, caused Lucy to break sweat again. She heard it as if someone else were saying it, a neighbor or a teacher, offering it up as thoughtlessly as any other daily remark, about rain clouds or pie. *Still a head shorter!* As if all this time Lucy had been growing to grow as tall as this woman. As if the woman had been waiting for her to arrive. Longing poured into Lucy, filled her to her neck, brought her hand into a fist, daring to knock: *Take me in!* But before she could work up the courage, Beatrice Cohn grimaced, spun away from the window, and put out the light.

★ ★ ★

Bea finished her rye in darkness, set the glass on the floor, wove a wide arc to make sure she cleared the glass, and lay beside Ira in the dark, her back to his side, her head spinning. She could no longer see the window but she knew it was there because she could see the quarter moon. Her eyes closed. The moon hung in the private room behind her eyelids, a white, wiggling echo of itself. She opened her eyes again, closed them, let the moon swim through her, putting her and her circles to sleep. Her eyes fluttered. Then they were open, and she was looking at herself, on the other side of the window, a child, Bea-Bea, staring in.

★   ★   ★

Briefly, Lucy's mother seemed to have disappeared. Lucy pressed her face to the glass. She felt her body drain of hope, felt her knees turn to mud. Then two pricks of light gazed out at her, as startling a sight as a raccoon's eyes in the woods. Like a raccoon's eyes, they glinted, lit by the moon and apparent menace. Like a raccoon's eyes, they seemed to look straight through her, as if in warning.

Lucy ran. She ran off the terrace, across the lawn, past the pine, over the wall, through the orchard. She found the coat and grabbed it up. She looked back, up toward the house, but saw no light. Had the woman seen her? Lucy waited. She had not seen her. Of course not. She was a woman who looked at herself in windows. She didn't care enough to see Lucy. And if she had

275

seen her, she wasn't coming. No noise came from above, no light. Lucy's stupidity was crushing. Beatrice Cohn had left her. She hadn't asked her to come back.

Still, Lucy waited, her arms hugging Liam's coat. The pear within split as she waited. She took a step backward, then froze, took another step, froze. She punched a low branch, knocking pears to the ground, froze again, waited. She waited until she could not bear the disappointment, until fatigue darkened her senses, until all she could do was shake the pear chunks from the coat, twist her hair into the cap, and start the long walk home.

Part Three

26

'Post for Mrs. Cohn!' the mailman sang, his voice resounding through the house, for he had taken the trouble to kneel down, poke open the flap, and push his lips into the hole. His words arrived in all their snide glory in the great room, where Bea lay on a sofa with her arms covering her face, Albert stood looking out the window, and Ira and Henry sat with three newspapers between them. Sacco and Vanzetti were supposed to have been executed the night before, but thirty minutes out, as Robert G. Elliott, widely admired as the gentlest executioner in New England, checked his voltage, Governor Fuller sent a last-minute reprieve, giving the defendants twelve days to find a judge willing to retry their case.

Bea appeared to be asleep but wasn't, Ira knew, because when the mail flap crashed down she rolled over at once and sat up, her response as automatic as a dog's.

Poor Bea, who had gone finally, truly, mad, who swore she had seen her baby, grown into a girl, peering in the window one night. She had told Albert, who had told Ira and Henry, and then Henry had told Lillian, which made Bea even crazier — she accused Albert of betraying her. Ira just shook his head. He knew she had drowned the baby, but he couldn't possibly say that to her now. Henry kept reminding Bea that the baby (as far as he knew) had gone to the orphanage, and that the orphanage kept no records. Bea had nothing sensible to say about any of it. 'But the pears,' she kept saying. 'They didn't come this year, for the pears. They're still on the trees, they'll go soft . . . ' As if that explained anything.

They stopped responding to her. Ira kept waiting for her to admit she was wrong — if not lying, then mistaken. She had been dreaming. *Everyone gets confused sometimes,* he said, *Vera used to get confused, even I sometimes think not entirely thought-through, thoughtful — what do you call them? — thoughts.* He tried to make her laugh. But she looked at him without any sign of confusion or torment and said, calmly, I know what I saw. Her certainty was the worst part, proof of how fully she had unraveled. It sat heavy on Ira, and there was his guilt, too, at how Bea's suffering had brought his brother back to him. The shipwreck seemed to have roused Henry from his tunnel of commerce, and then Bea's hallucination had roused him further, so that he had come to visit each weekend and on some days, like this one, in the evening after work. Ira couldn't have predicted the pleasure Henry's company would bring him. For years, he had thought of his brother as a statue, made of wax, but he was real, with warm, hairy forearms and, across his balding brow, a shock of black hair which by this time in the day, in the middle of August, had started to frizz and fly. Henry hadn't been hard about Bea all those years, Ira decided, but

280

overcome. Or, if he'd been a little hard, Lillian had bossed him into it. But that wasn't entirely fair, either. Ira was less inflamed by thoughts of Lillian now that Henry had returned. Even Lillian herself didn't seem so hateful. She'd joined Henry on his weekend visits, along with Albert, who was good to all of them, taking Bea out on long walks, pushing Ira down to Mother Rock, making tea for Lillian and Henry, going out on his own once Bea and Lillian had gone to bed, walking for hours — they didn't see him until morning — so that Ira and Henry could play chess.

Bea sat, rubbing her face with her hands, preparing to go fetch the letter. 'Nah nah *nah*-nah!' the mailman might have shouted. The picketers had dispersed but venomous missives continued to arrive, accusing Bea of crimes ranging from attempted manslaughter and bribery to excessive wealth. Many referenced Sacco and Vanzetti in some way, suggesting that Bea was directly responsible for the persecution of the working class. Their letters mobbed Bea's desk, spilled onto the floor, while nearly every day another piece about Bea's fiasco ran in the *Gloucester Daily Times*, next to headlines about Sacco and Vanzetti. Today's article exposed the number of extra ambulances the city had to maintain year-round for the two months when the population boomed with summer people like Beatrice Cohn. If she had been a Protestant, Ira thought, her fellow vacationers might have stood up for her. But she wasn't. They didn't.

'Sweetheart,' Henry said. 'Don't bother with

281

the letter. Let me burn it. Come. Sit with us awhile longer.'

'I wasn't sitting with you.'

'Lie with us. Lie back down. We'll read to you.'

Bea stood. Ira shook the *Globe* in her direction. 'Look! They're cheering in Buenos Aires and Paris! It's progress, at least.'

Bea took the paper and read for a minute. 'I wonder what made him change his mind.'

'The bombs,' Ira said with joy. 'The demonstrations! London, Chicago, Brussels, everywhere. Workers standing up as one!'

'You think a few bombs scared Fuller?' Henry huffed. 'They sent one to his house in May, didn't change his mind. You think he cares about the mighty granite cutters threatening to strike?' Henry shook his head. 'He's got two hundred million in riot insurance, tear gas by the truckload, machine guns stacked like wood. It's not up to him anyway. It's the judges who decide.'

'That's what Fuller would have us think,' said Ira.

Bea handed the paper back. 'They should get a fair trial. I do believe that, even if the throngs think I'm a beast. But it won't make any difference in the end. They criticize America. Their English is bad. I wouldn't execute them. But they'll be executed.'

She left the room.

'I wouldn't bother her with the news while she's still in it,' Albert said from his spot at the window. He was thinking of Lyman Knapp, the man who owned the huge, strange house on the

282

harbor and who was a great success in interior design in Boston. On the afternoon Albert had dared climb onto his raft, Lyman had swum out to say hello. He was gaunt, with an easy grin and a hairless chest. They were lovers now.

Ira and Henry looked at each other, then Henry shut the paper and slid it under his left buttock. Ira smiled. Even as his ever-roving mind drew lines from Sacco and Vanzetti to Bea (for wasn't it all about money, in the end? didn't class oppression work both ways?), his brother's boyish charm titillated him. So what if Henry was, politically speaking, a simpleton and a jackass? He knew how to get things done, which was more than Ira could say about himself. Ira slid the *Globe* under his own haunch and circled his hands on his wrists, then straightened his right leg and circled his foot, then straightened his left leg and circled that foot, and the maneuvers, undone for decades, brought him back to the loud, tiled lunchroom at the William Cabot School for Boys, where each morning, before lunch, the headmaster would direct them to rise from their chairs, stretch their arms and legs, and perform twenty jumping jacks. Ira remembered how anxiously he had watched the gaggle of younger boys. Where were Henry's hands? Had he fallen? Did he not understand the rules? Later, Ira learned that Henry had been sitting calmly on the floor, out of the headmaster's view: already he had devised the most efficient route to success. His brother was extraordinary, Ira thought now. Even in that bouncing sea of silken, Gentile hair, Henry had understood how to win.

Bea walked in swinging a torn envelope. 'What am I supposed to do now?'

'Sweetheart, why don't you sit down?'

'It's from Luis Pereira's wife.' Bea shook the envelope upside down, releasing a flurry of torn paper. 'My check. They don't want my 'dirty money.' The Murphys haven't deposited theirs, and now the Pereiras rip theirs up. What am I supposed to do?'

'Bea — '

'Why don't they believe me?'

No one answered.

'Oh,' Bea said. 'Of course. You don't believe me either. You're awful. All of you. I *did* see her. I saw her. She was here. The pears . . . '

'Sweetheart.'

'She was! Besides, I'm not talking about that.'

Albert turned. 'What is it you want them to believe, Bea?'

'That I'm sorry.'

'You've written your apologies. You've sent your checks.'

'Exactly!'

'Exactly. That's all you can do. You can't make anyone believe anything.' He laid out his palms as if he himself were proof.

'I used to be able to,' she said.

'You think the women who came to your speeches didn't have their minds already made up?'

Bea whimpered. 'I'm like poor Sacco.'

'I wouldn't go that far,' Ira said.

Bea rolled her eyes. 'I feel that way.'

284

'Bea.' Albert walked softly toward her, and cupped her shoulders in his hands. 'Does it matter if they believe you? If they took the money, if I got them to take it, would that be enough?'

Bea squinted at him. 'Enough to do what?'

'To satisfy you. To stop your train wreck.'

'I am not a wreck!' Bea shook him off. 'I am not a nut and I am not a wreck, and if I were a wreck it would be because of you!' She swung her glare at each of them. 'But I'm not. I am fine! I am absolutely fine!'

'FINE!' pinged off the chandelier, flew around the room, shimmied into silence. Ira looked at his slippered feet, next to Henry's shining Haven wingtips. Henry looked away, wishing Lillian were there. Albert stared at Bea, as if daring her to say it again. She shook, frustration and humiliation warring in her limbs. She had seen her daughter as clearly as she saw Albert now. She had followed her, but not fast enough: by the time Bea reached the orchard, she had lost her. Bea had crept, then listened, crept, listened. She did not want to frighten the girl away — this was one reason for her caution. But it was also true that Bea herself was afraid: she did not want to discover that there was no girl, that she had, in fact, made her up, drawn her from her haze of Templeton and self-pity. She trained her eyes on the darkness, willing the girl to reappear. She nearly called, *Hello?* but lost her courage, so neither she nor Lucy heard the other — they were both, mother and daughter, too good at hiding, too practiced at silence. And they moved

285

synchronously, like two second hands on the same watch, driven by the same gear. By the time Bea reached the gap, Lucy was gone. Bea had seen her! But then, what if she hadn't? Each time she had to defend herself, she felt her certainty split a little more.

She could not say this, of course. She would not give them any more reasons to think she was a loon. She held Albert's gaze. 'It would be something,' she said. Then she gathered up the confettied check and the hateful note and went upstairs, to throw it onto the piles with the others.

27

The paper would speculate that Josiah Story, holed up in his office with the quarry gates locked, was afraid — afraid of what his striking workers would do if he opened the gates for the scabs, afraid of the scabs themselves, Sicilians who had been trucked in from Lowell and who paced, dark-skinned, at the wall. Sacco and Vanzetti's execution had once again been scheduled — they would die tonight, August twenty-third. No judge had saved them, not William Howard Taft or Harlan Fiske Stone, who were both summering in the North, not Louis D. Brandeis, whose wife had grown close with Sacco's wife. Brandeis recused himself. There had been more bombings, more demonstrations, more strikes. Steelworkers, textile workers, miners (many of the same miners who would be massacred in Columbine, Colorado, that winter), mill workers, granite cutters. In Gloucester, the wreck of the *Mendosa* was like kerosene on an already blazing fire.

If Josiah Story wasn't afraid, wrote Jonathan Hardy, a young reporter who had been praised in school for his impeccable logic, why wouldn't he let them in? Why wouldn't Caleb Stanton's son-in-law let the scabs in?

But he wasn't afraid. His men were peaceful. His engineer had come early to bank his fire, then left to stand with the others on Washington

287

Street, holding signs: FREE SACCO AND VAN-ZETTI; SUMMER PEOPLE = MURDERERS; WE STAND WITH THE FISHERMEN AND THE FISHMONGER; LAND OF LIBERTY; and Josiah's favorite, JUSTICE FOR ALL, which so neatly condemned his absurd slogan — Prosperity for All — on the east rock that Josiah felt relieved of having to condemn it himself.

In fact, he was so unfamiliarly calm he experienced it as a kind of elation. There was nothing he wanted to be doing apart from what he was doing. Just as extraordinary, he was doing nothing. He was standing in his office watching the empty pit: a bird drinking at a sludgy puddle, a pile of bright, rusted bits, a vision of himself down there, drill in hand. This vision mesmerized him. He knew the figure was himself, Josiah, yet from this height and distance he couldn't see his own eyes and so he doubted what he knew. The figure moved like him, but maybe it was his father as a young man. Josiah and his father had the same high-arched feet (like ballerinas, his brothers laughed) and walked a bit on their toes, chests forward. They were steady with their hands but slow, the way Josiah down in the quarry was with his drill, setting it, seeming to consider, setting it again half a foot farther along the seam. Josiah's father had never worked in a quarry, but his father's brothers had. They had worked in the quarries and Giles had worked in the shop just as Giles now worked in the shop and Josiah worked in the quarry. Not in it — above it. But there he was in it, busy with his drill, not allowing Josiah to tell if he was Josiah.

288

Josiah thought it extraordinary, how immersed he could be in the vision and also aware of it as fantasy. What was it in him that he could stand here, doing nothing, allowing his men their strike, pretending — almost — not to consider the consequences? He felt so calm. Unified, really. With himself, with the lone bird, the thrown-off bits, the quarry, its green mouth open to the sky. It wasn't sexual, he didn't think so, though the only thing he had to compare it with was what he felt when he slept with Emma, his urges narrowed, his priorities clear, his clear urging toward the light. But that was in his body, whereas this was everywhere. The word 'spiritual' occurred to him. It rode across his mind the way he'd seen kites, bearing advertisements, slip across the sky behind airplanes, a surprising, doubtful sight. It rode out again. Down in the pit, he had chosen his spot. He was readying his drill, without wonder or guilt.

It took Josiah a full minute to register his father-in-law in his face, throwing a finger, hauling it back, throwing it again, his face contorted. First, Josiah heard his men chanting, though he couldn't make out their words. *My men*, he thought. *I've been brainwashed.* He saw the white hat in front of him dripping with sweat, saw dark maps appear at the armpits of a custom-made poplin shirt. Only then did Josiah feel the worm in him waking, anxiety slithering up his innards.

'What are you doing?' Caleb growled.

Josiah realized he'd heard a pistol shot. 'Did you shoot them?' he heard himself ask, his voice far away and oddly measured.

'Are you insane? I was simply announcing . . . I was making . . . Why am I defending myself to *you*?'

'I don't know,' Josiah said. He waited for his father-in-law to rear up and attack again, to say he knew about Josiah's affair. Even if Susannah, against all odds, didn't know (when she'd asked about his mangled hair and he told her he cut it himself, she believed him! she laughed, then fixed it herself without another word!), wouldn't Caleb? Josiah waited for his self-sabotage to be complete: the quarry, the campaign, and now his marriage. But Caleb simply stood there, shaking his finger. Josiah was struck by what a remarkably undersized finger it was. He leaned left to see around Caleb. Down in the quarry, the figure was gone. Josiah lowered himself into his chair.

'This is my office!' roared Caleb. 'Stand!'

Josiah sat. What could Caleb do? He was small, and old.

'Please,' he said. 'Sit.'

Caleb leaned across the desk. 'You will end this strike or I'll destroy your campaign.'

'Would you really do that, sir?'

'I don't give a damn about you becoming mayor.'

'Of course you do,' Josiah said, in awe of his own steadiness, a warm courage through his throat, the worm held at bay. 'It's your campaign. And it looks like you might lose anyway. People are a little fired up, if you haven't noticed. Sacco and Vanzetti. Beatrice Cohn. The

290

tide is turning. Fiumara's looking like a beleaguered butterfly right about now.'

Caleb breathed like a bull.

'I'm doing my best, you know. Trying to play up my working-class roots. Reverting to the accent you taught me how to lose. Did you let the scabs in, sir?'

'It's nearly one! Let them in to go down and come back up? I got a call from Babcock. He got covered trucks to bring men in from New Hampshire. His stone is moving! He wanted me to know mine wasn't. Do you have any idea how much you're costing us? Of course you don't, you have no idea about how anything is actually done, you just shake the hands, make the deals.'

'I thought that's what you wanted me to do.'

Caleb narrowed his eyes. 'After everything I've done for you. Your speeches, your car. It's all mine.' His lips drew back, baring his teeth. 'If you had a daughter, you would understand. You wouldn't screw with me. If you had any children at all.'

'That's very cruel, sir.'

'It's not half of what I'll do to you. You'll be out of a job! Mark my words.'

'But who will take my place? One of your sons?'

Caleb sat then, on the chaise against the wall, which was so low, and his descent so abrupt, that once he was down, he appeared helpless. He didn't look at Josiah — he looked at the wall behind Josiah, where a portrait hung of Caleb Fiske Stanton, Caleb's grandfather. Caleb was thinking, Josiah supposed, of his family's greatness, and of their imminent ruin at the hands of Josiah Story. Exaggerations both. Why should Josiah feel such pity for him? Not the glinting slash of pity he'd felt in odd moments before, when Caleb was in front of him, telling him to do something. That pity was for Caleb's not being able to tell whether Josiah obeyed out of respect or duty; that was for how vulnerable Caleb's power made him. That pity quickly evaporated because Josiah wanted power, too. But in this moment, having disappointed Caleb in the worst ways possible, Josiah was free of obligation and could see the man's tired sorrow.

'If they strike tomorrow, you'll bring in the scabs.'

Josiah didn't even nod. He pretended at nothing, only sat with his hands in his lap, his chest open to whatever Caleb would say next. The man in the pit was within him now. The chant was clear. *Justice*. That was all.

'So you think those wops are innocent,' Caleb said.

'I have no idea,' Josiah said.

'You read Thayer's decision? Fuller's report? You think a man like Lowell, a Harvard president, would lie?'

'I think all sorts of men lie. I think maybe that's the whole point, sir.'

Caleb was silent. He looked toward the pit, where nothing moved but the bird, and two more that had joined it at the puddle. The birds hopped, flew off briefly, and returned, pecked at each other's wings. Josiah watched Caleb watch them, his fingers propping up his chin, his face

292

slowly softening, like clay. His silence stretched on for so long Josiah started to worry he'd had a stroke. Then Caleb looked up.

'Our poor Susannah,' he said. 'She's had enough.'

Josiah waited, unsure what his father-in-law meant. But Caleb only looked at him, his face soft, and expectant, and because what he'd said was true, Josiah nodded. He nodded and nodded, until Caleb got up and left.

28

The men were executed, their heads encased in Robert G. Elliott's ingenious leather helmets, their stomachs full. There was some picketing outside the State House — the poet Edna St. Vincent Millay and a few others would appeal their ten-dollar fines — but mostly the people were tired, the crowds small. All the insurance the city had bought against riots and bombings, the mobs of state troopers armed with rifles and tear bombs, the former was regretted, the latter sent home. In Paris, thousands of people marched in the streets shouting, 'Death to Fuller!' They smashed the windows of restaurants serving American diners, mauled billboards advertising American artists, hurled stones and seltzer siphons at police — the papers called it the worst violence Paris had seen since the war. In Buenos Aires, Johannesburg, Havana, Sydney, Mexico City, Geneva, London, workers marched, their heads bared; U.S. embassies were bombed; boycotts were called against American goods. The *Giornale d'Italia* declared: 'Democratic and liberal in theory, the United States desired to show that in practice it does not admit other laws than its own, not even the law of humanity.' But Boston, the morning after, nearly echoed with silence. In Gloucester, quarrymen returned to the quarries, dockworkers to their docks, and by late afternoon the Heschel brothers, Ira Hirsch and Henry Haven, sat in lumpy, intricately carved armchairs built for the Bents a century before, their eyes traveling between the papers and Bea, who lay in her usual spot on the sofa, her arms heavy across her face.

'See here,' said Henry, 'even the *New York Times* says Fuller did what he was supposed to do. 'Civic inflexibility.' 'Steadfastness.' See? They say even if you don't agree with the decision you have to admire him for standing by it.'

Ira picked up the *Globe* again. ''Sacco's Father Weeps at the News. Screaming inarticulately and trembling in every limb, the aged man finally managed to say, 'They have killed my innocent son,' and then fell back into his chair weeping and muttering maledictions.''

'Hysterical reporting,' Henry said. 'And to be embraced by a newspaperman such as yourself.'

'It's a bit hysterical,' Ira admitted. 'So I picked the wrong bit. That doesn't mean change isn't called for.'

'The *Times* agrees with that, too. It's really a very balanced piece.'

'Since when did balance become a virtue?'

In Lanesville, Josiah Story left the quarry early and went home to Susannah to ask her forgiveness for what he'd done.

'The strike,' he prompted.

'The strike,' she repeated.

She took his hand. 'I forgive you, Joe. It's all done.' Then they read the paper together, in silence.

At Sven's, Emma poured coffee and listened to the men talk. She liked the job Josiah had gotten her there, liked how in the afternoons light poured in the front of the shop and neglected the back so that the place seemed to be two places, and how she knew by now, after only a couple weeks, which men sat in the sun and which in the dark, and how well their choices fit their faces. She liked not being in the house with Roland. But today the air in the shop felt too close. The men looked sick with disappointment. They spoke softly, as if a baby were sleeping nearby, and Emma found herself thinking of her own babies: of the ones who, like her, had been pale, almost translucent; and of Lucy. At the back of Lucy's neck, and on the backsides of her ears, and along the tops of her toes, there grew a black, downy fur that Emma touched helplessly, incessantly, as she nursed her. She had nursed all her babies well but often without thinking of it — she had mended clothes and stirred porridge and fed the fire and shoveled snow with babies attached to her breasts. With Lucy, she was transfixed. Even now, if Lucy was in sight, Emma watched her. She had watched her new skittishness sharpen in recent days. Lucy looked at Emma like a rabbit, ready to bolt. Thinking of her now as she poured coffee for the grieving men, Emma felt a nauseating fear rip through her. Lucy! What was wrong with Lucy? She spilled the coffee, enough to drip off the counter and stain her shoes, but the men, eyes on their mugs, barely noticed.

In Charleston, Admiral Seagrave believed the execution unjust but had no one to talk about it with — not the other officers, who would disagree, nor his wife, who didn't like 'the world' disrupting family time. He tried his older son, but the six-year-old said, 'Those wops? Jack Jessup says they got 'em good!' And all Seagrave could think to do was send him to his room and wonder — as he often did now — about the daughter he would never know.

On Eastern Point, Bea interrupted Ira and Henry to ask, 'Did you see the two-inch about Mother Jones?' Her voice was rough from not speaking. 'She's ninety-eight years old, in the hospital, and nobody will tell her they're dead. They're telling her they've been given an indefinite reprieve. She's lying there shouting things like, 'They'll never dare to kill them, it would stir up the whole world!' And nobody will tell her the truth. They say it would kill her, but I don't buy that. The same article says she lost her husband and four children in one week to yellow fever. If that didn't kill her . . . I think they're just scared.'

'Of what, sweetheart?' Henry leaned forward, preparing to stand. He felt buoyed, more like his usual self, his boss self. Bea had not said so much in days. But when she looked at him, her cheeks wrinkled and red from where her sleeves had pressed into them, her eyes pinned him to his chair. 'That she knows something they don't,' she said, in a tone bordering on disgust, as if he had asked her the color of the sky. Then she left the room, leaving him alone with his brother and their papers, every inch of which they had already read.

29

Once upon a time, Caleb Stanton himself handed the quarrymen their pay, and now, as a symbol of his mistrust and a warning to his son-in-law, he began the practice again. On the first Friday after the execution, the last whistle sounded and there he was, all five feet two inches of him, standing straight as a mast in his white suit and white Panama hat against the backdrop of the *Berenice*, the hulking, shining, incomparably aggressive 0-4-0 tank-type locomotive named after his late wife.

Caleb always told any man who asked — and more asked than you might expect, which confused one of Caleb's basic divisions of the world, into the sorts of people who wondered about things and the people who didn't — that Berenice was an old lover of his. This seemed to amuse them. Maybe it even made them like him a little more. At least it used to. But that had been before the strike. Before the *Mendosa*. Before, now that he thought of it, the Scare. It had been years since Caleb stood before his men.

They lined up according to how long it took them to get to the *Berenice* from their positions: *Berenice*'s engineer, her brakeman, the boys who work the chains and pull the pin, the loaders, the draftsmen, the carvers, the cutters, the surfacers, the derrick operators, the fall men, the drillers, the chip men, the men who set the powder kegs and lit the match. Every one of them colored gray. 'Asa Hood,' Caleb said, prompted by Sam Turpa, who stood to his right and knew the faces. 'Jacob Soltti, Urjo Matson, Dominic Toneatti, Henry Hanka, Andrew Pearson.' Caleb knew how to pronounce these sorts of names — he had hired a tutor, years ago, to teach him. This had seemed to him a good idea. But as he looked down the line at the gray faces, Greeks, Finns, Swedes, Italians, Yankees, Irish, and called out the syllables that had taken not a small amount of effort to learn to pronounce, an effort he had thought of as wholly selfless — 'Peter Lilja, Angelo Buzzi, Toivo Nikola' — as he waited for Sam Turpa to hand him each check, which Caleb then deposited into a gray hand, he felt a steam rising off the line, a thickening agitation, as if their strike had brought them no satisfaction at all, as if in their impeccably pronounced names they heard Caleb joking with the other quarry bosses: *One left-handed Finn is worth three right-handed Yanks. Pay the Irish, watch them drown.* As the line steamed, Caleb felt physically vulnerable for the first time in his life, and bewildered. Why were his men so angry? He paid them fairly and on time, let them have their little union meetings, never asked them to sign any yellow-dog contracts. He was not the tyrant his grandfather had been. Why should they fight to save a couple of anarchists? If it weren't for the state, who would have stamped their papers when they arrived in America? Who would pay for the streets that took them from home to work? 'Silas Procter, Octave Marcelles, Liam Murphy, Jeffrey Murphy, Johnny Murphy . . . '

Caleb paused. The Murphy boys didn't look at him, but that's not what made him stop — most of the men didn't look at him. It was something else, a fleeting doubt that made him think of Berenice. She had been so small, like a child, so finely jointed at her wrists and knees, so tiny at her waist you could hook an arm round her and reach the same hand into your own pocket. Even Caleb could manage this. It was the pose of a carefree man, an adventurer.

Maybe it was his longing for his bride that made him turn to watch the Murphy boys depart. Maybe it was the steaming line, his exhaustion, his feeling that the men might rise up at any moment, light torches, run shrieking through the sheds. Generally, as a boss, Caleb did not abide doubt — in another era he would have gone on to the next man without hesitating. But he hesitated, and turned, and saw what he must somehow have sensed: that Johnny Murphy's cap was bulging in the back, and that there, just above his collar, one dark curl had escaped.

★ ★ ★

Emma's first thought was that the car sounded almost but not quite like the Duesenberg. Her second, seeing the small man she recognized as Caleb Stanton jump from a Rolls-Royce in her yard, was that the boys had been involved in

300

some way with the strike. Watching Liam and Jeffrey climb out of the car, she felt a seam of pride, thinking of her father nailing up his Land League posters along the main road in Banagher.

She wasn't expecting another boy to follow them, and she didn't understand, at first, why the boy's hair was so long, or why someone else's child had been brought to her, until it struck her that Lucy Pear wasn't standing with Janie and the others, who had come out of the perry shack to watch. Emma had arrived home from Sven's half an hour ago — she hadn't checked on the children yet.

Mr. Stanton pushed Lucy toward the house. 'The quarry's not a place for a girl,' he said as he deposited her in Emma's arms. His voice was gentler than Emma would have guessed, nothing like his cold blue eyes.

'Emma?' Roland called.

'Everything's fine!' she called back.

'Her father should know,' said Mr. Stanton, striding for the door, but Roland was already there, on his one leg, the first Emma had seen of him in sunlight in the month since he'd come home. His beard, she saw, had grown to be wider than his ears. Bits of crumbs stuck to his shirt. He was out of breath from hopping. 'What's going on?' he asked, but no one answered. He stared at Lucy in her costume. 'Get inside!' he shouted. 'Get your arse inside this house!'

It was shameful, how glad Emma was that Roland could not climb down from the step. She said, 'I'll bring her in, Rolly. Go sit.'

'What the *fuck's* been going on?'

301

'Rolly! Boys, help your father get back to his chair.'

'I don't need help getting anywhere,' sneered Roland. He would not move from the doorway, Emma saw, and no one could move him — even on one leg, he was like a mountain.

Mr. Stanton said, 'Mr. Murphy, if I may . . . '

'You may not,' Roland mocked back.

'Thank you,' Emma said to Mr. Stanton. 'Thank you for bringing them home. We'll manage from here.'

Mr. Stanton took off his hat. His eyes were wet, Emma saw. 'It's not such a crime,' he said, 'a girl wanting . . . ' Then he trailed off, got into his car without looking again at Roland, and drove back down the hill.

'Was there leather on the seats in there?' asked Joshua.

Liam and Jeffrey nodded, but their eyes were on their father, who stared at Lucy as if repulsed.

'Is like a galloping sofa!' Joshua cried.

'Here,' Emma said, taking pennies from her pocket and giving one to each child. 'Go down to the store, buy a piece of candy.' She led Lucy into the perry shack, where she sat her down on the potato bin, sat herself down on the 'turnip bin,' and took Lucy's hands into her own. It was a way of comforting the girl and steadying herself. Emma was frightened by Roland, in the doorway. And she didn't know what to make of Lucy in her brothers' clothes, an old cap in her grip (and now in Emma's), her curls in a plantlike tangle around her head. Emma felt closer to understanding something about Lucy's behavior all summer — her itchy glances, her pleas for Emma to go back to work — but also farther, because why? Why would the girl want to do such a thing?

Before Emma could speak, Lucy started to cry. She shook silently, then let out a soft wail, her mouth opening to a raw, shocking size, her fingers pulling away from Emma's. The cap dropped to the floor as she hid her face in her hands. Emma leaned forward, taking the girl into her arms. 'It's all right,' she said. 'Shhh. You don't have to explain.'

This was true, she realized — she didn't need to know, if it meant having Lucy back, the way she'd been. But Lucy was already explaining, through her tears: 'I wanted the money . . . I thought the pears . . . but then I . . . This year . . . I just wanted . . .'

Emma put the snotty, broken parts together. The pears. Lucy was falling apart over the pears, the change of plans since the *Mendosa*, the neglected Schedule of Ripeness pinned to the shack wall. The children played jacks in the perry shack now, or marbles — they passed time here to avoid Roland. The fruit they had harvested was nearly pressed and there would be no more — despite Roland's urging, they had been too rattled by the Feds to go out again. But not Lucy, Lucy was saying. Lucy was not afraid of those men! Lucy wanted to finish what they had started. They had made a plan and they should stick to it!

Her vehemence startled Emma. How had she come to care so much about the pears? She took

Lucy gently by the shoulders and began, 'Sweet girl, we're going to be fine, it'll all be fine, you don't have to go dressing . . . ' She wanted to tell her the money from Sven's was enough, tell her part of growing up was accepting what you couldn't change, but Lucy pushed her hands away. 'It is not fine!' she shouted, and started to sob.

Emma waited then, until Lucy began to tell her, between choking gulps of air, not about the pears or the quarry but about a trip she had taken a few weeks ago, late at night, while the rest of the family slept. She described a ride in a truck full of whiskey, her near capture, a man's foot on her back, heavier than her carry bag at the quarry, his foot bruising her ribs. There was some kind of search, lights beaming through the coat that covered her, the man's foot pressing harder, a deal struck, her nose smashed against the truck floor. Emma hardly breathed as Lucy spoke. Apparently it wasn't just the job: Lucy had a whole life, a species of courage, Emma knew nothing about. You found a newborn and she seemed blanker, somehow, than the newborns you had birthed, free of any history, exempted from her own ties, more *yours*. But of course she wasn't any more yours than they were, which was to say less and less all the time.

Still, Emma did not understand where the story was heading, not until Lucy described climbing out of the truck at the Eastern Point Yacht Club. Even then, Emma could not believe it. How could she? She was late, as usual, with

304

laundry. She had not yet found the torn newsprint with Beatrice Cohn's likeness in the pocket of Liam's pants. But then Lucy told her about slipping through the gap in the honeysuckle, walking up through the pear trees, swinging a leg onto the terrace of the house where she had been born.

She looked at Emma and said, with sudden coherence: 'I saw my mother.'

'Lucy . . . ' Emma started to say, but Lucy went on, not noticing or caring about Emma's astonished tears.

'She looks just like me! Anyone could see it! Why didn't you tell me?'

'I — '

'What were you doing working for her?'

'I — '

'How could you not have told me she was right there all this time?'

'Lucy — '

'You take me from her, then you go back and don't even tell me?'

'I didn't take you.'

'You did!'

'She left you.'

Lucy glared at Emma. Her breath was ragged from crying, her hair wild, poor Lucy with her wild hair Emma had no idea how to care for.

'Where did she leave me?' Lucy asked quietly. She had started to shiver.

'In the orchard.'

'Where?'

'Under a tree.'

'Which tree?'

'The middle one.'

Lucy shivered harder now. Emma reached for her hands, and when Lucy didn't pull away, she blew onto them. She rubbed the girl's arms, but nothing helped. She wasn't cold, she was inconsolable, she was weeping without tears. 'Wait here, don't go anywhere,' Emma said, and ducked out of the shack. She had forgotten Roland, filling the doorway of the house.

'Excuse me,' she said.

'What's going on in there?' he asked.

'Later,' she said. She tried to squeeze past him, but he tilted on his leg, blocking her way.

'Now,' he said.

'She found Mrs. Cohn,' Emma said quietly. She was so determined to get inside she only noticed the fact of Roland giving way. She didn't see the rise and fall of his Adam's apple, or the color leaving his face. On her way back out, she nearly tripped on him — he had lowered himself to sit on the threshold — but she ran on toward the shack, afraid Lucy would be gone.

She was there, still shaking. Emma, wrapping the blanket around her shoulders, said, 'This is what you were bundled in. When Peter found you.'

Lucy looked at the blanket.

'It's yours,' Emma said.

'Peter?'

'Yes.'

Lucy nodded. She appeared to be thinking hard. The chatter of her teeth slowed. 'What is she like?' she asked.

Emma didn't understand at first. The question

306

was almost bewilderingly obvious. It was so simple, and yet impossible to answer. What was Beatrice Cohn *like?* She wanted to be kind, for Lucy's sake, but not overly kind, for her own. She wanted to be truthful, but Beatrice Cohn did not hold still in the mind. She was sensitive, selfish, fearful, overconfident; she was a Jew; she was homely, lovely, ancient, immature; her kindness was helplessly aggressive; she was lonely. 'Lonely' would be the word, if one was forced to sum her up. But that did no one any good.

Finally, Emma said, 'She means well.'

She would not forget how Lucy's face sagged with disappointment then. Instantly, Emma regretted the paltriness of her answer. It had been so ungenerous! So sterile and meticulous as to be a lie. Yet Emma could not think how to say anything else. Lucy's curiosity, however natural, was painful to behold. Emma felt as if a scaffold were buckling inside her.

'I almost died walking home, you know.' Lucy's tone was heartbreaking in its matter-of-factness. 'I thought I was going to die. And then by the time I got here the sun was rising and you hadn't even noticed I was gone. You were asleep!' She lowered her voice. '*I* noticed every time you left in that car.'

Emma's face grew hot. She filled with rage — how dare Lucy? — swept quickly under by shame: instinctively, she glanced toward the house. But Lucy had been quiet, careful, protective of Emma even as she confronted her, and Emma recognized the more essential crime

307

of her affair: each time she had disappeared in Story's Duesenberg, she had left Lucy lying awake and alone in the night.

Her throat burned. 'O Lord. I am sorry.'

'Will you take me back?'

Emma felt relief bloom inside her. She thought Lucy meant one thing, until she saw that the girl's eyes were bright with tears. Determined to hide her disappointment, Emma held her gaze. 'We'll see,' she said. It was a thing she said often to her children, a seemingly innocent way to put off their requests, but she heard now the trickery in it, for it implied a helplessness on her part. It belied — and therefore strengthened — her power over them.

'Please,' said Lucy, who rarely begged for anything, but Emma was too full of feeling to think, too overcome to promise anything. She didn't want to promise anything. 'We'll see,' she said again. Then she went to help Roland up from the stoop.

★ ★ ★

An hour later, a different car drove up the hill. A different man got out, taller and leaner and darker. Not since Roland first arrived home a hero had so many people come to the Murphy house in one day. Everyone came to see, except for Lucy, who after her conversation with Emma had climbed down through the turnip bin into the perry cellar. With the blanket Emma had given her wrapped around her shoulders and a large stick in her hands, she crushed pear pulp,

308

not with any of the techniques described in the
PEAR VARIETIES pamphlet but in a way that
made as much sense and was far more satisfying:
again and again, with all her might, she drove the
stick into the pulp.

Were they expecting him? Albert sat a minute
in the car, taking in the Murphy family, all lined
up in the yard. Emma's children looked just like
her, but she did not look like herself — the
moment she locked eyes with him, her usual
warmth faded. Her jaw locked. Her husband
tilted in the window like an enormous broom,
not saying a word. Albert recognized the danger
in him — he saw that he was not always silent,
saw that he exacted silence as Teddy had, as
warning. Driving up Leverett Street, Albert had
been hopeful, for Luis Pereira's wife had
accepted the cash he had brought there, but
when he saw the Murphys his hope lost its shine.

'Mrs. Murphy!' he called, striding toward the
line they made, reminded for the first time since
childhood of the game Red Rover.

'Mr. Cohn,' she said.

'Albert Cohn,' Albert said to Roland Murphy,
braving his scowl. Albert nodded at the children
in turn, working to appear lighthearted. 'I don't
mean to bother you,' he said to Emma. 'I only
came to bring you this.' From his vest pocket he
produced the envelope. The heat had not
broken, but Albert was a banker, used to wearing
a three-piece suit in any weather. He was used to
impressing people in this way, used to getting
what he wanted.

Emma peered in the envelope. 'Thank you,

Mr. Cohn, but we don't need it.'

'Don't need what?' asked Mr. Murphy.

'Mrs. Cohn's sincerest regrets,' said Albert.

'We're grateful,' Emma said. 'Please tell her that we're grateful. But we can't accept.'

'But she insists. You haven't deposited her check.'

'What check?' Mr. Murphy asked.

'I have no idea,' Emma said flatly, staring at Albert. 'I never got any check.'

'I don't know what happened,' he said. 'I'm very sorry, as is Mrs. Cohn. Please.' Again, he held out the envelope. 'It's the least we can do.'

'She was a good employer,' Emma said. 'She paid me well.'

Albert said nothing about the fact that it was Josiah Story who had paid her — or that Bea suspected the two of an affair.

'We don't blame her,' Emma said emphatically. 'Tell her that.'

Mr. Murphy spoke. 'Emma, take the money.'

'We don't need it,' she said without turning to look at him.

'What makes you think you won't lose your job at Sven's tomorrow?'

'I won't lose my job,' Emma said.

'Do you know something I don't? Has the world changed in a remarkable way since I last saw it?'

'We'll talk about this later. Mr. Cohn, your generosity is much appreciated, but please, you should go.'

He put the envelope back in his pocket. What could he do? Emma was not Luis Pereira's wife,

310

Rosalva, ready to eat Albert's handsome face. But Albert could not give up. He would fall onto his knees if it would help. *Mrs. Cohn needs you to have it. I need you to have it!* He needed her to take it so that Bea would calm down. He needed Bea to calm down because he loved her, and because he was ready, at last, to divorce her. Albert was still sleeping with Lyman Knapp. He wanted to keep sleeping with him. Perhaps divorce should not matter — why should a real divorce be necessary to end a sham marriage? Yet it did matter. He wanted to leave, officially. But first Bea had to be leavable. He looked once more to Mr. Murphy, hoping — awfully — that the man might shout at Emma, make her take the money. But Mr. Murphy was looking beyond Albert now, his expression altered. It was softer, somehow — Albert glimpsed fear in it. He turned to see a girl walking out of the small shack. Lucy had left the blanket in the cellar but its furs clung to her sweaty face. She was red from her crushing. She hollered, 'Time for your bath, Joshua!' before she saw the assembled crowd, and stopped.

'Lucy!' The littlest boy ran to her, and hugged her by the leg. 'It's Mr. Cohn! The husband of the lady who wrecked the ship!'

'What were you doing in there, Lucy Pear?' In the doorway, Mr. Murphy folded his arms. His voice singsonged, as if teasing, but he squinted like a bully. 'Building a nest?'

She didn't answer. She was looking at Albert. She was Bea in miniature, he saw, the resemblance so plain he barely registered his

311

shock — he thought of the bosomy nurse, at his office door, telling him how she and Ira had found Bea asleep among the pear trees. *But the pears,* Bea kept saying, *but the pears . . .* Even if he hadn't heard the girl's middle name Albert would have known this was Bea's daughter. Her question, as she stared at him, was clear. Was he her father?

He was sorry not to be. He was sorry he couldn't take her away, right then, and tell her the story, what he knew of it. Lucy Pear! But she was not his to take. His question, as he stared back at her, was how quickly he could get back to Bea and assure her she wasn't crazy. The money in his vest was immaterial now. The point was to apologize, bid them adieu, jump in the car, ta-ta! The point was his rising heart.

30

It had rained only once in August and the track to the cove was dry, without grass to cover the middle berm where the children usually walked. They carried sticks and fishing line and worms dug up from Emma's scrap heap. They walked fast, wanting to secure their favorite spot on the seawall, but Lucy's feet had grown soft from wearing shoes at the quarry and she fell behind, picking on her toes across the gravel. She moved slowly enough to notice colors in the crushed stone, to see lizards poke themselves onto the path, then dart back into the brush. She stopped to inspect the painful bottoms of her feet. Not so long ago, Lucy had had a child's sense of her body, which is to say she was unaware of it as such. She moved, it moved, she was, it was. Lately, though, she found herself watching it, noting a hardness beneath her nipples as if pennies had been sewn in there, noting hair in places it had not grown before. She was divided from herself, a spectator. And she was divided further from the family, too, for Janie did not seem to be undergoing any of these changes yet and Lucy knew the reason: Janie's mother was like a ruler, while Lucy's was not. Seeing her mother had confirmed Lucy's sense that she was alone. And it fed a fantasy that maybe she didn't have to be.

She sat on the track so she could rub both feet

at once. The pale skin under her toes was red, the pads of her feet howled. How had she gone so soft in only a couple months? Still, her feet weren't as bad as the welt on her right hip — if she concentrated, she could feel it there, the blister chafing against her skirt. Last week, after Mr. Stanton brought her back from the quarry, after Emma had heard Lucy's story and promised her nothing in return, Roland had called her to where he sat, in his chair. Lucy went bravely — everyone was watching. Maybe all he wanted was an apology. Even when he pulled her onto his lap, she remained hopeful. She was helpless not to hope: maybe he would only tickle her, rub his knuckles against her head a little too hard, then let her go. Maybe she had imagined the times before. She worked to keep her balance on his one leg. She started to say, 'I'm sorry. I shouldn't have gone . . . ' but Roland put his hot, moist palm over her mouth. 'So you made a mistake,' he said. 'We all make mistakes, Lucy Pear.' His voice was reasonable — she believed he meant to be kind. Even his hand over her mouth she forgave, for his smell was familiar, comforting. Meanwhile with his right forefinger and thumb he began squeezing at the back of her leg, near her buttock, his hand under her and well hidden, squeezing first and then twisting, twisting her skin until she blinked back tears. Meanwhile she sensed Roland stirring under her, a man's stirring. This was new. This was terrifying. Still, she withstood it — her tears were easily interpreted by her audience as remorse — until Joshua, blessed

314

Joshua, whined for his bath. Roland released her. Only as she scrubbed Joshua's back did Lucy peek behind her and inside her skirt and see that her blood vessels had burst, that Roland had twisted a circle of skin the size of a pencil clear off.

Lucy picked up her fishing stick and began to walk. She was so focused on shaking off the memory, and on watching where she set her feet, that she barely registered the woman in a long, dark dress, sitting on a boulder at the side of the track.

'I'm sorry. I didn't mean to scare you.'

Lucy stared.

'I would have come to the house . . . I went to the bottom of the street. My husband drove . . . Somehow I knew you would go swimming today.'

Beatrice Cohn was visibly shaking. *I knew.* Emma would call that a boast, but Lucy liked that her mother had known (even if she did have the sport wrong). She wondered at the woman's boniness, wondered, if she were to go closer, if she were to reach out to touch her, would her hand go straight through? Had the others not seen her, in her weird dress? Was Lucy dreaming? She felt as if her blood had been replaced by boiling water. 'You're here,' she said tentatively.

'My husband saw you. I saw you, at my house. But no one would believe me.'

Lucy blinked slowly. The woman had not disappeared. There were Lucy's thick eyebrows.

'You're very brave.'

This is my mother, Lucy told herself. *This is your mother.* This was her mother, praising her. Surely she was meant to feel grateful. Perhaps she should move closer. But her limbs might have been rubber. Her feet held to the berm. The longer she looked at Beatrice Cohn's face, its familiarities seemed to recede and the fact of her utter strangeness came forward. Lucy knew nothing apart from what the paper said. She didn't know what this woman liked to eat, or what her laugh sounded like — *did* she laugh? — or whether she drank tea. And the woman had kept it that way. She had not come looking for Lucy. Lucy had been the one to look — she had stowed herself in a whiskey truck to find this woman who sat so stiffly now, with her stiff face and her stiff hair in its bun and her hands in her lap like she was waiting for Lucy to tell her what to do. What did she want, for Lucy to say, *Thank you, you're brave, too?* Emma taught the children to always repay a compliment but Lucy couldn't make herself do that now because it just wasn't true and the longer she looked at the woman's face, the less true it seemed. Lucy felt an excruciating loneliness. Why hadn't Janie and the others come back for her? Did they think she had gone back to the house? Did they think she had run off again to the quarry? She heard herself say, with a firmness that belied her confusion, shored her up against tears: 'I'm ten now.'

The woman's face changed then. The parts she'd been holding seemed to give way. She covered her eyes with her hands. 'My husband

316

told me your name,' she said pitifully, and Lucy's pride withered. She crouched down, trying to see beneath the woman's hands. 'Would you like to see my perry shack?' It was the only thing she could think to say. 'I built it. I was the boss. We can wait there, for my mother.'

Slowly, Mrs. Cohn lowered her hands.

'I have to tell my mother you're here,' Lucy said, using the word purposefully now, watching it hit Mrs. Cohn. It was like watching wind hit a sheet — the sheet's flailing gave away the strength of the wind.

'Of course,' Mrs. Cohn said at last. 'Emma.'

'Yes. But not my father. Not yet. He'll be angry.'

Mrs. Cohn nodded. 'I don't know if today . . . I don't know if I should . . . '

Lucy filled with despair. 'Please!' she begged, feeling fizzy, frantic. She should not have said *my mother*, not twice. She would drive the woman away, lose her all over again. 'I've been asking her to take me to you. I've been asking and asking. Come on. We'll wait in the perry until she's back from Sven's. I'll show you everything. Come on.'

When the woman still didn't move, Lucy took her hand — and she didn't disappear, and it was just a hand, after all, bony but soft, and oddly cold on such a warm day — and dragged her like a stray toward home.

Bea followed the girl's instructions: racing across Washington Street, high-stepping up through the woods instead of on the road, watching the ground for roots. She was grateful

317

for the precision mimicry demanded, antidote to her mind's flailing. *Run away, run away!* her mind cried, though of course she had known she would wind up here, known since Albert ran in calling, 'You were right! You were right!' He had ignored Ira and Henry, dropped to his knees by the sofa, shaken Bea hard by the shoulders. 'Sit up! You were right. It's her. I saw her.' Bea rubbed her eyes. Was he mocking her? She doubted, again. Perhaps she had dreamed the girl, and Albert was only trying to placate her. 'Where? Are you sure?' Albert cupped her face in his hands. 'I couldn't be more sure.'

He was crying, she saw. Birds winged in her chest. She began to tremble. Her father said, '*Oy mein goht,*' the first Yiddish she'd heard him speak, in a bare, strange voice. 'Where?' she asked again. 'Lanesville.' Why had Bea assumed the girl had gone so much farther? She had been to Lanesville. She could be there within an hour. She stood. 'You'll drive me.'

That was when Albert let his hands fall away from her face. 'She's been raised by Emma Murphy,' he said, and Bea sank back onto the sofa.

She had needed a few days after that, to wallow in shame, to work up to her courage. 'You have no choice,' Albert kept reminding her. She thought of sending a letter to tell Emma she was coming, thought of driving to the house when Emma would be home, going to Emma first, falling at her mercy. But she did not, finally, have the courage for that. She was too afraid that Emma would keep her from seeing the girl. So here she was, behind her daughter, her very brave, very fast daughter, struggling to catch up, to step where the girl stepped, even as her mind hissed, *Run away!*

But now they tiptoed into the yard, now they ran into the shed so the father wouldn't see, now Bea caught a glimpse of the house and realized she had been here before, on a diaphragm mission. Her hand clapped to her mouth — she must have shoved the thing at Emma! How humiliating, how crass! She had not connected the address she had sent the check to with this house — how could she have? The Ladies did not go by addresses, they went by the look of things. They went to the places that looked poor.

'She'll be home at three,' Lucy said, and again Bea's mind told her to run, but the girl told her where to sit and Bea sat, on a low pine box, and tried to listen as Lucy explained, in a loud, excited whisper, the box's trick. Lucy's hands flapped. Her eyes shone. 'The bottom drops out and there's a ladder! Do you climb ladders?' Bea moved her head in a noncommittal way, struggling to pay attention. She was thinking of Emma, who surely remembered Bea coming to this house, moralizing, scolding. She had been thinking of Emma constantly: Emma washing Ira's sheets, bathing him, caring for him so well while she cared haphazardly for the rest of the house, scattered Bea's shoes, disappeared her pens. She had been wearing a mask, Bea understood, in every moment, every time she smiled or nodded or spoke. Bea remembered making Emma ask her questions over Pinkham's.

She remembered her own stupid, lonely bossing, and Emma's reluctance, almost a truculence as she complied. How superior she must have felt to Bea. *And what about children, Mrs. Cohn? Did you never think to have any?* She was not purely kind, as Bea had thought — nor should she have been. It had been her voice, low and calm, that had soothed Bea in the orchard. It had been her hands that changed Lucy's diapers, fed her, bathed her. Ira, too. All Bea's duties — Emma had done them.

'The trouble is,' Lucy was saying, 'it takes a full year for the perry to come right, so you have to wait.' She folded her arms, looking suspiciously at Bea. 'You don't approve, I know. I read about it in the paper.'

Bea realized her expression was grim. She smiled, as much as she could smile. 'I don't care, really, not anymore,' she said, but the girl was already at the window, peering out. Her face caught the light and Bea saw, in her profile, the lieutenant's long jaw. She took in the curve of the girl's nose, the particular flatness of her forehead — she tallied these in her mind as her own. The girl turned to face Bea. 'He's probably sleeping,' she said — meaning the father, Bea understood. 'He sleeps a lot now. He's getting fat.' Lucy giggled, revealing the lieutenant's tall, straight teeth. She moved carelessly, her arms jumping as she spoke. Bea had the thought that if Lucy had grown up with Bea, in Lillian's house, she couldn't possibly have been like this, her eyes full of mischief, her cheeks ruddy, her hair poufing plantlike around her head. She imagined Lillian, the first thing she would notice that jaw. *Good for her,* she would say, ignoring history, her vision singular and bitterly optimistic. *It won't droop.*

'What time is it?' the girl asked.

Bea checked the piece around her neck, taking the opportunity to close her eyes for a little bit, fix the girl's face in her mind. 'A quarter to three.'

'She'll be home soon.'

Fresh panic bloomed in Bea's stomach. She said, 'She doesn't expect me. Maybe I should come back when — '

'You can't go!' Tears pooled in the girl's eyes. She stood flat-footed, arms at her sides, just as Bea stood — Bea knew because Lillian had always instructed her otherwise: close your legs, do something with your hands, you'll frighten them away. Bea saw now how the stance could be imposing, how completely Lucy blocked her way. Bea's cowardice hung between them in the dark shed like fly tape.

She sat.

Emma did not come at three. Bea watched as Lucy showed her how the scratcher worked, where the pears went, how to turn the crank, how the pulp, when you hooked up the chute Lucy had devised, slid down through the turnip bin to the press. She wanted desperately to entertain Bea, to keep her — her desperation made Bea ill. She tried not to think of Albert, waiting for her in the little village. Was there anywhere to go, she wondered, other than the coffee shop? And it was closed now, according to

Lucy. So where was Emma? Lucy pulled Bea to the scratcher, urging her to try. Bea was astonished at the crank's weight. She managed to produce a mere fistful of pulp before she had to stop — it fell into a bowl beneath the scratcher with a slimy thud. She had an urge to feel the girl's arm, touch the muscle there, touch her at all. But Lucy was already off in the corner, gathering up more pears. 'I was trying to make enough money to go to Canada,' she said. 'But we had to stop, after the boat wrecked. These are all that's left.'

Bea smiled, assuming a joke. 'Canada?' she asked.

Lucy shrugged, her hands full of pears. 'My brother Peter's there.' Her voice was breezy but Bea glimpsed, in the lieutenant's long chin, a quivering. 'I had a job,' she said, 'but not anymore. I pretended to be a boy, in the quarry. Then I got caught. Now I have to wait again, a whole year.' The pears sounded hollow as she dumped them into the press.

'You want to leave here?' Bea ventured.

'Please don't tell.' Lucy flashed a painfully eager smile. 'I was thinking . . . maybe . . . you could help?'

'Help?' Bea couldn't hide her surprise.

'With the ticket, I mean.'

Bea swallowed hard. Again she tried to smile, but it was a lopsided effort — she could no longer process the conversation, she knew so little about Lucy's life. Did she want Bea to help her with some kind of escape? Bea had left her daughter when she'd barely been able to see.

322

Why should the girl trust her now? 'But your mother . . . ' Bea sputtered.

'Look!' Lucy lifted her skirt, turned sideways, set her foot on the box next to Bea's. High up on the backside of her leg, Bea saw a wound the size of a quarter, bright red at its center, fading to pink at its edges. It could be a burn, she thought. She had seen plenty of burns. Nearby a few old bruises lay quietly under the skin, like dim moons around a sun. Bea felt her temperature rise — her ears and fingers swelled with blood. Rage shot through her. What had she allowed to happen? She asked as calmly as she could: 'What is this?'

Lucy let her skirt fall.

'This is why you want to leave?'

Lucy turned away and resumed cranking. 'What is my father like?' she asked.

'Your father?' It was a natural question, and connected, Bea presumed, to the wound, yet she was not prepared for it. 'Lucy.'

'Is he Mr. Cohn?'

'No.'

'Is he dead?'

'No!'

Lucy looked doubtful. 'He's dead.'

'He's not dead.'

'Then what?'

'He was a very honorable man. He would have wanted you to be — '

'You talk like he's dead!' The girl bit her lip. She appeared in awe of her own impertinence. 'You didn't know him,' she said, realizing. 'He didn't know me.'

Bea reached a hand toward Lucy. Lucy didn't take it.

'That was how it had to be done.'

'Why?'

Bea thought how to explain it. But the explanation was about certain types of people and schools and mothers and concerts. It was about a sort of life, a world, that didn't sound so hard. She tried another tack. 'Imagine one of your sisters . . . '

'My mother got pregnant with Juliet before she was married,' Lucy said. 'I did the math.'

Bea took a deep breath. She could smell the girl. She smelled of sun and sweat, girl sweat — Bea remembered — tangy but appealing, like citrus. 'Forget it,' Bea said. 'What I mean to say is that it was a mistake. Not to have kept you. I mean to say I'm sorry. I know he is, too. Which sounds completely useless, I know. I'd understand if you hate me. But I am. I'm sorry. I'm here now. I — ' She nodded vaguely at Lucy's leg. 'Maybe I can help.'

That was when Emma peered in. She was backlit, and breathing heavily from her walk up the hill, her shoulders rising and falling, and Bea's first thought was of Nurse Lugton, here to stop the strangeness, wake her, tell her it was all a dream.

* * *

Emma was so quick to think of Roland, to account for him, to smooth the world for him, to protect the children from his wrath, which was

324

mounting again, a toothier, maimed cousin of its earlier self — he was unwilling to try a prosthetic or even leave the house yet too large and roving to be contained in a chair — that she made no sound. A howl of lightning from her head to her heels, a twisting through her ribs, a silent, wrenching mewl. Why had she thought it could go on forever? She had been stupid, delusional, as if Lucy would forget, as if Mrs. Cohn might not have seen her, as if Mr. Cohn were blind. *We'll see*, she'd said to Lucy. *Maybe, mmm, we'll see*, though Lucy begged. *We'll see*, and off Emma went to work in the mornings, *We'll see*, and off she went in the night with Josiah Story, *We'll see*, and twice more to the woods with him during the day. She had been there now! He had picked her up from work, saying to the room that one of her sons was hurt, while he whispered in her ear, *Not true*. The memory of it filled her with horror, their thumping against the car door, his hands pulling her roughly. He had been rough and she had liked it, liked thumping like that, liked it so much heat flooded her lap at the thought of it, even as she stood in the window, looking at Lucy and Mrs. Cohn. *I'm here now. Here now.* Lucy, Lucy, her eyes brimming with tears.

'Go in the house,' Emma said.

Lucy shook her head.

'Go.'

'I won't.'

'Go somewhere.' Emma's voice was sharper than she intended, her hands in fists. She moved to the doorway, her hair clinging with sweat, her shoulder sore from where he'd bitten her. A piercing shame. Was this her punishment? *I'm here now.*

'I won't!'

'Lucy!' Emma hissed.

The girl didn't move. She was afraid, she must have been terrified, but she looked at Emma with such utter defiance that she appeared almost languorous, mocking, her face close to a smirk. If not for Roland, Emma could have yelled. Instead she was inside the shack, her hand raised, her hand falling with such force that when Lucy dodged it, Emma's wrist met the scratcher's edge with a sickening twang. She yelped. Lucy stared at her from the corner, then started to cry.

Emma shook out her arm. 'Stop staring at me,' she said to Mrs. Cohn without looking at her. 'I've never hit her. Lucy, tell her. I've never hit you.'

'You've never hit me,' Lucy said miserably.

Emma rubbed her wrist. 'Do you remember, Mrs. Beatrice Haven Cohn, coming to this house once before?'

'I do.'

'Should I be flattered, that you remember?'

'I didn't say that.'

Emma's wrist was maybe broken. It hurt like hell, like she might fall down and weep. But Lucy was weeping. 'You told me not to have any more children,' Emma said.

'I remember. I'm sorry.'

'You're sorry.' Emma looked at her now, and was astonished to find Mrs. Cohn staring at her with an expression so free of guile or cover, so

326

bare and young and thin — so thin! the bones in her forehead showing through — that Emma heard herself laugh. 'You are sorry!' she said. 'Well. I haven't had any more.'

'I know.'

'What do you want?' Emma asked.

Mrs. Cohn said nothing.

'You can't take her.'

'I didn't . . .'

'Proof? Is that what you want?'

'All I wanted . . .'

'Don't lie to me.'

'I wanted proof. I'm sure I did. I did. Of course. But . . .' Mrs. Cohn glanced at Lucy, then back at Emma with a pointed look. 'You should know — '

'You should knowwww,' Emma mocked. Her wrist soared with pain. 'No. You don't tell me anything. You don't come here and tell me what's what. Oh, Emma, let me give you my dress, let me help you, oh, Emma, you should know . . . Oh, Lucy, maybe I can help. We don't need your help. We — '

'Stop! I'm sorry. I'll go. We'll arrange another time.'

Mrs. Cohn stood.

'That's it?' Emma said. 'You're sorry? You'll go? You'll run away, go cry to your uncle?'

'I don't know what I can do.' Mrs. Cohn looked desperately at Lucy, who looked at Emma, her eyelashes stuck into clumps, reminding Emma of a bird she'd found as a child, after a storm. This was in Banagher, not long before her father died and she left for

327

America. One of the bird's wings was broken, its feathers stuck together like Lucy's eyelashes were now. Emma brought it home. Her father, out of work again, wrapped it in a towel. But then Emma's mother walked in, took the creature from her father, and twisted its neck with one quick maneuver. 'It's better off that way,' she said. Thirty seconds later, Emma saw her throw the carcass to the dogs. That was her mother's order: healthy or dead, righteous or bound for hell. Emma didn't let her father see her cry. For a few days, the bird unsettled her, then she forgot about it. Now she thought of her father's helpless deference, how it had driven her to be another way, strong and separate, and how she had managed that, in some ways, and in other ways failed, allowed herself to be bossed and intimidated. She turned to Mrs. Cohn. 'I keep house poorly,' she said. 'But not as poorly as I did for you.'

Mrs. Cohn nodded. 'It wasn't what you were hired for. You shouldn't f — '

'I shouldn't what. Tell you how I enjoyed your dismay when you couldn't find something? How I despised you when you admonished me, making jokes you thought I wouldn't understand? The pillowcases and lions looking for their mates? You of the pure marriage.' Emma remembered Lucy, and saw that her eyes were swimming. She was younger, Emma realized, than Emma had been the day she found that bird. In a calmer voice, she said, 'There are other things I would like to say to you.'

'I understand.'

'Imagine me saying them.'

Mrs. Cohn watched Emma as if in a trance. She nodded slowly, her face bobbing in and out of the light. From the scratcher came the grainy sigh of a pear stem puncturing another pear.

'What can I do?' Mrs. Cohn's voice was barely audible, her eyes dark, sorrowful pools. Emma's wrist throbbed. She remembered Lucy, as an infant, looking up at her with those eyes. Lucy's claim on Emma had been so surprising, so complete. And the others had known. Roland especially had known. Roland, perhaps, had been the most jealous. Lucy's mouth had been full, her suck steady, bottomless, drawing Emma down into a quiet room where her muscles went soft. She was used to feeling like a kitchen table, at the center of everything yet barely noticed, a repository for hunger and want, but in the quiet room with Lucy she was seen. And the other children, her children, had waited while she stayed there, often longer than necessary, after Lucy was full. They must have been confused, perhaps hurt. But they had been patient. They had made way.

'You played piano,' Emma said. 'I read about it. You were supposed to have become a pianist. You were supposed to have been very good.'

Mrs. Cohn nodded, barely. Her eyes appeared to cross slightly, as if she were trying to retreat.

'So that's what you'll do.'

31

Susannah was not home. Josiah was late enough she should be home. She was home almost always. She didn't go anywhere unless it was to swim, or if Caleb drove her to the quarry, but she swam in the mornings and Caleb's car was here, parked in front of his house. At this hour, five o'clock, Susannah waited for him. She dressed for supper and waited, reading or pacing, until Josiah walked through the door. Then she was there, kissing him, handing him a drink, asking him to tell her the latest news from the quarry. He hated telling her about the quarry! He should be relieved that she wasn't home, he thought, asking him about the price of paving stones, or whether he'd instituted a company lunch on Mondays, as she'd suggested after the strike, to keep the men happy, by which she meant quiet. But he was not relieved. He needed to tell her about Emma. He had screwed her like an animal this afternoon. He had wanted to smash her for his helplessness, for the fact that he couldn't stop going to her even after the strike, after his apology and Susannah's forgiveness. He needed Susannah to stop him.

He took the stairs two at a time. Their bedroom was empty, as was the room with the twin beds, where he had slept since the last miscarriage, a full month ago now. The third bedroom was empty, its double poster bed as tightly tucked as ever. He knocked at the bathroom door. Sometimes Susannah took a bath after a swim. He pushed his way in. The tub was empty, and dry, with no stray hairs — it had not been used since the housekeeper came that morning. The silence of the house oppressed him. He pressed his hands together and brought them to his nose. They smelled of Emma. He turned on the sink faucet, then turned it off. He would not wash them. He would stick them in Susannah's face if he had to!

But where was she?

He walked to Caleb's house and opened the door without ringing. 'Susannah?' No one came. He pressed his ear to Caleb's closed office door. Nothing. (Caleb snored softly, a true gentleman.)

She was not at the bathhouse, or in the pool, so Josiah started down the path to the bay. Maybe he should have confessed to Caleb on the day of the strike, be done with it then, out of a job, out of his marriage, out of waiting for a baby. He might go back to Mason Street. He would live with his parents, work with his father, listen to his mother sigh each evening: *Oh, what does our Jo-Jo want?*

He did not know! He didn't know what he wanted any more clearly than he had when he was a boy. He strode quickly among the stunted trees that grew close to the water, the ground brittle under his feet. He could not remember the last time it had rained. Stepping out from the last cover of the cedars, he shielded his eyes. 'Susannah,' he said aloud.

He saw her robe, in a heap on the dock, and next to it her towel, laid flat to catch the sun. It was the first week of September, the bay already cooling — just standing here thinking of it made Josiah shiver. Thick tangles of seaweed floated up from the rocks. When the tide was low, Susannah headed up the river's narrow channel toward Conomo Point. But it was high now — she would have swum up the creek that wound through the marsh. The tide was very high, Josiah saw, so high she would have been able to swim straight across the grass in places, a thing she loved to do. He didn't know how she could stand it, any of it, the grass against her skin, the seaweed, the crabs and fish and dead things she couldn't see. Josiah had seen deer skulls wedged into the mud of the creek at low tide.

He squinted up the creek, but didn't see her.

He sat on the rocks and waited. She could not swim for more than thirty minutes, he didn't think, and she was fast. She would be back soon.

But thirty minutes later, she had not returned. This made no sense. He had not seen her swimming away and he did not see her swimming back. He saw only cormorants, and seagulls, and a lone egret standing out in the salt hay.

He worked over the situation calmly at first, considering without believing. He had thought before of Susannah dying, not with malice but with curiosity, as he assumed all married people did from time to time. He had imagined his own sorrow. He had imagined in some detail the emptiness of the house, and the people who would come to her service, Caleb's associates, the quarry workers, most of them people Susannah had met only once or twice, for Caleb had not kept his children anywhere long enough for them to learn how to make friends. He had imagined the Vermont black granite Caleb would choose for her headstone and the words Caleb would choose to be carved into it, and because this stirred up in Josiah the sort of irritation he was used to feeling toward his father-in-law on a daily basis, the exercise of considering Susannah's dying had seemed a somewhat mundane activity, not at all alarming.

But twenty minutes later, when he still could not see her, he did not feel curious. Panic rummaged through his joints, his digits began to shake.

Susannah!

Josiah started to see her where she was not, in patches of sunlight on the water, in the scrubby, rustling trees out on the little island. He had killed her, he thought. It came to him plainly. Sure, he had told himself it was out of respect that he did not return to their bed. He told himself couples slept in separate beds all the time. But it wasn't respect — she had asked him to come back. And it wasn't to punish himself that he squeezed onto the twin bed each night, the bed meant for a child, across from another bed meant for another child, both beds equipped with hidden trundles, for the children's friends. It was to punish her.

Susannah! His blood tried to leap up the creek, to fly out beyond the dock, over the river.

He had blamed her, he realized, not only for her failure to bear children, and her unwillingness to give up, but for involving him in it, for choosing him in the first place. From the beginning he had been suspicious of her affections — he had felt mocked by the vehemence with which she'd pursued him, and by the seeming joy with which she'd upset the hopes of an entire cadre of young men, the college-educated, world-traveled sons of Caleb's associates. He felt at least a little bit mocked by her all the time, he supposed, a state he survived by judging her. His judgments were so rampant and fundamental he had stopped noticing them. He judged her for wearing a swimming costume without a skirt, and for the fact that she had had it custom made. He judged her for her confidence, for the way she pointed, throwing her arm into it. He judged her for her long, shiny hair, hair he loved, and for her long, firm, blue-blood thighs, which he also loved. He judged her for the dock, all that teak stretching into the bay for a little swimming and one boat, and for the inboard tub her father kept tied to the dock. He judged her for the fact that her father didn't know how to sail, which was especially absurd, since Josiah judged anyone who could sail, too.

He was sorry. He saw her winging, a cormorant, and he saw her standing, a stump at the edge of the far woods. His vision seemed at once to contract and grow stronger, so that he saw, at his feet, through a pool of water gathered in the pink crease of the rock, how the pink was made of white and gray and red, how the

334

individual nubbles of white grew upon the gray and the gray upon the red. Susannah. He could not look up again to find her everywhere and nowhere. He had withheld affection from her, thinking it would toughen her up. He had feared if he loved her fully that her grief would become his own.

'Josiah!'

He scanned the water again, turning wildly, his sun-bleached eyes leaping with worms. He parsed out wind on the surface from a woman breaking through. Nothing.

'Joe!'

He felt mocked. He spun to face the trees. Had Caleb been watching him all this time?

'Over here, dummy!'

Susannah, out beyond the dock. Treading water. Waving. She was not coming from any direction he had expected her to come from. She must have swum straight across the bay, all the way to Crane Beach or Hog Island. More than a mile each way, and against the wind all the way back! Josiah started to laugh, a helpless, choking, hysterical laughter that heaved him forward, elbows to knees, then knees to rock. It took all his strength to lift his face to her, to lift an arm and wave. He was too pained by his laughter to call out. Susannah dropped under the water, stopping his heart. Then she was swimming toward him, her sharp, fine elbows pointing to the sky.

32

It was Lucy's idea that the children should use Mrs. Greely's piano for their lessons. Emma did not want them going to Mrs. Cohn's house, and besides, transporting them there would have required a coach, so a deal was struck: each Saturday Mrs. Cohn would come to Leverett Street and, on the Steinway Mr. Greely had given Mrs. Greely as a wedding gift, teach the children and Mrs. Greely how to play. The piano was a black-painted upright with vines carved into its front, through which you could see the hammers strike and retreat.

The first Saturday, Lucy sat beside Mrs. Greely on Mrs. Greely's cat hair-covered sofa as Jeffrey made his first tentative pokes at the keys. She had seen Mrs. Greely only once, on her way to the woods one night. Mrs. Greely had been leaning out an upstairs window without any clothes on, her breasts swinging like sinkers. Lucy had run. But up close, apart from a jiggle in her chin and her long white hair, the woman did not appear crazy: her skin was smooth and pink, her cheeks almost plump, her eyes sparkling. After Jeffrey went Liam, then Janie, then Maggie, then Anne, and all the way down to Joshua, who giggled as Mrs. Cohn showed him how to hold his wrists. Lucy winced, waiting for him to be admonished. It was her turn next. But Mrs. Cohn giggled back, and Lucy, bewildered, jealous, went outside to the porch, where she found Emma sitting by herself on the top step, her back to the music, like a guard dog.

'I don't want my lesson,' Lucy said.

Emma looked up. 'Are you sure?'

'I don't think I'll be any good at it.'

Emma nodded. She looked surprised, and also, Lucy could tell, pleased. Lucy sat down next to her. And so it went. During the fourth lesson, from their spot on the porch, Lucy and Emma listened to Janie, who had a natural talent, it seemed — already she was playing something recognizable as a song. It was almost October, the shadows purpling across Mrs. Greely's cluttered yard, the flame-colored leaves of sugar maples drifting steadily down from the woods. Mrs. Cohn had had the piano tuned and it sounded so nice Lucy regretted, a little, not taking the lessons herself. She might be a natural, given her resemblance to Mrs. Cohn in almost every other way. She handed Emma one of the pears Mrs. Cohn had brought with her that morning, and bit into another one herself. Emma had told Lucy the story now, of the night they found her in the orchard. Still, Lucy saw her go pale when Mrs. Cohn lifted the sacks of fruit from the trunk of her uncle's car. Mrs. Cohn had been learning to drive so she could make the trip to Lanesville by herself. 'They're overripe,' she apologized, setting bag after bag on the ground. 'I forgot about them this year.'

'Sweet,' Emma said now, as juice dripped down her forearm into the sleeve of her dress. 'Too sweet.'

Lucy nodded. The pears were too sweet, and a little mealy, but they would make good perry, she hoped. She peeled skin from hers with her teeth, and chewed that for a while before biting into the juicy part. Slowly, she made her way around the fruit like this, before she spoke the words she'd been rehearsing all morning. 'Mrs. Cohn's parents want to meet me.'

Emma wiped her arms on her skirt. She faltered with the right one — it hadn't broken, but was badly bruised. 'I guess that's not surprising.'

Lucy waited. A loud, dissonant chord came from inside. Mrs. Greely.

Emma squinted into the yard. 'Would you like to meet them?'

Lucy shrugged, her blood pounding.

'You can.'

Again Lucy shrugged. She thought she would cry if she started to talk. She couldn't have said why. She wasn't old enough yet to know that having choices could be as hard as not having them. She did want to meet her grandparents, of course she did. How could Emma not know that? Lucy squeezed the pear and it fell instantly apart, mush oozing through her fingers. In moments like this, Emma's grip on Lucy made Lucy want to escape her, too. Last week, in Emma's book, Lucy had found the address for Peter, a post office box in Quebec City, and, with the help of the postmistress, sent a postcard (*Are you still their? Your sister Lucy*) but immediately after she wondered if the postmistress would mention it to Emma and then she realized, if

338

Peter wrote back, that Emma would see his response first. And she might show Roland, which would defeat the whole exercise. *What are you, planning to go to Cah-nah-dah? Ha.*

And just to send the postcard had cost a penny, so she was even further now from her ticket to Quebec.

Emma squinted into the yard. She gazed up at the trees. She turned at the sound of a chipmunk. She looked everywhere but at Lucy.

'I do. I want to go,' Lucy said. 'I haven't had any grandparents,' she added, meaning it as a kind of excuse or apology but hearing, as it came out, how it might hurt Emma further. Emma got letters from her own mother once a month, but none of her children had ever met her. Lucy wiped the mess she'd made of her pear on the underside of Mrs. Greely's stair and Emma didn't scold her. She didn't seem to notice, or even to have heard what Lucy had said. But she had. Emma was thinking about how for so long she had let herself believe that she had saved Lucy from her beginnings — she had taken the girl's maturity personally, felt deserving of her peculiar contentment. But Lucy was no happier than anyone else. She must have known, even before she saw Beatrice Cohn, that she had been abandoned, unwanted. If she had seemed happy, it was out of desperation. If she had been protective of Emma it was so that she would be protected. Her extraordinary love was her need.

Emma threw what was left of her own pear into the trees, then said, 'I shouldn't have done that. That was very rude.'

'To Mrs. Cohn?' Lucy asked.

'Oh. No, to Mrs. Greely.'

Which gave Lucy an excuse to slip off and look for the pear, which she pretended took a long time, which was plausible because the ground was buried in leaves.

33

Lillian brought three gifts. First, a trio of rings her own mother had given her, not the finest pieces but they would mean something, she hoped, and they sparkled like a young girl should want, one ruby, one emerald, one sapphire, each with a tiny diamond at its center. The bands were gold and skinny, good for young fingers that didn't puff or swell. When Lillian's father had given them to her mother after she closed her shop, Lillian had thought, *Why bother now? Why not give her something when she could still appreciate it, wear it out to parties?* She was partially right — her mother had lived only two more years — but mostly wrong, she understood now, not only because her father hadn't had the money before that time but because he hadn't yet felt the need to give them. Last week, in the office of her analyst, Dr. M., Lillian had come to the realization that gifts were mostly for the people who gave them.

During her first session, lying on his couch, Lillian had waited for Dr. M. to tell her something. She had grown impatient. It seemed he should have answers. But by now, her fourth visit, she was used to the fact that he mostly asked questions, which she then tried her best to answer. It turned out she knew a lot about her own life, which shouldn't have surprised her, she supposed, but did, which was another thing, perhaps, to discuss with Dr. M. But for now she was agonizing over what to give the girl. It was nearly her first thought when Henry told her. A granddaughter! The details about pear trees and robbers slipped right past her. A gift! Might a dress be more appropriate than jewelry? Or maybe a beautiful box, to hold trinkets? Dr. M. interrupted her to ask, 'Is it possible with these gifts that there is something else you mean to say?'

She could not think how to answer his question. She went on to describe her mother's rings, and in describing them to decide they were right. But later, it struck her that Dr. M. was wrong. She didn't mean to say anything. She meant to change the girl in some way, leave a trace of herself, a mark.

This was the sort of thing she wasn't sure she even wanted to know about herself. It led to all the dresses she'd given Bea, the hairpieces and stockings and assorted undergarments she likely never wore.

Lillian had not told Henry about Dr. M. She was fully clothed on his couch, of course — though she had wondered, the first time, she could not deny wondering. She was a woman, he was a man, here was a couch, he gestured for her to lie down. It was impossible to know what was expected of her! But that was not the point. The point was money, or rather Henry's way of thinking about money: Either you bought a thing with your money or you saved it. If you paid for a service, it should be necessary, or at least measurable in some way — school for Bea,

342

Fainwright for Bea, the hair salon for Lillian, who was too old for all the rest. If Lillian wanted to fix her nose, as she'd been talking about since the war, Henry would pay for that. But how could she argue that going to Dr. M. was necessary? She wasn't clearly troubled. What proof would she have that it had worked? In Dr. M.'s office on Clarendon Street, amid the heavy furniture, behind the heavy door, reclining on his couch, Lillian forgot to hold her stomach in. She entered a loose, woozy state, as if she could be anywhere, anyone. This sensation crept up on her outside their sessions, too, Dr. M.'s baritone singing into her thoughts, *But why? Why did you lie to the women at the club? Is that really so? And what is it you dream?*

The second gift was from Estelle. Estelle had been unsurprised that Lillian and Henry weren't bringing her to meet Bea's baby, but not unhurt. She had given a twenty-dollar bill to Lillian that morning, and asked her to please pass it on to the girl. Lillian had protested — it was nearly a week's wages — but Estelle held firm. So Lillian had that, too, though she'd stuck it in a little box with paper and a bow to make it look less crass than paper money.

The third gift was a doll. In the car with Henry and Albert, on their way to meet the girl, clutching her gifts, Dr. M. asked, *Are you sure?* The doll had been Bea's, one of many Lillian had given her, though Bea had never especially liked dolls. This one had been sitting for years in her old bedroom, looking at the window. It was a collector's doll, more valuable perhaps than the

343

rings, with pale, porcelain cheeks, rosebud lips, blue eyes, yellow hair. For the trip to Gloucester, Lillian had put it in a white dress and tied back its hair with a pink ribbon. She held it in the crook of her elbow. But as the car neared Niles Beach, she started to doubt the wisdom of her choice, not just now but twenty years ago, when she'd given it to Bea. Not only did the doll look nothing like Bea, it was the very *opposite* of her, in every respect.

Lillian looked at the side of Henry's face. His cheeks had slackened since the news about the girl. Even his chin looked more relaxed. He tapped his fingers on his leg. The worst gift Lillian had ever given Bea came back to her now. It was the day of Bea's discharge from Fainwright. In a new mink coat Lillian waited, torn between satisfaction and alarm: Bea was done with this; but what would she do now? What could she be? At last Nurse Lugton appeared at the door to the reception lounge, holding Bea's hand, and Lillian led Bea out to a waiting car as darkly tinted as the limousine that had disappeared her to Gloucester. Bea did not look at her. She looked out her window. Lillian applied lipstick, which cracked at once — it was deep winter by then. As the car left Fainwright's grounds and pressed toward the city, she said, 'Don't worry. Estelle made you soup. I bought you a new robe.' She paused, looking out her own window, at black trees half etched with snow. There had been a storm, but the sky was blue. The robe waited at home on Bea's bed, wrapped in tissue and ribbons. It was long, and

344

mauve, and made of cashmere — Lillian had spent a full week shopping for it. She had missed her last visiting hour with Bea so she could find her the perfect robe. Outside the car, the trees began moving fast. She rested a hand on her daughter's leg and urged, 'Darling, it's from Milan. It's soft enough to wear all day.'

What did you want from her?

I must have wanted her to stay.

Now, again, a car. Trees. Hedges. Then they had turned up Ira's drive and Lillian, reaching automatically into her handbag, realized she had forgotten her lipstick.

'I don't have my lipstick,' she said. 'I left it in my other purse. I planned to wear that purse but then I changed my dress. I'm so stupid! How could I have forgotten? I never forget. How do I look? How do I look?' And Henry, looking at her carefully — always, he looked carefully, when other women's husbands glanced or ignored — said, 'Beautiful.' And Albert, turning in the front seat, said, 'He's right.' But Lillian didn't even know why she'd asked because she could never believe them.

Why not? Why can't you?

'I can't get out of the car,' she said. 'I won't, I can't. I can't look like a dead lady when I meet her. She'll be frightened! She'll hate me. How could I forget? I had days to prepare . . . ' And so on, until the driver pulled the car to a stop and Lillian, seeing her granddaughter's face, so like her daughter's face had been at one time, childish and bare, inquisitive and brave, waiting for her life to begin, was quieted by her own

345

tears. The doll was wrong, she understood, because it symbolized a baby. When Albert opened the door for her, she left the thing in the car.

★ ★ ★

Lucy had not seen a grown woman cry openly, but that was what her grandmother did now. At last week's piano lesson, Mrs. Cohn had taken her aside to say, 'My mother means well, but she can be a little standoffish,' so Lucy, once she figured what standoffish meant, had prepared herself for that. But not for this: the woman's shoulders jumping under her coat, tears dripping from her chin. Most disconcerting, she didn't bother to cover her face with a handkerchief. (Lillian had left that, too, in the other purse, with the lipstick.) She stared at Lucy as if hungry for her. Lucy might have yelped had soft hands not enveloped hers then — Mr. Haven's, cupping and smoothing Lucy's hands as if they were rare jewels. She had never known a man to have hands like her grandfather's. He murmured something about pleasure, then disappeared, leading Mrs. Haven away from the group, then Mr. Cohn was introducing himself with a warm, easy smile. He did not refer to their first meeting on Leverett Street — instead he began to ask Lucy entirely normal questions about school, which had started up again. And what grade was she in, and who was her teacher, and what was her favorite subject? Mrs. Cohn had said Mr. Cohn was not her father but Lucy couldn't help

346

searching his face for some evidence to the contrary. His features were sharp, his ink-black hair combed into neat waves, his eyelashes dark as a woman's, his cheekbones tall. Lucy wondered if her own cheekbones could be described as tall, if maybe this was why she had succeeded as a boy in the quarries for as long as she had.

'I'm very good in math,' she said hopefully, but Emma's clear disapproval — at Lucy's boast, at her secret, deep hope, which shamefully Emma could see — made Lucy close her mouth, and Mrs. Cohn, who had been standing next to Lucy all this time without saying a word, appeared to be in some kind of shock, and the four of them stood around in a stunned sort of shyness for a moment until Emma asked Mrs. Cohn how Mr. Hirsch was doing and Mrs. Cohn answered that he was well. Actually — emerging from her daze — he was very well. He was walking again, not far but walking. He was up on the terrace, eager to meet Lucy. And to see Emma, she added. She took Mr. Cohn's hand, as if for balance. At last Mr. Haven led Mrs. Haven back into the circle. Her eyes smudged with makeup, her hands trembling, she held out a blue velvet box to Lucy.

Lucy looked to Emma, who nodded.

Inside the box were three golden, sparkling rings.

'They're lovely,' Lucy said. And they were. Janie or Anne or Maggie would gasp. They would flap their hands on their wrists, commanding everyone to ooh and aah. But Lucy's thought

347

was that the rings must be worth something — maybe a lot. 'Thank you,' she said.

Mrs. Haven drew a ragged breath. 'You . . . ' She paused. Lucy waited. But her grandmother said nothing more. She handed Lucy another box, wrapped in a satiny, dark blue bow, then closed her mouth, swallowed audibly — a wet click — and, almost as if unbeknownst to her, began to smile. It was a tight smile at first, but soon her lips parted to reveal her teeth, and then her tongue, and then her obvious delight.

★ ★ ★

Lucy would wait to open the second gift. She was being ferried up to the terrace, where Mr. Hirsch sat, a lumpish man with a blanket on his lap. She felt tired suddenly, walking toward him. So many people to meet, and for what? She had wanted to come, but wasn't sure, now that she was here, what was happening. Did they expect she would visit regularly? Be part of the family? She couldn't tell what that would mean, or even what sort of family this was. There were no other children, as far as she could tell. Cousins had been mentioned, but weren't to be seen. The brothers' surnames didn't match, nor did their appearance: Mr. Haven had a thatch of coal-colored hair, Mr. Hirsch one white wisp winging at his ear. They were rich. Richer than anyone Lucy had ever met. And they were Jews. Lucy had never met a Jew, though apparently, at least somewhat, she was one.

Ira stared at her with such wonder that she

flinched at first. He reached for her and she bent, relieved when his kiss was dry, quick, and stubbly. 'Ahhhh,' he said, holding her away again. 'Henry's granddaughter.'

What could Lucy say to that? The entire situation was strange enough — why did it need saying, and with such drama? She felt at once overimportant and tiny, as if the adults were playing a game whose rules she didn't know, and she was their little checker.

★ ★ ★

Sometimes a change changes everything that came before it, too. For Ira, this was like that: it was as if a new color had been thrown across the past ten years, as if the energy he felt now, the optimism, was retroactively applied, so that when he looked back, his mood was better than it had in fact been. He felt expansive. The baby had not been drowned. Bea had not drowned it. She had left it in the care of the pear thieves! Henry was here, and Lillian, who for the first time since Ira had known her had nothing to say. And Emma, whom Ira had missed. She was drained of color, but of course.

Lucy Pear. What a name. Found amongst Ira's Braffets, imagine that! How horrible he'd been, to think Bea capable of drowning her. She looked so like Bea Ira felt a chill run through him — but her character, he thought, her essence, the pit of her, was different: if Bea was made of compartments, separated by doors that rarely opened, the girl was all one piece. Yet Bea had been like that, too, at this age, when she was Bea-Bea, running around with Julian. Seeing Lucy made that time vivid again. But Lucy wasn't Ira's, and he felt surprisingly fine about this — he had no desire whatsoever to rescue her, or even to know her particularly, only to know that she was.

Ira had his own granddaughter now, and perhaps that made a difference. Marlene Aimée, born to Julian and Brigitte on September 15 in New York City. It seemed a very serious name for a baby, but that would sort itself out.

But it wasn't just the babies. It was Bea, too, who had started playing again, who as she watched the girl now seemed to have slipped from her fortress, forgotten all self-censorship: her mouth hung open, her eyes were clear. And it was Vera, who had at last — quite abruptly — lost her solidity inside Ira, meandered into something else, a gentle, scintillating wind through his limbs, waking him up, pushing him on. A staggering relief. A blessing. Finally, he was giving them back.

★ ★ ★

Bea knew Henry's speech would fail from the start. She had never seen him so nervous, picking at his sleeves, shifting from one shiny Haven shoe to the other. 'On this lovely autumn day . . . I must confess I never imagined . . . a pleasure and an honor . . . befitting, to overlook such a prosperous harbor . . . ' He was trying to welcome everyone but was uncertain of his terms

350

— it wasn't his house, after all, and what was he welcoming them *to*? He was used to speaking, but about matters he'd already pronounced upon, meetings he'd already run in some other incarnation, versions of versions of the same speech. He ended abruptly, with a perhaps involuntary bow: 'We are so very pleased to meet you.' But he forgot to address this to Emma or Lucy — instead he looked at Bea, who looked back, aware suddenly that her father had aged. His large hands shook at his sides. The shaking was drastic. It appeared oddly celebratory, almost musical, like his fingers were sending off little fireworks. He looked happier, she thought, worn to a soft patina.

'Anyone for tea?' asked Lillian. She had stopped crying and stood awkwardly, not knowing what to do with her hands now that she had given up her gifts. When no one answered, she said brightly, 'I do. I need a cup of tea. I'll just say it. I'm saying it. Henry, come. Help. We don't want to protrude.'

Bea saw Emma bite back a grin. She smiled, trying to catch Emma's eye, to tamp down the thumping at her clavicle: *Please, look at me!* It was so childish yet powerful, her longing for Emma's attention, for some sort of acknowledgment. Each Saturday Bea went to Leverett Street to play piano with the children, but Emma barely looked at her. She stayed out on the porch with Lucy, acknowledging Bea only to say a curt 'Good morning' and 'We'll see you next week.' Even when Bea had brought Cousin Rose to look at Emma's wrist, Emma had thanked Rose

351

heartily yet said little to Bea. She had spoken to her plenty back when she was working in the house, but Emma had had her secret then, Bea supposed — it had been a thing she held over Bea. She had pretended to be kind but now she could not.

Still, Bea liked the visits to Mrs. Greely's house. She liked the disorder, and that no one ever remarked on it, liked that Mrs. Greely was so straightforwardly batty, which somehow did more for Bea than any treatment ever had to convince her of her own basic sanity. She liked teaching, too. It had been far simpler than she had imagined, to begin to play again: with Janie sitting beside her and the other children waiting, she had had to do it, to set her thumb upon the middle C and feel the ivory give as easily as water, and then it was done and she was doing it, just as she had begun speaking again, once upon a time, after her muteness. It was surprisingly easy, to make a different choice. It was easy to remember. She liked teaching the Murphy children. She liked seeing Lucy Pear, even if the girl shied from her and didn't want her lessons. Bea brought a check each week, enough to cover groceries and more, which she handed to Emma inside a bag of something else, bread or sometimes chocolates, and Emma was cashing the checks now — so there was that. Bea had not managed to raise the issue of Lucy's wound, or Mr. Murphy, though each time she passed the house on her way up the road a slickness rose at her neck. He didn't want to meet her, clearly, and Bea didn't especially want to meet him. She couldn't imagine what she would do with her eyes — look at where his leg had been? Not look? Would she apologize? Would she ask him what he had to do with Lucy's leg? And if she didn't, wouldn't she fail again, as she had failed from the beginning, to protect her? But Lucy's injury was hard to categorize, and relatively minor — you could not go leaping to conclusions about such things or even asking questions without seeming hysterical. She could raise it with Emma but feared Emma would take it badly, as if Bea were accusing her, if not of inflicting the wound then of turning the other way. So she'd said nothing, only handed Emma the bag with the check tucked discreetly inside. She behaved in the most appropriate way possible, she thought, given the circumstance. She tried not to intrude. Protrude.

She could not expect Emma to *like* her. So what was it she wanted, when she stood here trying to chase down Emma's eyes? What was it Bea wanted her to acknowledge?

Bea couldn't have said exactly, but Emma knew. Even as she avoided Mrs. Cohn's eyes, she understood that the woman now grasped what she had done, and that she was sorry, and sorrowful, and grateful, that she felt she owed Emma her life. Mrs. Cohn couldn't say this, which was fine by Emma. For her part, she would not tell Mrs. Cohn that she had seen how she suffered. She would not tell her she was forgiven. There were certain things — simple, yet immeasurable things — that could not pass directly between two people without seeming false, even crass, and these were among them.

'I'm happy to make your tea,' Emma said to Mrs. Haven. 'But first . . . ' She squeezed Lucy's shoulder. 'Tell Mrs. Cohn where you'd like to go.'

Lucy stared at Emma. She had said nothing about wanting to go anywhere.

'It's all right. Tell her.' Emma tilted her chin toward the end of the terrace, where the stairs led down into the trees. 'You'd like to see the orchard.'

Lucy's cheeks flushed the color of plums.

'Oh!' Mrs. Cohn cried, a beat too late, as stunned as Lucy. She smiled. 'Of course!'

'It's all right,' Emma said again, giving Lucy a tiny, invisible push. 'Go on. I'll be in the kitchen, then I'll be right here. I'm not going anywhere.'

★ ★ ★

The orchard was not as Lucy had understood it to be. In the dark, it had seemed to her vast and pungent, a whole country of pears. But it wasn't an orchard so much as a field with a few pear trees in it. They were bare and gray. The middle one — Lucy's tree — looked no different. The ground was splotched with rotting fruit and overgrown with thorns. Mrs. Cohn talked about how the soil was this and the pears were that and then she started to say that she wasn't actually sure about anything she was saying because she'd heard it so long ago, and from Uncle Ira, when Lucy, unable to listen any longer, broke in to ask, 'Will someone clear it?

354

Before it's back to brambles?'

Mrs. Cohn stopped walking. 'I don't honestly know.' She pointed. 'That's the old fish pond my aunt Vera used to keep.'

'Did she die?'

But Mrs. Cohn was looking up, at the tree above her, or the sky. Lucy caught a low branch and started to pull it back and forth as she watched the long stretch of Mrs. Cohn's neck, its slight undulation as she spoke. 'I told you, before, that I forgot about the pears this year. That was untrue.'

Lucy said nothing. It seemed to be a mild lie.

'I thought you should know.' Mrs. Cohn looked at her. 'I don't forget.'

Lucy nodded. 'Okay.'

'Shall we sit?'

Lucy sat. A look of regret came over Mrs. Cohn's face. 'Are they painful? The prickers?'

'Not really.'

Slowly, Mrs. Cohn knelt next to her, taking care to tweeze the brambles back with her fingers, though once she was seated in her little clearing, they popped back into place, surrounding her. She smiled an effortful smile. A gull called. From the slide of its shriek, Lucy could tell it was diving. She watched a caterpillar crawl onto her mother's skirt. It was the black and gold kind, so fat and furry its progress was barely perceptible — Lucy knew it moved only because its colors rippled, and because after a little while it rounded Mrs. Cohn's knee and began the long trip up her thigh. For a long moment Lucy allowed herself to imagine that this was her life,

355

that there was no Emma or Janie, no quarry, no hoarding of pennies, that it was just Lucy and her mother sitting in a field together until they decided to walk back up the hill to their enormous house. She imagined piano lessons in her own living room, trips to Boston, marble floors in department stores, plush red seats in theaters.

'Lucy. Remember when you showed me the wound on your leg?'

The caterpillar paused. It lifted its fat head and swung it around.

'Was it your . . . Was Mr. Murphy responsible for that?'

Woolly caterpillar, Lucy remembered. Peter had taught her that. Also, Peter had shown her how the gulls got their meat. *Look*, he'd said, pushing her cheek to make her turn, focus: he wanted her to see how one gull dropped a mussel from the sky and another gull stole it before the first could fly down.

'Lucy?'

She didn't like how Mrs. Cohn said her name. Loo-See. The syllables were too distinct, the thing broke into pieces. Lucy had shown her. But that didn't mean she wanted to talk about it. She wanted it to be solved, wanted it to stop. There was a new blister on her other side now, in the crease where her leg joined her hip. But it, like all the others, didn't look so bad. It could be from banging into a chair at school. It could have happened in any number of ways. It could be that Roland never meant to hurt her. It could be he couldn't stop himself. He loved her. She knew

356

he loved her. She felt shame roll through her, a black, heavy sludge through a small, small space.

'Lucy. I don't mean . . . What I'm saying . . . I want to help you.'

Lucy jumped up. She was sure she should run, and equally sure that she had nowhere to go. The field seemed private, the road hidden, but Lucy had walked from here to Lanesville — she understood now that neither was as it appeared. Any distance could be closed, any secret stolen. Everything she'd had for herself — the quarry, Emma's nighttime wanderings, Roland's punishments, Lucy's own beginnings — had been taken from her, or exposed.

She hoisted herself into the lowest notch of the middle tree and began to climb. Up, the sky blue, open wide. But the tree was short, the trip over too quickly, and from the highest branch she couldn't see anything she hadn't been able to see before. Mrs. Cohn looked up at her and Lucy saw that it wasn't easy for her to watch Lucy up there, balanced, no hands, and so she stayed, the sun hot in her hair, and called down: 'You want me to come live here, with you? That's what you're saying?'

'No! No.'

Mrs. Cohn's vehemence was startling. 'You wouldn't want me . . .'

'Of course I would! I would. But Emma . . . What I'm saying — '

'She would never.'

'Never.'

'Plus you don't want me.'

'Lucy.'

357

Loo-See.

'What I'm saying . . . '

'Why don't you just say it!'

Lucy waited. She wanted to be scolded, punished, but she didn't know this — she knew only that the sun was hot and her throat full with the shame. Then she saw that Mrs. Cohn was standing. She wasn't looking at Lucy anymore but at something ahead of her, something Lucy couldn't see. She noted the top of her mother's head, the pale part amidst the dark, kelpy hair, how much paler it was than the rest of her. Lucy had the urge to curl up in that narrow place, protected and unseen.

'Lucy. Come down.'

This was said firmly, by Emma. It had been her job from the beginning, to enter quietly, and now she had done it again, she had found she couldn't not do it, she had placed the teacup and saucer in Mrs. Haven's lap and excused herself, followed them, heard everything.

Lucy stayed in the tree.

'This is what you were trying to tell me? He's done something to her?'

Mrs. Cohn's voice was a threadbare string. 'You couldn't have known.'

'Of course I could. I'm her mother.'

Lucy crouched in the branches. She stared at her shoes, which Emma had polished for this occasion.

'You're not to blame,' said Mrs. Cohn.

'We're all to blame.'

They were silent. The gulls, having moved on, called gently. Lucy watched as Mrs. Cohn discovered the caterpillar crawling up her arm and did not scream but — surprising Lucy, and comforting her, and breaking her heart all over again — took the thing and cradled it in her hand.

'Lucy. Come down.'

But she couldn't think how to go down, not with Emma knowing what she now knew. Not the motions of it, feet, arms, hands, and not what she might do once she was there. She couldn't imagine meeting their eyes, or letting them touch her.

They waited.

34

Bea told Albert the truth that night, after everyone had left and Ira had gone to sleep. The lieutenant's courteous stride, undersized for such a tall man, as he followed the admiral into her parents' parlor. How delicately his large hands held his lowball as Lillian cornered and harassed him. How genuine his smile had been, as if he knew nothing about his own astounding teeth. How Bea had not minded at all when Lillian pushed him toward her. *A walk, a walk!* A shock, especially ten years ago, that Lillian had encouraged such a thing. But the streets would not have been empty. The common was lit. If they had gone outside, they would not have been alone.

They had not gone outside. On the stairs, instead of down, they had gone up to Beatrice's bedroom, her little writing table, her dolls, her brass bed. It was shocking, she was shocked, the whole way, the entire time. There was some talk, as if he were a friend of her father's, but she was fully grown, and she was not occupying the part of herself that spoke and nodded and smiled and fiddled with the loose knob on the bedpost as if she would momentarily lead him out of the room and back downstairs. She closed the door. A shock. But Estelle was busy downstairs. The gramophone played loudly. To blame Lillian was not entirely wrong — she had been neglectful, crass, she had thrown her daughter at the man like a souvenir — but neither was it accurate. Lillian had meant for them to walk, as Bea and Albert were walking now, on the road out to the point. Lillian had in her mind a stroll, however ill conceived. But it was Bea who closed the door, Bea who stood, waiting, having no idea what to do, aware only of the heat that ran through her. She had felt this heat before, in the company of Julian — she knew it would scatter eventually, ache a little, wane. But she did not think far enough ahead to think of that.

Deep down, maybe, she wanted to punish Lillian, show her. And Julian? She did not want to punish Julian, she wanted to marry him. And yet. She could see her life so clearly, now that he'd come out and asked, now that she'd nodded Yes: Radcliffe (or really, why bother with Radcliffe?), marriage, babies, the piano's natural retreat into hobby, a toy into its corner. Lunches with Lillian. She would be the exact woman she was raised to become.

Some part of her might have flinched at this. Some part of her might have wanted to blow it all down. But even that wasn't fair — she wanted to do what she was doing. She stood, and waited. He hesitated, and she waited, and then she lay under him on her own bed, not against a wall, not even crying out when it hurt, which it did, though not badly. He was very gentle. Mostly what she felt was fascination; mostly what she wanted was to know. He was apologetic, flustered. He left the room immediately and waited for her in the hall.

It was a terrible lie she had told. It was cheap, and she had told it enough that she had come to a way of believing it: she had built in her memory his forcing, her resistance.

'When I think of Lucy,' she said (she had told Albert what Mr. Murphy did to the girl, just on the periphery of violence, just bizarre enough not to warrant straightforward punishment), 'it's like I've been mocking her.'

They had passed the yacht club and were nearing the end of the point. The lighthouse rose up before them, forever like a man to Albert, spreading its affections, one, two, three, four, until it shone for him, briefly, and withdrew again.

'It was what was expected of you,' he said. 'To cry rape. Lillian practically fed it to you.'

'I never had any trouble refusing her food.'

'She cooked?'

'No, though that's not my point and you know it. Estelle cooked.'

'Good. Then I'm only in for one surprise tonight.' He laughed, throwing an elbow at Bea, but she walked heavily, her eyes straight ahead.

'I've told worse lies, you know,' he offered.

Without pausing, Bea stepped out onto the first slab of the breakwater. She thought he meant their marriage, he realized — she thought he was exaggerating his sins for her benefit, making a joke.

'Really,' he said. 'In college . . . '

'I'm planning to give her money,' Bea said. 'To help her get to Canada.' She was taking the stones in large strides, though the moon was

362

skinny, the night dark — apart from the intermittent sweeps of light, Albert could barely make out the gaps between the rocks, some as long as a man's foot.

'You can't do that,' he said.

'I told you, didn't I, about her brother?'

'Still, you can't do that.'

'I can.'

'What about Emma?'

'She'll understand.'

'Bea. Think about this.'

'I have. The girl is stronger than she looks.'

'You think strength has served you well?'

Bea didn't respond. Albert stopped walking. He let her get two stones, four, six ahead. 'You think you can just step in with your money and be forgiven?' he shouted.

She was a shadow. The breakwater ended in a few hundred yards — she would have to return. He sat down to wait, the granite damp through his trousers, his fingers finding a snail that had been tossed up by the last high tide. He put his thumb in the hole, felt the thing retreat. He thought of last week's party, at Lyman Knapp's house. Like all of Lyman's parties, it had consisted of small groups around cocktails, people spilling onto the terrace, mostly artists and musicians and poets who, thank God, didn't bother to ask Albert what he did, the women in short dresses and the men without neckties. The talk was of travel and music and politics and, sometimes, in low tones, of baseball, as if Ruth and Gehrig's home-run race should not be of interest to imaginative people. There was a general apathy at the news that Coolidge would not run again — what difference would it make? After the execution there had been a communal moment of silence, followed by a debate over whether the communist intelligentsia had really wanted them kept alive or whether they were worth more to the movement dead. But last week, the guests were raucous again, dancing and laughing. Albert, as usual, stood at the edges — he had been taught wit with different sorts of people — feeling stiff and too obviously handsome, watching as Lyman poured and greeted, waiting to see if he would be chosen again. He always was — each time, when all the guests were gone, Albert was the one Lyman chose, the one he brought to various bedrooms, each elaborately decorated in a different style, with angled ceilings and oddly shaped windows, Albert he laughed with about the name Knapp, for he loved to nap, and the name Lyman, and about Albert's long ago hearing Lyman's house described as 'the homosexual house' (Albert didn't mention whom he'd heard this from). Albert was attracted to Lyman's boniness (like someone else's), to the traveling knob of his Adam's apple. But last week, hours into the party, he started to despair, for beyond filling his glass, Lyman had yet to acknowledge him. The decision, it seemed, had to be made again. The entire procedure — waiting to be picked, being in a place as himself, belonging (in the most unacceptable way) and not belonging at all (in more acceptable ones) — felt like a small chastening. It made Albert feel a little better. A little cleansed. But unhappy. Until at last Lyman brushed hard against him, and Albert flushed.

He hummed to the snail. Ira had taught him this, down at Mother Rock — it drew the things out. Ira said Vera had taught him, and one of her brothers had taught her. (Who had taught the brother?) Albert guessed the snail might mistake the humming for water, or maybe the company of another snail, *something*, in any case, to see or do or eat, which is why, half a minute after he'd started humming, he stopped, feeling guilty. His growing sense was that promises were almost impossible to keep, even if you seemed to have kept them, because by the time the thing panned out, whatever you had imagined and wanted when you had made or received the promise had changed. He and Bea had done what they had said they would do, they had borne each other up, they had loved each other, if one was flexible with terminology. Their vows had served them, to a point. But the point was behind them now — they had outgrown the arrangement. Bea would not ask him to tell her about his lie. She had barely heard him. And so they had failed, in fact, to do what they had promised, which was, if you stripped it all down, yanked off the pretty shell, to protect each other from themselves.

'Let's not talk about that anymore.'

She stood over him, her voice gentle. He patted the rock, realizing too late that he was growing cold. But Bea was warm from her brisk walk, and leaned into him, apologizing, so he leaned into her, fending off his chill.

'I'm going to find my own apartment,' he said.

Bea shrank. 'Because I'm giving the girl money?'

'That has nothing to do with it. That's your decision to make. But you won't make it. You'll bring her here. You'll bring them all here.'

She was silent for a minute.

'But you don't need your own apartment.'

'You've lived in a box,' he said. 'I'm letting you out.'

'You can't. You didn't put me there.'

'But I can let you out. I'll push, if I have to. Imagine a mother duck, shoving her young from the nest.'

'Don't flatter yourself.'

'Imagine a man, then, pushing you out of a box.'

'You're talking about yourself. Every time you say 'you,' you mean 'I.''

'I mean both of us, maybe.'

'I can't keep the house myself. Where will I go?'

'You're already here.'

She shrank further. It always surprised him, how well he knew her body though he had never seen it unclothed, how he could perceive the slightest shifts in her temperature or heart rate. He held her hand. 'It's not a tragedy, Bea, to do what you want to do. Even if it feels right — or easy, God forbid.'

She was silent for a while. 'Ira won't live forever.'

'And you can drive now,' he said encouragingly. 'You can travel. I'll travel with you.'

She sniffed softly, in a way he knew to be

laughter. 'You'll travel with Mr. Knapp.'

'Do you know, Beatrice Haven Cohn, that in some parts of the world, twenty-seven is not so old?'

He'd forgotten the snail, tucked into his palm between their hands, but she took it from him now and chucked it into the water. They waited for the plonk. 'So you're not asking me.'

'No.'

'Will you go to Knapp's tonight?'

'Probably.'

He followed her gaze across the harbor, to the lights of the town. She sat for a while, seeming to consider, then leaped to her feet. 'Let's get you back, then,' she said, and started to walk.

'Slow down,' he said. 'You'll twist an ankle.'

'Again, you're worried about yourself. Enough. I'm hungry,' she added, with a bare little whimper that made him want to cry. But she slowed, and they walked home arm in arm, and after he had warmed soup for her, and toasted bread, and toasted more bread — he had never seen her eat so much — he went out again. It was later than he'd gone before, the guests gone home, and still, again, Lyman let him in.

35

If you flew above Essex Bay — thirty years later Josiah would do this, holding Susannah's hand, bound for a month in Paris, astounded as the familiar curve of beach and dune and river came into view, the place they lived flattened into color, white and blue and green, the effect bizarrely tropical — you would have seen a rowboat and a swimmer charting a slow, steady course between the shore and Hog Island. This was the deal they had struck the night after Josiah thought she'd drowned. He'd taken her to their bed, and made love to her, and it was good, and afterward, he said, 'I'm done trying to have children.' She was quiet for a long time, curved against him, her hair smelling of salt. Finally, she said, 'I'd like to swim the Boston Light. I know I'm not Trudy Ederle, but I'd like to try.'

It was an eight-mile swim, nearly four times as far as she had swum before.

She needed him to come home from work when the tides were right and follow her out into the bay. Josiah's pulse began to throb. He had the sensation, as he told her he was afraid of the water, that he was meeting Susannah again, for the first time. She looked quizzical, and for the briefest moment, disappointed. 'You're quite a man,' she said, and he pulled his hand away from her leg, seizing with regret for having told her. But she put his hand back. She wiggled closer to

368

him. 'So you'll have something to reach for, too.'

They had until next July to train. It was the middle of October now, the water cold enough Josiah wouldn't even put his feet in, but Susannah hated swimming pools and insisted on two more weeks in the bay. Josiah rowed. His worry for himself had shifted easily onto Susannah. She had slathered herself in petroleum jelly and lard, but what if she froze anyway? What if she swallowed water, or was taken out on the tide, and he could not save her? What if the whitecaps that rose up quickly some afternoons overwhelmed her? But he understood that she had to swim, and so he rowed. He was used to seeing the sandbar rise up beneath the boat now, the water so shallow he could see the ridges on the backs of horseshoe crabs. He was getting stronger on the oars. In a few more weeks, he would be elected mayor. Fiumara had pulled out, forced by allegations of terrorist involvement. The allegations were vague (Josiah's father had been involved in stirring them up, though Josiah would never know this) but there was the man's socialism, too, and with Sacco and Vanzetti dead, people's tentative sympathies in that direction had shriveled. The men were on their way to being forgotten.

Josiah was resolved to his fate, but determined to serve only one term. If Coolidge could pull out in front of the whole nation, Josiah thought, he could do the same in Gloucester. Granted, Coolidge's son had died — some people said this was behind the president's decision — but Josiah had his reasons, too. There was, for instance, the fact that he didn't want to be mayor at all. This, too, he had told Susannah. That had been a relief.

In the meantime, in the abstract, he would continue overseeing the quarry. But Susannah would be manager now. She would do the work she already knew better than he how to do, in the corner office that had belonged first to her father and then to her husband and from which she could see, if she pressed her cheek against the wall, an unimpeded view of Ipswich Bay. She would close the doors some days, unable to speak for the grief that seized her, for all she had agreed to let go, but with time this happened less. She was free now, her mind unclouded with thoughts of her body, her body no longer bound by doctors and false hope. She lost track of her cycles. She kept Sam Turpa on. Her door stayed open.

Caleb was not there to naysay these changes. A month ago, he had dropped off a card inviting Josiah and Susannah to dinner in his formal dining room, where he had laid out one of his prized maps on the table. *South America!* he had cried as they entered. He would go for a few months, maybe a year. Chile, Argentina. He would see about a trek into Patagonia. He would write them. It would be good to get away.

He had gone, leaving almost no instructions about the quarry or the estate. Josiah and Susannah were left to handle paydays, the union, the shrinking demand for stone. Despite pressure from his father, Josiah had not added his own name to the company sign. He would not try to replace Caleb. The trees on the estate had not been trimmed. When Josiah looked back at it now from the middle of the bay, the buildings were barely visible, the bathhouse a little white lump behind the pines.

Susannah stopped to rest. She didn't hold on to the boat — holding on was a disqualification — but treaded water, her eyes on the still distant mound of Hog Island.

'Your lips are purple,' he said.

'I'm cold.'

'Come in.'

She swam on. Her pace was slowing, but he would say nothing more. His fear was nothing compared with her desire. The muscles in her arms twisting and pulling, the gust of her inhale when her face lifted from the water. Her beauty stunned him, and not in a brotherly sort of way.

The day after their dinner at Caleb's, he had picked up Emma at the coffee shop and surprised her by staying parked on Washington Street, in full view. He was the opposite of artful. His sternum felt bruised. He could not look her in the eye. 'I can't see you again,' he said. Why was he surprised when she did not weep or berate him but sat still as a rock, forcing him to look at her face in profile, her hard jaw, her throat visibly working back tears? 'I'll get myself home,' she said after a few minutes in silence. Then she was gone from his car and walking toward Leverett Street. Josiah, feverish, thinking what did he have to lose, thinking, *Go, go, finish cleaning up the messes you've made*, drove straight from there to the Hirsch estate, to

371

apologize to Beatrice Cohn for the way he'd dropped her from the campaign. She looked different — less standoffish. She listened. He was focused on getting back to Susannah, determined to do the deed and run, but Mrs. Cohn's face, listening, was so reminiscent of Emma's dark girl, who had looked out at him from the perry shack with her dark eyes that bore through you, asking for something, though he couldn't figure what, it shook loose a quaking in Josiah. And though he did not put it all together the way it was, he did have the thought, as he drove home to Susannah, that some people try very hard to have children and others not to have them but that there is never, ever a way to even it all out.

'Okay.' Susannah's bone white fingers gripped the gunwale. 'I'm done.'

As Josiah moved to help her up, the boat tilting drastically, the dark water sloshing beneath him, he saw that he could never do what Susannah did. No matter how strong he got at rowing, he could not get into that water and swim. Nausea choked him. But he remembered to spread his legs and hold the back one firm for counterbalance and he managed, grunting, Susannah's legs nearly useless with cold, to haul her up onto the bench. He wrapped her in blankets, poured her the chocolate he'd brought, and turned the boat toward the shore. The beach swung into view, then a pair of seals, flopping up onto an edge of exposed rock. The tide was turning. He rowed harder. 'It'll be all right,' he said. 'Even Ederle trains in a pool, you know.'

Susannah nodded. Her teeth chattered. Her goggles had left deep circles around her eyes. A chunk of lard had congealed at the tip of her nose. She smiled. Even her gums were purple. He had not noticed Susannah's gums before. 'It'll be fine,' she said, and closed her eyes, letting steam from the cup warm her face. 'I can see now that I'm going to make it.'

36

In the dug-out cellar under the perry shack, Emma and Lucy faced the barrels. There were four — a little better than Emma had feared but not a fifth of what they dreamed in their dreaming days, which seemed dream-like now: Emma hunched over the PEAR VARIETIES pamphlet, Lucy reading over her shoulder, trying out the words, 'bung,' 'bunghole,' 'wintering.' Now Emma held the bungs, and Lucy the hammer. She had been full of her usual questions last night — were the bung-holes in the barrels in fact big enough, and was the juice actually done fermenting, and what would happen if they put the bungs back in before it wasn't? — but now that they stood here, ready to complete the task, which was simple after all, and so much smaller than they had hoped, she was silent. The other children had left for school. They had lost interest in the perry long ago.

'Don't be blue,' Emma said. Though she was blue, too. She had walked Lucy through all the reasons the perry didn't really matter anymore: There was the job at Sven's. The weekly check from Mrs. Cohn. There was the fact that Lucy no longer needed to go to Canada. Any time Roland called her to him, Emma called her away. What should they care about the perry? Yet they did. Perhaps its meagerness made them care more.

'Where should we start?' Emma said. 'You choose.'

Lucy walked to the nearest barrel, holding out her free hand for a bung. It was cold and dark in the cellar, the only light what drifted down through the turnip-bin hole from the already-dim shack above, and as Emma passed Lucy the bung, she was suddenly uncertain that Lucy's hand was as close as it appeared to be. This was an illusion — the bung made a flawless trip from Emma's fingers to Lucy's — but it left Emma with a kind of vertigo, the sense that she was drifting, only half real, through a shifting scenery, the edges of things blunter or sharper or further or closer than they'd been a moment ago, the known world untrustworthy. She experienced this frequently since she overheard Mrs. Cohn and Lucy in the orchard, since she looked for herself at Lucy's leg — it was her hip, really, that nascently curving hip — a dizziness close to dread except it wasn't dread because it was a feeling about something that had already happened. And it wasn't as straightforward as rage, either, because Lucy's wounds were nothing Emma recognized, they weren't slaps or burns, they were in a category she had no name for. Lucy would not speak about them — they had to speak for themselves. Their very strangeness, their inexplicability, allowed Emma, most of the time, to be more mystified than she was angry. She was repulsed by Roland's behavior, but because she could not understand or classify it, it didn't seem quite to count. Yet she couldn't discount it either — even if Emma

375

had been able to, Lucy would not let her. Every day at some point Lucy asked why, after the perry was put up, they couldn't go away, to Mrs. Cohn's, for instance, or somewhere else? And Emma would say, in a placid, queer voice, *He's a broken man, Lucy-boo. He'll come out of it. We've got to give him time*, even as her innards rebelled, twisting and snagging. She had the runs nearly all the time now.

Lucy set the bung in the hole, hammered once, twice.

'All set?' Emma asked.

Lucy nodded.

'Want me to do the next one?'

'I'll do it.'

No matter how many times Emma said to Lucy, *I won't let him do it anymore*, the girl's edge would not loosen. Emma tried not talking about it, but that didn't seem to help. She tried spoiling Lucy, giving her extra honey in her porridge, singing her two songs at bedtime, but Lucy didn't want anything extra. She wanted to be like everyone else. She wanted Emma to leave her alone — if they weren't going to leave, she could at least leave her alone. Emma understood this, but she couldn't do it. Instead she crowded her, watched her incessantly. She was physically incapable of anything else.

The second bung, the third. *Thwing*, went the hammer. *Thwing*. The fourth. Lucy tapped it once more, then said, 'I should get to school.'

Emma nodded. Sorrow jammed her throat like a fist. Lucy was extraordinary. Capable. Self-sufficient. Mature. But all her precociousness seemed to Emma double-sided now: a thing to behold, a thing to regret. And her body, too, how fast she was growing, changing, compared with her sisters — Emma could not think of that and she could not avoid thinking of it. If Lucy wasn't so special, Emma felt certain, Roland wouldn't have hurt her.

Which was the worst way of blaming the girl, really. It made Emma like everyone else in the world. And because it wasn't something she had said — because it didn't need to be said — it was something she couldn't take back. She could only nod as Lucy started up the ladder. The girl's trials had leaped even further beyond Emma's own — there seemed to be no way to catch her now, no way to know or comfort her.

'It's going to work,' Emma said. 'You'll see. In the spring. We'll pour it out and boom! Perry of the highest order.'

Lucy turned. 'How do you know?'

Emma looked around at all the barrels they hadn't filled (barrels paid for by Josiah Story, who had rejected Emma with such abrupt certainty she felt she'd been slapped). She didn't know. She didn't know how the perry would fare — or Lucy, either. She didn't know how to help her. She found herself wishing the girl would say it for her, accuse her outright: *You don't know.* But Lucy wouldn't do that. It wasn't her job to do that. Emma was a coward. If she weren't such a coward, she would tell Lucy the truth. If she weren't such a coward, she would leave Roland. She did think of it. Of course she did. Before they left the orchard Mrs. Cohn had offered her uncle's house as a sort of way station for Emma and the children. *I know you wouldn't want to live here, but for a while . . .* she'd said, as Emma braced herself. Saying yes, she was almost certain, would be an admission of failure on an intolerable scale. She considered asking Sven's wife if she would temporarily take them in; or going to Sacred Heart, asking there, though the parish knowing the situation was almost unimaginable. Emma even wondered if Mrs. Greely would take them for a time, until Roland . . . But what? What would Emma wait for Roland to do or not do? Emma had not confronted him. She couldn't imagine what she would say. Each time she thought of it, she heard him laughing, heard her own confusion — Emma would leave because of the nonsense with Lucy, was that all? — saw herself slithering away.

Lucy waited on the ladder. Emma didn't have to talk to him, of course. She could just leave. Women did this. They left. But Emma was scared. She was scared of what she knew people would think. Leaving was sin enough — *A woman might as well run naked through a butcher shop*, Emma's mother used to say — but to leave the poor, maimed fisherman? She was scared, too, about the chimney catching fire. How would Roland put it out? How would he fetch wood in the first place? She worried about his loneliness. She worried about his dying from it, worried he was the sort of man who might, who fought people off but needed them to survive. She loved him, though the love was deformed now, much of it piled up behind her, though she felt hate for him, too. She envied Josiah, going back to stay with Susannah with such apparent confidence. That was how he'd phrased it, coldly: *going back to stay.* As if otherwise Emma might stand around waiting for him to defect again. No. She had gone and confessed. At last. Then she had knelt on the bare wood floor of her bedroom and done what Roland wanted her to. That was not how the priest phrased her penance — *Go tell your husband you love him*, he'd said — but it was Emma's interpretation.

'I don't know,' she said at last. 'I don't know if the perry will work.'

Lucy, on the ladder, looked at her with impatience. 'I'm sorry,' Emma said, but Lucy was already disappearing through the hole above. Emma followed her up and out into the yard, where the breeze coming up off the cove bit through her dress.

'Lucy!' cried Joshua, running out of the house. 'Don't go to school. Stay with me.' He jumped up and down, tugging on Lucy's hand, begging her, 'Don't go!' A fresh fear spun through Emma. She dressed Joshua, and bathed him when Lucy didn't. She had not seen marks on him, but was there something she missed? She had seen nothing of what Roland had done to Lucy. When he tickled and squeezed the other children, did he hurt them in some way, too? She had thought it sweet — before the accident, he had not touched them at all. She had gone on pretending it was sweet even after seeing Lucy's leg — she refused to watch him obsessively, refused to suspect. Who could live like that? But what if she was wrong? What if her delusion ran that deep? Nausea rolled through her. They would have to leave, she understood — it was the only way forward, the only way to live right again. She cradled her wrist, though it was fully healed now, the cradling a habit that would break of its own accord once she and the children were gone from him. She did not think to worry about herself. Other people would do that, later: her children, Sven and his wife, Mr. Hirsch. Mrs. Cohn, though she did not offend Emma by saying it. The men whose coffee she poured in a different shop, in Rockport, where she and the children were living — in Juliet's house — by the time summer came around again. The women in her new parish. Everyone worried that Emma was lonely. And she was, sometimes. Sometimes she woke to find that she was groping herself — she woke from dreams of Roland, or Josiah, or another man, a stranger. But that kind of loneliness lived in one corner. Her days were filled with people. She did not often have time to dwell. And when she did, she found that her thoughts were not unhappy. She had a great capacity, inherited from her father and passed on to Lucy, for close, consuming observation. This was a discovery, once she broke through her pride and asked her own daughter to take her and the children in; and later, when she found a place she could afford on her wages alone; and later still, when her children did not need her so acutely: how long and with what pleasure Emma could sit watching a bird building a nest or a flag snapping in a wind or other people's children running in circles.

'Play with me, please?' begged Joshua.

'I've got to go to school, boy-boy.'

Joshua's face crumpled as Lucy patted his head. He whimpered, 'Don't go.'

Lucy looked to Emma for help, but Emma shrugged. She wanted Lucy to stay, too. She could take them both to work with her. She could set them up in the sunny part of the room, buy them pencils and paper at the penny store, watch them draw as she worked.

Lucy squatted next to the boy. 'I'll be back. Cheer up. Be good. Take care of Mummy. If you're good, I'll help you make a Halloween costume tonight.'

But she didn't go. It was as if her will had deflated, as if she'd used it all up in the cellar, shutting the bungholes. She took Joshua's hand and walked with him at his slow, tottery pace to the coffee shop and sat with him in the sunny half of the room and drew and took him down to the cove and brought him back and spent the rest of the day where Emma could see them, just as Emma had hoped.

37

By the middle of November, Bea had gained twelve pounds. When her cycle came, she bled heavily. She had forgotten how nearly black the blood could be, forgotten amid the meek, irregular dribbling of the past decade that there was something reassuring about a dark, monthly, soil-smelling exodus. She had forgotten her body. It returned to her now, flesh at her hips, her chin. Proof. Padding. Shelter. She slept more deeply. Her face took on color. She hadn't realized how unreal she had often felt, how close to breaking or floating away. She started pushing Ira down to Mother Rock once a day — he could walk again, but not for any distance — and her legs and arms grew strong.

On the weekends, Albert came to do the pushing, and to sleep with Lyman Knapp. He was in the process of selling the house on Acorn Street, and looking for an apartment. A separation, they told their parents, trying to ease them in, but the realtor's assistant had snitched to the *Herald* and so it was out. Bea was surprised to find herself temporarily devastated, though about what exactly she could not say. Lyman Knapp. The house. The hissed public censure. Albert. It was almost entirely Albert. She could still point to the moment she began to love him: he said something like, *If that's politics, you must be a fine actress,* and proceeded to look at her, and look and look, with his startling blue eyes and not a hint of judgment. They had both been in hiding. Bea had seized on this as fair, as if they were nothing more than parts in a mathematical equation. She had thought it right that they should know each other so baldly, good that they had protected themselves against surprises. But for a few days after the *Herald* ran its piece, she felt the full tragedy of their pairing — regret that it had been necessary, grief that it was now over. As if to prove the point, it was Albert who drew her out, making her laugh with stories about his colleagues at the bank, who had immediately set to work locating single women they wished *they* were free to fuck. Albert politely declined. Eventually, they would draw whatever conclusions they drew and let him be. One boss, a few years later, would close the door to his office and ask Albert outright, 'Are you a faggot?' and Albert, mystifying, enraging, and humiliating the man all at once — all this he reported to Bea — would say, 'As much of one as you imagine me to be.'

Down at Mother Rock, the leaves of the beach rose had bleached a bright yellow. Bea sat between Albert and Ira, thinking about Lucy Pear, who was still on Leverett Street with Emma and the others. Bea had invited them to Ira's house, but so far Emma had not come, nor said she would come. Bea kept up her lessons, sick each time she drove past the house with Mr. Murphy inside it. Soon, she thought, she would take the girl aside, give her the money, show her the timetables and routes. Or she would drive her to the train herself. Bea knew what it was like to not belong in a place. She would lock the girl into memory — her wide eyes, her long chin, one curl stuck into the corner of her mouth — and wave good-bye. But here her mind swerved. She could not do that. How could she possibly say good-bye when they had only just met? In a crook of her heart Bea fantasized about boarding the train with the girl, becoming her mother in a new place, starting again. But that would be a kind of kidnapping, of course. And Lucy, Bea knew, did not actually want her. And Bea could not start again. She had made a life, as much as she had told herself over the years that it was temporary. She had shed the cause, and made true commitments. To care for Ira (though she would soon hire people to help, with him and with the house, and another woman to cook, forgoing martyrdom so she could do things like visit Eliza Dropstone — whom she'd recently contacted through the *Quarterly* — and her three children in Needham, and go with Rose and her new boyfriend to the theater in Boston). To teach the Murphy children. Janie was very good. If she remained disciplined, Bea thought, if she agreed to more lessons and practiced each day, eventually she might win a scholarship to the conservatory. Or Bea might pay her way.

Bea was starting to teach other children, too. Janie had told a friend, who had told her mother, and so on. In a couple years, Bea would marry the father of two of her students, a widower, a doctor, not a Jew but Lillian would forgive that.

They would make a home in the house his parents had left him. Bea would become an authentic year-rounder, one of the winter people. They would have a baby, a girl. But that would not be starting over, either. It would turn out to be the opposite, a continuing, Bea awake this time, animal, humbled and astonished, and staying as the baby grew, a corner of her mourning all she had never known of Lucy while the rest of her fell deeply into her days, the baby, the stepchildren, her husband's laughter, his gratitude, his fingertip way of touching her at the hip each time he passed, his awe at her stamina, disbelief even, though she had already told him everything. They would let Lillian and Estelle take the baby to Granddaughters' Day at the Draper House, which had become a thing. They would visit Ira often. He would live to be ninety-one.

That — the new baby — was in 1930, the same year that Mother Jones finally died and Bea donated the humidor to Howard University in Washington, D.C., for its slavery collection, and other objects to other places and people who valued them more than Ira or Bea or her cousins ever would. It was also the year her father lost so much money he closed Haven Shoes and moved himself and Lillian to Gloucester. Only Lillian kept up the trips to Boston — to shop, she claimed, though she went for her appointments with Dr. M. Henry bought a storefront in downtown Gloucester, started up a department store called Heschel Brothers, and taught his granddaughter how to measure feet, but really measure them, length, width, corns, and all.

★ ★ ★

Long before any of that, though, the yellow
leaves would fall off the beach rose and the first
snow would blow through and Bea would find
herself and Ira taking in Emma and Lucy and
the other children. *Only until spring*, Emma
would say, and Bea would say, *Whatever you
like. Whatever works*. The house would be loud.
Lucy would be everywhere. She would show Bea
the old shawl and Bea would bury her face in it.
Over at Leverett Street, the third week of
December, the perry would freeze and be ruined
— the one danger neither Emma nor Lucy had
accounted for — but no one knew about that
yet. The children's cheeks were bright with
displacement — if it made them sick, they
smothered their sickness in glee. Ira nodded,
following the sound of their running with his
eyes, rubbing his face in disbelief, shaking his
head at the noise, the house filled with life. Bea
would think, *Maybe this will be enough*.

★ ★ ★

But today, Bea was leaving Albert and Ira down
at the rocks and going to pick up Julian and
Brigitte, who were arriving from New York with
their baby, Marlene Aimée. They were climbing
haggardly down from the train, surprised to find
Bea waiting for them, Bea behind the wheel,
waving out the window. They were placing a

386

crying Marlene Aimée into her grandfather's arms.

Yesterday, Bea had gone into town to have Brigitte's locket fixed. For weeks, she had avoided looking at it, at first impressed by her self-discipline — as she had been so many times before, repeating scales until her fingers cramped, surviving for weeks on apples, writing speeches she loathed — and then, finally, appalled. It was like being suddenly nauseated by the scent of her own skin. She scooped up the pieces, drove them to the jeweler, and said, 'I'd like to fix this, for a friend.'

She felt lighter today. A fist had unfisted. Ira clucked and cooed at the screaming baby, swinging her vigorously left and right, the effort making him red and happy. Bea let herself look at Julian and he looked straight back and said, 'Bea. Father tells me you've been reunited with your daughter. It makes me glad to know it.' Bea thanked him. Then she gave the locket back to Brigitte — 'It was trampled,' she explained, 'but they made it good as new' — and went to the piano, where she began to play Brahms's lullaby. Julian shouted, 'You've started to play again! That's wonderful!' and though Bea knew Ira had already told him this, she forgave him his exuberance. He worried, of course. He still expected Bea to envy them the baby. He feared, perhaps, that she would do something rash. He feared her more generally, Bea supposed, and had for a long time, ever since she had become a woman before he became a man.

Later, after supper, but not so late that the

answer was sure to be no, not hesitantly or apologetically or half trying to sabotage herself, Bea asked if she could hold Marlene Aimée. The baby was quiet, and wide awake, her blue eyes wandering from Bea to the lamp behind her and back again. Julian mumbled something about how she didn't often smile at this hour, Bea shouldn't be offended, but Bea barely heard. She was looking at Marlene Aimée: her radish pink lips, the upper curling over the lower in such a way that she appeared to be on the verge of laughter, the fluffy thatch of dark hair that sprouted like a mushroom from the top of her head, the pert, puggish nose. And the things that would not last: the yellow flaking at her scalp, the fur that grew at her temples, the rash on her cheeks. Now, too, Bea thought, *Maybe this will be enough.*

38

She boards the train as if climbing a tall, precariously tilted boulder in the Lanesville woods, her steps quick, already committed. Like a rock, the train seems to her at once alive and unthreatening, animate yet without preference — it lets her on but is unmoved by her weight. Lucy has with her clean underwear, two new dresses bought by Mrs. Cohn, the blanket Emma gave her, and a sack of sandwiches she made this morning in the dark kitchen before even the cook woke. Also, a book of children's poetry Uncle Ira left on her pillow one night, inscribed: *For Lucy, full of light.* She was going to take Mrs. Haven's rings, but then she found a stack of twenty-dollar bills in the top drawer of Mrs. Cohn's desk, so she left the rings for her sisters. The wad is stuffed deep into one of Liam's socks, though she keeps one bill, the gift from Estelle, separate, in the other sock, understanding that it did not come easily. She wears one of Liam's sweaters, too, and a pair of his trousers, and Jeffrey's extra cap, low over her eyes. Around her chest she has wrapped one of the bandages Emma saved from Roland's first weeks home. The sweater is roomy, Lucy's breasts still nearly imperceptible, but she wears the bandage anyway, as a cautionary measure. It keeps her warmer, if nothing else. She left her winter coat behind, unable to wear it — clearly a girl's — or to fit it into her bag, a brown canvas duffel Roland used to bring on his fishing trips. Emma took the bag and nearly everything else from the house, including the bandages, the curtains, all the pillows but one. She left only Roland's clothes and a few kitchen things. The children weren't there when she did this. They were at school, except for Lucy and Joshua, whom Emma had sent down to the coffee shop. Afterward, she would say nothing of what happened, not even to Lucy. She did say that they could go back in the spring, for the perry. And she said that she had arranged for a nurse. The nurse would go to the house twice a day to check on him, keep the fire lit, keep the house. Emma looked, saying this, much older, and very beautiful.

If she were a girl, Lucy thinks, she would wrap the blanket around her shoulders, but because she is not supposed to be a girl, she hugs the duffel to her while she waits for the car to warm up and rests her feet on the opposite seat, like a boy can do. The train is not full — still, she was surprised when the conductor moved her to a place where she could have two seats, facing each other. At night, when the beds are set up, Lucy will have both the top and bottom bunks, a sort of closet all to herself. She doesn't understand how the seats will change into beds — she sees no mechanism. She tries to look out the window, but instead stares at the porter as he carries another suitcase through the car. She hasn't seen a colored person before.

For hours, as the train rolls north, she speaks to no one. She eats her sandwiches and wonders, as they disappear, if she has made a mistake. She was safe now, after all, with her siblings and Emma and Mrs. Cohn and Mr. Hirsch, with the cook and housekeeper and nurse. It was a kind of family — a good family, in many ways. The only man was old and sweet. There were two women, two mothers, home almost all the time. The children had space to run. There were enough beds that each child had one to herself — though often, by morning, she had found a sibling and crawled in with her — and enough money that it was no great hardship that Emma could no longer work at Sven's. The men at the long counter glared at her. Lanesville was done with her. So she was home, and Mrs. Cohn was home, the house large enough to let them pass each other comfortably, like moons. But they were warming. The other day Lucy had seen them talking quietly on the screened porch, huddled close in their coats, Emma's new — she had relented, accepted — so that they looked like equals. Like two women, friends even, having a conversation. Then, sensing Lucy, they'd looked up, their faces instantly lit, vying for her attention, praising, worrying, making way. She was everything to them.

But that was it. They wanted to help her but they needed her, too, and their need was heavy. They thought she was older than she was, but she wasn't. You couldn't actually be older than the number of years you had lived. She was ten. She felt as if they were sitting on her head.

This morning, hours before the train to Boston was scheduled to depart, she had slipped out through the basement bulkhead, walked off Eastern Point, and ridden the bus to Lanesville. A few quarrymen sat in back but none seemed to recognize her, and even if they had, it would have been Johnny Murphy they saw. Leverett Street was dusted in snow. She climbed the hill in the trees, the duffel pulling her back, her concentration so great she nearly passed the house. The Davies' chimney trickled gray smoke, residue of last night's fire. The Solttis had bought a car — it sat like a black rock in their yard. Even Mrs. Greely's house was dark, and silent. A wan light spread through the trees. Lucy had stayed on Eastern Point through Christmas, had gone to Mass with Emma in a new church, had done what she could to avoid cruelty. January was setting in now. The door to the perry shack squealed at her touch and she stepped in quickly to find the place scentless. Her breath jumped in front of her. She moved cautiously to the window.

With the curtains gone from the house, she could see easily into the front room, and in the front room, to her surprise, she saw Roland sitting in his chair, asleep. She had imagined that to see him she would have to creep to the bedroom window, but this — it was almost too easy, and sad. Had he slept there the whole night? She left the shack and went closer, until her face met the window and she saw that this man, covered in a blanket, was not Roland. She nearly banged on the window. What had happened to Roland? What had Emma done? Then the man's face fell to the side, exposing a peculiar, lobe-heavy ear. Roland's ear. He had shaved, that was it. She had never seen him without a beard. His face looked strange, doughy in places, the lines around his mouth deeper than she would have guessed, his skin fish white and soft. His sudden bareness seemed to suggest he had nothing to hide. Lucy went hot with guilt. She had overreacted. She had ruined him. He had brought her up as his child and she had ruined him. She let her forehead fall against the window and stared. But the noise made Roland flinch. His eyelids quivered and his hands emerged from the blanket to pull it tighter across his middle and his fingers were the same, thick and scarred, and Lucy's fear was simple enough to flatten her doubt and push her down the hill, running the whole way, the duffel banging her knees, until she reached the bus stop, a panting boy.

The trees change. The hills grow steeper. A family of deer stares calmly at the train as it roars past. Lucy wonders how they know not to be afraid.

The sun sets. Her sandwiches are long gone.

In the dining car, where the walls are still decorated for Christmas with musk-scented wreaths and velvet bows, Lucy chooses a table in the corner and keeps her eyes down. But the place is nearly full and a woman asks if the seat across from Lucy is taken. Lucy shakes her head, resisting the urge to check that her hair is still well tucked into Jeffrey's cap. She hopes Janie will forgive her for taking all her pins.

The woman is built like a tree trunk, Lucy thinks, the same from top to bottom, her brown velour dress probably bought for this trip given how she picks at it as she gets settled, pulling at the shoulders, tugging at the neckline. Her expression is similarly scattered: apologetic yet eager. For a large woman, her eyes are small. Her fidgeting calms Lucy — it suggests the woman will not look closely.

'Are you going all the way to Quebec by yourself?'

Lucy nods. The motion is like a hand opening a gate — it shakes loose her loneliness.

The woman smiles as she examines the menu. 'What are you, twelve?' she asks. She raises a thick, gloved finger for the waiter, and Lucy nods again.

Over dinner, the woman — Mary Morse — tells Lucy her story. Her parents were poor, the children always hungry, Miss Morse the oldest and hungriest. She has lived in Medford, Massachusetts, since she was sent there, at thirteen, to take care of her dying aunt. The aunt was her father's favorite sister. She was good to Miss Morse, made sure she kept up with school. She died, Miss Morse said, the way you hope a person will die, already used to the idea, and because she'd taught Sunday school, her funeral was well attended. Miss Morse became a history teacher. She met a man to marry but he ran off with her best girlfriend. ('Don't you go doing that,' she says to Lucy with a coy, surprising grin.) For a while after that Miss Morse thought she would die of heartbreak — that was like a separate life, that time, a black pit between her first life and this one — but now she knows nothing like that will kill her. She likes her students, but she's going back to Quebec, where she was born, to take care of her dying mother.

'See how it goes? New year, old journey. Nothing extraordinary in it, not the least little bit. Most people want to be extraordinary. Make a mark in the world. But for what? In my experience it's the extraordinary people what aren't happy, always expecting something better than they get. Whenever anything at all happens to me, I tell myself it's happened to everyone else, too. It's actually very comforting. I feel steady almost all the time because I know that nothing out of the ordinary will ever happen and if it did, or if it seemed like it did, it wouldn't be, anyway. Well, aren't you patient. I bet you want to be the next Charles Lindbergh when you grow up. But don't you see how that makes you ordinary, too?'

Lucy nods vaguely. She hears little of the woman's words — it's the cadence of her voice she likes, its carelessness, an almost frothy cheer, and that it keeps on coming, like a tide.

★　★　★

Her bunks have been made up. She climbs into the top one and opens the book Uncle Ira gave her to a poem about a bluebird who is saying good-bye to a girl, but he can't tell her himself because he has already flown away. He has told a crow, who tells another child, who will have to tell the girl. But before that happens, the poem ends. Lucy reads it twice, then shuts the book and turns out the light. Tears spill down her face. Her stomach is full in a way she's unused to, the passing sky milky with clouds. She longs to be in bed with Janie. There are questions she would have liked to ask Miss Morse: *Did you know, when you left, that you would one day go back? Why did your father live so far from his favorite sister? How can you be sure that the dangers you already know are worse than the ones you're heading for?*

The conductor passes through the car, telling a few people to talk more quietly, and Lucy is sorry for the silence that spreads behind him. She hears his accent as he nears her bunk, *Quiet down, please, a bit quieter, please* . . . Irish, she thinks, a different kind of Irish, maybe from a county near Emma's, and Lucy lets this idea soothe her a little. She thinks of the first letter she will write, and wonders what she will have to say. (This: that she has found Peter, that he is the same, that he makes her go to school, that she has learned a little French, that they are neither rich nor poor. And this: She is sorry. She misses Emma. She misses them all. She addresses the letters to Emma, though everyone who can write writes to her, including Mrs. Cohn. She thinks she will devastate Emma if she writes to Mrs. Cohn and she is right, though this devastation would be nothing compared with what Lucy has already put them through. For months they wake to footfall and think it is her. They wonder silently which of them is more to blame for her leaving. They wish out loud that they had chained her to her bed.)

Lucy is wrong about the conductor. He is British. Thirty-one years ago he was hired to watch over a bunch of pear trees en route from Sussex to Massachusetts, and he never went home. He has worked as a water boy in the quarries, a messenger in Boston, a busboy in Providence, a conductor for the last fifteen years, always carrying things, or people. He knows where Lucy is. He noticed the boy alone, of course. He notices everything. He stops at the kid's bunks. Hasn't said a word. Doesn't seem to know about the curtain. He's lying there in full view, facing the window, not asleep — the conductor can tell by the stiff way his head doesn't quite rest on the pillow. He hasn't taken off his cap. Most people who ride the Pullman think it's going to be their chance to play high class. Then he sees their faces change as night falls, sees their fear. He hears them call for the porters, a glass of water, an aspirin, this or that, and the porters think it's despotism — which maybe in part it is — but the conductor knows it's also fear. The ghostly shapes of trees, the moon behind a cloud, old stories of wolves. He lets the people be. By morning they have forgotten. They revise the night's demons, boast to their fellow passengers how civilized it is, traveling this way. But the boy can't be more than ten, maybe eleven. The conductor wasn't much older when he left home. He rises on his toes next to the bunk and, though this is the porter's job, asks quietly, 'Is there anything you need?' After a pause, still facing away, the boy shakes his head. Black curls escape from his cap, snarled, but not dirty. Long. The conductor itches to touch one, pop it, see just how long. 'I'll be back in the morning,' he says. But he doesn't go. He won't go back to his compartment tonight. He'll stay awake, watchful. He lifts himself closer. He murmurs, 'It'll be all right.' Then he pats the long pile of the kid, pulls the curtain, and snaps it shut.

Acknowledgments

For this book's inspiration, thank you to my father, William Greenbaum, for telling me far-fetched stories about our family's pear trees.

For help with research, Sarah Dunlap at the Gloucester Archives was unfailingly generous, creative, and prompt in her responses to my incessant queries. Richard Wyndham put *The Saga of Cape Ann* into my hands. Barbara Erkkila passed away before this book's publication but spent hours talking with me about the old granite industry on Cape Ann; her book *Hammers on Stone* served as a critical text. Erik Natti and Scott Stewart took me straight to the quarries. Terry Bragg gave me a stirring tour of McLean Hospital. Zoe Argento shared her knowledge of the navy and brainstormed disastrous scenarios with me. Stephanie Buck and Erik Ronnberg at the Cape Ann Museum went out of their way to help. Many others shared what they knew: Ann Abrams, Annie Adair, Sarah Baer, David Bianchini, Joey Ciaramitaro, Marni Davis, Sarah Deutsch, Jody Georgeson, Sheryl Kaskowitz, Steve Ledbetter, Frederick Nowell, Ellen Smith, Andrew Todd. Others wrote books I returned to time and again, including *Last Call* by Daniel Okrent; *History of Woman Suffrage* and *The Woman's Bible* by Elizabeth Cady Stanton; *The Psychiatric Persuasion* by Elizabeth Lunbeck; *Hystories* by Elaine Showalter; *Studies on Hysteria* by Joseph Breuer and Sigmund Freud; *One Summer* by Bill Bryson; *The Jews of Boston* by Jonathan D. Sarna, Ellen Smith, and Scott-Martin Kosofsky.

For space and resources: I began writing this book at the MacDowell Colony, wrote parts of it at Wellspring House, and received generous support during the process from the Rhode Island State Council for the Arts. Thanks also to the staff at the Sawyer Free Library in Gloucester, the Schlesinger Library at Radcliffe, and the English department at Brown.

For support, friendship, and good ideas throughout the writing of this book: Deborah Barron, Beth Bisson, Jenna Blum, Austin Bunn, Clare Burson, Chris Castellani, Deborah Cramer, Anne Deneen, Elyssa East, Eve Fox, Abigail Greenbaum, O'rya Hyde-Keller, Sheryl Kaskowitz, Rachel Kulick, Edan Lepucki, Julia Mitric, Rekha Murthy, Britt Page, Anna Painter, Yvonne Piccirillo, Heidi Pitlor, Eli Pollard, Mitzi Rapkin, Jane Roper, Avital Rosenberg, Kim Snyder, Amy Scott, Lawrence Stanley, Sarah Strickley, Beth Taylor, Marina Toloushams, Sarah Wildman, Samara Yeshaiek, Gina Zucker.

For reading early and late drafts with wisdom, honesty, and heart: Mike Burger, Eleanor Henderson, Hester Kaplan, Abigail Cahill O'Brien, Taylor Polites, Jessie Solomon-Greenbaum, Evelyn Spence, Lisa Srisuro.

Thank you to everyone at Viking who has poured their energy and time into bringing this book into the world. To Kate Stark and Lindsay Prevette and their teams, including Lydia Hirt,

Mary Stone, Allison Carney, Meredith Burks, and Emma Mohney. To Brian Tart and Andrea Schulz for welcoming me to Viking. To Hilary Roberts and Shannon Kelly, as well as all the Penguin sales reps who championed *The Little Bride* and continue to support my work. To Sarah Stein, who believed in this book, made it better, and continues to shepherd it and me with wisdom and humor, I am ever grateful.

To my extraordinary agent, Julie Barer, thank you. And to everyone else at The Book Group, including Gemma Purdy, Meg Ross, Anna Knutson Geller, and William Boggess, thank you for making this business a pleasure.

Thank you to my family, for cheering me on no matter my mood. To my in-laws, Barbara and Andrew. To Alfie, Jessica, Charlie, Courtney, Pam, Anton. To Gajan and to my sisters, Jessie and Fara, sources of laughter and comfort. To my father, for always checking in. To my mother, Ellen Solomon, for her boundless encouragement. To Sylvie, for her insatiable curiosity and huge imagination. To Sam, for kisses and smiles. To Mike, for everything.

We do hope that you have enjoyed reading this large print book.

Did you know that all of our titles are available for purchase?

We publish a wide range of high quality large print books including:
Romances, Mysteries, Classics
General Fiction
Non Fiction and Westerns

Special interest titles available in large print are:
The Little Oxford Dictionary
Music Book
Song Book
Hymn Book
Service Book

Also available from us courtesy of Oxford University Press:
Young Readers' Dictionary
(large print edition)
Young Readers' Thesaurus
(large print edition)

For further information or a free brochure, please contact us at:
Ulverscroft Large Print Books Ltd.,
The Green, Bradgate Road, Anstey,
Leicester, LE7 7FU, England.
Tel: (00 44) 0116 236 4325
Fax: (00 44) 0116 234 0205